Breaking
the
Mould

Books by Victoria Hamilton

Vintage Kitchen Mysteries

A Deadly Grind
Bowled Over
Freezer I'll Shoot
No Mallets Intended
White Colander Crime
Leave It to Cleaver
No Grater Danger
Breaking the Mould

Merry Muffin Mysteries

Bran New Death
Muffin But Murder
Death of an English Muffin
Much Ado About Muffin
Muffin to Fear

Breaking the Mould

Victoria Hamilton

BEYOND THE PAGE
PUBLISHING

Beyond the Page Books
are published by
Beyond the Page Publishing
www.beyondthepagepub.com

Copyright © 2018 by Donna Lea Simpson.
Cover design and illustration by Dar Albert, Wicked Smart Designs.

ISBN: 978-1-946069-89-4

For Bill H., WBE (World's Best Editor), whose unfailing generosity, kindness and staggeringly good editing are endlessly appreciated. He invariably finds the weakness in a book, and with great kindness points it out. With even greater kindness he gives valuable hints on how to rectify it. I've become a better writer because of him.
Thank you, Bill.

Cast of Characters

in the Vintage Kitchen Mystery Series

Jaymie Leighton Müller: newlywed, new stepmom, and collector of all things vintage kitchen-y!

Jakob Müller: her husband, dad to Jocie, Christmas tree farmer and junk store owner.

Jocie Müller: *little* little person (as she says!) and happy daughter to Jakob and Jaymie.

Dieter and Helmut Müller: Jakob's oldest and next oldest brothers

Becca Brevard: Jaymie's bossy older sister and co-owner of Queensville Fine Antiques, aka QFA.

Kevin Brevard: Becca's husband and co-owner of QFA.

Georgina Brevard: Kevin's older sister and manager of QFA.

Valetta Nibley: pharmacist and lifelong friend to Jaymie and Becca

Brock Nibley: Valetta's older brother and Queensville's best real estate agent.

Heidi Lockland: Jaymie's friend.

Bernie Jenkins: Heidi's best friend, Jaymie's good friend and local police officer for the Queensville Township Police Department, aka QTPD.

Mrs. Martha Stubbs: Jaymie's elderly friend and confidante.

Bill Waterman: Queensville's favorite handyman.

Austin Calhoun: Jaymie's acquaintance from a past investigation and new Wolverhampton College (aka WC) student.

Mrs. Bellwood, Trip Findley, Haskell Lockland, Imogene Frump, Mabel Bloomsbury, Johnny Stanko: Queensvillians and Jaymie's friends.

Detective Angela Vestry: QTPD's first female detective.

Hoppy and Lilibet: Jaymie's Yorkie-Poo and Jocie's tiger-striped kitten.

Cast of Characters

in *Breaking the Mould*

Mr. Evan Hollis Nezer: Tenured professor of economics at Wolverhampton College (WC) and noted author.

Mrs. Bella Nezer: his second wife and decorative accessory.

Mrs. Sarah Nezer: his ex-wife, mother of his son.

E. (Evan) Benjamin Nezer: aka Ben, his son, recently un-estranged.

Jacklyn Marley: Evan's ghostwriter.

Erla Fancombe: Nezer housekeeper.

Finn Fancombe: Erla's son and WC grad student and former master's candidate.

Hazel Belcher: WC president.

Carter Crossley: WC provost.

Andy Markham: WC dean.

Pastor Vaughan Inkerman: WC interfaith chaplain and author of *Living Your Best Life Through Scripture*.

Amos: Wandering soul who collects booze bottles from recycling containers.

Shannon Parker: WC college student and Müller Christmas Tree Farm hire.

"If I could work my will," said Scrooge indignantly, "Every idiot who goes about with 'Merry Christmas' on his lips, should be boiled with his own pudding, and buried with a stake of holly through his heart. He should!"

– *Charles Dickens,* A Christmas Carol

⚡ One ⚡

A COLD BREEZE swept along the main street in Queensville, Michigan. Jaymie Leighton Müller wrapped her jacket around her more tightly as she held the hand of her stepdaughter, Jocie. Though nine years old, Jocie was much smaller than other kids her age because a condition, achondroplasia dwarfism, had made her, as she put it, a *little* little person. They stood together opposite the triangle-shaped plot of land known to Queensvillians as the village green, and watched Bill Waterman, local handyman, at work. Preparations were under way for the holiday season, Jaymie's favorite time of year. Other villagers were out in force, too, stringing white lights from pine tree to oak, hanging festive wreaths, and erecting wood cutout snowfolk and other displays on front lawns and porches.

Jocie pulled her hand out of Jaymie's and buried both of them in her coat sleeves, her breath coming out in puffs of white. "Are you warm enough, sweetie?" Jaymie asked, looking down at Jocie. Her daughter's pudgy cheeks were rosy from the cold, and with her blonde ringlets jammed down by a pink tuque and her powder-pink padded jacket, she looked adorable.

"I guess," she said. Her big brown eyes were fixed on Bill and his namesake grandson, Billy, who was nine as well and in Jocie's class at school. He was a handsome dark-skinned boy, his black hair cut close to his skull, and he helped Bill with quick, deft movements, a testament to years in the shop alongside his grandfather. He glanced over at Jocie, then ducked his head bashfully, like a silent hello.

Jocie started forward to join them, but Jaymie grasped her shoulder. "Not unless you're invited. They're working, and we don't want to get in the way."

"I wasn't going to get in the way, I was going to help!"

"Unless you know what you're doing, that's also called getting in the way," Jaymie said firmly. Jocie pouted, her lip starting to push out. Though she was generally sunny-tempered, she did have moments of stubbornness. "Jocie, we ask first, we don't just assume we know what to do. It's like in the kitchen, where you need to ask if you can use the cooking tools."

1

"Your mom's right," Bill said with a kind smile. He was a tall man, into his seventies, but sturdy and strong. Dressed in overalls and a striped cap, he looked like a train engineer, appropriate since one of his hobbies was model train construction. "I'm swinging a hammer. Wouldn't want you in the way of it, honey. Billy knows when to step back."

She thought for a moment, then asked, "Can I stand with Billy?"

"Okay with you, Jaymie?"

She nodded. Jocie raced over and stood talking to Billy while his grandfather worked. The boy was pointing to things and explaining, and Jocie was paying close attention. Her father and grandfather often included her in their work, so she understood more than many kids her age would have.

It was the Sunday of Thanksgiving weekend. Dickens Days was scheduled to start on Friday, and Jaymie was excited! The village of Queensville would soon be decked in white lights and festive ornaments for the annual Christmas festival, one of the year's two fund-raisers for the local historical society. Helped by a couple of volunteers from the heritage society, Bill had moved the adorable cider house into its position on the village green, and now he was hammering nails back into place that had come loose in the move. From it, volunteers would dole out steaming cups of warm cider to folks who would wander from shop to shop while Victorian-garbed carolers strolled the village streets, pausing by the Victorian-style light posts to sing of holiday cheer and joyful celebration.

Unless . . . the village Scrooge ruined it all. That was a fly in the ointment this year, that the house behind the village green was now occupied by Professor Evan Hollis Nezer, when in past years it had been rented out by various casual occupants who hadn't cared what was happening on their doorstep. Jaymie hoped Nezer didn't cause them any grief.

Bill tethered a rope to a hook at the peak of the booth's roof and pulled it taut behind the booth to a spot in the middle of a line of tall pines. Billy followed and handed him his hammer as Jocie returned to Jaymie's side. Bill raised the heavy mallet, ready to pound a wooden stake into the ground to anchor the line.

A man bolted from among the pines and confronted the handyman, grabbing the wooden stake and throwing it through the open booth toward the road. Jaymie let out her breath, holding Jocie to her side with one arm. Her wish hadn't come true.

"You've got no right to infringe on my property!" Evan Hollis Nezer shrieked, *literally* hopping mad.

"Hey, now . . . you shouldn't be throwing that, especially not with kids around!" Bill stepped back and let go of the rope, gesturing toward his grandson nearby and Jocie with Jaymie.

Nezer's property, on which his big Queen Anne historic home stood, abutted the Queensville village green. That greenspace had always been used as public land, central as it was in the village, within view of the Queensville Emporium and across from a small public parkette that was separated from other homes on the street by groves of trees. The Nezer property line was thought to be the line of pines in front of it, but there was no actual indication, no fence or barrier.

Red-faced, fists clenched, the property owner hopped up and down twice as he faced the Queensville handyman. "I don't *care* who's around, you can't use my property. *Get off!*"

"Now, Mr. Nezer, it's just a peg to tie a rope to, to keep the cider house stable. Nothing more. I promise." Bill Waterman, calm and good-natured, loomed over the other fellow. His grandson had retrieved the stake and handed it back to his grandpa, who still held the mallet.

Nezer, who had longish silvery hair, a trim beard and mustache and brushed-silver-framed glasses, would have been distinguished-looking if not for the choleric expression on his face. "I don't care. Cease and *desist!*" he demanded, his cheeks scarlet. "This moment!"

The villagers who had been decorating were attracted by the shouting. Dark-haired Cynthia Turbridge, owner of the Cottage Shoppe, and flame-haired Jewel Dandridge, proprietor of Jewel's Junk, whispered together, joined by their shared employee, Petty Welch. Gracey Klausner stood in the Queensville Emporium window, arms folded across her chest, and gazed out. Others, who had been helping decorate, stood in groups chatting and watching the commotion.

Bill glanced around, passing one hand over his thin hair and beginning to look irritated. "It's barely six inches on your property! You've lived here all your life and know it gets windy in our town in

November and December. It comes off the river and sweeps through Queensville. Surely you don't want the structure to blow over. It could hurt someone." At six feet plus, Bill was a big guy, but despite the fact that he carried a rubber mallet and a long stake, which was incidentally pointed right at Nezer, he meant no harm. He stepped forward. "C'mon, Evan . . . let me—"

"Don't you threaten me, Waterman!" the man screeched in alarm and backed away. He held one hand out in front of him. "I'll sue you; I will!"

Billy's eyes widened and he looked scared. Jaymie dropped Jocie's hand and lurched forward. "Mr. Nezer, please, there are children present. Calm down!"

Belatedly it occurred to her that the worst thing to say to an excitable person was "calm down." The man exploded in rage, his face turning even redder and puffing up alarmingly. "Don't tell *me* what to do!"

Jocie watched in fascination. She moved forward and grabbed Jaymie's hand.

"What, Jocie?"

"Why is he getting so red?" Jocie whispered.

"I'll sue! I will *sue*, Waterman, I swear it!" Nezer shrieked, dancing like a marionette, arms flailing.

Jocie's eyes lit up and she pulled away from Jaymie. She screeched with laughter, and began dancing around like Mr. Nezer. Billy turned and watched her, laughing out loud in glee. Some among the gathered crowd laughed too, and pointed at the man and the little girl, both dancing like maniacs.

Nezer stopped and shook his fists. "Waterman, and you, lady with that child . . . you're both on notice. I'll sue you for—"

"What, Mr. Nezer? *What* will you sue them for?" Valetta, her sweater wrapped around her and shivering, had come from the Queensville Emporium, where she ran the pharmacy. More folks had gathered to witness the spectacle. "For making fun of you? That's not sue-able, I shouldn't think." She pushed her glasses up on her face. "Or you'd be suing everyone in town."

Jaymie bit her lip, trying to keep from laughing at Valetta's acerbic comment. A young woman about Jaymie's age stood by Valetta and applauded, a grin on her face.

"Val, you're not helping," Jaymie muttered. "What are you doing at the pharmacy on a Sunday anyway?" she asked.

"Sick customer needed antibiotics."

"Ah, I see. Jocie, please don't antagonize the man anymore." She grabbed her stepdaughter's shoulder and pulled her close.

Nezer calmed and blinked, his face still red. He was a tidy man, dapper in his clothes—he wore a stylish gray wool trench coat with a red silk scarf under the collar—and with that silky mane of thinning gray hair. He had owned the house, a family inheritance, for a long time. Over the years he had rented it out as office space and a vacation rental. Most recently it had been rented to an accounting firm. But he had sued the accounting company, and they had vacated the property rather than settle. Then he had been about to sell it in October. However, according to Brock Nibley, a local real estate agent, Valetta's older brother, and the source of all of Jaymie's information on the house, Nezer had tanked a sure sale by demanding more money, nitpicking contract details, refusing to do required work, and otherwise being a jerk. He eyed the gathered crowd, perhaps looking for supporters and finding none.

Jaymie set Jocie behind her and moved forward. "Mr. Nezer, honestly, Bill was doing what has always been done for the Dickens Days celebra—"

"*Confound* your Dickens Days! Humbug on it," he said, his eyes a frigid blue. He stuck his thumbs in his lapels and strutted forward. "Why should your silly festival infringe on my property? I have rights, don't I? And that includes the right not to be bothered by chanting and cider-swilling idiots traipsing over my property. And stakes being pounded in, damaging my turf! What about *my* rights? If you all don't leave me and my property alone I'll sue every solitary person in this town. Starting with you, Bill Waterman!" he said, jabbing a finger in the handyman's direction. "I'll end it all, or my name isn't Evan Nezer!" He whirled and strode away.

Most of the crowd dispersed, knowing the show was over and feeling the icy chill of a late November day in Michigan seeping through their coats. It was time for home, and hot soup and hotter tea. Jaymie shivered, a presentiment of trouble chilling her as much as the cold wind.

"You go on home, Jaymie," Bill said, an exasperated and weary expression on his face. He clapped his grandson on the shoulder. "Billy and I will head on home. That Nezer . . . he's a bunch of hot air. I'll continue tomorrow. Maybe I can rig something that doesn't anchor it on his property."

She examined her old friend. He didn't seem completely well, and she was worried. "You let me know if you need any backup though, Bill. Honestly."

"I'll be fine. I'm done for the day. Moving it into place was enough of a chore for a Sunday. Billy and I will probably head on out for cocoa."

One person clapped. Jaymie turned to see the young woman, dressed in a long coat, who had been standing by Valetta. "Well met, Ms. Leighton Müller," she said, her voice melodious.

Jaymie nodded and smiled, then grabbed Jocie's hand and turned to leave the scene.

"Oh, don't go! I had hoped to speak with you about joining your heritage society."

Jaymie turned back to her. "Come to our next meeting, Miss . . . uh—"

"Jacklyn Marley," she said, thrusting her hand out and taking Jaymie's, shaking it vigorously. "I will indeed attend the next meeting. Is this your daughter?"

"Yes. Jocie, this is Ms. Marley. Jacklyn, this is Jocie." Jaymie examined her. She was smooth and self-assured, a woman about Jaymie's age, but with dark brown hair in a chignon, and dressed chicly in a gray tweed skirt, black boots, and a gray plaid cape. Who was she, though, and what did she want of Jaymie?

"You may be wondering why I'm approaching you. I've read your column, 'Vintage Eats.' I'm a writer and wondered if you had ever considered gathering your columns into a cookbook."

"Mama *is* writing a cookbook," Jocie said, tugging on Jaymie's hand. "Aren't you?"

"Hush, Jocie."

"Are you indeed?" Ms. Marley said with a smooth smile.

"You're a writer?"

"I am. Or rather . . . have you ever heard of a ghostwriter?"

"Sure."

"A ghostwriter?" Jocie stared up at the woman, her blue eyes large and round. "Mama says there are no such things as ghosts. At least not in my room, at night."

"I'm not that kind of ghost," the woman said, crouching down. "I'm the kind of professional ghost who quietly goes about my business, writing, writing, writing for other people and never getting paid or getting any of the attention. Also known as . . . a ghost-writer."

There was an edge of bitterness to her words.

Jocie spotted elderly Mrs. Klausner at the door of the Emporium, holding out a candy cane and beckoning Jocie. "Can I go see Mrs. K?" Jocie asked. The woman, who with her husband had run the Queensville Emporium grocery store for years, was renowned for her crabbiness, but she had a soft spot for Jocie.

"You can, but five minutes, no more." Jaymie eyed Jacklyn Marley as she stood and straightened. "Who have you ghostwritten for?" she asked, glancing over to see Jocie skipping up the steps to Mrs. Klausner.

"Well, you've just met my most notorious client, Mr. Evan Nezer. That clutch-fisted old Scrooge with a corkscrew for a heart still owes me thousands of dollars in back royalties that he won't let go of."

"Oh, really?"

"Yes, really. I'd sue him, but he'd *love* that. Do you know, he has a double degree in economics and law and teaches at Wolverhampton College, but the joke on campus is he became a lawyer so he'd never have to pay one to represent him. He *loves* to sue!"

"That explains so much," Jaymie said faintly, thinking that the heritage society and Dickens Days was likely in for some rocky times.

"Like his threatening to sue the handyman, yourself, the township and anyone else in his path. And he'll do it."

"I *do* know him," Jaymie muttered. "Or at least *of* him." Evan Nezer had lived for years in the newer section of town near Heidi's ranch-style home and had sued many more folks in Queensville, including his annual lawsuit to keep the Dickens Days celebration from proceeding. It never went anywhere, but it was a nuisance. If she recalled correctly, he had sued neighbors, his ex-wife, and even fellow academics whom he claimed stole his work. It was annoying, and him moving to the center of town to the historic Nezer home meant the members of the historical society would likely have to deal with him much more often. They must prepare a strategy.

A young man pulled up and parked by the village green, eyeing the cider house with distaste. He got out of his silver sedan, checked his phone, then slipped it into his coat pocket. Catching sight of Jacklyn Marley, he strode over. "Jacklyn, my stepmother just called. She was taking a fit, screaming at me to get over here. Something about Dad getting beaten up by a handyman?"

Jacklyn laughed. "Benjamin Nezer, this is Jaymie Leighton Müller. Ben, here, is Evan's son." She turned to the tall young man. "I thought you two weren't talking?" she said with a sly smile, her eyes wide. She paused, then added, "Or do you communicate through La *Bel*-la?" She glanced over at Jaymie. "The lovely Bella is Nezer's second wife. He screwed every last drop of life out of Sarah, his ex, and now he's working on number two."

Jaymie eyed her uncertainly; there seemed to be some undercurrent to her words and phrasing, some digs at Mrs. Nezer that she didn't understand, not knowing the parties involved.

"Jacklyn, that's not fair!" Benjamin said, his eyes narrow. "My mom and dad had their differences for years before they split."

"I thought you were on your mother's side," she said, jamming her hands into her pockets. Her tone was spiteful, but Ben didn't respond. "Nice to see *you've* turned on her, too," the young woman added, staring steadily at him, digging the spite in deeper.

Given what Jacklyn had already told Jaymie about Nezer's unpaid bill for her ghostwriting, maybe she was taking her anger out on the whole family, but working on a book must have been a long process, certainly long enough to get to know and dislike the whole family.

Ben leveled a concentrated look at her. He looked like he wanted to say something, but his jaw tensed, his lips pursed into a hard line, and he turned to walk away.

"By the way, he wasn't being beaten up by any handyman," Jacklyn called out, cupping one hand around her mouth to increase the volume. "That's Bill Waterman over there, working on the cider house for the Dickens Days festivities. Your father threatened to sue him, that's all. Business as usual."

Benjamin shoved his hands deep into his pockets and walked on, pausing to watch Bill winding up the rope he had intended to use, then striding past through the fringe of pines and across the lawn toward the Nezer home, flickers of his progress showing through gaps in the tree trunks.

Jaymie turned to Jacklyn Marley. "That felt personal. Do you know him well?"

She shrugged. "I worked for his father for the better part of a year, so . . . yeah. We know each other."

"What does Ben do?"

"He's a lawyer specializing in contracts."

"His father must be thrilled, given his litigious nature."

"Not so much. He's disappointed in Ben, actually. They didn't speak for a long time because of that. Until recently, when Ben decided to start sucking up to his father again." Jacklyn chewed her lip and looked off in the direction Ben had disappeared. "Evan wanted him to go into financial planning and estate management and was disappointed when Ben became a lawyer."

"Sounds like a complicated family dynamic," Jaymie commented.

Jacklyn snorted in laughter. "You said it! That Bella is a handful. She married Nezer thinking she was moving up in the world, only to find out how deadly dull a professor's life is, and how a professor's wife has to make nice to the whole board of governors and college leadership. No glamour in that. Add to that the Nezer family housekeeper who lives in, the much put-upon Erla Fancombe." She cast a glance at Jaymie, a wry smile twisting her lips. "Erla's son, Finn, was a student at WC until Nezer accused him of plagiarism and got him kicked out."

Eye's wide, Jaymie reflected that Nezer seemed to have made a second career of angering and alienating people. "You know the family doings *very* well."

"I've made a study of the Nezers, I suppose," she mused. "I've spent a lot of time with Evan as his ghostwriter, and much of that was in his home office. They're an interesting tribe. Do you know he is actually an author of some note? Back in the eighties he published a couple of novels that made a big splash. I guess writing wasn't lucrative enough. He was a professor of economics at that point but got a second degree in law and started suing people as a hobby."

"Nice hobby; making people miserable for fun and profit. I did not know any of that. You'd think once a writer, always a writer." At least that was Jaymie's experience from knowing a writer who was obsessive, always in the middle of at least two novels, and often more than two, as well as publicizing the latest book and planning the next. "So . . . I'm puzzled. Why did he need a ghostwriter?"

Jacklyn shrugged. "It's been years since he got those books published." She twisted her lips and squinted. "He's odd in some ways. Somewhere along the line he got . . . warped. The whole suing thing, for example, seems to have started in the nineties. He would sue you as soon as look at you." She sighed. "He's such a bitter Betty. Sarah, his ex-wife, he screwed out of every possession she ever had, even her heirlooms, and she's not willing to fight it. I don't know why not, since her husband moved on to Bella, wifey number two, even before they separated."

"You know that for sure?" Jaymie said, always uneasy about gossip.

"I do. They didn't always cohabit, from what I understand; she spent a lot of time . . . away. But they were married. Bella is younger, buxom and gorgeous, a virtual Nigella Lawson clone." She glanced over at Jaymie. "You know who Nigella Lawson is, right?"

"Of course. British cooking celebrity. I love some of her food."

"Well, Bella has the bod and the accent. Why she's with an old geezer like Nezer, whose nads are probably shrunk up into his body, I'll never know."

"What about Ben? Is that whole career thing the only reason they were estranged?"

Jacklyn regarded Jaymie and grimaced. "I learned early, with Evan there's always more. Originally, when the marital split first happened, Ben made the mistake of siding with his mother in the divorce proceedings."

"It's too bad kids seem forced to take sides."

"I don't think Sarah was forcing anything, it was all Evan."

"You seem to dislike him. How did you work with him for so long?"

"I didn't know him when I first started on the book. Ghostwriters need work. I got to know him, Bella and Ben over the year I worked with Evan. Anyway, it looks like maybe Ben has switched sides. I can't *imagine* how hurt Sarah must be about her son sucking up to

Evan now. But I suppose Ben has to think of his future," she said with a nasty sneer.

Jaymie, taken aback by her tone, said, "What do you mean?"

"Papa holds the purse strings. Evan Nezer is quite possibly the Scroogiest fellow to ever stroll the bedizened streets of Queensville."

"Maybe he'll undergo a miraculous ghostly intervention and will embrace Christmas and the Dickens Days festival," Jaymie said lightly.

"That would take more than visitation from four ghosts, it would take a heart and soul transplant. Not that he has a soul to begin with." She paused, then with a dark look toward the Nezer property, she added, "Or a heart."

ᑲ Two ᑲ

THE WEEK STARTED BUSY, as always, with a Monday full of obligations large and small. Jaymie submitted her "Vintage Eats" column to Nan at the *Wolverhampton Weekly Howler*, and her editor ribbed her some about not finishing her cookbook yet. She had been working on her new take on vintage recipes for a couple of years, but the idea had morphed so much since her original inception that she had to keep playing catch-up with herself. And now, with a husband, a daughter, her food column, radio shows, food blog and multiple jobs, she was constantly racing to try to make it all fit.

So dinner was a frozen pizza for Jocie and Jakob and a salad for herself. After a huge family weekend of turkey, stuffing, cranberry sauce, sweet potatoes, green bean casserole and mashed potatoes drowned in gravy, as well as Oma Müller's German specialty food, *käsespätzle*, a cheese noodle dish, she felt like a tightly stuffed bratwurst. She did up the few dishes while Jocie read a book for a report—one of Jaymie's childhood favorites, *The Lion, the Witch and the Wardrobe*; she may have influenced Jocie's choice a skosh—while Jakob set up his yearly spreadsheet for the Christmas tree business, which would start in earnest soon.

Their evening promised to be busy, too. Jakob and Helmut were going over the business plan for the next adventure, the Müller Family Holiday Store, and they were meeting at the cabin since Jaymie was going to the Queensville Heritage Society meeting. She made a point of attending at least one a month, and this was the night for the final planning for the Dickens Days festival, set to go in just days.

She had raced upstairs, carrying Hoppy and followed by Jocie and Lilibet, who climbed up on her and Jakob's bed while she dressed in the attached bathroom. She came out and stood in front of the mirror. She eyed her reflection, while Jocie sat on the bed with Hoppy flopped on his back. She sorted through Jaymie's jewelry tray while Lilibet lunged at necklaces and beads, batting and tussling with each piece. She was far from a kitten anymore, but had stayed small, a petite tabby darling with a coquettish personality and too much energy, kind of like Jocie.

Jaymie wore a long navy sweater over patterned leggings, her favorite outfit at the moment, but it felt wrong for some reason. She twisted and turned in front of the mirror, unhappy with how she looked. Some women were full-figured but still managed to look elegant and put together. Jaymie could wear the same darn thing as the plus-size models wore and it looked dumpy on her. And she *had* to do something about her hair; it was long and shiny, a not-bad medium brown, but she never actually did anything with it other than tie it up in a ponytail or twist it into a bun.

"What about this, Mama?" Jocie said, holding up a long silver chain with a blue and white Dresden bead and silver silk tassel on the end. "I gave that to you for your birthday." She held it away from Lilibet's outstretched paw, which paddled and batted the air frantically, trying to grab hold.

Jaymie took it and held it up to her. "Good choice, honey," she said, slipping it on over her head and pulling her long hair up and over the chain. She eyed it and nodded, then twisted around again, studying herself in the mirror. "I wish this sweater didn't make my bottom look so wide," she muttered to herself.

Jocie stared at her in consternation, her big brown eyes filled with concern. "But you look so nice." She slipped off the bed and stood next to Jaymie, only coming up to her waist. She turned, mimicking Jaymie's movements perfectly. "My bottom is wide too."

Jaymie's heart skipped a beat. What was she *doing*? She had morphed back into the teenage girl whose mother kept cutting back her portions because she was too heavy and needed to slim down. She knew her mother didn't mean to be cruel; Joy Leighton had fretted that Jaymie would never find love, or peer acceptance. But it had left her daughter mortified by her own body, her growing breasts, her plump butt, her thick thighs. Weight was such a freighted issue for girls and women whose bodies wouldn't conform to society's dictates, but even those whose bodies were deemed perfect ended up self-conscious somehow. It was *never* easy.

Tears welled in her eyes. This stopped here and now. She sat down on the bed and helped Jocie sit up beside her. "Thank you, honey," she said seriously, holding her daughter close.

"For what?" she asked, her voice muffled.

Jaymie released her and met her gaze. Anything worth saying

was worth looking someone in the eyes for. "I was wrong to criticize myself that way. You reminded me to be thankful for my healthy body, and remember how lucky I am to have it. Sweetie, a big butt, or thick thighs, or double chins . . . *none* of that matters. We're healthy, and we'll stay that way, if we can. We will exercise and eat vegetables and love ourselves no matter what. We're lucky our bodies move and dance and jiggle and we can laugh and run and play."

"I like to dance," Jocie said.

Jaymie hugged her, inhaling the fruity fragrance of Jocie's shampoo deeply. "Sometimes grown-up women need to be reminded to be grateful for all we have and all we are." She let her go and met her brown-eyed gaze, tucking one blonde curl behind her daughter's ear. "*And* thank you for helping me choose my jewelry. This is the perfect necklace for such a lovely blue." She made a silent vow to never criticize her own or other people's bodies again, not in front of Jocie, and not away from Jocie.

They descended the stairs followed by the pets, and Jocie raced around the big open living room with Hoppy and Lilibet, the little dog barking as the young cat tore up a sofa and stood at the top. The two men sat at the kitchen table with the planning books for their next venture out in front of them.

"This time next year we'll have the Christmas store up and running!" Helmut said, his narrow face shining with happiness.

"And we'll all be ten times as busy," Jakob added. He looked up at his wife. "You look beautiful! That color blue . . . so lovely on you. It brings out your eyes." He got up and kissed her. "Mmmm . . . love you," he murmured in her ear, just for her to hear.

Her breath caught, as always. "I love you, too," she said, framing his face with her hands and staring into his dark brown eyes. "Don't work too hard." Jaymie kissed him goodbye and headed out into the autumnal twilight, pausing by the SUV to take in a deep breath and whisper a prayer of thanks. She was a lucky woman, and she must never forget it.

It was a crisp autumn night, the wind rustling in the leaves along the drive, sweeping them into piles. The forest opposite the cabin was a velvety dark mystery and the moon peeked through leafless limbs, silvery light glossing her vehicle. She got into the Ford SUV, started it up, and headed down the country road, bypassing the village proper on her way to the gathering. They were meeting, as always, at the Queensville Historic Manor. She was grateful for the warmth, the updated HVAC blowing warm air out of registers along the perimeter of the rooms. The sitting room and parlor had huge sliding doors that opened to make a room large enough for a meeting, or a wedding even, as Jaymie's and her sister Becca's had been held there in May. This was expected to be a large meeting, so the doors had been opened, and rows of chairs had been set up to face a dais by the far wall.

Ever since the heritage society had purchased a wheelchair lift to give access to the front porch, Jaymie's elderly friend, Mrs. Stubbs, had attended every meeting. So, among others who Jaymie knew and/or recognized were Mrs. Stubbs, her cousin Miss Perry, and her cousin's niece, Morgan Saunders. They all sat in the front row. Mrs. Bellwood and Imogene Frump sat together; Jaymie had come to think of the Bellwood/Frump team as the Snoop Sisters for their insatiable curiosity and fruitless search for a hidden treasure in the manor. Trip Findley (Jaymie's back-alley neighbor in the Queensville home), Bill Waterman, and even Heidi Lockland, who had recently become more active with the historical society, were in attendance.

Petty Welch, who had moved to Queensville and started working at a couple of local vintage shops, as well as joining the historic society, was sitting near the front. A month or so ago she had started dating Haskell Lockland, the historic society president who was, of course, at the front standing near the dais looking over his notes and calling out to folks who entered. A murmur of voices in low conversation provided a background noise to Haskell's louder voice. Off to one side at a low table sat Mabel Bloombury. As of the summer elections she was treasurer for the society. Jacklyn Marley had approached and was paying the fee to join, it appeared. She then took a seat nearby and rummaged in her bag, taking out her phone and scrolling through messages.

After greeting all her friends, Jaymie, clipboard in one hand and purse in the other, took a seat about midway back next to Heidi's chair, where her designer bag sat in lone splendor, waiting for the meeting to commence. The young woman herself was talking to Mabel at the front. Jaymie had to make a brief presentation, so she went over her notes to be sure she had everything ready. Heidi sat down beside her and had her phone out, texting someone, her thumbs rapidly flying over the onscreen keyboard.

"Who on earth are you texting from a heritage meeting?"

Heidi blushed and slipped the phone into her tan leather Louboutin bag. "No one," she said primly, folding her hands on her skinny jean-clad lap.

Jaymie smiled. Heidi had a new beau, one she was not yet ready to talk about, clearly. Later, maybe. Or another day. Conversation buzzed, and Jaymie glanced around at the beginning of the seasonal decorations. A few faux pine swags topped paintings and doorways, and the fireplace mantel was already decked with a collection of antique oil lamps snuggled among the branches of a faux greenery garland. The only Christmas tree in the house would be set up in a week or two, and would come from the Müller family Christmas tree farm, of course.

At the last minute, as Haskell looked up and cleared his throat, with a smile, there was a bustle behind them all, at the doorway. Ben Nezer and a lovely dark-haired woman who must be his stepmother entered. They marched to the front and took seats at one end of the first row near Mrs. Stubbs and Miss Perry, who whispered to each other and examined them openly. Jacklyn glanced over at them, snorted in amusement, and returned to scanning her phone. Haskell appeared taken aback, and returned to his notes, hastily scribbling in the margins.

All in all there were about thirty-five people in attendance. With everyone eyeing the newcomers, the room was abuzz with whispers and mutterings. Haskell called the meeting to order, and they dispatched a number of items of business. The minutes of the past meeting were read, no new business was introduced, so they got down to the Dickens Days committee reports.

"We'll now hear from Jaymie Leighton Müller. Jaymie, if you'll come up?" Haskell made room for her on the dais.

She took a spot and looked over the room, the variety of happy, calm, sleepy, disgruntled and attentive faces. "As you all know, I'm head of the food subcommittee for Dickens Days. I'm happy to report that several home cooks and a few commercial bakeries are providing treats to both give away and sell during the four weekends we will be celebrating. The pastry chef at the Queensville Inn will be creating some wonderful treats, and Tansy, of Tansy's Tarts on Heartbreak Island, will be making miniature butter tarts from her special recipe for us to give away, with a dollar-off coupon for their bakery attached."

There was an *ahhh* of appreciation at that. Anyone who had tasted the Canadian treat, made by Tansy from her Canadian family recipe, became hooked. Free tarts were a surprisingly big deal.

"I will be making hermit cookies and brownies, as well as miniature two-bite muffins. Treats will be sold, of course, at the cider booth."

She glanced down at her clipboard. She had covered everything, but had one more thing to say. Looking back up, she met the gazes of Mabel Bloombury, Jewel Dandridge, and a couple of others. "I'm looking forward to our Dickens Days this year. For anyone who needs it, even for our shops, I have holly bushes growing profusely in our Queensville yard. Becca has cut a few branches to use in her Queensville Fine Antiques holiday displays. If you need any, I'll be happy to cut some. I'll be using some for my secret project, but we still have plenty! Let me know how many you need and I'll cut the appropriate amount." She returned to her seat and sat down, smiling around her at the faces of her friends.

Mrs. Bellwood and Imogene Frump stood up together, an inseparable duo since their long feud had been laid to rest, but they did not move to the dais, staying by their chairs. Together they were in charge of the cider booth, and had organized teams to cover all weekend evenings. They had a new recipe to try, Mrs. Bellwood said, and had sourced local apple cider, which they were purchasing at cost in exchange for an advertisement for the cider mill at the booth. "Jaymie, we'll take you up on the offer of holly branches to decorate the booth. We'll need . . ." She leaned over and consulted with Imogene Frump. "We'll need four bunches. If you have enough." She sat down.

"I'll get them before we open this coming weekend."

After that was dealt with, Bill Waterman stood and cleared his throat. He, too, stayed by his chair. Everyone hushed as he surveyed the group, his gaze finally resting on the Nezers before he returned his attention to Haskell. "We've got trouble," he said. "I don't know if anyone heard, but Evan Nezer is kicking up a big ole fuss about

Dickens Days, as he does every year. Trouble is, this year he's living in that house of his right on the village green."

His tone was dry and creaky, his face pale. Was he okay? Jaymie again wondered.

"So, he was whining about me hammering a stake into his grass to anchor the cider house," Bill continued. "He's threatening to sue, and you all know what he's capable of, 'cause he does it every dang year. Usually we can count on the judge throwing it out as a nuisance suit, but this year, with him living right there, it may hold water. What are we going to do?"

The woman with Ben Nezer stood and turned toward Bill, a troubled look on her lovely face. Jaymie recognized her immediately from Jacklyn Marley's description as the Nigella Lawson look-alike: dark hair, lush figure, full lips, classically beautiful face. Jacklyn was watching her with an avid gaze. "My name is Mrs. Bella Nezer, and I'm Evan's wife. He means well, Mr. Waterman, really he does. He's misunderstood, that's all."

A ripple of laughter drifted across the room, spreading, then dying as folks saw she was not kidding.

"Mrs. Nezer, we mean no disrespect toward your husband," Haskell said, his courtly manner, well-trimmed mane of white hair and lanky stature giving him a commanding presence. "But we have had dealings with him in the past, as I'm sure you know."

"I have been married to him for two years. I'm quite aware of his feelings on the subject of Dickens Days," she said stiffly, tapping the chair in front of her with one beringed hand.

Haskell eyed her with some doubt. "Bill is, unfortunately, correct. In the past Professor Nezer's suits have been dismissed as frivolous. Like last year, when we had that trouble and he went to court to try to halt Dickens Days, saying it was disrespectful to continue. And the year before, when he said that traffic drawn from other towns for Dickens Days was cluttering his street."

"That 'trouble' last year, Mr. Lockland, was a *murder*!" Bella said, her cultured, English-accented voice trembling over the word.

Jaymie felt a squeeze of anxiety; it was indeed just one year ago that she had found a young woman dying in Bill's shed. It was a terrible tragedy, true, but shutting down the festival had not been the answer. There was so much sadness in the world and it needed to be countered with joy, not defeat. Reflexively, she jumped up and said, "Mrs. Nezer, I know you're supporting your husband, but Bill was doing nothing that we haven't done for years."

"Just because you've done something for years doesn't mean you should get to keep doing it," she retorted, her voice crisp and clipped.

Jaymie couldn't argue with that, so she sat back down.

Haskell put up his hands in a calming gesture. "Ladies, Bill, let's take a step back. Bella, I understand your husband's concern. Perhaps if I were to oversee the placement of the stake Evan would allow it?"

She smiled brilliantly. "I'll speak to him about it, Haskell."

They left things at that, but Jaymie, concerned, headed toward the front to speak with Haskell and Bill Waterman as people dispersed.

"Haskell, you have to stand firm with that Nezer character," Bill was saying as she approached. "If you give an inch he'll take a mile."

"Let's see what Bella can do. We worked together on a committee last year. She's a very persuasive woman," Haskell said with a sly smile.

"I do *hope* I'm persuasive," Bella Nezer said, joining them. Her stepson awaited her at the door, self-consciously examining the coffered ceiling. "We're having a little seasonal soiree Friday evening at our home. Haskell, you're coming, correct?" she said, glancing at the society president. He nodded. She turned to Jaymie. "Would you come too? I feel we've gotten off on the wrong foot, and I want to prove my husband is no monster. You could bring *your* husband?" she said, glancing down at Jaymie's engagement and wedding set of rings. "And I believe I know a friend of yours, the delectably eccentric Valetta Nibley, from the Emporium? She is a *true* character. Will you invite her, too?"

Jaymie bristled at the description. The woman made it sound like Valetta skulked around town wearing a tinfoil hat and tuning in alien mindwaves. And she had pointedly not invited Bill, who stood silently by. But it was important that the Dickens Days festival proceed, and the Nezers were critical to that. She didn't want to offend Bella, so she nodded. "Sure. I'll see if Valetta can pry herself away from her cat skeleton collection."

Bella Nezer stared at her, eyes wide, then she smiled. "Oh, you're joking. How clever you are!" From her, that sounded like an insult.

"Hey, am I invited too?" Heidi said, approaching with a luminous smile on her lovely face.

Bella, her own smile fading, nodded. "Certainly. I'll make sure you're added to the list. Heidi, correct? It's a very exclusive party, mostly Evan's work friends from college. You may be bored."

"Oh, no, not at all! If Jaymie and Val are there, I'll never be bored," she said, grabbing Jaymie's arm.

Jaymie hugged her friend's arm to her side, noting Bella's determinedly neutral expression.

"We're having it catered," she said, apropos to nothing. "Some of the students from WC are working as servers."

"That's very kind of you, to give them work," Haskell said. "So many of them need to supplement their scholarships."

"We do our best to be good neighbors and good citizens," Bella said with a gracious lady-of-the-manor nod and smile.

"You know, we were neighbors," Heidi said, eyeing the taller woman. "I'm not sure you remember me."

"Of course I do," she said coolly, looking down at the younger woman. "My husband's son made sure to be in the front yard every time you went jogging." She cast a look toward Ben, at the door, who was now examining the door frame.

Jaymie bit her lip to keep from smiling too broadly.

"And your husband once called the police on me because I wore a bikini top to mow the front lawn," Heidi said, still staring at the woman. Her tone had become unexpectedly flinty.

Jaymie glanced over at her in surprise. Heidi was a sweetheart, but she occasionally showed fangs, like a kitten with needle-sharp teeth.

Bella's cheeks shaded a delicate pink. "Evan thought it was . . . distasteful. Said it brought down the tone of the neighborhood. There are . . . standards."

"Standards?"

"Well, we don't approve of lawn gnomes, do we?" she said, still showing that smile that was a thin veneer over a sneer.

"What, *seriously*?" Jaymie said as Heidi rolled her eyes. "First, lawn gnomes aren't everyone's cup of tea, but they aren't illegal. And I'm sorry, but every guy in Queensville mows his lawn in August with no shirt on. It's not a big deal, apparently, but a woman with a top *on* is?"

Haskell looked alarmed. Bill, who had remained silent until now, huffed in disgust; normally the most equable of men and charitable to a fault, Nezer's willingness to make others miserable rubbed him the wrong way. "Doesn't surprise me," he grunted. To Jaymie he said, "I'm finishing up the cider house tomorrow, come hell or high water, and I'd appreciate your help."

Jaymie glanced over at Haskell, who shrugged. "I hope we can find a compromise. Haskell, you said you'd be there? You and Evan can talk it over."

"That's settled then!" Haskell said, clapping his hands. He put one arm over Bella's shoulder and strolled away, down the aisle between the rows of chairs toward her stepson at the door, murmuring soothingly to her.

"Tomorrow is going to be interesting," Jaymie said to Heidi. "Let's help Mabel and the others put the chairs away," she said, setting her purse aside and starting to fold chairs as the treasurer and one of her daughters began.

"You be careful tomorrow, Jaymsie," Heidi said, squinting after Bella and Haskell as she began to stack chairs on the dolly cart used to store them. "That Nezer dude is a real pill. I didn't want to say it with his wife there, but he used to leer at me as I mowed my lawn." She took two collapsed chairs from Jaymie and stacked them on the dolly cart. "He'd slow his car down and cruise past, staring at me, then when I called him out on it and said he was a creep—I don't mind guys looking, but there's a difference between looking and leering—he called the police to complain." She shuddered. "I told Joel about him," she continued, naming her former boyfriend (and Jaymie's before that) who had moved on and left Queensville. "But all Joel ever said was, what did I expect, mowing in a bikini top?"

"Typical Joel," Jaymie said. No one's life was poorer for him having moved on. They finished the last of the chairs, hugged Mabel and walked out of the big double room into the entrance hall and toward the front door. "I'd better get going. See you Wednesday night for girls' night?"

"You bet."

They hugged, strolled out into the autumn chill, and Heidi hopped into her blue sports car, zooming off while Jaymie fished around for her keys and unlocked her SUV. She was ready to step up into it when, by the light over the garage, she saw Ben Nezer talking to a woman Jaymie vaguely recognized, someone she had seen around town lately. She was older, maybe in her sixties, pear-shaped and wearing a navy peacoat over long skirts, and with a white mane of long hair bound back in a braid.

The two murmured to each other, seemingly arguing, then Ben walked away, to Bella, who was saying a lingering farewell to Haskell. Jaymie wouldn't even have noticed, but it appeared so furtive. The older woman strode away, got into a small rusty Volvo, and drove off, her car rattling and roaring as if on its last legs. Jaymie shook her head, put it out of her mind, and headed home.

Jocie was already in bed, but Jakob was sitting on the sofa, examining the business plan his brother had drawn up. Jakob and Jaymie, in partnership with his brother Helmut and her brother-in-law Kevin, had purchased the land abutting the Müller property and were starting the process of planning a Christmas and holiday store, along with a family fun venue in back and a tobogganing hill, among other things. They had decided on the name Müller Farms Holiday Store because they didn't want to limit themselves to the Christmas season, and they wanted everybody of every faith to feel welcome and included.

After seeing to Hoppy, who danced around her feet and yipped until she picked him up and snuggled him, Jaymie plunked down beside her husband, setting her little dog on the sofa beside her. He slung his arm around her shoulders. Jakob was a handsome fellow, broad-shouldered, dark-haired, brown-eyed, with a beard that grew thicker and more luxuriant as winter approached. He kept it soft and touchable with beard balm, a bearded man's best friend, he kidded. He kissed her enthusiastically. They got distracted for a while and then, hair delightfully mussed, sat back up, breathless.

"Whew, Mr. Müller, you are one heck of a kisser."

His dark eyes even darker, he chuckled. "And you, Mrs. Müller, are quite the temptress."

"Mmmm . . . coming to bed?"

"In a minute. I'm checking Helmut's figures. He asked me to, though I don't know why. He's always so precise."

"He likes another pair of eyes, he always says."

He went back to examining the business plan. Helmut, who had a business degree from Wolverhampton College, had drawn up a proper formal business plan, since they would need to approach the bank for financing and the township for zoning. Jaymie read over his shoulder, the sections labeled *Market Analysis* and *Financial Plan*, among others, and the attached spreadsheet of projected costs, including the first-year break-even point.

"Do you really think we can have it up and running by this time next year?" Jaymie asked softly.

"If everything goes according to plan," he said. "*I'm* hoping we can have it going by October first. I thought maybe we'd start in the spring with creating a pumpkin patch. We used to grow pumpkins when we were kids, and my dad is the best at it."

"Spring is a busy time of year for everyone," she said, worried about them taking on too much. Most folks thought Christmas tree farmers rested and watched the trees grow from January until October, but in truth every season had its work. Spring was especially busy, with new planting, fertilizing, pulling stumps from the previous year's cut, and a million and one other tasks.

"We'll have to hire extra help. We'll be using some of the back acreage for more pine seedlings, and maybe . . . Sonya was thinking of a big garden of herbs." Sonya was Helmut's significant other; her kids by a previous relationship were Helmut's too, now. He turned to look into Jaymie's eyes. "What do you think of that? She said she could make herb wreaths and herbal whatevers for the store."

Jaymie laughed at "herbal whatevers" and put her head on his shoulder. "Knowing Sonya, whatever those 'whatevers' are, they'll be beautiful. She has a knack for that kind of thing, and everything she touches, actually." She raised her head and met his gaze. "Jakob, I was thinking . . . maybe Sonya could be the store manager."

"Would she *want* to?"

"We were talking about it the other day, when we were at your folks' for Thanksgiving dinner. Remember she went for a walk with me, Hoppy and the kids? She's planning to take a retail management course at WC. She'd *dearly* like to manage the store, but she doesn't want to push herself in. She thought I was going to do it, since I've already worked at so many stores and know the ropes." Jaymie sighed. "I told her I can't handle one more job, and that though I want to *work* at the store, I have no desire to *manage* it. Not my strength."

"Okay. What *exactly* did she say?"

She examined him and petted his beard. "She asked me to talk to you."

He frowned. "Why didn't she talk to me herself?"

"She's afraid of putting you in a tough position. Think about it, Jakob; she's with Helmut, and he's our partner in the business. She was worried that if she approached Helmut, he'd feel like he *had* to agree, and that if she approached you, she'd hurt Helmut's feelings. She asked my advice."

"And you said . . . ?"

"That I'd talk to you."

Jakob nodded. "I think a family meeting is in order. If she's going to be manager, she needs to be able to talk to any one of us about anything. No secrets, no hurt feelings, no hidden agendas. In fact, maybe we ought to make meetings a regular part of the business, so that all of us have a venue for expressing our thoughts without dragging it into family gatherings."

"Agreed. So offer her the job," Jaymie said, and kissed him. "Now, one more question: will you be up for going to a party at the Nezer residence in Queensville this Friday evening? Maybe Jocie can stay with your mom and dad and we can dress up and hobnob with the college crowd?"

"Isn't Nezer that guy in town you don't like? The one who was complaining about a stake hammered into his grass?"

"Yes, but his wife invited us, and I'd like to try to keep the peace for Dickens Days."

"Okay. Do I have to dress up?"

"Mmm, sports jacket and slacks would be appropriate, I would imagine. No tie."

"All right, we're on. We haven't had a date night in a while. Now, let's go to bed."

"Good idea. I have a big day tomorrow."

"Oh?"

"I may have to head off a confrontation between one surprisingly hotheaded handyman and a snarky college professor."

✄ Three ✄

JAYMIE SPENT THE MORNING testing recipes for her cookbook and updating her food blog. The cabin was a peaceful place to do both, with the view through the kitchen window and across the road of the spare black limbs and deep green of deciduous and coniferous trees in the woods opposite. The whole forest was edged in low stands of sumac, a hardy bush that grew in ditches and on hillsides throughout the countryside. Scarlet staghorn sumac, with their brilliant red leaves now gone, proliferated, the hardy long-tapered clusters of wine-colored berries remaining on the furred branches from which it got its name.

It was a beautiful view, one she cherished after half a year living there.

She had finally decided, after trying a few ideas, that her cookbook would be a collection of vintage recipes reimagined two ways, one for modern palates, and one elevated. She had, for example, taken a heavy meat loaf and made it with ground turkey instead of beef, for the fat-conscious among her readers. For a second version she had taken ground beef and, using a food processor, ground it finer; she then formed it into a pretty oblong loaf, with spinach to add color and a layer of chopped hard-boiled eggs. She finished by wrapping it in prosciutto.

Her new approach had made the cookbook writing more complicated and it was taking a lot more time than she had originally anticipated, but there were so many cookbooks on the market that she needed a hook for hers, and the two-way treatment of vintage recipes was it.

The cabin smelled delicious, and after doing some initial photographs of the meat loaves, she wrapped both in foil and set them to cool, after which they would go into the fridge to be reheated for a simple supper.

Meanwhile, as she wrote the cookbook, she was doing what had been suggested to her by an editor she had approached. She had convinced the local newspaper to give her a food column, "Vintage Eats," had started a blog that was gathering followers, and she had even done two radio interviews with a fellow who hosted a talk

25

radio show about antiques and vintage collectibles! All of that took a lot of time, but it was a joy to do.

Life was never boring.

The meat loaves were going to be a quick-and-easy dinner for another night, so she started dinner in the slow cooker—a stuffed rolled pork loin that would cook all afternoon with no fussing—had lunch, played with Lilibet, took Hoppy for a walk, then got in her SUV ready to meet Bill at the village green by two. Her jeans from the previous winter wouldn't do up anymore, the result of too much recipe testing, so she had bought some new jeggings, which fit in wide calf boots nicely. Jakob had bought her a leather jacket, and she topped it with an infinity scarf in a lovely pumpkin color with a fall leaf pattern. She felt smart and was comfortable.

The sky was overcast and there was a distinct chill in the air. The forest across the road from the cabin had been splashed in a palette of yellow, orange and brown, but the leaves were almost all gone now. Soon a blanket of white would overtake it all. It would be her first winter living out here, though they did, as a family, spend time at the Queensville house, too. It was a balancing act, maintaining both homes, but Becca and Kevin spent about a week or two each month in the Queensville house, so it was well tenanted.

She parked at the Leighton house and walked to the downtown area, but Bill had not yet arrived. She walked over to the Emporium to check in on Valetta, her new boots making a satisfying *clunk clunk* on the old board floor of the historic store.

Her friend was in her glass-fronted pharmacy booth at the back of the store. She slid the window open. "Hey, Jaymie . . . didn't expect to see you today."

"Hey, Val. I'm waiting for Bill. We're going to finish up with some of the Dickens Days preparations. You missed the heritage society meeting last night."

"I was looking after Will and Eva," she said, naming her nephew and niece. "You know I'm not as avid a hysterical society gal as you are."

"The second Mrs. Nezer was there, with her stepson."

"Oh, lovely Bella-the-Ball?"

Jaymie chuckled. "She asked me and Jakob to a party on Friday night and wanted to know if I'd ask you, too."

Valetta pushed her glasses up on the bridge of her nose. "Why would I go? Why would *you* go? Jaymie, that man has been a pain his whole life and spends most of his time thinking up new nuisance lawsuits, and wife number two treats me like I'm some kind of oddball."

"Yeah, why *is* that? She called you delightfully eccentric or something like that."

"Code for a whackadoodle," Valetta said darkly.

"I *may* have suggested you collect cat skeletons," Jaymie said, struggling not to laugh out loud.

"*Jaymie!*"

Chuckling, she tapped on the glass and added, "Relax, she realized it was a joke. *Finally.* It took her a moment. Why does she treat you like that?"

Valetta sighed and rolled her eyes. "I have no clue." She paused, counted out some pills, then checked the prescription and counted them again—her mantra was count twice, bottle once—then swept them into a vial, sealing and carefully labeling it. "The only substantial interaction we've ever had was talking about books one day when she was in for a prescription and said something about Jane Austen. I said I didn't care for her novels and preferred Charlotte Brontë. From then on she started treating me like I was a weirdo."

"And that's it?"

"That is *it*."

"Okay. So . . . will you go?" Valetta sighed. "C'mon, it'll be fun," Jaymie pleaded, folding her arms and leaning on the counter, staring into the glass booth. "Heidi's going. Much to Bella's chagrin, if I'm not mistaken. I'm hoping I can prove to Nezer that we're just community-minded folk, not out to annoy anyone. We'll get to see what they've done to the place. We can dress up and drink wine and pretend to be fancy. Think about it! We'll hobnob with the glitterati, trip the light fantastic, mambo along the buffet line." She wiggled her shoulders and grinned. "*And* we can gawk and make fun of the stuffed shirts."

"All right, but just for you."

"Yay!"

"I'll bring Brock as my plus one. He likes to hobnob."

"Oh. *Not* yay." Jaymie did not like her friend's brother at all.

"That's the price you pay, kiddo."

Jaymie sighed. "Okay. I'd better go in case Bill is over there and gets into a fistfight with Nezer. Hopefully the old Scrooge is at the college today. Bella was supposed to talk to Evan and get him to co-operate, and Haskell is supposed to join us, so maybe that will help."

Jaymie left the Emporium and stood on the porch, shifting out of the way as a couple entered. A breeze had sprung up and the sky had lowered, thick clouds rolling across it in ominous dark clots, like spoiled cream. The Emporium was on a slight rise above the village center, and from there she could see that Bill's beat-up dark blue pickup truck was now parked by the village green and he was already walking around the cider house checking it structurally. The village had put in a waterproof electrical outlet on a post for such events, so he had to place the booth close to it. But in doing so, he was inevitably also close to the Nezer property.

Jaymie descended from the porch and crossed to the village green. "Hey, Bill, how's it going?"

He straightened, his lined face wreathed in a smile. "So far, so good. Can't complain for an old guy."

There was a comfort, Jaymie thought, in the day-to-day banalities of life, the *can't complain for an old guy* and the *can't complain, who'd listen?* responses to the usual question. But she wondered, was any of it true? Bill sometimes appeared to be in pain, a grimace crossing his weary face when he straightened. He had had back surgery three years before, and knee surgery before that. Maybe saying "can't complain" was shorthand for "I don't want to bother people." She touched his shoulder and smiled. He covered her hand with his huge, arthritic mitt and nodded.

"Where is Haskell?" she asked.

"He called me this morning. Something's come up and he can't join us."

She sighed. That figured. "But you're still finishing up here?"

Bill nodded. "I'm not going to let Nezer interfere with what this town has been doing for years."

Jaymie felt a twinge of foreboding but pushed it to one side of her mind. Everything would be all right. It wasn't like Bill was actually doing anything harmful, after all. "So, can I help?"

"You're a strong girl, sure. I need to shift the whole booth about five inches so it's close enough to the electrical. If you could put your shoulder to it with me, I think we can do it."

They grunted and pushed, but it wouldn't budge. Jaymie stood back, sighing in exasperation. Her hands were freezing and she was regretting not bringing gloves. Or mittens. She had some in her car, but it was at the Queensville house, too far to run and get. She and Bill tried again. It moved a bit, but not enough.

A blonde young man wearing a hooded khaki jacket paused and watched them for a moment. "Uh . . . can I help?" he finally asked.

Bill eyed him and nodded. "That would be great. What's your name?"

"I'm Finn . . . Fancombe."

"Erla's son?"

He nodded.

"Jaymie Leighton, this is Finn; I know his mom, Erla." Bill glanced at Jaymie and winked. "She's housekeeper for the Nezers."

Which made the man's aid a delicious irony, Jaymie thought, given his connection to the Nezer household. She examined him, remembering the story from the paper, his being expelled from WC because of a plagiarism complaint from Nezer. He was a serious, attractive fellow, probably in his thirties. She wondered what he was doing now that he no longer was welcome at WC. Would another college take him? And would his work at WC be transferable given the scandal? She knew little or nothing about academia, having been satisfied with her arts degree from a Canadian university.

They all put their shoulders to it, and the cider house was pushed into position, close enough to the electrical outlet for the heavy-duty outdoor plug to reach so the heritage society could hook up lights and the slow cookers of cider.

"Maybe we don't need to put in the anchor line. This thing is pretty heavy," Jaymie said, hand on the cider house structure.

Bill squinted and curled his lip, two circles of color on his cheeks. "I'm going to anchor it. I don't give a good goldarn what Mr. Evan Nezer says!"

Finn looked up quickly but didn't say anything. Bill was feeling mulish, Jaymie could see. That didn't happen often, but when it did, there was no use arguing with him. Nezer had put his back up, and he would not retreat.

He got the length of rope out of his truck, and the wooden stake, along with the mallet. He slipped the loop of the rope over the hook screwed into the cider booth roof, then hunched down by the pine trees and swung the mallet, pegging the stake into the earth at an angle. He then tied a loop in the other end of the rope and slipped it over the stake. The rumble of a motor broke the Tuesday afternoon peace, and an old gold MK2 Jaguar throbbed closer, then stopped.

"What are you doing on my property!"

Nezer leaned out the driver's-side window, which in his case was the right side of the car. Jaymie stared, and Finn looked up.

Bill did *not* look up at Nezer's irate shriek.

"I told you not to touch my property," Nezer yelled again. "You're ruining my grass. What you're doing is illegal. I'll sue!"

The siren call of a public dispute brought folks from many places. Georgina, who managed Queensville Fine Antiques for Becca and Kevin, trotted down the store porch and moved toward them, up the slight incline past the Emporium, hugging her cardigan tightly around her slim body. Jacklyn Marley emerged from the side door and down the stairs from the apartment above the grocery store.

Mrs. Bellwood, walking her pug, Roary, paused on her afternoon stroll. This directly concerned her as one of the two ladies who ran the cider booth. She ambled up to the car as her pug leaned back, tugging on the leash, barking furiously with its choked, muffled grunt. "Mr. Nezer, the anchor will not harm your grass in the slightest. In fact, aeration of any kind is beneficial to turf. You must be reasonable!"

"Didn't your wife talk to you about it, Mr. Nezer?" Jaymie asked, joining Mrs. Bellwood and eyeing the driver.

Nezer squinted, glancing from Jaymie to Bill—who had stood and watched, awaiting the outcome—to Mrs. Bellwood.

"We met Bella at the heritage society meeting last night, and she said she'd speak with you," Jaymie said, hoping to derail the argument.

"She did not say anything and would not because she knows my feelings on this. She knows when to shut her mouth, unlike *some* people." He glared up at Jaymie.

Bill bent back to his work, hammering the long stake into place.

"I said *stop* it!" Nezer climbed out of his car and slammed the door, the powerful engine still throbbing. He strode over to the handyman. "Cease and desist this *moment* or I'll call the police!"

The handyman kept at it, but the rigidity of his shoulders revealed to Jaymie exactly his feelings. He was angry, his ears becoming red with his ire. He disliked anyone who wasn't community-minded.

Nezer's face turned brick red. He did not like to be ignored. He charged at Bill, grabbing his shoulder and shoving him. Bill toppled sideways. Finn, eyes wide, looked on. There was a cackle of laughter and Jaymie spotted the woman she presumed was Sarah Nezer standing over by the Emporium stairs, hand over her mouth and glee in her eyes.

"Stop!" Jaymie yelped, scooting toward her friend and reaching out. "Bill, are you okay?"

Bill staggered to his feet, face red, and yelled an expletive—the first time Jaymie had ever heard him swear—and roared, "Nezer, if you lay a hand on me one more time—"

"You'll *what*? Tell me, hammer boy," Nezer taunted as he whipped out his cell phone and held it up in front of him, hitting an onscreen button.

"So help me God, I will plant you in the ground, you condescending little turdwipe!"

"Don't you threaten *me*, Waterman!"

"That's not a threat, Nezer. Threats are empty," Bill said, face twisted into a grimace that Jaymie thought indicated pain. "That's a *promise*! I'll plant you six feet under your precious turf."

Nezer, a smirk on his face, lowered the cell phone. "Got it on video, you Neanderthal. Now let's see what the police say about that!" He hustled to his car, jumped in, and roared off.

"Bill, are you okay?" Jaymie asked, her voice shaking. She went to her friend. His face was red and he was panting. "He pushed you pretty hard. Did he hurt your back?" He looked dangerously close to a heart attack or something similar, and the pained grimace was even more pronounced. He didn't answer, he just shook his head. "Take deep breaths. Calm down. Was that wise, tweaking Nezer like that when we're trying to get his cooperation?"

"*Someone* has to stand up to him, Jaymie, or he's gonna ruin this year's Dickens Days." He straightened with a grimace, one hand to

31

his back. "Bullies need to be faced. Otherwise, somehow, some way, Evan Nezer is going to ruin Christmas for everybody."

Jaymie understood his point, but felt that sometimes people like Nezer must be appeased, or the consequences could become calamitous. Finn Fancombe, who had backed away during the argument, turned and headed around the pine trees toward the Nezer residence. Sarah Nezer climbed the steps into the Emporium and Jacklyn Marley retreated as well, climbing the steps back up to her apartment over the store.

Jaymie sighed. "Let's take advantage of the fact that he's gone to get to work and set up the other structure."

"The diorama?" Bill took a deep breath.

"You have it made, right?"

"I do, but it's in pieces."

This year, in keeping with the Dickens Days theme, they were setting up a life-size diorama of the Cratchit family's Christmas feast, complete with a child-size mannequin dressed as Tiny Tim, a painted Mrs. Cratchit and a Bob. On the table was going to be the flaming pudding bedecked with a sprig of real holly from Jaymie's own backyard.

"Would it take long to put it together?"

"Nope. It's made to go together in a jiffy. I figured if you wanted to keep it for another year it would store better in flat panels so I attached hinges. All we have to do to set it up is screw the hinges to the side panels. Let me bring them down here on a handcart, and you can hold them in place for me while I attach them."

"Are you up to doing this?" Jaymie asked, still concerned.

Bill's face was a better color, and the merry twinkle was back in his eye. "It takes more than that humbug college professor to take *me* down!"

He had constructed it carefully, but inevitably there was more to it than screwing the pieces together. Finding a level spot was vital, and next was arranging where to face it. Jaymie postulated that there would likely be folks stopping to examine it and maybe even take photos, so they didn't want it to interfere with potential lineups at the cider booth. They settled on a spot by one of the Victorian light posts that lined a paved path through town. It was closer to the Nezer home but still on public property, and had the row of pines as a backdrop. It would look lovely if there was some snow, Jaymie thought.

Together, they began. Townsfolk passed by. A few stopped to talk and take photos, asking what it was. She had wanted it to be a secret, but in Queensville the gossip increased by social media would make that impossible, so she explained to each. Everyone in the village was excited about Dickens Days, and her diorama would probably be posted online before the day was over. That was okay; it increased excitement and possibly would help get a larger crowd out for the opening!

As they finished putting it together, a police car cruised to a stop. Bernie, dressed in her uniform and with a heavy police bomber jacket over it, got out. She looked embarrassed and unenthusiastic. "Jaymie, Bill."

"What's up, Bernie?" Jaymie asked, noting the reluctant gaze.

Bernie walked around, investigating the cider booth. She eyed the rope and the stake, buried now among the pine trees, then returned to the two, who stood, awaiting her purpose. "We got a call from a Mr. Evan Nezer saying that Bill, here, threatened his life."

Bill chuckled. "What a chowderhead!" He met Bernie's gaze. "Oh, not you, Bernie, I'm talkin' about that Nezer character!"

"That wasn't a threat, Bernie, truly, it was more—"

"Mr. Nezer showed us a video and Bill's exact words were, and I quote—" She flipped open a notebook and read, "'*So help me God, I will plant you in the ground, you condescending little turdwipe,*' unquote."

"I did say that," Bill admitted with an unrepentant grin.

"And there was more. You also said you'd plant him six feet under his precious turf."

"He didn't mean it, Bern!" Jaymie cried. "Mr. Waterman wouldn't hurt a flea."

The senior handyman's smile died. "I mighta gotten a little annoyed. Like Jaymie says, I didn't mean it literally. It was said in a moment of anger, and didn't reflect any intention of doing bodily harm. Pure exasperation."

Bernie nodded, her dark eyes twinkling, though her expression remained neutral. "Having met the gentleman on many occasions in my capacity as a peace officer, I can imagine a context where I might get exasperated with Mr. Nezer. However, Bill, I *have* to warn you not to say anything like that again. Are we clear?"

"Yes, ma'am," Bill said, his eyes twinkling in the dull light. "I'll tell Mr. Nezer what you said. I suppose my job here is done."

"What about the stake in the ground he was complaining about?" Bill asked, motioning to the cider house.

Bernie hesitated and walked back to the structure, which she circled again. "Where is his property line?"

Bill followed her around the back of the cider house. "You see this electrical post?"

She nodded.

"Right on the other side of that."

"You can't keep the stake on public property?"

"Nope. If I could, I would. Honest. But that's too close to the structure."

"Have you asked Nezer formally for an easement?"

"He'd never agree to that."

"You don't know that," Bernie said.

"We never had to do that before!"

Jaymie exchanged a look with Bernie. "Bill, things change. He wasn't living in the house before. We can at least consider asking."

Bill nodded. "I'll consider it."

"Okay, then," Bernie said.

Jaymie eyed her handyman friend; something about Nezer rubbed Bill so wrong that he was being stubborn about the whole affair. Nezer was being a jerk, yes, but it didn't help to make him angrier. Sometimes to obtain an objective one had to swallow one's pride and plead. She'd have to check into why Bella hadn't done what she said and asked Evan to reconsider.

"Thanks, Bernie," Jaymie said. "We'll find a way to make it right."

The diorama structure put together, Jaymie said farewell to Bill, who trudged off to his workshop pulling his handcart and box of tools. He left for her the tarp and twist ties he had used in the workshop to keep the diorama clean and dry. She examined the internal painting closely, smiled in satisfaction at the scene, then attached the tarp to the front opening, slipping the long twist ties through the tarp grommets and the holes Bill had drilled in the top and sides of the diorama.

By the time she was done her nose was dripping and her hands freezing. She backed up across the road, slid her hands into her jacket sleeves to warm them and eyed the result, the blue tarp over the plywood structure. It looked like an ugly box. She'd have to think of a better system because she hadn't considered how it would look from the outside, and it was hideous. For now the tarp worked to keep it protected from inclement weather.

It was a letdown.

She was going to head back toward the Queensville house but, out of curiosity, took a detour and wandered past the line of pines, toward the Nezer house. It was large, a lovely old Queen Anne, similar to the Leighton house but bigger. A Wolverhampton renovation company truck was parked outside, and two men were working on the windows, with Bella Nezer standing outside huddled in a heavy cable-knit cardigan, watching.

"Lots of work to do on the house," Jaymie commented, joining her.

Bella glanced over at her. "Oh . . . yes. We haven't had much time to get it ready for company, but we'll be almost there by the party on Friday. It's been sadly neglected over the years."

"Whose idea was it to move here? Yours or Evan's?"

"Does it matter? It's a lovely home, and shouldn't have been neglected for so long," she said with an airy wave of the hand.

"I agree. As a fan of historic homes, I'm truly happy the Nezer family is back in it. Does Ben live here too?"

"Oh, heavens, no. Just me and Evan, rattling around this big place all alone."

"Except for the housekeeper."

"Oh, of course. Erla. She has her own suite of rooms."

"In the house?"

"Aren't you a curious little busy bee," Bella said, her voice tight with tension. "Of course in the house. Do you think we keep the help in a shed out back? No, not that way!" she shouted.

Jaymie was startled, but Bella glided away, flapping her hands at a fellow who was putting up a shutter.

"That's upside down, you tosser!"

The worker took it down and turned it the other way, moving to the other side of the window.

Jaymie walked on and passed by the driveway and the back of

the house. A door opened and Finn Fancombe emerged, then turned back as a woman followed him out, handed him a shopping bag, and pushed him to a back path that led away from the house and toward a sturdy shed at the back. A robust, strong-looking woman, she appeared worried and glanced around, her gaze resting for a moment on Jaymie before returning to Finn. She shook her head ever so slightly. The young man looked toward Jaymie, then circled the shed and disappeared behind it.

So that was Erla Fancombe, the Nezer housekeeper. It must be awkward for her to work for Nezer, when her son had been bounced from collegial life because of her boss. Or more accurately, if the plagiarism claim was justified, because of something her son had done.

Lots of bad feelings surrounding Nezer in this town, Jaymie thought. *The Friday evening party should be interesting.*

⚘ Four ⚘

JAYMIE WOKE ON WEDNESDAY WITH A KNOT IN HER STOMACH. She had to appear in court at a preliminary hearing to determine if the accused in a tragic crime the month before would stand trial. It had been delayed time and again over the last month by the killer's attorney troubles, but today was the day. She dressed carefully, and, accompanied by Jakob, who held her hand through the whole thing except when she gave evidence, did her duty, avoiding looking at the accused.

After it was over, they walked out of the courthouse into the brilliant November sunshine, brittle and cold. She was so relieved she wanted to celebrate. She and Jakob went to lunch at the donut shop where they had had their first coffee together, then headed home and had an intimate hour before he had to work. She spent the rest of the day writing as best she could. The court case in the morning had thrown her off-kilter, but she was not going to let it stop her from getting something done.

• • •

WEDNESDAY EVENING WAS GIRLS' NIGHT. Bernie was working a double shift, including the graveyard shift, never popular for police officers, so it was just Jaymie, Valetta and Heidi gathered in Valetta's cottage-style home a block or so from the Emporium. It was a low-key evening of gossip and munchies, with much of the talk centering around the upcoming Dickens Days festivities and the holiday season. Jaymie had used it as an opportunity to test a couple of bar cookie recipes, which everyone enjoyed.

"What do you think Nezer's problem is, with the Dickens Days festivities?" Jaymie asked, sitting back in a snug chair and stroking Denver, her used-to-be crabby tabby, now become purring master of all he surveyed since he had moved in with Valetta. He lolled across her legs, perfectly at his leisure, something he had never done while living with her.

Valetta stretched out her long legs, her feet clad in fluffy cat slippers complete with yarn whiskers and bead eyes, propping them on an ottoman in front of her shabby-comfy sofa. "I don't think it has anything to do with Dickens Days," she said.

"He's always been like that," Heidi said. Like Jaymie, she wore leggings and a long sweater. "Like I said in the historical society meeting, he called the cops on me for wearing a bathing suit top while mowing, but only *after* I confronted him about leering at me." She shivered. "He used to drive by real slow and smile at me. Creep!"

"So when he's caught doing something shady, he doubles down," Jaymie said.

"We've all seen that kind of personality, haven't we?" Valetta remarked. "Politics seems to teem with people who can't man up, admit they were wrong and let something go. *Petty* people."

"But no one has confronted Nezer about Dickens Days."

"Except Bill," Valetta pointed out, "who won't back down either."

Jaymie smiled at Val's comment. "You're right about that. I've known Bill a long time, and I've never seen him so *angry*. He was red-faced."

"I've known him most of my life," Valetta said. "The thing about Bill is, he's a real old-fashioned gentleman. He doesn't like men who abuse women, and he doesn't appreciate people who make a big deal out of small things. He doesn't like folks who aren't community-minded. Nezer is all of those things."

"He abuses women?" Jaymie said.

She shrugged. "He talks down to females, at any rate."

"Oh, no," Jaymie said, watching her friend, her smile growing. "Don't tell me . . . he didn't try talking down to you, did he?"

"Once," Valetta said, her chin going up, the soft light of the TV screen glinting on her thick glasses. "He told me that I clearly didn't understand the economics of government debt."

"Do you?"

"I know enough," Valetta said. "I knew enough to tell him he was spouting crap."

"How do you know so much?" Jaymie was genuinely curious. Valetta was intelligent, as proved by her pharmacy degree and knowledge of medicine, but she had a broad range of other esoteric knowledge that often puzzled Jaymie.

"I read! You know me; I read everything. I read NPR online, and

The Atlantic, and Slate and *GQ, Rolling Stone.* I read anything and everything."

Jaymie smiled. "My Google friend. I always know to ask you first if I don't understand anything. When was this and where?"

"At my pharmacy window, where else would I see him? He isn't choosing to socialize with me, I can tell you that. Until Friday night, anyway." She smiled wickedly. "While I filled out his prescription he was on his phone spouting crap, and I called him on it. He said as an ignorant woman, I could never understand the complexities of government domestic debt. He said that's why there were so few women in economics."

"What did you do?" Heidi asked.

"I told him that maybe there were so few women in economics because females of my generation—and I experienced this myself—were actively discouraged from math-related subjects." She grinned. "And then I reminded him that I fill his prescriptions. It would be a pity if this poor wittle silly woman couldn't count or understand the prescription dose and did it wrong." She looked over the top of her thick glasses and waggled her eyebrows. "Then I handed him his bottle of pills."

Jaymie collapsed against the back of her chair in peals of laughter, which Denver did not appreciate, adjusting himself on her lap with a sour expression. "Use your *'Don't make me drug you!'* coffee mug around him."

"I wish he'd stayed where he was, in your neck of the woods, Heidi, instead of right in the middle of town." Val looked over at their friend. "Sorry, hon; I know you're probably glad to have him gone as a neighbor."

Heidi shrugged. "Bernie had a little talk with him when he complained about me wearing the bikini top while I mowed my lawn. He didn't bother me after that."

"Did she wear her uniform?" Jaymie asked.

"She said that would be . . . what did she say? An abuse of power. She just headed on over in her civvies and reminded him that I had done nothing wrong, and she said as a friend and neighbor she hoped she could say the same about him." Bernie lived a few blocks away from Heidi.

Jaymie chuckled. "Smart woman."

"Is he going to sell that house?" Val asked, and Heidi shrugged. "I don't know who he's going to get to sell it, now that he's crossed Brock off his list of real estate agents."

"Oh, he'll bring someone in from Wolverhampton," Jaymie said. "No doubt. But now I get why you're bringing Brock to the party Friday night. I thought there had to be a reason; it's to tweak Nezer."

"Maybe," Val said.

Jaymie yawned. "It's been a long week so far, and today was stressful. I'm going to call it quits and head home." She gave Denver a big kiss on the top of his fuzzy head, then moved him off her lap over onto the sofa. "I do not know what you have done to this cat, but you've transformed him."

"He likes being king of the castle," Valetta said. "He's the Evan Nezer of cats."

Jaymie laughed in horror. "Oh *no*! Don't *say* that about poor Denver. He was never as mean as that jerk. And he's a lot cuter." She stood and dropped another kiss on the cat's head. He sighed and snuggled down into the blanket on the sofa.

They all rose, and Jaymie retrieved her coat from the coat tree, nabbing Heidi's cute ski jacket at the same time and handing it over to her. She grabbed her purse and fished around for her keys, jingling in the bottom somewhere. "Aha, got 'em," she said, grabbing her key chain as the sound of sirens filled the air, coming closer. "Wonder what that's all about?" She pulled on her favorite plaid wool jacket, one with toggle buttons and a hood, over her cardigan and leggings.

Valetta opened her front door and stepped out onto the porch, wrapping her long cardigan around her body to protect against the frigid air of late November. She cocked her ear, a troubled look on her face. "That sounds like it's . . . good lord, I hope it's not the Emporium! I've been bugging the Klausners for years to get the wiring checked."

Heidi's eyes grew wide, big and round like two blue saucers fringed in navy mascara. "Can you see anything? Or smell smoke?"

More sirens. "Let's see what it is," Jaymie said.

They piled into her Explorer SUV, and Jaymie backed out of Valetta's driveway, then followed the sound two blocks over toward the Emporium. Valetta, leaning out of the passenger-side window, frosty air pouring in battling the heater warmth, yelped, "Hurry up. I see smoke! It looks like it's the Emporium all right. Crap . . . it's a good thing all the paper information in the pharmacy is backed up to the hilt on the cloud. But I'll have to order all new stock! *Darn* it."

Jaymie ducked her head, peering out the front windshield. "I don't think it's the Emporium, Val. Look . . . the smoke is drifting south, but not from the hill where the store is. It's from a little south of that." She pulled around the corner, narrowly avoiding the fire truck that careened to a stop by another. Firefighters were already on the scene pouring water on . . . "It's the cider booth!" Jaymie cried.

She bolted from the SUV, slamming the door shut, followed by Valetta and Heidi, and stood watching as the firefighters shot water on the booth, cutting branches from the pine trees nearby to keep them from catching. The sound of chain saws competed with the din of more sirens, shouts from the firefighters, and the crackle of the fire. The odor wasn't bad at first, but the smoke billowing from where the hoses were dousing the booth was acrid and filled the air with cinders and ash. Townsfolk gathered, knots of worried people chatting, moving from group to group, huddled in coats and blankets, dogs barking, teenagers gaggling, seniors reminiscing about bygone fires in Queensville.

Jacklyn Marley joined them, bundled up in a hooded puffy parka that reached down to her knees. She snapped photos with her cell phone, and Jaymie suddenly realized she should be doing the same. She whipped out her cell phone, handed her purse to Valetta, and took thirty or forty shots, first of the flames and the firefighters, and then, after some time, when it had been quelled, of the burnt, smoking wreckage of the small structure. She strode over to the lamppost, scanned through the images, and sent half a dozen to Nan, the editor of her food column at the *Wolverhampton Weekly Howler*, with a brief explanation.

She rejoined her friends, who were huddled with Jacklyn Marley. Val looked up. "Jaymie, you have to hear this."

She joined her friends, and Val urged Jacklyn to repeat what she had been saying.

"Don't you think that it's suspicious, this fire, when Evan just moved back to his house right behind it and had a confrontation with that handyman guy?"

"What are you saying, Jacklyn?" Jaymie asked. She'd better not be implying that Bill had anything to do with this.

Impatiently, she shook her head, her face shadowed, her expression hard to read. "I bet Evan Nezer set this fire."

It was possible, Jaymie admitted. "But he would be taking quite a chance," she pointed out. "With his house right there."

"It's not that close," Valetta said. "The Emporium is actually closer. If the wind had been blowing from the southeast and stronger, embers and sparks could have flown. It would have been trouble for us."

"But winds were from the northwest, as they usually are," Jaymie pointed out.

She caught a glimpse of an older woman staring avidly at the quenched fire, the red flashing lights giving a grim illumination to her lined face. Jaymie moved closer. The woman was standing by a bicycle, watching the firefighters. She stood out because she was alone, no chattering neighbors for her, and her expression as Jaymie got closer, was . . . troubling. It was the same woman she had seen a couple of times before, most recently at the historic house after the heritage society meeting, speaking with Ben Nezer. She had to be Sarah Nezer, Ben's mother. "Does anyone know that woman?" Jaymie asked, returning to Valetta, Jacklyn and Heidi.

They all glanced where she was motioning.

"*That* is Mrs. Sarah Nezer, abandoned ex-wife of Evan Nezer," Jacklyn said, confirming Jaymie's guess. In a puzzled tone she said, "It's weird; why does she look so happy to see the cider house on fire? Unless . . . well, the fire is awfully close to her ex's house, isn't it?"

"What are you saying?" Jaymie asked, turning her gaze to Jacklyn Marley. The ghostwriter appeared troubled.

"Nothing. Nothing, really!" She stood staring. "It's just . . . what is she doing here in the middle of town at this time of the night?"

Jaymie looked back, but the woman was gone.

✑ Five ✑

IT WAS A GLOOMY NOVEMBER MORNING in downtown Queensville, suiting Jaymie's mood. She hugged her arms around her purse and yawned. Suspicion and anger had kept her awake all night, tossing and turning, Jakob snoring serenely at her side. As annoying as this was, she was still determined to somehow make Dickens Days a success, and so had filled her SUV that morning with all the stuff for her Dickens diorama and had parked close by so she didn't have to tote it too far.

But right now Jaymie stood with Bill Waterman watching the township fire inspector surveying the damage to the cider house.

"Who do you think did it?" Bill asked. He had not been on the scene the night before as he lived out of town, and didn't hear about it until the *Wolverhampton Weekly Howler* broke the news with Jaymie's pictures in the online edition.

"It could have been an accident," Jaymie said, but her tone was half-hearted and unconvincing.

The inspector, a broad-shouldered middle-aged man wearing a navy blue uniform, red and gold Queensville Township Fire Department patch on his shoulder, was crouched down, clipboard in hand, examining the electricity post and shaking his head. Bill strode over to speak with him. "Dale, there wasn't even anything plugged into the electricity last night and there wouldn't be until we were actually up and running," he said, his voice loud enough that it easily carried back to Jaymie standing twenty feet away. "No matter what you think about the electrical outlet, it is *not* the source of the fire."

"Bill, don't get your unders in a knot. I'm just checking." The man stood and finished making notations on his clipboard, which he then tucked under his arm. He was a smidge taller than the older handyman.

"What *do* you think caused it?" Bill asked, craning his neck at the booth, trying to see all the details.

"You know I can't hazard a guess at this point, and I wouldn't even if I could. I've got a few more things to do, then I'll be making my report to the police."

"So it's arson?"

"I didn't say that," the fire inspector said patiently, his lined face weary. "I would be making a report either way. You'll have to wait like everyone else."

Bill paced back to Jaymie. "I *know* Nezer had something to do with it."

"We *don't* know that, Bill," Jaymie said, thinking of Sarah Nezer and her expression as she watched the fire.

"I'm gonna make sure they consider it." He strode off to follow the fire inspector, who stopped and turned, listening to the handyman.

Valetta brought Jaymie a hot cup of tea in a thermal mug and stood with her across from the village green, staring at the burned wreck of the cider booth. It had been so cute, a simple square structure, about six by eight feet, with a marquee over the counter on which Bill had painted some sheet music. "O Come, O Come, Emmanuel" was picked out in black notes, with the words in gold script, holly sprigs painted in the corners. Now it was a blackened shell, debris and burnt chunks littering the grass around it, the paint that was left curled and cracked, just one O showing. There was still an acrid smell coming from the wrecked husk whenever the wind wafted through it.

What were they going to do now? Their annual Dickens Days festival featured free hot cider for tourists who had come for the beginning of Dickens Days. It was heavily advertised on their website, in their brochure and in all Dickens Days print and radio ads. The cider booth being destroyed changed everything, and was devastating to one of the heritage society's two moneymaking events of the year.

"What are we going to do?" Jaymie fretted, giving voice to her worries. "There's no time to build another one."

Valetta, in deep thought, didn't answer for a long moment. Finally, though, she leaned in to Jaymie and murmured, "You know, we do have a security camera mounted up on the top of the Emporium now. I don't think it looks over this far, but it may have some footage of value on it."

Jaymie looked up in surprise but quickly looked back to the burnt-out booth, her heart and mind racing. "I did not know that."

She glanced up quickly and spotted a very small addition to the roof of the Emporium. "How did I not know that?"

"It's recent, and we didn't exactly make it public."

"I hate to ask, Val, but would you . . . could I—"

"Have a look at it before I tell the police? You know it, my friend in investigation. If you hadn't asked, I would have suggested it. Let's go."

They headed up the slight rise to the Queensville Emporium. As they entered and passed by the cash register, Jaymie waved to Gracey Klausner, granddaughter of the owners and soon-to-be manager, but followed Valetta to the back. There was a lunch room behind her pharmacy that doubled as an office that was rarely used in this digital age. The Klausners now had another one of their granddaughters, who was an accountant, looking after the books, but with everything available digitally now, she did that off-site. Mostly the room held boxes of overflow goods for the shelves. They lined the walls, piled high, cartons of baked beans, soup, juice boxes and pop.

Valetta used it more than anyone as a lunch room when the weather was too foul to eat her meal outside, either on the porch or at the picnic table under the oak tree by the store. She pushed a chair over for Jaymie and sat down behind the desk, accessing an elderly computer. She tapped the mouse and brought up a split screen of wavery images that appeared to be a live view of all sides of the Emporium. "We've got four cameras set up and they digitally record everything, one month's worth of video, before it begins overwriting old footage."

Jaymie squinted and stared at the screen. "So that's the view we want, right?" she said, pointing to one of the four boxes. "Can we get that full screen?"

Valetta adjusted her bifocals and tapped away at the computer keyboard, then moved the mouse pointer, accessing the correct video camera. "Look, you can see to the cider booth, just barely," she said, pointing out the view of the village green. "I didn't think you'd be able to. Maybe we hit the jackpot." She wound back through the hours, the timer spinning backward. "When should I go to?"

"Uh . . . maybe eight or nine last night?"

"That early?"

"We can scan quickly until we see movement, right?"

"True."

"You never know what will be useful."

She found eight p.m. Jaymie leaned forward as Val scanned through quickly. It was weird, seeing the town's activity in such a way. She caught a glimpse of her own SUV as she headed through town to Val's place. Mrs. Bellwood scurried past in quick time with Roary, her pug, which stopped to pee on one post holding up the Emporium porch; Petty Welch speed-walked through town, then ten minutes later returned, her routine fitness walk now that she had moved into Queensville; cars came and went.

A thin figure with a bulging shopping bag bustled across the street and disappeared behind the Emporium, then reappeared, the bag empty.

"Who was that, I wonder?" Jaymie asked.

Val stopped the film and glanced over at her. "You know, I noticed a while back a lot of gin and wine bottles in our recycling bin. I wasn't worried about it, but . . . I noticed. Now, seeing this, I have a feeling I know who puts them there."

"Who?"

"Really, Jaymie, you don't know?" She backed up the video footage and restarted it at normal speed. "Look at the angle the person took as they crossed the road."

Jaymie watched. Her eyes widened and her mouth dropped open. "That's Georgina, my brother-in-law's sister!" *And* manager of Kevin and Becca's store, Queensville Fine Antiques. "She's a secret drinker!"

"And she hides it by bringing her empties and disposing of them in the Emporium's recycling."

"I wonder if Kevin knows?"

"Probably. How could he not? Maybe as long as she does her job well he doesn't care."

"Does her job well? She's rude, even to customers sometimes!"

"Part of the shop's charm, from what I've heard," Val said dryly. "You would not believe how many tourists come in here chattering about the British manager over at QFA, and how she was so hoity-toity. Americans *love* being abused by a Brit."

Jaymie rolled her eyes. "Not me. But she does give excellent customer service. I've watched her. She's knowledgeable and can source something in minutes. She'll go out of her way to help a customer find something, and she can spot a fake and give a value within, as she says, a farthing."

"She's never drunk on the job, right?"

"Not that I know of," Jaymie admitted. "I've never seen it, at any rate, and I've spent hours with her. It's none of my business what she does in her off hours." But was Georgina happy in her new job and new town? Did she miss home? She vowed to take more time to get to know her brother-in-law's sister. In the past she had been so determined to stay out of other people's business that sometimes she missed a cry for help, or an extended hand of friendship. Georgina was standoffish, but maybe that masked a friend waiting to be made.

They kept watching and saw a shuffling fellow push a shopping cart along the street. He left it on the curb and took the same rout Georgina had, disappearing behind the Emporium, then reappearing with a bulging bag, which he put in the cart. He then continued on.

"And that, my friend, is why I leave the gin and wine bottles in the recycling bin at the back," Val said. "That's Amos."

"Amos? I know him," Jaymie said. "He was homeless, but now he rents a room from Johnny Stanko in his house down near the river."

"When I was a kid he was the school custodian, but he's fallen on hard times, I think."

"He was the designated town drunk for a while," Jaymie said. "Maybe staying with Johnny is helping his sobriety."

"I hope so, for his sake. He's such a nice old dude."

As Amos trundled away with his cart, Jacklyn Marley could be seen circling the Emporium from the direction of the stairs that led to her apartment above. She jammed her hands in her coat pockets and disappeared off camera. Nine forty-five, and no smoke yet. A large male figure lumbered into sight, moving from the river side of town down the main street. Jaymie squinted. "I think that may be Johnny," she said suddenly.

"Good call!" Val said. "It is." It was Johnny Stanko, who galumphed by with his recognizable gait. "He's probably on his way to Cynthia's." Cynthia Turbridge, who owned the Cottage Shoppe, was Johnny's sober buddy.

It was fascinating to see the village life in such a form, folks coming and going, driving, strolling, jogging and walking their pets. Amos headed back, passing by the Emporium once again, pushing his cart off in another direction, past the line of pine trees, disappearing into shadows and then beyond the camera's range.

There was a period of inactivity, and then movement. "Who's that?" Jaymie asked.

A figure approached the cider booth from the Nezer house side, pushing through the pine trees. With the distance, the grainy black and white of the video and the booth obscuring the person, it was impossible to even figure if it was a male or female. He or she appeared to be clad in a long coat, but it was hard to tell.

"I don't know," Valetta admitted, squinting at the screen. "But look!"

There were some odd motions of an arm, something glinted in the glow from the light standard, and then a flare. There was an arcing flash and then, as the figure retreated between the pines, a flame flickered and built on the cider booth.

"That's it. *That's it!*"

Jaymie and Val watched as the cider booth erupted into flames, the flare blinding the camera at times. They witnessed the arrival of the fire trucks, and the firefighters' swift action, then the moment that Jaymie rushed to the scene and shot out of the SUV.

"It's like a grainy black-and-white action movie," Jaymie said. "Well, you have proved positively that it was arson. The firebug looked like they came from the Nezer property. Do you think it was one of them?"

"I don't know. It could be. Or it could be someone wanting to hide. Those pine trees provide good cover."

"You mean you think they knew about the camera on the Emporium?"

"Not necessarily," Valetta said, pushing her glasses up on her nose and squinting at the screen, where she had backed up the video and paused it, with the person throwing some flammable liquid, presumably, at the cider booth before torching it. "It could have been a convenient way to hide his or her actions from anyone passing by."

"I guess that's true."

"I'm going to call the police. Can you see if the fire inspector is out there still?"

As Jaymie had hoped, the fire inspector had already determined that it was arson and called the police. The destroyed booth was cordoned off with police tape, and Officer Ng was standing by it, arms crossed, legs splayed. She looked around but Bill had retreated. Haskell Lockland and Mabel Bloombury, representatives of the Queensville Heritage Society, stood speaking with the fire inspector and Detective Macadams, who had been promoted and replaced a departed detective a year before. Drifting over to join the heritage society members and eavesdrop, she heard the fire inspector reassure them that everything was being done as it should be.

The mayor, Eddie Fletcher, an infrequent sight in Queensville lately as he sought a wider political arena, stood and talked to the detective. The fire chief joined them. Evan Nezer strode around the pines from his home and headed straight for the fire inspector and detective. He berated them for a moment, shaking one finger at them both.

The mayor put out one hand, touching his shoulder, trying to reassure him, it appeared. Nezer shook him off, then stomped over to Jaymie, Haskell and Mabel, his expression malice-filled. "I hope you bunch of plaguey do-gooders are happy now. I told everyone this whole thing is a fire hazard. And on my property!"

"I don't remember you telling anyone it was a fire hazard, Evan," Haskell said.

"It is *not* on your property, Mr. Nezer," Mabel said, her tone steely. A plump little partridge of a woman in sober colors and perfectly permed curls, she was nonetheless doughty and fearless. "The booth is on public property. And it wasn't a fire hazard any more than your house is."

Jaymie stifled a smile. *Atta girl, Mabel!*

"Madam, you display your ignorance by opening your big, fat mouth."

Gasping aloud, Jaymie stared at the man, appalled.

"I *beg* your pardon?" Mabel said, eyes wide.

"Beg all you want," he sneered. "I'm sure you're accustomed to it."

"Sir, you go too far," Haskell, who had stiffened into rigid dislike, said. "I will *not* tolerate rudeness to a lady."

Nezer examined him up and down. "Gasbag," he muttered.

Bella Nezer paced toward them from beyond the fringe of pines.

She was in an elegant white wool wrap coat, her glossy dark hair pulled up into a chignon, revealing her glorious cheekbones and creamy complexion. "Evan, dear, behave yourself," she said, taking his arm. She turned to the two members of the heritage society. "He doesn't mean to be rude."

Yes, he does, Jaymie thought. He appeared to enjoy being rude.

Her ungracious husband motioned to the burnt, soggy wreckage and grumbled, "*Look* at this ruin! It could have burnt down my trees, destroyed my house. Look at that . . . they hacked off branches!"

"To *save* your house. Would you rather they let the trees catch fire and spread to your home?" Mabel said.

Nezer ignored her. "Haskell, why don't you take this whole damn circus and put it out at that house you all paid a fortune to renovate?"

Interesting, Jaymie thought. If Nezer *was* the one to set the fire, as Bill suspected, perhaps that was his goal, to induce the heritage society to relocate Dickens Days. "Mr. Nezer, the whole point of the Dickens Days festival is to get publicity for the Queensville Historic Manor," Jaymie said. "Which, as you appear to know, is on the outskirts of town away from the tourism district. The holiday festival attracts people who have never been there; we hand out treats and flyers and free visit coupons to the house. We promote Queensville as a tourist destination, thereby fattening the town's business coffers, *and* making some money for the society. It's a win-win situation."

"Ah, yes, there you are, old Sobersides' sad-sack sidekick," Nezer sneered, eyeing her up and down.

"Sobersides?"

"Waterman, old fart that he is. And you . . . you're one of those plain hausfraus who throw yourselves into good works to force people to notice you."

Bella stared off toward the Emporium, either appalled or uncaring about her husband's rudeness. It was impossible to tell which by her deliberately neutral expression.

Nezer's intent was to needle and offend Jaymie. Instead she felt nothing but minor irritation. He was a blind pimple of a person. "And you're one of those sour *sad* little bullies who have a mean nickname for everyone, right?"

Mabel clapped her hands together in delight.

"I suppose that's your only shot," he said dismissively, stroking his beard and adjusting his glasses. "Too bad it is pathetically weak." He turned away. "Come along, Bella," he said, yanking her by the arm so she stumbled. "Let these bumbling ninnies try to recover from this."

Jaymie was tempted to tell Haskell and Mabel what she had seen on the Emporium CCTV footage, but that was a recipe for disaster. In minutes it would be all over town that Nezer or someone from his house had set the fire, and as Valetta had pointed out, that was not certain . . . it wasn't even probable. Instead she excused herself and walked away. Her phone pinged; it was a text from Nan thanking her for the scoop and asking what else she had. The editor appended a list of questions: What exactly had she seen? Who did she suspect? Was it arson? What was the heritage society going to do now? What was the fate of the Dickens Days festival?

Jaymie would respond later. Her mind turned to the heritage society's problems; what *would* they do now that the cider booth was gone? She took shelter from the chill breeze by the Emporium porch; she had an idea forming and texted Jakob to ask a question. She also needed to talk to Bill. He was the only one who could answer if there was any hope for the shell of the booth. She slipped her phone in her coat pocket and trotted along the street, then up and across the grassy area between the Emporium and Jewel's Junk, heading to Bill Waterman's workshop. He was a handyman, yes, but he was also a talented woodworker who restored antiques, rebuilt pieces for Jewel and Cynthia, and made cabinets from scratch in his spare time. His volunteer work with the heritage society saved it thousands of dollars every year, and it was done solely to help preserve the town in which he had grown up.

She approached the big barn and slid one of the huge doors open slightly. That it was unlocked was a good sign. It meant Bill was somewhere on the premises.

"Yoo-hoo, Bill!" she called out, her voice echoing within.

"In here!"

She followed his voice, inhaling the aroma of wood, damp earth, and something else. He was in the dark depths with a task light on over his sawhorses, staining a lovely old set of drawers he had stripped. The pungent smell of shellac assailed her nostrils, and she breathed in deep. "I love the smell of fumes. Weird, right?"

He chuckled, his good humor returned. "My daughter says whenever she smells paint, stripper, shellac or vanish she thinks of me."

"So what are we going to do, Bill? I don't imagine the shell of the cider booth can be saved."

"Nope. That ship has sailed out of the harbor and wrecked on jagged rocks."

She laughed. "You sound more at peace now, Bill. You don't like Nezer, do you?" Understatement of the year.

He shook his head. "Classic bully: mean, rude and unfit for human company."

"Or animals."

He smiled. "How that lovely woman, Bella, can stand him I do not know. He has names for everyone, did you know that?"

"I was getting that idea."

"He calls his ex-wife Old Graytop."

"What is *wrong* with him?"

Bill dipped his brush, spread a thin coat of shellac along the final raw strip and stood back, nodding. "He's like the Grinch. Has a heart two sizes too small."

"Or Scrooge. He actually said 'humbug' the other day!" Her phone pinged, and she took it out of her pocket. Aha! She looked up from her phone. "So, Bill, the cider booth can't be saved and it's too late to build one from scratch, but . . . what about repainting something already built?"

"What do you have in mind?"

She brought up the photo her husband had sent her in reply to her text, positioning the phone under Bill's task light so he could see it. "Look at this. Jakob rescued a bunch of buildings from the old fairgrounds near Wolverhampton. Now they're sitting in his warehouse taking up space. I laughed at him and asked him what he was going to do with them. He said he might be able to use them on the farm someday, you know, make one over into a roadside vegetable booth or something. But today I thought . . . could you repaint this one to be the new cider booth? It's about the right size."

He wiped his hands then took it from her, squinting at the screen. The booth in question was about the right size, and though it had been a hot dog stand, the marquee on top could be repainted. A big smile lit up Bill's homely, lined face. "Jaymie Leighton Müller, you are one smart cookie. This will be perfect, and the best part about it is, it's going to drive Nezer bonkers when we tote that over and put it in place. How soon can we get it here so I can paint it?"

๕ Six ๕

JAYMIE RAN TO SPEAK WITH HASKELL AND MABEL. Among them they made the decision and arranged with Jakob to bring the booth out on his flatbed trailer right away. Bill hustled off to the nearby Lowe's to get the paint he needed.

Meanwhile Detective Macadams had responded and Valetta was showing him the surveillance footage. An official investigation had begun.

Jaymie sat on a bench in Bill's work shed and texted Nan some answers. She couldn't comment on the fire, as that was a police matter, but Dickens Days would most certainly be going on, she wrote her editor. Nothing would stop it; they were all working together to ensure that.

She heard a commotion and rushed out into the chilly gloom. Jakob had arrived with the booth strapped into the back of his long-bed pickup; he expertly backed it up the hill and into the workshop, with much shouting and directing from the handyman. The two men, with Jaymie and Valetta's help, wrestled it off the flatbed truck to sit in the middle of the concrete workshop floor. As Val returned to the pharmacy and Jakob helped Bill clean the booth to ready it for painting, Jaymie strolled to the door of the workshop and leaned against it, viewing her village from the slight rise.

The destroyed shell of the booth was a dark blot on the lovely outlook. Bill was certain that the cider booth had been set ablaze by Nezer, but Jaymie wasn't so sure. However . . . who else had a motive? She mulled that over and couldn't think of anyone else who had a problem with Dickens Days, which had become a lighthearted nondenominational celebration of the festive season. She turned back to look into the depths of the workshop and smiled. There was Jakob, up on a ladder, already starting to paint a primer coat. "You guys going to work here for a while?" she called out, her voice echoing in the cavernous depths.

"Don't blame me," Bill said, pointing his brush at her husband. "I told Jakob to go home, or back to work, but he said I needed help. So . . . I been told."

"If you want to have any shot at all of having this ready to go

Saturday, you need help, Bill," Jakob said firmly, winking down at Jaymie. "I've got time today, and some tomorrow. Let's knock this out in twenty-four hours."

"I'll leave you two gentlemen to it. I have work on the diorama to finish."

She returned to her SUV where it was parked along the street that led away from the downtown. Using a handcart, she moved the small table and chairs to the diorama, pulled off the tarp, and placed them inside. She then returned to her vehicle and retrieved some other bits and pieces. She set the box of decorations from her SUV on the ground beside the scene.

Bill was better than a mere workman, he was an artist. The diorama was a three-sided open structure with a floor and top . . . kind of like an open box set on its side. Bill had painted, on the inside walls, a scene from *A Christmas Carol*, the Cratchit dining room and parlor. It was like a backdrop for a play. There was a fireplace, with Tiny Tim's crutch painted leaning against it. Mrs. Cratchit was depicted, her comically rounded face and rosy cheeks worthy of a book illustration; she had her hands up in the air, as if she was about to clap at her plum pudding's delectability!

The police officer who was still guarding the burned-out cider booth looked on in puzzlement, but no one had said she couldn't proceed, so she continued. Finn Fancombe skulked by at one point, but only paused and watched her working for a moment before moving on. Bella Nezer strolled by from the direction of the Nezer home, pulling on gray wool gloves. She was about to walk past toward the Emporium but she paused. "What is that supposed to be?" she asked.

Jaymie joined her on the sidewalk and surveyed her work so far, as she explained. "It's the scene in *A Christmas Carol* when Scrooge is visited by the Spirit of Christmas Present and the ghost takes him to see the Cratchits' Christmas. The plum pudding, bedizened with a sprig of holly, is set alight and served, to the delight of them all."

"So that's the Cratchit kitchen?" She eyed Jaymie's set decoration.

The small wood table from The Junk Stops Here, along with two rickety chairs, were the largest furnishings. She had some chipped old china on the table, and a copper pot, with a glossy fake baked chicken in place of the goose. Something was missing, but she couldn't think what. "It is, kind of. I mean, at their income level their home would have limited rooms, so the kitchen and parlor and dining room would likely all be one." She glanced over at Bella. "I'm about to place the mannequins. The Bob Cratchit one is a little heavy. Can you help me with it?"

Bella looked surprised, but agreed, and followed Jaymie to the SUV.

"I'm so glad you're lending me a hand," Jaymie said, handing her one of Bob Cratchit's arms. She giggled, but Bella seemed coolly unamused.

She and Jaymie hauled it from her SUV and pushed and prodded it until he was sitting in the chair at the head of the table, fork in hand. He was far too good-looking to be Bob Cratchit since he was a mannequin from the fashion department of a store. He had dark, crisply waving hair and a square jaw, and an intense model-gaze. But he'd have to do; lucky Mrs. Cratchit. Well, if Scrooge wouldn't pay his bookkeeper more, maybe old Bob could model for the Burberry catalogue.

"And now for the pièce de résistance," Jaymie said, racing and skipping back to the SUV and getting the last item. She hauled the mannequin to the scene and placed little Tiny Tim—a child mannequin—at the table and adjusted his newsboy-style cap on his wig, tugging it askew to a rakish slant. The lad was overlooking the big, fake plum pudding Jaymie and Jocie had made using papier-mâché over a balloon. Painted a rich chocolate brown, it was adorned with blobs of color to represent almonds and figs. She had Jocie stick glistening red plastic cabochons all over it to represent candied cherries, and they had glued construction paper flames to it. She placed it on a chipped plate and stood back.

"Darn!" she explained. "It needs a couple of things. I forgot to get the holly to deck it with, and . . . something is missing." She twisted her mouth into a grimace. "What the heck is missing? I'll need to think about it."

Bella stared at it for a moment.

"What do *you* think?" Jaymie asked.

"It's . . . odd," the woman replied. "I have to go now. If I'm going to get everything done in time for the party I can't waste a minute." She turned, walked up to the Emporium and disappeared inside.

"Well, all right then," Jaymie muttered. There was still more to do. She opened the tote that held the strings of lights and pulled them out. Using zip ties, she strung them around the sides and top of the diorama, then ran a long outdoor extension cord to the electrical outlet, sneaking under the yellow crime scene tape to do it. The burnt smell of the booth was acrid in her nose, and she backed off, turning back to her joyful little diorama. Too bad it looked so bleak from the outside, the plywood dull. Too late to do anything about that now.

She finally remembered what was missing: the pudding mould! She had a cheap damaged vintage one at home that would do, and she wouldn't worry about it being stolen. Everything in the scene was placed with that thought, that anything portable might be stolen. She had doubles of everything: more chipped china, more rickety chairs. She even had access to a couple of extra mannequins if she needed them, though she hoped she wouldn't. With any luck father and son would stay in place over the holidays. She patted Tiny Tim's thin shoulder. The best thing about *A Christmas Carol*, to her, was its inclusion of a little boy bravely struggling with a disability, and a family that stuck together, no matter what.

She dusted off her hands, finally, and stood back to examine the scene. If she thought of anything else, it would have to wait until Saturday morning, when Dickens Days would officially kick off. She sure hoped the fellows could get the cider booth done by then. Now it was time to replace her hastily rigged twist tie closures. She got out her tool kit and hammered pilot holes, then screwed in hooks for the corners of the open side of the diorama. She hooked the corner grommets of the tarp on those, then used pieces of nylon rope to tie the tarp securely to the holes Bill had already drilled all along the top. She then packed up her tool kit and put it back in her vehicle.

Time to go home, but first she wanted to see how Bill and Jakob were coming along. They had a crowd of onlookers at the door to Bill's workshop. Haskell Lockland bustled up and pushed through the crowd, not noticing Jaymie as he elbowed past her. Ostentatiously dressed in crisp new workmen's overalls, available at any home improvement store, he held a brand-new paint brush. "I'm here to help save Dickens Days, my fellow workmen!"

Jaymie bit back a snicker. Good to know that now that Haskell

Lockland had shown up in crisp new overalls, which would likely never see a spot of paint, everything would get done.

• • •

FRIDAY WAS ANOTHER BUSY DAY. Cynthia and Jewel had been fighting over who would have Petty help them when, so Jaymie stepped in and offered her services. She worked all morning helping Cynthia arrange Christmas displays. She stopped in on Georgina at Queensville Fine Antiques and moved the table in the front window and vacuumed, something the older woman, slight and fine-boned, wasn't strong enough to do. She snuck looks at her, and sniffed her breath when she got close enough. No gin breath that she could tell, and the slim woman certainly didn't stagger or slur. Georgina might drink like a sailor on shore leave, but every single day *every* gray curled hair was in place, her sweater set and ironed trousers were impeccably neat and her pearls in place.

Georgina finally said, as Jaymie hovered close, "What is *wrong* with you today, girl?"

"Nothing. Nothing at all," Jaymie said, moving away hastily. "Hey, will you be coming to the start of Dickens Days tomorrow evening?" she asked, hoping to become friendlier with the frosty woman.

"Not bloody likely," she said, ferociously polishing a silver candlestick. "I'm going to dinner tomorrow evening."

"Oh. Okay. Well, I hope you'll have a look at my diorama," Jaymie said, and described it.

With a nod, the woman said, "I'm sure I'll see it . . . sometime."

Jaymie slipped her coat on and walked up to Bill Waterman's workshop to check on the handyman and her husband. They had finished painting and the cider booth was amazing, maybe even better than the original. "Bravo, gentlemen. *Bravo,*" she exclaimed, applauding as she examined it in the light from the big open double doors.

Haskell had not shown up that morning to work on the booth. That wasn't surprising; there would be no admiring crowd gathered. But Johnny Stanko had; he had swiftly worked to lay a coat of weatherproof varnish over the whole booth. He was about to slip away, but Jaymie stopped the big fellow with one hand and said,

"Thanks so much, Johnny. Your help was unexpected, but appreciated."

He ducked his head, his face turning red. "It's nothin'. Cynthia always says to look for opportunities to help. When you find one, she said, you can be an angel to someone."

Jaymie smiled, her eyes welling. The fellow had had trouble in his life, and tragedy and sorrow, but he was determined to do better, stay sober, and work hard. Cynthia had been a good influence on him, but Jaymie knew that Johnny was an immeasurably good influence on Cynthia, his sober buddy, too. Everyone needs someone to help, especially in Cynthia's case, when she had had a break in her sobriety. Helping others was a vital source of pride, and gave one a full heart, and in Cynthia's case, a powerful motive to stay sober.

"Come by the booth when it's up and running during Dickens Days. If you like brownies or cake, I'll be making both. On the house, for all your help."

He ducked his head, said he'd be back whenever they wanted to move the booth, and galumphed away. Jaymie checked in with Jakob, who was positioning a fan to blow on the building to dry the varnish completely, while Bill went to speak with the fire department, to see if they could clean up and remove the debris. A fan wouldn't normally be used. There was a risk of dust and sawdust sticking to the booth. But time was of the essence, and it was important that it dried completely.

Jaymie sauntered over to her husband. They shared a long, lingering kiss, and Jakob, leaning back against a table, pulled her closer, holding her as he stared down into her eyes, his own glowing with contentment. "How did I get so lucky?"

"I could ask the same thing."

"Are you looking forward to the shindig tonight at the Nezers'?"

"It'll be interesting. I saw Bella earlier, but she's a frosty one, for sure. I don't know why I agreed to go, but I'm curious about the inside of the house. We don't have to stay long."

"We'll play it by ear. If we're enjoying ourselves, we'll stay. As long as you want."

She reluctantly pulled away and bid him adieu, bought some things at the Emporium, then headed to her SUV. Becca and Kevin were coming back to Queensville that afternoon after a few weeks in

Canada, so she had done the shopping for them—bread, milk, coffee, and other staples. She drove over, stocked the fridge in the house, then headed out the back door. Remembering just in time that she needed it, she cut a few holly branches from her shrubs for the cider booth and her diorama, then headed home.

She took Hoppy for a long walk, cutting some long wild grasses for a dry arrangement in a vase, then spent some time updating her food blog, ruminating on Christmas treats her grandmother made when Jaymie was a kid. Hoppy and Lilibet napped in a basket near the fireplace. She looked up to the clock; it was a quarter to four. She wrapped herself in a thick cable-knit cardigan and headed outside, letting Hoppy out with her to snoop and sniff. He had been used to a measure of freedom in town, in their fenced backyard, but the only time he got outside now was with one of them. Too many coyotes in the country!

Along the front of the cabin was a bench, some planters brimming with chrysanthemums and two Adirondack chairs. She sat down in one, setting the Melody Heath novel, *The Duke's Delicious Distraction*, a Regency historical with a duke as the hero and an earl's daughter masquerading as a baker's apprentice as the heroine, on the arm. Melody was an old friend and housemate from university. Jaymie sipped her hot tea and listened to the breeze rustle through the bare branches and pine trees across the road, and sniffed the air: poplar leaves, fresh earth, and the scent of her tea, like honey. It was peaceful. Occasionally a car zoomed past kicking up a cloud of road dust, and sometimes someone waved, but for the most part it was quiet.

She needed these moments of solitude. Her adult life had been spent living mostly alone except for a brief period when she lived with Joel. It had been a big adjustment having a husband and child. A half hour of alone time, just herself, a mug of tea and a book centered her the way yoga or meditation did others. Maybe it *was* her form of meditation. She wasn't a shy person . . . never had been. But when she went to events, or was in a crowd, sometimes she needed to disconnect for a few minutes.

She read for a while, losing track of time, and then suddenly heard a roar in the distance. She looked up, traveling through the years from 1815 England to present-day Michigan in seconds, as she set the book aside. Hoppy, who was sniffing a clump of weeds along the fence line, heard the heavy noise, too. He wobbled and bounced to Jaymie's feet and sat, watching, his ears pricked up as he stared down the road expectantly. Funny how quickly he had learned that sound, and what it meant. The big yellow school bus roared down the road and stopped in front of the cabin, the brakes squealing and the door opener screeching. Jocie clambered down, jumping the last step, as Hoppy went mad with excitement, yipping and whirling in wobbly circles. He loved his little girl fiercely, which warmed Jaymie to the core of her being. Jocie turned to wave goodbye to her friends, then ran toward the cabin, throwing her book bag down in the dirt, hugging Jaymie, and running off to dash about with Hoppy for a few minutes.

Jaymie's cell phone buzzed and she picked it up, laughing as she answered. It was Becca, back in the Queensville house, and they went through the usual check-in after the couple had been in Canada for a couple of weeks. Jaymie asked about their grandmother, who was doing well, and business, which was also doing well. Becca thanked Jaymie for filling the fridge, and asked about Jocie. Jaymie described the scene going on in front of her.

"So, are you two free tonight?" Becca asked.

"Well, actually, it's one of those rare occasions when we have plans," Jaymie said, telling her sister all about what had been going on, including the cider booth arson.

"Holy mackerel, excitement in our little village!"

"I know. Big-time excitement." She went on to relate the party invitation, that Valetta and Heidi were attending as well, and . . . "Valetta is bringing Brock. Ugh!"

"He's her brother, little sis. You *know* he's gotten better the last year or so."

"I suppose," Jaymie said, rolling her eyes.

"I heard that! I *heard* you rolling your eyes."

Jaymie laughed. "So . . . we're busy tonight. In fact, as soon as Jakob gets home we have to take Jocie over to her Oma and Opa's to stay. I hope they don't mind. We've been doing that a lot lately, and I know they have an evening alone tonight. Sonya and Helmut and their brood are off to visit her relatives this weekend since they couldn't get there at Thanksgiving."

61

"How about Kevin and I come over and babysit on premises?"

"Really?"

"Sure. I was going to suggest we come over tonight anyway, you know, bring snacks and a kid-friendly movie. So instead we'll have the kidlet all to ourselves!"

Jaymie swiftly agreed and hung up, then told Jocie the change in plans. She called her mother-in-law, had a bit of a chat, got a recipe, and told her the change in plans too. Renate was good with that, and hung up. "Time to go in, Jocie. Dinner and bath, then Aunt Becca and Uncle Kevin are going to be here."

• • •

WOLF WHISTLE.

Jaymie whirled to see Jakob staring at her as she did last-minute primps in the mirror, before they were off to the party in Queensville.

"You look . . . wow," he said softly, appreciatively.

She smiled and felt her cheeks burn as she smoothed the dress down over her hips. She curtseyed. "Why, thank you, sir. Heidi picked it out." She turned back to the mirror and adjusted her updo, a simple twist fixed in place using the holly-bejeweled comb Becca had brought back from a vintage shop in Scotland on their delayed honeymoon.

"Remind me to thank Heidi," he said, coming up behind her and encircling her in his arms, squeezing. His kissed her ear, his beard tickling her neck. "Not that you don't always look gorgeous, but you must admit, this does play to your attributes." He stared at her in the mirror and winked.

Jaymie always thought of warm colors like rust, crimson and gold for autumn, but on their last shopping trip Heidi had insisted that for her coloring she should consider blues and greens even in fall, so together they had chosen a long soft dress in swirling shades of blue and teal. With delicate filigree silver jewelry she thought it looked pretty good. When she bought it she hadn't been sure what she'd wear it for, but this was the perfect occasion.

"You look very handsome yourself," Jaymie murmured, turning in his arms, hands on his shoulders.

Jakob wore a navy sport jacket over a taupe sweater and oxford shirt, with taupe chinos and boots. His dark hair glistened, as did his beard, and he smelled delicious. She didn't particularly want to leave right that moment, but they had to.

Becca and Kevin had arrived an hour ago, so they were well-entrenched. Jaymie and Jakob descended to find Becca on the floor with Jocie pasting pictures into a scrapbook, as Hoppy sat watching and waggling his butt, hoping for attention. Kevin sat on the sofa with Lilibet stretched out on his lap and flicked through the TV stations.

"Woo-hoo, you two look *good!*" Becca said, her glasses reflecting the light from the TV screen.

Jaymie pulled on a long-sleeved black faux fur shrug while Jakob got his coat. Becca clambered to her feet and helped Jaymie pin a glittering diamante snowflake brooch on the shrug's shoulder, making it glitter festively in the firelight. Jocie was entranced and wanted a picture with her mom right that minute. Jaymie obliged, of course, and then it became a picture-taking session with Jaymie and Jakob both, embracing by the hearth.

It took another fifteen minutes before they got out of the house, and another twenty to get into Queensville, but finally they pulled up by the Nezer home, which was ablaze with light in every window. Jaymie found a parking space wedged between another SUV and a Lincoln. "I'm nervous," she admitted. She unlocked her seat belt, threw her keys in her evening bag and took in a deep breath. "We don't normally go to fancy functions. What if I'm not dressed right? What if I'm *mmph —* "

Her protestations were stopped by a big kiss. Jakob, leaning across the center console, held her face in one hand. "You look gorgeous. I am going to be the envy of every man there, and you could never be inappropriate."

"You messed up my lipstick," she said breathlessly, and turned on the vanity light to fix it. She glanced at him. "And thank you. Every woman there is going to envy *me.*"

Hand in hand they followed a sidewalk from the parking lane by the house and strolled up toward the front door. Jaymie paused. Bella had done wonders to the exterior in the couple of months she had had access to the house. It had been painted a soft dove gray, with details and trim picked out in a creamy white. It was an unusual design, though in the Queen Anne style. A central square tower rose above the hipped roof, which was tiled in gray slate accented by lines of darker gray.

Some Queen Anne homes had a wide wraparound porch, but the Nezer home did not, just a square porch covered by a roof supported by double pillars. The big double doors had crimson glass sidelights, as well as a transom-style window over the door with the street number in silver gothic scroll. Lace curtains filtered the interior light through the windows in the lovely wood doors.

They approached the steps, but Jaymie paused and released Jakob's hand when she heard a rustling in the snowball bushes to the left of the porch. She bent over and peered into them. "Hello? Who's there?" she said. The rustling continued for a moment, then stopped.

"Probably a raccoon," Jakob offered.

"I suppose."

She was about to continue in, but the rustling began again and she glanced over once more, seeing a flash of white. "Wait!" She stared and saw the face of a woman, with white hair, in a dark cloak. Jaymie opened her mouth to say something but the woman smiled, mischievously, and put one finger to her mouth in a hushing gesture.

"What is it?" Jakob asked.

The woman held out a piece of paper to Jaymie. She reflexively reached out and took it.

"What's going on?"

"Let's go in," Jaymie said as the woman rustled away. Jakob frowned and looked into her eyes, his own dark and shadowed in the dim porch light, but she shook her head, troubled and unsure. "It's nothing. Let's go!"

What had the woman handed her? It would take longer to explain than it took for it to happen. She'd tell him later. She slipped the paper into her clutch as they entered.

A young woman in a black skirt and black vest over a crisp white shirt took their jackets; a rudimentary cloak room had been set up in one corner of the den or office, racks of coats visible beyond the open pocket doors. She pointed them to the right, to a big parlor accessed by another set of pocket doors. Through the doorway they could see an enormous Christmas tree set up in the far corner. It was decorated with gold and silver faux mercury lights and tinsel, with a glittering star on top. There was a gorgeous wood fireplace along the far wall, which was painted a deep wine color, and atop the mantel was a snowy scene of a white ceramic village, with mercury glass globes interspersed.

Jaymie took Jakob's offered arm and they strolled through, nodding to those they knew and smiling at those they didn't. Quite a few people had already arrived. Haskell and Petty were there with a group of folks, laughing and chatting, drinks in hand. Haskell, who must have set aside his quarrel with Evan Nezer, was handsome as always in a dark gray suit, and Petty was lovely and sparkling in a floral damask skirt and silk blouse, in tones of rose and gold.

Haskell summoned them with a wave of his hand. "Pastor Inkerman, this is Jaymie and Jakob Müller," he said as they joined the small group, and Petty gave her a brief hug and a smile. "Our little Jaymie is quite the author too, you know, as well as being a docent at our historic home; she writes for our local paper, a column called 'Vintage Eats.'"

Jaymie held her breath, sure that the pastor would sneer at a food columnist being called an author.

Instead he smiled and nodded. "I have read your column! Quite entertaining. Not that I'm a cook at all. But I have *heard* of you, young lady. You've solved a few crimes around town." He gave a mock look of alarm, one hand on his chest. "Should I be wary of you?"

"Not unless you've killed someone lately."

He gave a sharp bark of laughter but looked discomposed.

"Jaymie, behave yourself, now!" Haskell said. "Pastor Vaughan Inkerman has written and published a wonderful book entitled *Living Your Best Life Through Scripture*."

The man was slight and pale, with a lovely wave of dirty blonde hair across his forehead. He shook Jakob's outstretched hand, then bowed over hers. "Haskell is too kind. Critics were rather savage, unfortunately." He colored slightly, a peachy pink mantling over his cheeks. "One, a particularly vicious reviewer nicknamed Book Bookman, called it a Panglossian wonder."

Jaymie traded puzzled looks with Jakob.

"Pangloss was a character in *Candide*," the pastor explained. "He was a foolish optimist."

She had read *Candide* in university, but the reference had passed her by. It had been more than a few years since she had read the work and it clearly had not made a lasting impression. "I'd rather be a foolish optimist than a clever cynic," Jaymie said with a slight smile.

Inkerman's eyes welled. "Thank you, young lady. You are both lovely and wise beyond your years."

Jaymie spotted Valetta and Heidi lingering in the next room by an enormous marble-topped mirrored Eastlake sideboard that held platters of treats and an exquisite china tea set. She tugged Jakob away with a parting smile and nod. "He seems an emotional sort," she murmured to her husband.

"Maybe all writers are?" he said.

"Not in my experience! My friend Melody—you know, the romance author—is as cynical and hard-nosed as they come. She says she can turn on the romantic spout and turn it off just as easily."

"She married?"

Jaymie waggled her hand, thinking of Melody's hurried and now regretted wedding of a couple of years before. "Kinda-sorta."

"Lucky guy."

She chuckled. "He's no prize, let me tell you." They strolled over to her friends and were enveloped in hugs. Heidi was gorgeous as always, in a slim-fitting long-sleeved black sheath dress topped by a silver shrug. Valetta, on the other hand, eschewed the fashionable lack of color embraced by others. She had chosen a long red velvet skirt and with it wore a green satin blouse, topped by a Christmas cardigan bedazzled with jacquard squares depicting holiday scenes picked out in sequins and tinsel thread.

"You're . . . *breath*taking," Jaymie said, examining Val's outfit.

"Is it too much?" Val asked, eyes wide behind the glinting lenses of her glasses. It was hard to discern, but she may have been kidding.

"Not at all," Jaymie said warmly. "You're *gloriously* festive." She fished in her bag and took out her little digital camera. "You two, stand together," she told Val and Heidi. She snapped a shot, and then took photos of the treat trays and sideboard. Val insisted that she take one of Jaymie and Jakob by the fireplace and the Christmas tree. They threaded through the convivial, chattering crowd and took photos of each other, giggling and chatting.

Brock joined them, glass of scotch in one hand. With a drink or two under his belt he was more bearable, friendly and happy, rather than sarcastic and judgmental. As he buttonholed Jakob, Jaymie took a glass of wine from a server and drifted away from the two men, ambling off to tour the house with her friends.

The main floor was all public rooms, the parlor and dining room on one side, then across the central hall a sitting room that led through another set of pocket doors to a library, all full of small groups of people clustered everywhere, their chatter drowning out the seasonal orchestral music that floated through the house on some kind of central sound system. The fireplace in the sitting room was topped by a gorgeous Eastlake-style mantelpiece, with family photos and mementoes. A large carved wood frame held a photo of Evan and Ben together, the handsome, dark-haired son behind his distinguished-looking father's chair, hand on his shoulder, family ring displayed prominently. It looked very new, within the last few weeks, perhaps. There was another, matching, of Evan and lovely Bella, her beauty shimmering in the perfect professional lighting. It was a good-looking family. No photo of the ex, of course; no older photos at all.

They kept circling back to the dining room and snacking as they went, fighting through a crowd when some new delicacy had been served. But as well as the sideboard buffet and trays of food on the ten-foot-long table in the dining room, waitstaff dressed in black and white circulated with plates of hors d'oeuvres. So far she had seen neither her host nor hostess. Odd. As she speared a mini meatball with a tiny sword from a tray on the table, having lost contact with Heidi and Valetta for the moment, Jaymie edged close to a group composed of an older woman, very august and staid, with two middle-aged men. Pastor Inkerman approached them. It appeared that he was well known to them, as they greeted him by name.

"Good to see you, Vaughan," the older woman said affectionately, hugging him and exchanging air kisses. "You look . . . happier."

"Somewhat, Hazel," he said. "I'm still wounded. It's never easy when you're criticized and don't know where the disparagement is coming from. Listen, I've been told recently that that horrible reviewer, Book Bookman, is a local man. Who could it be, do you think? I've wracked my brain. Who would be so set on destroying me that he'd trash my book in such a manner?"

"Vaughan, you *must* let go of this," the woman said, glancing over at the other two men and raising her heavily penciled brows. "Carter, Andy, please reassure him. Among many positive reviews, one negative should not hold so much sway."

"If only it were just one criticism, but this Bookman fellow . . . he has stalked me online and continues to do so! Anywhere I blog or write, he follows and . . . what is it called? Trolling? He *trolls* me, makes disparaging comments, sarcastic jabs." There was a plaintive edge to his voice. "I don't know what I ever did to deserve it. I wish he'd leave me alone."

The woman exchanged looks once more with the two men. There was something knowing in her gaze, something that arrested Jaymie's attention. "Vaughan, whoever this unpleasant individual is, I have faith you will deal with him with grace and humility." She turned once more to the other two men. "Isn't that so, gentlemen? We must keep our college pastor happy, mustn't we?"

The woman knew *something*, Jaymie was sure of it. She stole a look, as the two fellows obediently burbled about how the reviewer was probably some outsider, someone who didn't understand, someone who . . . they trailed off, watching their host approach. Inkerman examined them, brow furrowed, lips pursed. When he saw where their gazes were directed he whirled around to find Evan Nezer standing behind him, a derisive expression on his face.

"Having a bad day, Inkerman?" he said, his lip curled.

The pastor's face told Jaymie as clearly as if he'd said it aloud. In that moment he knew, and so did Jaymie: Nezer was the offending book reviewer, Book Bookman.

⌀ Seven ⌀

INKERMAN'S EXPRESSIVE FACE blotched with red. He set down his drink, his hand shaking so much it sloshed, and fled the group. Jaymie watched as he bumped into Valetta, apologized, and moved on. Val joined her, looking over her shoulder. "What was that all about?"

Jaymie explained.

"Poor guy," Valetta murmured. "What a thing to find out at a party, that your host is your mortal enemy! Let's look around some more. Where's Heidi?"

Heidi was nowhere to be found and Jakob had been absorbed into a group of men near the Christmas tree, as had Brock, so the two friends went along on their own. Valetta, even snoopier than Jaymie, led the way. At the end of the hall was a dark space and a door. They pushed it open and peeked. There was a dowdier area beyond the front of the house, which explained why there was no lighting in this end of the hall. Bella Nezer had no doubt had her hands full getting the rest of the house ready for the party. She couldn't do everything in two months. This space had peeling wallpaper, stained with moisture, and chipped floor tiles.

But there were no signs commanding them to keep out and the door was unlocked. Jaymie and Val passed through the heavy door. They noticed a small washroom, which Val used. Then it was Jaymie's turn. She did her business, then opened her clutch to get her lipstick. There was the note the woman in the bushes had handed her. She held it to the light, too weak for a bathroom, but designed to hide the tiny room's flaws.

The note was folded over and taped, and on one side was written *Ben* in a large scrawl. So, this was for Benjamin Nezer? Her curiosity, always an itch under her skin, tickled. What did it say? Why hand it to her?

She ran her lipstick over her lips, smacked them together in the mirror, then pushed the note back in her clutch and exited the bathroom. She'd have to find Ben, at some point, and give it to him. Valetta was peeking into the room beyond. Jaymie joined her at the door. It was the kitchen, bustling with caterers who whipped trays of hors d'oeuvres out of the oven and filled platters that servers awaited as they chattered among themselves.

It was a huge, open room with sparse furnishings and centered by a large high worktable. The housekeeper—Jaymie assumed it was Erla Fancombe, anyway—leaned with one hand on the counter as she faced Finn Fancombe, her expression tense. "You should *not* be here tonight, you *know* that!" Her son hung his head, looking more like he was ten than the thirty-something-year-old he must be.

"Jaymie Leighton!" gasped a familiar voice nearby.

She whirled. "Austin Calhoun! What are *you* doing here?"

Austin was an acquaintance who had helped her sneak into a business building a year ago when she was trying to solve a murder. They hugged and she introduced Valetta as her partner in crime, the woman with whom she had gotten locked into that office building. He giggled. When she stood back she could see his plump form was clothed in the black and white of waitstaff. "You're *working*?"

He rolled his eyes. "I need money for the holidays. My mom wants the latest iPhone and I'm a poor student now."

"Student?"

"I've decided to *do* something with my life," he said, beaming. "At least that's what my mom says." He rolled his eyes. "She's relieved I've got a goal. With my sparkling personality and ready wit I decided hospitality is a natural, so I'm taking the hotel management course at WC."

"Oh, WC!"

"It's cheap," he said with a shrug. "And local. I moved back in with my mom to save money."

"You *will* be a natural," she agreed. It was a perfect fit for him. He loved people and could talk to anyone.

"I'm still working at the call center part-time, but when the listing was posted on the college work board for this party I signed up. Extra moolah for Christmas."

"I was surprised to see waitstaff, actually," Jaymie said, her attention still straying to Finn and his mother, arguing by the back door. Valetta had moved into the kitchen and snatched a treat from a tray, bouncing it back and forth between her hands until it cooled, then popping it into her mouth as a caterer gave her a censorious look. "Most parties in this town are *there's the buffet; help yourself.*"

"That would *never* do for Mrs. Bella Nezer," Austin said with an edge to his tone, as two of his fellow waiters pushed past through the door. "When she arrives at the college to check up on her hubby she always makes such a *production* out of it, swanning through campus, Louboutin shoes, Hermes handbag and matching scarf wound into a turban over her hair like Joan freaking Crawford. The students call her La Bella."

Erla Fancombe glanced over, perhaps hearing her employer's name. Finn smiled woozily at Jaymie and shrugged. What was he doing there on the night of a party? Surely Evan didn't know about this. His mother handed him a bag and pushed him toward the back door, then sent an unfriendly look at Jaymie and Val.

"Austin, you'd best get one of those trays and get going before the shrimp goes off," she said loudly, her gruff voice tinged with impatience. She bent over and pulled a heavy roasting pan out of the oven and easily hoisted it up onto the counter. "Mr. Nezer doesn't wait for anyone. Get a move on."

"Yes, ma'am," he said, rolling his eyes at Jaymie.

"We'll follow you back to the front of the house," Val said.

As they pushed through the door to the front hall another server was on her way through, returning to the kitchen with an empty platter for more food.

"Jacklyn?" Jaymie exclaimed.

It was indeed Jacklyn Marley, dressed in black and white. Her face burned red and she grimaced. "Yeah, well, I'm getting money out of the bastard one way or another," she joked as she shouldered past them.

"That is *odd*," Jaymie said as she followed Val.

"Why?"

"Why would she work here, given her animosity toward Evan Nezer? And why would Bella hire her, knowing their history? That makes zero sense."

Val knew Jacklyn as a new tenant of the apartment above the Emporium, but she didn't know the whole story. As Austin waved and mouthed *toodles*, then headed back toward a crowd of people with his platter of shrimp, Jaymie strolled with Val and told her friend about Jacklyn's bitterness toward Nezer for his failure to pay her, as his ghostwriter, what she was owed.

"What does he write?" Valetta asked.

"A couple of fiction books back in the eighties, according to Jacklyn, but his more recent work that she ghosted, I haven't a clue."

"Ladies! I'm so happy you both could come," Bella Nezer said, drifting over to them. She was, of course, gorgeous, in an off-the-shoulder body-hugging black gown, ruched across the stomach, and with a glittering halter of rhinestones that held it up, as the front plunged deeply, displaying her impressive décolletage. She emanated a cloud of good wine and expensive cologne. "Where is your little blonde friend, Heidi whatever her name is?"

Jaymie exchanged a look with Val. That was the most passive-aggressive way to describe Heidi Lockland imaginable. Her last name could not be difficult to remember, as it was the same as Haskell Lockland, whom she seemed to remember quite well.

"She's around here somewhere," Jaymie said. "Lovely house, Bella. You've done an amazing job with it in such a short time. I don't know how you did it!"

"It wasn't easy. We haven't even been here long enough to have our mail delivered properly, for heaven's sake! Evan has had it all routed through the college until we're settled properly. *Très incommode,*" she said with an airy wave of one elegant hand. "But my dear husband wanted to host all his friends from the college and community, so I knew I had to make it happen. He's busy with all his work, and teaching, and writing. It's the least I can do to provide a lovely home for him."

There was no answer to that and fortunately she appeared to need none, drifting off to graciously speak with others, touching a shoulder, smiling beneficently, beaming at her husband, air-kissing the college president.

Austin, Jacklyn, and the other waitstaff, probably students at WC as well, threaded through the crowd offering a variety of appetizers and hors d'oeuvres: crostini, smoked salmon bites, stuffed endive, rumaki, and a dozen more were endlessly supplied from the caterers. Sparkling wine flowed, punch was available, a traditional wassail, as Bella announced, to celebrate the season. Funny, Jaymie thought, when all Nezer seemed to want to do was *end* the festive Dickens Days, where such traditions as fellowship, wassail and gathering with friends were celebrated.

Jakob, standing with Brock, looked across the room to her and winked. She winked back and rolled her eyes. Jacklyn Marley sailed past with a tray of tiny quiches and she snagged two, handing one to Valetta, who stood next to her chatting to a stranger.

Her question about the host's writing was soon to be answered. Nezer, at the heart of a circle of folks, including the college president and her minions, held forth about the meaning of Christmas, and how if they were going to be true to it and their society, they needed to embrace the commercial aspect. It was only through unfettered buying that the lower orders could be gainfully employed and thus lifted out of the poverty in which they toiled. "If our society would toughen up a little, those who are laying around on food stamps would be forced to get off their butts and work for a living. Otherwise — "

"Otherwise?" Inkerman said, standing up from his sofa seat behind the group. "Otherwise where should we put them? Your book *The Literary Economics of Charles Dickens* says the Victorians had the right idea and Dickens was full of bunkum for painting such a grim picture of the prisons and workhouses. Am I right?"

Nezer swiveled his gaze and stared at the pastor over the top of his glasses. He raised his wineglass in a salute. "So you've read it. I hope you found it illuminating."

"I found it horrible," the pastor said. "Rife with heartless judgment and void of compassion."

"Interesting. I suppose you have to say poppycock like that, being a man of God — " Nezer paused and glanced around, as if waiting for a laugh, even though he hadn't said anything particularly funny. A couple of the college colleagues politely tittered. "But I stand by that one hundred percent, Inkerman. False hope of some miraculous deliverance isn't doing them any justice. Not like that 'best of all possible worlds' crap *you* peddle."

"*Now* we get to the heart of it!" Inkerman howled, jabbing his finger at his host as he pushed through the crowd toward him. "Now I understand you, why you haunt me and torment me wherever I go. You're a heartless contrarian who can't bear anyone having a different opinion than you."

Jaymie noticed Jacklyn Marley standing close, transfixed, her platter drooping dangerously, the tiny quiches sliding to one side, then looked back to the two men, edging closer and closer. Jakob was paying attention too, from his spot near the front window, where he stood with a drink in his hand chatting with Nezer's son, Benjamin.

"You're just angry your book was panned as pie-in-the-sky silliness." Nezer turned away.

"By *you*, you . . . you sour, faded, hack Scrooge! You're *jealous* of Dickens because besides being a brilliant author and devoted humanitarian, he had a heart. You wouldn't know what that was if someone ripped out the vital organ dripping with blood and slapped you with it!" That violent and evocative image was followed by a physical attack of sorts. Inkerman threw his drink at Nezer's back. It splashed his expensive suit, the silk blotching in drips.

Nezer whirled, shards of ice scattering around him. "Why you wheedling little pathetic excuse for a writer." The words grated from between gritted teeth. From coolly amused, he had transformed into fuming fury, his skin red above his trim beard. "Get out of my house. I don't even know why you're here."

"Your wife invited me, you louse." Inkerman set his empty glass aside. "She, at least, is graceful and gracious. How she ended up married to a doddering old has-been like you I'll never understand."

"Has-been? *Me?*" Nezer bellowed. "Look who's talking! A *never-was*. Your book was so bad that when I reviewed it, I had to hold back the worst points." He looked around at the crowd gathered. "Yes, that's right, folks. No one would have believed its awfulness until they read it for themselves!" He turned again and glared at the pastor. "I probably did you a favor. At least I steered a few people away from it. Readers are laughing at the drivel you've spewed."

Inkerman launched himself at Nezer, but the older man held his ground and grabbed the pastor, whose blonde locks were in his eyes, interfering with his vision. "Give it up, Inkerman," he said, shaking him. "You know you only wrote that piece of crap to try to hide your past *affairs*."

The pastor roared in anger and swiped ineffectually at Nezer, who was certainly stronger than he looked. Jakob calmly set his drink aside as people started to shout and gabble. He pushed through the crowd, stepping between the two men and physically separating them with his bulk, grabbing a handful of fabric from each man's shirt. "Gentlemen, let's remember where we are," he said gruffly, lasering stern looks at each of them. "And that there are ladies present."

Inkerman retreated first, his pale face blotched in red spots of color that stretched in blobs down his neck. He swept his fair hair back off his forehead, gasping and wheezing in distress. Nezer, with a sneer still on his face, shifted his glasses up to the bridge of his nose again and stood his ground, even as Jakob kept his big hand on the professor's chest.

"This poor fellow is suffering humiliation over the devastating failure of his book in comparison to mine," Nezer said.

"I'd rather have a tender heart than one of stone," Inkerman said, his eyes welling and his voice breaking. "I'll be leaving now." He stepped back, settled his rumpled shirt, turned and bowed to his hostess, who stood, hand over her mouth in mortification at the quarrel. "Bella, beauteous lady, radiant morning star, my most *sincere* apologies to you, and my condolences on wedding the worst human being I have ever met in my life." He threw a disgusted look over his shoulder. "I'll take my coat now and leave."

Alone, he walked to the door, where the coat check attendant retrieved an elegant black wool trench, handing it to him.

Nezer chuckled. "Bravo, little peacock," he said loudly as the pastor exited. "He handled that better than I expected." Some of his friends, including the college president's minions, chuckled. He nabbed a glass of champagne from a tray being carried by Jacklyn Marley.

Jaymie blanched; given how Jacklyn felt about him, he'd better hope there was no poison in that glass. He didn't appear to notice who held the tray, but then, that was the fate of most servers, as she knew from serving tea at their annual Tea With the Queen event.

"You're a spiteful old gasbag, aren't you," Brock said, his voice slurring as he stumbled toward his host.

"Oh, crap," Valetta mumbled, setting her drink aside and dusting quiche crumbs from her fingers.

"I beg your pardon?" Nezer said, turning slowly. "Nibley, are you drunk?"

"Maybe."

"Then you ought to shut up. Or I'll tell everyone what I *really* think of your skills as a real estate agent."

"Darn. How do we stop this?" Val asked, almost vibrating in agitation next to Jaymie.

Jakob, nearby, put his hand on Brock's arm. But the fellow shook it off. "You tell 'em whatever you want, Nezer, about me. Everyone here may kowtow to you, but every single one of 'em knows exactly what you are. Poisonous old Farty McFartpants."

"Wow, he's been hanging out with his kids too much," Jaymie said, stifling a laugh.

"Tell me about it. Farty McFartpants is Will's favorite insult this week," Valetta said about her nephew, Brock's son. "And lately Brock has been calling me 'dude' a lot."

Jaymie laughed out loud, and Brock turned with a sideways smile. He straightened, pounded his chest, and said, "I'm a *good* real estate agent." He nodded drunkenly and turned back to Nezer. "But *you* were a lousy client," he said, stabbing the air with a finger as, increasingly, those around them hid smiles.

"*Lousy client?* How can the customer be a lousy client?" Nezer appeared aghast. "Without clients you would be nowhere. Your client is your boss!"

"Hey, it happens. A lousy client is one who won't take good advice even when it's spoon-fed to him. No harm, no foul." The situation was defused as Brock ambled off and collapsed on a sofa in the space Inkerman had vacated. "Farty McFartpants," he mumbled with a drunken giggle.

As Brock snoozed, the party continued on a more subdued track. Nezer spent much of the next while huddled with the president and her two colleagues. Hazel Belcher appeared to be taking him to task. Heidi reappeared, shadowed closely by Benjamin Nezer, seemingly infatuated with her. She decided to call it a night early, and after hugs all around, headed out.

Jaymie sighed in exasperation after her friend left. The night was not going as she had anticipated. She had thought that after charming Nezer with her witty banter, she could subtly ask him to discard his animosity toward Bill Waterman and allow the historical society an easement on his property to anchor the cider booth. It had always been a long shot, given that she suspected he was the one who set the cider booth afire, but you don't get anything in life without asking, as she was learning. However . . . nothing had gone according to plan.

Valetta was soon yawning, too. "I'm taking my dear brother home," she said, motioning to Brock, who was snoring on the sofa, his head on a bemused young woman's shoulder. "My feet are killing me, and Denver is waiting up." She hauled her brother to his feet, slung his arm over her shoulder, and departed.

Jaymie leaned her head on Jakob's shoulder. "Can we escape too, do you think?"

"I don't see why not."

Together they found Bella Nezer by the front window, looking out as her party went on all around her, albeit somewhat muted.

"Thank you for inviting us," Jakob said.

"And thank you for a lovely evening. You've done a wonderful job with the house in such short order!" Jaymie said, taking her hand and shaking it.

She sighed and her eyes looked slightly teary as she squeezed Jaymie's hand. "I had hoped inviting Pastor Inkerman would be a good move to get the two men to behave politely to each other, but their animosity is too deeply held, I suppose. Poor Vaughn loathes Evan."

"Did you know that your husband is the reviewer who slammed Pastor Inkerman's book so badly?" Jaymie asked.

"I did *not*," she said indignantly. "My husband is a very private person and his work is his own. I don't interfere." She gazed earnestly into Jaymie's eyes. "You know, Evan means well, he just has strong opinions."

"So their animosity predates the pastor knowing your husband was the negative reviewer?"

Bella sighed and rolled her shoulders. "Both work at the college, you know, and . . . they have philosophical differences. I *knew* they didn't see eye to eye, but I never would have expected it to end with such . . . animosity." Her gaze hardened and her lips thinned. "I'm a little shocked at Pastor Inkerman, in truth. That was *not* Evan's doing, that altercation."

It sounded like Bella was defending her husband, which was understandable, but Jaymie felt there was bad behavior on both sides. Nezer was a name-calling taunter, and surely had inspired his share of fights before the pastor threw a drink at him. Bella had certainly invited and employed a whole host of folks who were antagonized by Nezer . . . Inkerman, Brock, Jacklyn Marley . . . even herself, who had

had her own run-in with Nezer. She didn't know what to say, so she said nothing and moved on, deciding on diplomacy over honesty in that moment. "We'll be heading out now. Can't let the babysitter wait up too late. Thank you for your hospitality."

"Good night," she said, grabbing Jaymie's hand. "I truly hope you all have a lovely Dickens Days festival. I'm so excited about it, you know. Living here, I feel we'll be a part of it, right in the thick of things! I look forward to strolling the town and enjoying the amenities."

Jaymie was speechless, and beside her she knew Jakob was struggling not to laugh. How could Bella say that, given her husband's intent to ruin it with one lawsuit after another? Jaymie even considered Nezer the prime suspect in torching the cider booth, so deeply did his animosity toward their lovely little town tradition appear to run.

Bella returned to her husband's dwindling group and stepped between him and the president, who were having an animated disagreement. Life with him must be a tornado of stomping out the fires he created with his fractious personality and divisive behavior. She almost pitied the woman.

"I need to use the little girl's room first, Jakob," Jaymie said and headed to the back hall. The guests had been pointed to an elaborate washroom up the stairs, but she preferred the closer option Val had used earlier.

She did what she had to do, then thought she'd stop and thank Erla for all her hard work. She ducked into the kitchen. Austin and the other servers were gone, and there were only two of the catering staff left, now that food service was done. They were packing their equipment. But Erla was busy; Pastor Inkerman must have circled the house and entered the kitchen, perhaps with the same mission she had of thanking the housekeeper for all of her labor. Inkerman stood near the back door speaking with Erla Fancombe most earnestly, his fair hair gleaming in the light from the pendants that hung over the counter.

Jaymie decided not to interfere and headed back to join Jakob. He was chatting with the coat checker, who must be another of the hired college students. She was by the office door, but it was closed.

"We'd like our coats," Jaymie said.

Jakob handed the young woman the numbered ticket. "It's a dark gray parka and a faux fur cape or . . . what do you call it?" he asked, turning to Jaymie.

"It's a shrug," she said to the young woman. "A black faux fur shrug with a diamante snowflake pin on the shoulder. That and the dark gray parka ought to be together."

The girl looked embarrassed. She looked over her shoulder, shifting from foot to foot, folding the coat check ticket in her hands, looking nervous. "Uh, can you wait a minute?"

Jaymie glanced at the closed door. "Why? What's going on?"

"N-nothing, it's just . . . it's . . ." She shook her head. "I . . . I can't . . ." She shrugged helplessly, a frightened look in her blue eyes.

"We'll get them ourselves," Jaymie said, deeply weary and unwilling to wait a moment longer. She slipped around her, pushed open the office door and marched over to the rack, with Jakob following. "Why have a coat check girl if . . ." She stopped and turned to look at a weird glow behind the desk. Someone was there, in the shadows, she could hear them tapping away. She walked across the room to find Jacklyn Marley huddled behind Nezer's desk, the computer screen illuminating her pale face.

"What are you—"

"Shh!" Jacklyn said, looking past Jaymie to the open door.

"What are you doing, Jacklyn?" Jaymie whispered. "This is crazy."

Jacklyn glared up at Jaymie, the white reflected glow making eerie long shadows under her eyes. "That butthole is hiding revenue from me. He's claiming the book I helped him write hasn't made any money," she muttered. "If I can find royalty payments on his computer it'll make it worth my while to sue him. But I have to have info first, to know I'll win. He's a maniac jerk about lawsuits! I *need* that money."

"Can't you ask the publishing company?"

"*Shhh!*" She bobbed up, looking toward the door, which had been closed by the coat checker. "My agreement is with Evan. The publishing company won't even return my calls or answer my emails. *Please*, Jaymie, go away. Pretend you didn't see this!"

"You've got that poor girl standing guard for you," Jaymie

whispered, pointing toward the door. "She's scared to *death*. What is she, a student at WC?"

Jacklyn nodded.

"And you've got her standing guard for you? That's not right. Any second Nezer could come here and she'd be in *big* trouble."

"Look, I'm almost done." She shoved a flash drive into the USB and tapped the keyboard. She looked back up at Jaymie. "Get out and let me finish! I'm almost there. *Please!*"

Conflicted, Jaymie shared a look with Jakob. "What do you think?"

He shook his head. "Look, I don't know the whole story here and you do," he murmured, putting his arm over her shoulders and giving her a squeeze. "This is *your* call, Jaymie. We'll do what you think best. No harm, no foul either way."

She stared down at Jacklyn, then back at the door. Sighing heavily, she said to her husband, "Let's get our coats and leave."

"I owe you!" Jacklyn softly called after her.

"No, you don't," Jaymie said, her tone firm, as Jakob found their coats. "I won't cover for you if Bella or Evan comes in here this moment."

Jakob helped her on with her shrug and they slipped out the door, closing it behind them, and headed past the coat checker, whose face was red and blotchy, her eyes full of fear.

"I didn't . . . poor Jacklyn . . . I mean, like, Mr. Nezer was so mean to her," she stammered. "And she was such a good teacher, and I . . ." She shrugged.

"I didn't know she taught at WC."

"Yeah. She was . . . cool. Creative writing and English classics."

"But she no longer teaches there? Why?"

"Well, uh . . ." The young woman glanced around, then leaned forward. "Mr. Nezer got her fired, I heard."

"Why?"

The girl shrugged.

"Enough," Jacklyn hissed, slipping out of the room as she pocketed the flash drive. "Good night, Jaymie. Thanks again." She stalked down the hallway toward the kitchen as another couple came toward them to retrieve their coats.

Jaymie took Jakob's arm. "Look out for yourself," she whispered to the student. She nodded with a tentative smile as she turned to her new customers and took their coat check ticket.

Jaymie and Jakob stepped out the front door. It was a frigid night, crisp and clean-scented, a hint of snow on the breeze. A few flakes fluttered down, but there were also some stars winking in the sky. Jaymie felt a calmness descend over her and she breathed in deeply. "I think I was tense most of the time we were there," she whispered, strolling down the path arm in arm with Jakob. "Maybe that's why I feel so relieved now."

"Why tense?"

She handed Jakob the keys so he could drive. "I'm not sure, but . . . the altercation between Nezer and Pastor Inkerman, for one, and Brock getting drunk and insulting the host."

"But neither of those were your doing."

"I know, I know. I guess I tend to worry about those things too much." She had a moment of clarity. "Maybe that's why functions have always been difficult for me. I usually need a few minutes in the middle to decompress."

"That's why you head off to examine the bookshelves at any house party we've attended."

"Well, partly, but mostly because I think you can tell a lot about a person by what books they read."

They circled to where their car was parked, along the lane near the back of the house. As Jakob unlocked and got in the driver's side, Jaymie glanced over to the back door and saw Finn Fancombe arguing with his mother again, his voice carrying clearly in the crisp still air.

"Mom, I *need* to talk to Professor Nezer. He *has* to write me that letter! I'm going to lose everything if he doesn't. The president would listen to him, I know she would. She as good as told me that all that was holding me back from re-admission was him."

"Let me handle it, Finn," Erla Fancombe said, grabbing his shoulder as he tried to slip past her into the house. "I *told* you I'd take care of it."

"You promise, Mom? You *promise*?"

"I promise, Finn. But you have to get out of here before Mr. or Mrs. Nezer sees you. Tonight's not the night."

"But the president is still in there. I saw her through the window. The prof could solve it all tonight, if he wanted to."

"*Not* tonight."

"It's his fault in the first place! I hate him so *much*," he said, his voice rising in anger, sounding on the edge of tears. "I *hate* that I have to beg him for help. It's not *right*!"

"Jaymie, you coming?" Jakob called out the SUV window.

Fascinated by people as always, and wanting to hear the rest of the conversation, Jaymie waved her hand, shushing him, and continued listening, lingering in the shadows of a large blue spruce that perfumed the cold air around her.

"Finn, *go*!" Erla said, trying to push her son away from the back door. "Let me handle this. I can't help you if the professor gets mad again. That's what happened in the first place. You wouldn't be in this mess if you hadn't made him angry by complaining he'd used your work."

"I know, I *know*! My effin' bad. I didn't think the stupid jerk would be such a big baby. He should have said he'd used my stuff accidentally and we'd all have moved on. But noooo, he has to take it out on me. He's such a frickin' liar!"

"You've known him your whole life, you should *know* what he's like," she said, her voice carrying through the cold, crisp air.

"Yeah, I've known him my whole life. I know enough to know he's a cheat and a jerk."

"Son, you shut your mouth right now and go away," the woman said, a hysterical edge to her voice. "You know if you put a foot wrong, or say something about him, he'll come back on you twice as hard. Look what happened to poor Mrs. Sarah."

"Okay, but Mom, this has to happen if I'm going to be able to restart my master's. I've sunk everything into this. I can't get a job, even, with a black mark on my academic record. Please help me!"

"You know I will, hon. Now go!"

"But you and I need to talk. Prof Nezer said he has something to tell me tonight, and I can't—"

"Go now!" She looked over her shoulder. "I have work to do. Go. *Trust* me."

He turned and fled into the darkness, down a path toward the back of the property. Erla retreated inside.

"Poor guy," Jaymie said as she got in and closed the door behind her.

"What's that all about?" Jakob asked as he started the SUV.

As they drove home Jaymie explained about Finn Fancombe, the plagiarism scandal, and his subsequent ouster from the studious halls of Wolverhampton College. She told Jakob how Finn had been in the kitchen earlier in the night, and had returned to plague his mother. It was weighing on his mind, and he clearly wanted to clear the air with the college president, who was so close, and yet so far away.

"Given everything you've told me, I'd bet that Nezer has some crooked angle on the whole thing."

Jaymie frowned as they pulled up to the cabin. "I never thought about that, but I wonder. The paper reported on it. I wonder what Nan's take was on the whole thing? That was a month ago or so."

"Let's not borrow trouble, as your grandmother says. It is time for bed, my dearly beloved," Jakob said as he got out and raced around to open her door for her. "Milady," he said with a deep bow and flourish.

Jaymie chuckled and took his arm. Jakob wasn't often playful, but when he was, it was a delight. *Dearly beloved*, indeed. She was a lucky woman.

✄ Eight ✄

BECCA AND KEVIN HAD STAYED OVER, sleeping in Jaymie and Jakob's bed while the younger couple spent the night on the pull-out sofa in the living room. They were all up early, Jaymie still yawning and stretching as she drowsily downed a cup of coffee at the kitchen table. It was the kickoff to Dickens Days, and they were already behind schedule. Kevin made breakfast, a decadent stuffed French toast with his own blueberry sauce. Jaymie groaned in delight through the whole thing, then raced back upstairs to don leggings, a long sweater and a scarf. Kevin and Becca were taking Jocie shopping at a pop-up Christmas market in Wolverhampton, and then to her grandparents', the rest of the day for Christmas arts and crafts with Sonya and her kids, Helmut's stepchildren.

Jakob was accompanying Jaymie into town, hauling the huge village Christmas tree in the extended box of his beat-up white pickup. Brock, Haskell and whoever else wanted to help were going to meet them in front of the Emporium. As Becca and Kevin did up the breakfast dishes, Jaymie grabbed the step stool and climbed to the top step, reaching for the vintage pudding mould from the rafters over the kitchen table. It was one of the two things missing in the diorama, which would be revealed that afternoon as the cider booth opened and the strolling carolers began their tasks. She already had the holly from the Queensville house, of course.

"You do find unique ways to store things," Becca said over her shoulder.

"You do what you have to do," Jaymie said, climbing back down. "There's not a lot of horizontal space left in the cabin, so I make use of the vertical!"

Dishes done and put away, Kevin helped Becca on with her Harris Tweed peacoat, purchased in Scotland.

"Come on, Jocie," Jaymie called over her shoulder as she checked to make sure she had everything: keys, cell phone, wallet, holly and pudding mould. *And a partridge in a pear tree,* she hummed to herself. "Aunt Becca and Uncle Kevin are waiting for you!"

Jocie and Jakob had returned from walking Hoppy. She unleashed the little dog to race off and find Lilibet. Since she was already dressed and ready, Becca and Kevin hustled Jocie out the door. Yawning, Jaymie took three containers of frozen treats out of the freezer to thaw, ready for giving away and selling at the cider booth, and put them in a cloth tote bag along with the pudding mould.

Thanksgiving through Christmas was life lived at an accelerated pace for Jaymie, even more so now with a husband and child, and the Friday night party had left her lagging. She was an early-to-bed, early-to-rise sort, but . . . she'd be fine.

Jakob ducked back in the door. "Are we ready to go? I've tied the tree down in the back of the truck. Can you follow in the SUV and make sure it isn't moving around too much?"

"Sure," she mumbled, holding her leather key fob in her mouth and hooking one arm through her purse strap as she fastened the toggles of her plaid parka with one hand and grabbed the canvas bag of treats with the other.

They drove slowly to Queensville, Jaymie watching the tree, which was securely fastened in the truck bed and up over the cab. It was eighteen or twenty feet tall and would take at least five or six people to erect. Jakob had already, wisely, strung lights around it and secured them to branches. Once they anchored it in the bucket sunk in the ground and tethered it, all that would be needed would be to plug it in that evening at the official tree lighting, hopefully. They were behind schedule, but everything should come together with cooperation.

The frosty promise of the night before was borne out in the frigid weather of the morning. She could have used one more cup of coffee, Jaymie thought as she parked near her husband's truck in front of the village green. The first thing she noticed was that the fire-damaged cider booth had been cleared away, and there was a layer of sand on the spot, making a clean start. That was a good thing, she thought, but then turned away to watch the tree going up.

The town tree would normally have gone to the right of the cider booth, but that was before Jaymie had planned the *Christmas Carol* diorama. Now it would go across from the cider booth on another smaller V of public land. The benefit of that was that there was a telephone post close by, perfect for attaching the tree to. Kevin and Becca had volunteered to provide electricity from their own shop, which was closest to the new location for the town tree, so they would reel an outdoor extension cord to it before lighting it up and plug it into their store's outdoor outlet. Haskell was already there in his faux working man overalls, talking to Bill Waterman. Johnny Stanko had been roped in and was standing by alone, rubbing his hands together and stamping his feet to warm them. Brock Nibley was there, nominally, but he sat on his car bumper, head in his hands, the very image of a man regretful about the night before.

"That is a man with a serious hangover," Jakob murmured to Jaymie as he walked with her toward the other men.

"The booze was free and his kids are at their Aunt Violet's place for the weekend."

"That explains his drinking . . . too much freedom. I've never known Brock to be much of a boozer."

Valetta had emerged from the Emporium to watch as the guys hoisted the tree into the deepset holder that Jakob had already secured. There was much grunting and groaning, and even more calls of *Is it straight?* But eventually they got it upright and secured with ropes tied off to trees and the telephone pole. The guys shook hands all around and there was much clapping on the back and hearty laughter.

But Jakob had to run. He raced over to Jaymie, gave her an enthusiastic kiss, bending her backward, and with a grin waved at the crowd that watched and laughed. Flustered, Jaymie laughed too and patted her flaming cheeks. He headed to his truck and roared out of town. From there he'd check in at The Junk Stops Here and work for a couple of hours, then he'd pick up Helmut and head into Wolverhampton to an employment agency. They needed two casual laborers to help them cut trees for sale for the season. It was a big job demanding considerable physical stamina and a knack with tricky machinery, since they had a Christmas tree baler, which wrapped each tree into a tight netted bundle, making them easy to stack. No one they had used before was free so they'd have to train a couple of new workers. The better of the two would be kept on to help sell trees until Christmas.

Mrs. Bellwood and Imogene Frump arrived at the site as Bill Waterman, with the help of Johnny Stanko, using the handyman's cart, arrived back on-site with the new cider booth. Bill kept ducking his head, looking through the line of pine trees toward the Nezer home, probably hoping the man of the house would notice what they were doing and come out to confront him. He and Johnny, with a little help from Jaymie, shoved the booth into place. It was considerably lighter than the previous incarnation. After directing Johnny on how to raise the custom-made shutter he had installed to open and close the booth, Bill set about hooking it up to the electricity.

The booth looked terrific, even better than the original. Bill had replicated the painting on the old one, and most people wouldn't notice that it was a different structure. There was a festive atmosphere all around as villagers gathered to watch the excitement of the tree being put up and the new cider booth being installed. Some were eyeing the Nezer residence, taking bets on how long it would be before Evan erupted from the house in fury to castigate Bill. Odds were even on five minutes or less. Laughter filled the air, and even those who had to get going did so with calls of *See you here later!* The first evening of Dickens Days and the lighting of the tree would be exhilarating and busy.

But Jaymie had another task, adding the finishing touches to her diorama. Dickens Days needed a scene of Victorian Christmas frolic, she had thought, and what would be better than the part where the Cratchit family go into ecstasies over the plum pudding? That was how she had put it to the Dickens Days committee when pitching the idea a month ago.

She practically had the plum pudding section of *A Christmas Carol* memorized and had recited it at the meeting, looking for approval for her diorama:

In half a minute Mrs. Cratchit entered: flushed, but smiling proudly: with the pudding, like a speckled cannon-ball, so hard and firm, blazing in half of half-a-quartern of ignited brandy, and bedight with Christmas holly stuck into the top.

Oh, a wonderful pudding! Bob Cratchit said, and calmly too, that he regarded it as the greatest success achieved by Mrs. Cratchit since their marriage.

She retrieved the vintage pudding mould and holly from her truck. The mould was not an expensive one. She had been ready to use a brand-new mould because the idea of leaving a vintage piece in the diorama to easily be stolen was frightening for anyone who valued old stuff, as she did. But Jakob, knowing her yen for authenticity, had surprised her by finding in his storeroom an old dented one that no one would want even for a display. If she positioned it perfectly in the background, no one would notice the ding. If it lasted, she'd keep it for next year. If it got stolen or ruined, oh well.

Bill had added a feature to the cider booth: music! A cheery chorus of "Jingle Bells" blared, and then softened as he adjusted the volume. The gathered villagers applauded and there was an impromptu *Hip hip hooray* for their local handyman. The air was frigid and the sky had closed in, clouds gathering overhead. There was a promise of snow that might fall for the first night of the festival. Jaymie smiled. Everything was going to be perfect, despite Evan Nezer's Grinchy attempt to ruin it. He could not dim their Christmas cheer; like the Whos of Whoville, they would gather around the tree and sing together.

Jaymie unfastened the tarp from over the diorama; one corner was ripped, she noticed. Wind must have tugged it free. Weird. Hopefully nothing was ruined. She'd have to make sure all the volunteers knew to fasten the tarp every night at all corners. She flipped the tarp up over the roof of the diorama and tied it so it wouldn't flap in the strengthening breeze, then stood back and looked it over. There was something wrong with the scene; the table had been moved, and the Tiny Tim mannequin had fallen over. Annoying. She went to push the table back into place, but it would not budge. She walked into the diorama and stared, a shriek of horror building in her throat.

Under the back edge of the table was a body, hairy legs sticking out from under a long linen nightshirt, and with an antique pudding mould placed like a cap on its head. Worst of all, a thick wooden stake pierced the chest, a big branch of glossy holly tied jauntily to the top. She ducked her head under the table to look; it was Evan Nezer! He had been handed a life sentence for his Scroogery, it seemed, for his part in the scene was unmistakably staged. She staggered backward, out of the diorama, faced the crowd of people and yelled, "Heeeelp!" before crumbling in a heap to weep in horror.

She quivered and wept into her hands as other people cried out at the sight that greeted them, and someone else called 911 on their cell phone, loudly, excitedly reciting the horrible, unbelievable details, and affirming that yes, the body was dead. And no, there was no doubt about it. Evan Nezer was dead as a doornail. But as Dickens so succinctly put it, it should be dead as a coffin nail, shouldn't it?

And now she was mindlessly repeating Dickens bits in her brain to keep from visualizing the horrid spectacle. Jaymie shuddered. But the scene . . . it was too, *too* appropriate. It was like in the book, when Scrooge muttered, *"Every idiot who goes about with 'Merry Christmas' on his lips, should be boiled with his own pudding, and buried with a stake of holly through his heart."*

• • •

"**I'M COMPLETELY BAFFLED** by how often this happens to you," Detective Vestry said as Jaymie sat in the open door of an ambulance, grimly viewing the police working on the scene of her lovely diorama . . . which she would never be able to look at again. "You seem like such a nice girl, but you find dead bodies with astonishing regularity."

"I'm starting to take it personally," Jaymie said, choking back a sob. "I have to believe it is wrong place, wrong time, or I'll go a little crazy."

Bernie took the detective aside, but not so far that Jaymie couldn't overhear the conversation. The new medical examiner, who had emerged from the diorama and removed her gloves, apparently conjectured that Nezer had been killed elsewhere and moved to the diorama. *Thank goodness,* Jaymie thought. For some obscure reason it made her feel better that Nezer had not been killed in her diorama. She caught Bernie's glance toward her; her dear friend had made sure she heard that part, knowing it would matter to her. She smiled through tears and nodded, mouthing *thank you*.

The stake of holly, Bernie continued to the detective, had been hammered into his body well after his death. The medical examiner said her preliminary finding would be that the cause of death was a blow to the head . . . a blow with very odd markings to it.

Feeling numb, not sure what to do but feeling she had regained her equilibrium, Jaymie stood, made sure her legs were not wobbly, and began to walk away from the dreadful scene. Valetta bolted toward her and pushed her shoulder under Jaymie's arm. "You should stay put, sit down. You've had a heck of a shock, kiddo."

Jaymie sagged against her friend. "I can't sit and do nothing. It keeps running in a loop, finding him like that. Val, who did this?" she said, turning and grabbing her by her cardigan-clad shoulders and staring into her eyes. "Why did they plant him in my diorama? Am I horribly selfish to be upset at that? What are we going to do? Dickens Days . . . *tonight* . . ." She shook her head, unable to continue.

"Come up to the porch of the Emporium and sit. You've had a shock; you need sugar. I'm going to get you a cup of hot sweet tea."

From the porch of the Emporium, where she had spent many an afternoon tea break with Valetta, the elevated view allowed her to see not only the village green but beyond, even to the Nezer home. Jaymie wondered if Bella had been told yet, or Benjamin. She huddled in weary anxiety until Valetta pushed a hot cup of sugary black tea into her hands, then draped a shawl around her shoulders for added warmth. "You're cold, my dear," Val said, concern in her voice. "I could close down and take you to my place to warm up. I'm sure the detective would be okay with that."

"I'm okay, Val." She took a deep breath and sipped the sweet brew. It was helping. She felt steadier, calmer. "Who killed him, I wonder?" Jaymie mused, cradling the hot cup of tea. "He had so many people mad at him."

At that moment Jacklyn Marley drifted closer, her gaze fixed on the scene, arms crossed over her chest, mitted hands under her arms.

"Like *her*. Last I saw her she was at Evan's computer stealing data from him," Jaymie whispered, her gaze not leaving the woman.

"What?" Valetta hissed, plunking down in the matching Adirondack.

Jaymie told her friend what she had seen the night before, Jacklyn hacking Evan Nezer's computer for proof he was defrauding her of royalties.

"How could he do that?" Valetta asked.

She shrugged. "She said her agreement was with him, not the

publishing company, so it's up to him to uphold his part of the bargain. I have to believe she has some kind of contract. Who would do all that work without one?"

"But who drew up the contract? Maybe she didn't know him that well before she signed. What we know about him now is that he's sue-happy. And he's a lawyer; if he drew it up you have to know it favored him."

Jaymie nodded, watching Jacklyn, who appeared rattled and upset, as she must be if she knew what was going on. "At any rate, she says she needs proof that he is making money from the book sales. With him dead, it may be a lot easier to negotiate with his estate than with him."

"Still . . . that's a heck of a stretch from hacking to murder."

"Depends on what she found," Jaymie said, sipping her tea.

Sarah Nezer, in jeans and a parka, riding an old-fashioned bike, stopped, putting her foot down on the dew-slick grass by the street. Imogene Frump and Mrs. Bellwood were standing and watching the goings-on. Sarah leaned in and said something to them.

Mrs. Bellwood loudly said, "It's that Evan Nezer character, the fellow who is always suing the town. He was murdered and thrown in Jaymie's lovely diorama."

Sarah staggered sideways, then threw the bike down and hustled over to the ambulance. "Is it true? Evan's dead? I want to see him!" she said loudly, the words carrying up to Jaymie and Val. A paramedic touched her shoulder and murmured something to her. She cried out and sank down onto the road. The paramedic beckoned to his partner and they attended to the collapsed woman, one laying her down and putting a cushion under her head while the other undid the top button of her sweater.

"Ma'am, ma'am, can you hear me?" the first one said as he tried to rouse her, checking her pulse.

A supercilious grin on her face, Jacklyn Marley turned and spotted Jaymie. Her smile died, her eyes widened, and she bustled away around to the side of the Emporium. The sound of her clumping boots up the exterior stairs thudded through the air.

Sarah was now sitting up, while a paramedic squatted beside her talking to her. His partner had gotten a compress out of the ambulance and held it to her head. Her color was improving already.

"It looks like she's going to be okay. It must have been a shock to her."

"I guess we can stroke her off the list of suspects," Valetta said jokingly.

"Maybe. Unless she's a pretty good actress." Jaymie watched the woman, who put one hand to her forehead and nodded at something the paramedic said. She was not weeping; she looked dazed as she stood, with his help, and climbed up to sit on a gurney the other paramedic had hauled out of the ambulance. "Val, I heard that Sarah didn't get anything in the divorce. Why is that? Shouldn't she have gotten a fifty-fifty split?"

Valetta shrugged. "Michigan isn't a community property state, it's an equitable distribution state. But I think that means if the couple works out an agreement of less or more than fifty-fifty the judge will go along with it."

"Why wouldn't she ask for her share? She's apparently destitute." Jaymie considered what she'd said. "We know what Nezer is like, though. Maybe he had something on her, some . . . scandal. Something to hold over her head."

"Maybe. We have no way of knowing. Why are you thinking of that?"

"You already said it, about Sarah being—or not being—a suspect."

"I was joking!"

Jaymie shrugged and drained her tea and set her mug aside. "You know how my mind works. Someone killed Nezer," she said, her voice quivering. "They then planted him in my lovely diorama with a stake of holly through his heart and a pudding mould over his head, and . . ." She stopped and sat up straight. "Wait, where did that pudding mould come from?"

"It wasn't yours?"

"I didn't have one there yet. I was bringing one this morning."

"What did it look like? The one over Nezer's head, I mean."

"It was . . ." She thought, and frowned, focusing on her memory of the scene, as little as she wanted to. "You know what? It's not a pudding mould," Jaymie concluded.

"It's not?"

"Nope, it's a decorative Bundt pan, which to the uninitiated might *look* like a pudding mould, I guess. It's one of those enameled ones meant to hang on the wall, not go into the steamer or oven." Though it still felt like it was targeted at her, it was done by someone who was clearly either not knowledgeable of vintage features or didn't care. It was absurd that it made her feel the slightest bit better, but it did.

"So, who killed Evan Nezer?" Valetta asked.

"I don't know." She couldn't feel sad about Nezer. As cold and awful as it sounded, there were some people whose leaving made the world better. He seemed to be one of them, though no doubt his son would be saddened. She covered her face with both hands, feeling remorse immediately; it was not like her to think that way. Evan Nezer was nasty, but even so, he was a human being, one who loved and was loved, had made mistakes, but who must have had some redeeming qualities. She could generally find it in her heart to have compassion toward anyone, and she must work toward it in this case.

However, it *was* a plain fact that his death solved problems for others, no doubt. "I wonder where this leaves Finn Fancombe?" she said aloud.

"What does he have to do with it?"

Jaymie told her friend what she overheard the night before, at the Nezer back door, about Finn needing Nezer to speak up for him and get his expulsion from WC rescinded. "Which makes me think . . ." She took out her phone and scanned through past online issues of the *Wolverhampton Weekly Howler*. "Ah, here it is." She found the articles regarding the scandal that forced the college to expel Finn Fancombe.

"What are you talking about?" Val said impatiently.

"Wait, let me read this and I'll explain."

Valetta smiled at a customer entering the Emporium and popped up from her chair. "I have to go in," she said to Jaymie. "Someone is here for a prescription. I'll be back."

Jaymie read all of the articles. When Valetta returned she had digested the gist of it, and thought she understood, though it seemed there might be more to the story, given what Finn had said to his mother. "So, Nezer wrote a piece for a literature journal comparing the economic aspect of Dickens's work to the realities of the financial industry of the day. I don't pretend to understand, but I suppose writing a nonfiction book, as an expert, you would have to condense or skim over some stuff to maintain the focus of the book. So the article was an extension of his book, fleshing out a part that had been briefly covered." She paused and squinted. "I think the book leaned more toward the economic theory aspect, rather than the literature, but I could be entirely wrong. Anyway, when it was published, Finn lodged a complaint with the college's ethics committee stating that significant portions of Nezer's article came from his master's thesis. Nezer was his thesis advisor, and as such he had read the draft version."

"But Finn was the one who was penalized . . . how did that happen? What did the ethics committee say about his complaint?"

"At first they supported him, but Nezer lodged a counter-complaint charging that Finn was the guilty one, and had used Nezer's notes on his thesis verbatim. So that portion of his thesis wasn't in his own words anyway, but in Nezer's. The professor couldn't plagiarize himself, so the complaint was void. Once Finn's complaint was dismissed Nezer then charged *Finn* with plagiarism. The ethics board found just cause and expelled Fancombe."

"For a first offense? That's harsh."

"It's a postgrad degree he's working on. He should know the rules."

"Still—"

"I know. But I think these things are looked upon rather differently in academic circles."

"Do you think the college board of governors would have some leeway, though, in how they assessed the punishment?"

"I don't know." Jaymie chewed her lip. "Finn was mad, but mad enough to kill the professor? That doesn't make sense, especially since he said he needed the professor's help to get back into the master's program."

"What if Finn confronted the professor that night, after the party, and they argued and he hit him and killed him accidentally?"

"But why would he stage the body in such a way?" Jaymie asked. She shook her head. "That sounds like a deliberate killing, not an act of passion."

"I suppose."

Jaymie was silent for a long moment. She picked up her cup to drink, but realized it was empty and set it back down. "Erla Fancombe said something else interesting though; she warned her son that if someone offended Nezer he'd hit back twice as hard, and that's what happened to Sarah Nezer."

"Oh, *really!*"

"Maybe that explains the first Mrs. Nezer taking a bad settlement in their divorce." She paused and glanced over at Valetta. "I wonder if she gets anything in Nezer's will?"

"Not likely. Why would Evan leave her anything when he divorced her?"

"Yeah, you're right. This whole scene . . ." Jaymie said, waving her hand at where Sarah was still being attended to by the paramedics. "It feels . . . contrived. I'm not saying it is, it just *feels* that way to me."

"You're speculating that Sarah killed Evan, planted his body, then 'happened' on the scene this morning and staged the faint. You're already trying to figure out who did it, aren't you?"

Jaymie sighed. "I can't help myself. It's second nature."

"And it keeps you from thinking about a human being done in that way, and what you saw," Valetta shrewdly guessed.

"That too." Jaymie sat in thought for a few minutes. "But in a weird way it felt like part of the scene. You remember that mystery series Dickensian? We watched it a couple of years ago at the same time; it was a murder mystery set in Dickens's world, only the murder was of Jacob Marley. It made me think of that. There wasn't much blood." She didn't say what she overheard, that Nezer had likely been killed elsewhere and moved to the diorama.

"I know what that means, kiddo—not much blood, though he died of a head wound—and I won't tell a soul," she said, giving Jaymie a sideways glance. "Head wounds bleed a lot, but the bleeding stops pretty quickly after the person dies. Coagulation begins, and once the heart stops pumping, no new blood rushes to the area unless gravity is a factor."

"You are a fount of information," Jaymie said, eyes wide.

"What can I say . . . the technical aspects of how the body lives and dies interest me. So, anyway, where was he killed?"

"Good question. And who staged the scene? It would take a particular kind of mind to set that up, I think."

"But *why*? Why do that at all? Why not hide the body, or leave it where it fell, or dump it somewhere? Why stage the scene?"

"I'd say that would take a lot of anger, or a weird sense of humor. Or, it was a message. But to who?" She glanced over toward the scene of the crime. "Uh-oh, there's Haskell," Jaymie said, standing. "I was wondering what we're going to do about the Dickens Days opening tonight. I mean, we'll postpone it, right? We *have* to!"

"Yeah, it would be a little grim to light the lights while the police tape is still fluttering in the breeze." Valetta stood and stretched. "You go talk to Haskell. I gotta go anyway. Time and medications wait for no man. Or woman."

Haskell strode over and spoke to the detective. It was a long, animated discussion, with much hand waving on Haskell's part, unusually expressive for the usually reserved fellow. Several of the Dickens Days committee members were milling about, so when he returned to the group, which Jaymie joined, they had an unofficial meeting and agreed. The Dickens Days opening and lighting of the tree would be postponed to the next Friday. Mabel Bloomsbury hustled off to make some calls to newspapers and radio stations on both sides of the border, as well as updating the Queensville Heritage Society website. Jaymie texted Nan personally to give her the news.

As they finalized the details, Bella Nezer, her face without makeup a pale, ravaged, tear-streaked mess, stumbled to the cider booth and beat on it with her fists. "Why? *Why?*" she cried, trying to pull the shutter off.

Bernie, who was standing guard on the diorama area, rushed to her side and gently restrained her, calling the paramedics over from Sarah Nezer's bedside. The two Missus Nezers were both, it seemed, distraught over the death of Evan Nezer, Scrooge.

๙ Nine ๙

BECCA HAD ARRIVED IN QUEENSVILLE to work at the antique store after dropping Jocie off at her grandparents'. When she saw the ambulance, police cars and clusters of townies, she bustled over to where Jaymie stood, tweed coat flapping open, purse hiked on her shoulder, a worried look in her eyes behind her glasses. "What's going on?" When Jaymie told her, she groaned. "Good lord, we're going to be called Murdertown, Michigan, soon."

"Don't look at me!" Jaymie cried. "I didn't *ask* for this to happen!"

"I didn't say you did," Becca exclaimed, startled.

"Sorry. I'm just . . . touchy. I loved the whole idea of that diorama and now it's r-ruined!" To her dismay, tears started welling and running down her cheeks and she sniffed. Valetta joined them and patted her on the back.

Ever practical, Becca fished in her purse and pulled out a tissue, handing it to her younger sister. "I would bet this bout of tears is less about the diorama and more about someone dying violently who you saw hours ago, alive and well."

Jaymie nodded and blew her nose. "You may be right. I didn't like him. But . . ." She blew her nose again.

"But he didn't deserve what happened to him," Valetta finished, hand on her friend's shoulder.

Jaymie nodded and took in a deep breath, letting it out slowly, her breath puffing a white cloud. "I'll be okay."

"What's going on over there?" Becca asked, pointing to the paramedic crews and the two women they were treating.

"That is the two Missus Nezers," Valetta said and explained.

Becca stared, blinked, and said, "I *know* Mrs. Nezer!"

"Really?" Jaymie exclaimed. But of course . . . Bella may have been in Queensville Fine Antiques while she was making over the Nezer ancestral home.

"I do! She was my history teacher in grade twelve for English literature!"

Jaymie frowned. "Bella Nezer?"

"Is that her first name?" Becca said. "At the time she was still using her maiden name, so we called her Miss Laughton, but I remember her married name. Don't you remember, Val? You, Dee, me . . . we went with her on a kind of informal field trip to some farmhouse in Washtenaw, near Ann Arbor. There was some old author there, uh . . . I'm blanking on the author name."

"Oh! I *remember*," Valetta exclaimed. She squinted, and continued, "Harriet Simpson Arnow who wrote . . . oh, what was the title?" She glared into the distance, pushing her glasses up on her nose. "Aha! It was *The Dollmaker*. They were making it into a TV movie, or something, with Jane Fonda. Miss Laughton . . . or Mrs. Nezer—I hadn't made the connection until you said it; can't believe I missed that!—wanted to visit her, so she took some of us girls with her on a field trip. But we got there, to the farm, and the woman wouldn't see us. She died soon after that. Miss Laughton . . . darn . . . *Mrs. Nezer* was extremely upset."

"You visited an author with your teacher?" Jaymie said, looking between her sister and her friend.

"Of course," Valetta said. "I remember the day mostly because it was freaking cold and her car didn't have a functional heater! So . . . winter, I guess."

It was one of those odd disjointed moments when Jaymie realized that though she was Valetta's best friend, Val was Becca's friend first. The two shared memories and a history Jaymie would never be a part of. She shook her head, puzzled. "Wait, Bella Nezer is only, what, mid-forties? Younger than you two, anyway."

"Don't be rude," Becca said. "Of course we mean the *ex*–Mrs. Nezer."

"Ohhh! *Sarah* Nezer. She was a teacher?"

Val nodded. "Yeah, in the mid-eighties. Still used her maiden name back then. We knew she was married and had heard her married name, but I had forgotten until Becca said it. She was my favorite teacher that year. Smart, funny, driven, a *great* teacher . . . I admired her."

"She was memorable," Becca added. "She had a loud laugh, and this big mane of golden brown hair that she held back with a colorful headband, and big chunky earrings that dangled to her shoulders."

"You *would* remember the clothes," Val said, bumping her shoulder against Becca's. "Until then I had preferred English literature, but she made me love American authors, like Faulkner. She admired women authors, and had met quite a few, like Betty Friedan, Toni Morrison, and she told us how she attended one of Flannery O'Connor's lectures before the author died. Miss Laughton . . . uh, Mrs. Nezer had a breakdown and left teaching, though."

"Still, you've got a heck of a memory, Val," Jaymie said, marveling once again at her friend's capacity for spongelike retention. She turned and pushed the hair out of her eyes. A stiff breeze had sprung up; it was drifting leaves along the town's main street and kept tugging at her hair, even though she had it pulled back in a ponytail. She watched the white-haired woman who was now sitting up, one shaking hand to her head, shooting malevolent looks at the woman nearby, who was arching her back and flailing about, a cluster of paramedics attending her. She shook her head, then slipped off the stretcher, unnoticed, retrieved her abandoned bicycle and walked it away.

Detective Vestry strode quickly toward them. "Jaymie, I want your statement soon. Keep me apprised of where you are." She turned and said, "Valetta, we're hoping the Emporium camera may come in handy again. Can we have a look?"

"Sure," Val said. She touched Jaymie's shoulder, but then led the detective into the store.

"How is Jocie?" Jaymie asked her sister, thinking with longing of her husband and child.

"She's good. There is some secret project going on at the farmhouse and there's a lot of giggling and hiding stuff." Becca smiled and clutched her purse to her chest against the stiffening wind. "I think they may be making gifts for their parents."

"I have a feeling I know what mine is going to be," Jaymie said. "Oma Renate had Jocie ask me if I had any allergies, and were there any scents I like in particular. I think it may be bath bombs for me and Sonya. We made some during the summer and I said how much I liked them."

"I have to go," Becca said, looking over her shoulder toward Queensville Fine Antiques. "Georgina has a lunch date she's eager to make, so I said I'd take care of the store for the rest of the day."

"A lunch date?"

Becca waggled her eyebrows. "A man!"

"A *man*?" It boggled the mind. Georgina was often sour, and did not seem to like Jaymie much. To know there was a softer, hopeful side to her . . . it made her want to get to know the woman. "Okay, you go on."

Becca touched her younger sister's shoulder. "Are you going to be okay?"

Jaymie nodded. "I am."

"Be good. Stay out of trouble."

Jaymie didn't respond. She *wouldn't* promise what she *couldn't* promise. Becca scurried across the windy street to the antique shop. Jaymie folded the shawl Val had given her and laid it on the chair, then hopped down the stairs and hustled to follow Sarah Nezer.

The woman was in her mid to late sixties, but she was fit, as evidenced by the speed with which she wheeled her bike along the walk against the wind. Jaymie raced to catch up with her and put a hand on her shoulder. The woman whirled with an *oof* of surprise and stared at Jaymie, who had to catch her breath.

"I'm sorry, Mrs. Nezer, to . . . to startle you that way." Huff, huff, huff.

"Who are you?" She blinked at Jaymie through thick glasses up on the bridge of her nose.

Jaymie examined her face, a collection of interesting wrinkles, soft skin sagging under her chin and a downturn to her thin lips. She wore heavy glasses, several years out of date, with tortoiseshell-patterned plastic frames. Jaymie tried to imagine her as Valetta described, vibrant and forceful, her favorite teacher. It was odd that, given how big an impression the woman had made on her, she hadn't remembered her until now, but it *was* a long time ago.

"My name is Jaymie Leighton Müller. My sister, Becca Brevard—Becca Leighton back then—had you as a teacher in high school, back in the eighties."

The woman frowned, but then nodded after a moment. "I remember her. Pudgy. Dark-haired. Thought she knew better than everyone else. Smart enough, but sassing back all the time."

Sassing back? Interesting. It sounded like Mrs. Nezer didn't have fond memories of Jaymie's older sister. "You have a good memory for your former students."

"I have a memory that is, at times, far *too* good."

"Uh, my best friend is Valetta Nibley. She was in that same class too."

The woman's expression softened. "I remember Valetta very well. Does she still live in Queensville?"

"Yes, in fact she's the pharmacist at the Emporium."

"Oh. Interesting. I've just moved back after being . . . away." She gripped and released the handles of her bike.

That explained a lot, why they hadn't seen the woman before, and why she had slipped from Val and Becca's memories. So much had happened in thirty years to fill their minds, memories and hearts. It made her wonder, briefly, why Sarah Nezer had such a perfect recall. Did that indicate a life sparse of pleasant recollections?

"Away?" Jaymie asked.

"*Away*," she said firmly, flexing her hands on the handlebars. "I remember Valetta fondly. She was friends with Becca, as well as DeeDee Hubbard. I called them the Fates."

"Why?"

"I don't remember now," she said with a weary sigh. "Because there were three of them, I suppose, always together." She turned and began walking again.

"Mrs. Nezer, I'm so sorry about Evan. You know, I'm the one who found him—"

The woman held up one hand in a *stop* gesture. Jaymie fell silent but stayed with her. They were heading toward the docks, but along the way she cut down a side street, picking up the pace as they descended the slope. There was only one neighborhood where they were headed, a narrow street near the docks where the houses, built in the late eighteen hundreds for workers, were small, rickety, and slightly off-kilter in many cases. There was a mixture of neat and trim cottages, alongside some that were decrepit, looking the worse for wear. Johnny Stanko's was near the end, still painted a vibrant shade of lavender from when his sister, who passed it down to him, was still alive. In the last year or so some gentrification had taken place, and there was a creeping sense that this funky little section of town was on the upswing. Amos pushed a cart past them, looking steadily down at his feet.

Sarah pushed through a leaning wrought iron gate and walked past her old Volvo in the drive up to a nicely kept home five houses before Johnny's. It was painted a deep rose, with russet trim. She lifted her bike easily and shoved it into a bike holder, then bent to chain it in place. She straightened and turned back to face Jaymie. "So what do you want? Why did you follow me?"

"I saw you last night," she said. "In the bushes by your ex-husband's front door. You handed me a note addressed to your son."

She looked startled for a moment. "Oh. You're *that* girl! You look . . . different."

"I'm not wearing makeup and don't have my hair up."

"Ah, that's it. You were attending my dear ex-late-husband and his shiny new bride's Christmas party celebrating an event he doesn't—didn't—even believe in."

Faced with that kind of asperity Jaymie had the urge to explain, but resisted. It was not this woman's business why she went to the Nezer party. "So . . . what were you doing in the bushes? Were you waiting for Ben to come out? Why did you hand *me* the note?" Which she hadn't delivered. It had been an eventful night, and she had completely lost track of it.

"Are you going to tell the police I was there?"

Jaymie paused and thought about it. "Probably."

"Then what's my incentive?" she said sharply, shoving her fists into her parka pockets.

"Why do you need an incentive? I'm just asking a question." How could this be the same woman Valetta so looked up to as a student? She was tetchy and difficult. Jaymie checked her first reaction, and dug deep in her heart, considering what life must have been like married to a man like Evan Nezer, and then dealing with her own mental health, only to be dumped by him for a younger woman.

And she didn't know Jaymie; why *should* she answer her questions? "I'm sorry," Jaymie said more softly, meeting her challenging gaze. "I don't mean to pry, but last night you took me by surprise. Usually I can imagine a scenario for anything, but I can't imagine one for you hiding in the Nezer bushes before a party waiting to hand your son a note. It doesn't make sense."

She smiled at that. "You look cold. Do you want to come in? It's not a palace, but it is all mine."

"I'd love that."

She followed Sarah up the drive to the back door, which faced a tiny pocket backyard, with a fenced enclosure that was mulched this time of year. It was fenced, Sarah said, to keep the rabbits and deer from eating her vegetables in summer. She had been there a year, she said. The kitchen was small, with a tiny table by a wall opposite a single line of kitchen cupboards, a window over the sink looking out at the neighbor's house.

"You've been here a year and you haven't been into the Emporium in all that time?"

"I have, but just for incidentals," she said as the kettle came up to a boil. She poured boiling water in a teapot. "I'm a minimalist."

Jaymie stared at her uncertainly.

The woman smiled. "I don't buy packaged foods. Most stuff I have to purchase I buy in bulk at the organic store in Wolverhampton. And anything I need from the pharmacy I also get in Wolverhampton. Would I even recognize Valetta after all this time?"

"Good question; I don't know." Jaymie paused a beat, then said, "I'm sorry about how you seemed to have heard of your husband's death. It looked like it hit you hard."

She shrugged as she set down two mugs of lavender-scented tea and shoved a tray of sweetener, sugar and milk to the center between them. She sat down opposite Jaymie, took off her glasses and set them aside, blinking and squinting. She rubbed the corners of her eyes with her thumb and forefinger. "I was married to him for thirty-two years and we share a son. I didn't like him, but he was a big part of my life."

All the questions Jaymie wanted to ask seemed off-limits, too personal, too nosy. "I've met Benjamin. He seems like a nice guy."

"No thanks to his parents."

"I'm sure his character is all you, Sarah," Jaymie said.

"Don't coddle me," she said, meeting Jaymie's gaze straight on. "I wasn't a good mother. I tried, but I had a lot of problems. Still do, but at least I recognize them now and do what I can to combat them. There was a time . . ." She paused and shook her head. "There was a time when I didn't, when I blamed everyone else, including Ben, for my problems. I was a rotten mother, and Evan was a rotten father. Ben being as wonderful as he is, is all him."

In the face of such bald self-condemnation, Jaymie wasn't sure where to go. There was an easy answer right in front of her. "I see you're a reader!" Jaymie said, picking up a book from the top of a stack on the table. *Feminism in Fiction and Poetry: Mary Wollstonecraft to Margaret Atwood.* "A little light reading . . ."

Sarah laughed, the first signs of mirth. "I know it sounds dry, but it's fascinating. The author—she's a friend of mine from college—traces feminist literature through women writers of fiction and poetry. She covers other authors in the book, but she picked those two to bookend her work. She asked me to give her a quote to add to her website." She shook her head. "Nineteen seventy-three . . . that's the year we started college. I was once that young. That hopeful. And then came Evan. We got married and almost exactly nine months later I had Benjamin."

Jaymie nodded, but then stopped. A quote? "Pardon me if I seem rude, but why a quote from you? Don't authors usually want quotes from other authors?"

The woman colored faintly. "Technically speaking, she is getting a quote from Brianna Hargreaves."

"As my grandmother would say, who is she when she's home?"

"Brianna Hargreaves is the name I go by in publishing."

Jaymie waited but the woman was silent. "Should I know that name?" she finally asked.

"Not unless you read literary theory journals used for feminist literature courses. She's hoping I'll give her a good quote, and recommend her book for course syllabi."

"Can't say I have taken a course like that." Jaymie paused, considering her next comment, but then decided to throw caution to the wind, stiffening her resolve. "I read romance novels."

"You throw that out like a challenge." Sarah smiled and picked up her glasses, polishing them on the edge of her tunic top. "You're expecting me to be shocked? To berate you? To tell you to read serious fiction?"

"Maybe."

She took a deep inhale of the fragrant tea and smiled. "My dear, many of us feminists believe we should include romance fiction of all stripes in the canon of feminist literature. After all, they are books written mostly by women *for* women. And a few gay men. Does that surprise you?"

"Yes, it actually does."

"Feminists, far from what online trolls will have you think, are smart, funny, and all-embracing. Apart from a few no-sense-of-humor fuddy-duddies, anyway. We recognize romance literature as a part of our . . . socialization. At the heart of most romance fiction is a woman's right to a good time in bed."

Jaymie laughed out loud in surprise. "I never thought of it that way. The romance novels I read generally don't have anyone going to bed."

There was a twinkle in the woman's eyes. "Ah, but there is the *promise* that there will be extraordinary sex in the very near future, am I right? Perhaps right after the closing pages?"

Jaymie acknowledged the truth of the woman's remark with a smirk and blush. "I won't let my nine-year-old read my books, that's for sure. Do you . . . have *you* ever written fiction?" Jaymie asked, thinking of her ex-husband's writing career, as explained by Jacklyn Marley.

Her gaze went cloudy and dour. "You're thinking about my eminent published author husband." She clanked her spoon around in her tea. "My book-stealing *wretch* of an ex and now late husband, who stole my manuscripts while I was grieving, locked me up in a mental hospital *'for my own good'* and published them under his own name."

⚡ Ten ⚡

STUPEFIED, JAYMIE SAT, EYES WIDE, thinking of all the implications of that statement. "So those novels he wrote in the eighties were *yours*?"

"You bet," she said with relish. *"Root of the Bitterfruit Tree* and *I Make This Solemn Vow*. My work. My blood, sweat and tears poured out onto the page."

"How did he get away with publishing them under his own name? You should have fought him! You should have—"

"Should have, could have, *would* have," she said, and hammered the tabletop, making the spoons dance. *"If* I'd been sane and not grieving. If I'd been independent and not needing Evan. If I'd not been nursing a little boy whose baby sister died in my womb." The last words were a groan of pain. She covered her face in both hands, her shoulders shaking, tears leaking from under her palms.

"Oh, *oh*! Sarah! I'm so sorry!" Jaymie jumped up and circled the table and impulsively hugged the woman to her, holding her as she shook.

The woman took a long shuddering breath and shrugged out of her grip. Taking another deep breath, like a fish gulping air, swallowing and choking back sobs, she steadied herself against the edge of the table and finally cleared her throat. "You'd think thirty years would have taken the edge off the pain, and usually it has, but learning Evan was dead . . . I guess it revived it."

She took another deep breath and closed her eyes for a moment. Jaymie silently sipped her tea.

"I got pregnant very soon after Ben was born," she said, calmer, her voice reflective and soft with emotion. "The doctors tell you that's unlikely; I'm here to say it happens. The pregnancy did not go well, but I didn't know for a while. It was . . . it was the worst time of my life."

Jaymie held her breath, tears welling, feeling the woman's pain, hearing it throb in her voice.

"Everyone thinks I should be over it. *That was thirty years ago,* they say. *Get over it already,* they say. And most of the time . . ." Her voice broke. She blinked back tears, licked her lips and took a deep breath. "I'm sorry. You don't need to hear all this."

"No, Sarah, *I'm* sorry. I was . . . I was judgmental and unkind, saying you should have done this or that, and that's not like me. I hope you believe that."

"I do believe that. You look like a kind young woman." She wiped her cheeks with a paper napkin and squeezed it in her hand. "I had already completed *Root of the Bitterfruit Tree* before Ben was born. But I wrote *I Make This Solemn Vow after* he was born. In a way it was about me and him, about a mother's vow to raise him to be a better man than his father. I finished it, kind of, but it never received a thorough edit. I was . . . I was in such pain, emotionally, and Evan was caught up with his work. I didn't think he even noticed my writing." She snorted and shook her head. "He noticed exactly what he wanted to notice. While I was convalescing, in no shape to do *anything*, he found the manuscripts and took them to a publisher."

"How did he justify stealing them?"

"He told me we needed the money. My care had cost a lot. He said there was no way I was capable of approaching publishers, much less being *with it* enough to promote a book." She sighed and rolled her shoulders, squeezing her eyes shut and opening them. "He wasn't wrong about that."

Jaymie thought about her friend, Melody, who wrote romance novels, and gave everything she had to the process. It left her drained and weary, but she then held it in her hands to love and weep over. It was a deeply emotional process for her. To have all of that stolen away would be a crushing blow. Sarah might shrug off the pain, but it had to have hurt, and on top of the loss of her second child . . . it must have been a devastating blow. "None of that justified him stealing your work."

"I know. But it was a long time before I came out of my fog and saw how he'd taken advantage of me. *Years* before I was functioning again, years when poor Ben relied completely on Evan and Erla. I couldn't afford to alienate Evan. And I had . . . setbacks. Months . . . years in a prescription fog." She sighed. "Life goes on."

Of all the people who may have killed Evan Nezer, it seemed to Jaymie that Sarah's motives were deepest rooted, a bitterness that may have soured into hatred over the years. "I think you're being far too kind about Evan," Jaymie said. She stood. There was more she wanted to know, but this had been a harrowing day for Sarah Nezer.

And for herself; finding a murder victim would never be easy. "I should go. Have you ever thought of telling the world that those books are yours?"

She shook her head. "The past is the past. It's taken me thirty years, but I'm at peace with it all."

At peace. Was she truly? "You *must* still write. I've never known a writer to just quit. Do you write fiction, still?"

"Not for publication anymore, just for myself. I've been broken so long that I want to heal and write and . . . be." She smiled, tears welling in her eyes. "You don't know how much pleasure there is in just *being*."

Jaymie hesitated. As much as she didn't want to torment the poor woman, the conversation felt unfinished. "I'm still curious, Sarah," she said, patting the tabletop. "What *were* you doing in the bushes by the front door of the Nezer house last night? Were you waiting to hand that note to Ben? Is that the only reason you were there?"

"What did he say when you gave him the note?" Sarah asked, searching Jaymie's face.

Jaymie felt her cheeks burn. "I . . . actually, with everything that went on, I never got a chance to give him the note. To be completely truthful, I forgot. It's still in my clutch purse."

Sarah's eyes widened. "You didn't give it to him. *Oh.*"

"Does it matter? What's in it?"

Sarah shook her head. "Oh, dear." She swallowed hard and looked up to Jaymie. "Could you do me a big favor? Could you return that note to me?"

"What's in it?"

"Nothing important, trust me. But . . . I'd rather have it back."

Jaymie watched her; she was upset about the note. She couldn't promise to return it to her. If it was evidence, if it had anything to do with the murder . . . it probably didn't have, but how could she be sure?

"Will you?" Sarah asked again. "Bring it back to me?"

"Why, Sarah? What does it say?"

She was silent.

Every question she had asked sounded, in her mind, like an accusation. What had Evan had over her that she took such a rotten settlement in their divorce? Where had she been before she returned to the village a year ago? What was in the note, and why did Sarah need it back? As accustomed as she was becoming to asking the hard questions, and as important as this seemed, she did have limits and she'd reached hers. Her nerves felt frayed and she felt anxious exhaustion welling up within her.

The woman didn't have anything else to say. She seemed troubled, but didn't appear guilty or worried, not as if she had killed someone, anyway, and she didn't continue to press for the return of the note. She hadn't been panicked, just concerned. Jaymie said goodbye and headed out, needed some solitude and time to reflect on what she would do with the note. Her phone dinged, and she answered as she walked. It was Nan Goodenough. In response to her editor's questions about the murder, Jaymie said, "I can give you *some* info, Nan, but not everything. It *is* a murder investigation."

"Don't be stubborn, Jaymie. At least give me a statement for the website. I'm recording."

Jaymie thought for a moment. "I was coming to set up my diorama; it's a scene from *A Christmas Carol*, the one where Scrooge is looking in a window with the Spirit of Christmas Present and watching the Cratchits with their Christmas pudding. I opened the diorama and found the body of Mr. Evan Nezer. The police are investigating."

There was silence. Then Nan's raspy voice and irritated tone: "Jaymie, come on. You *must* have seen the body. How did he die? Was his head bashed in? Or his throat cut? I heard there was a lot of blood; was there? What did you see? How do you feel?"

Annoyed, Jaymie stopped and took a deep breath. Sometimes Nan was too much, too pushy, too . . . news-editorish. "This is off the record, Nan; yes, I know more and saw more, but I can't tell you anything but what I just said. It could compromise the investigation."

There was silence from the other end for a long moment. Nan was tapping at her computer keyboard and scratching something down on paper. Conversations with her were often punctuated with silences, while the editor did several other things at once. The phone was muffled for a moment, and she heard voices in the background, probably Nan answering questions, or asking them of subordinates. Jaymie walked again, scuffing her shoes through leaves matted in clumps along the side of the road. She was in sight of the Emporium and could see police cars and people gathering.

Finally Nan came back as if there had been no pause and said, "Jaymie, I hate to say it, but at some point you're going to have to choose between being a newspaper writer and a police stooge."

"That's a little harsh, Nan."

"Maybe, but I mean it. What have they done for you lately? I know your cozy relationship with Ledbetter is gone now that he's retired, so what are you worrying about?"

Her stomach twisted. She hated confrontation, but Bernie, her police officer friend, recently told her to grow a pair and stop worrying so much about what people thought of her. She squared her shoulders. "Nan, as much as I believe in freedom for the press, and how precious it is, I will *not* be bullied into giving you more information than I feel is right. It's my decision to make, not yours. I only get this close to investigations because people in the police department trust me. If it comes down to choosing between you getting a scoop and the police catching the bad guy, then I'm going with the police every time. I'm sorry, but that's the way it is."

There was again silence on the other end of the line, and then Nan breathed out and chuckled, a rueful sound. "Okay. I guess I know where I stand."

Jaymie felt a moment's remorse, but steeled herself. She knew in her gut this was right and resisted the urge to apologize. In a relentless campaign to out-scoop other papers and news media outlets Nan could be manipulative. Guilting Jaymie into revealing more than she should was not beyond her. "This has nothing to do with *you*, Nan. This has to do with me living with myself, and being a good citizen in this town. This has to do with justice and catching the bad guys. Or gals. I've been too close to too many killers and I *won't* let one slip past the police because he or she found out what the police knew from my big mouth." She paused, then added, "That sounded . . . pretentious. I'll climb down off my soapbox now. I want you to understand where I'm coming from."

"Okay, *okay*, I get it," Nan said, and this time it sounded like she truly did and was irritated that she understood Jaymie's position more than she'd admit. "But keep me in the loop. Let me know *what* you can *when* you can."

"I will."

They hung up and Jaymie continued up the road to the Emporium then stood, uncertain and undecided, hanging back. It was rare that at this stage, hours after finding the body, that she knew so many reasons why so many people would want to kill the deceased, but events of recent days and the party last night had shown her much.

Pastor Inkerman loathed Nezer and had a violent altercation with him hours before the man's death. Nezer had ensured that Finn Fancombe lost his academic career. Jacklyn Marley was owed money and had been hacking his computer hours before his death; who knew what had happened between them after Jaymie left? Evan had deprived his ex-wife, Sarah Nezer, of her literary children—her novels—and perhaps the affection of their son, who seemed to be toadying to his father in the few days before the man's death. And that led her to consider Benjamin Nezer; had he been hiding his true feelings about his father, deciding to make up with him to make sure he didn't lose out on a family inheritance?

There were two more people of course, but Jaymie didn't consider either of them viable suspects. The police would have to consider both Brock Nibley, who had a run-in with Nezer the night before, his business reputation sullied, and Bill Waterman, who had been uncharacteristically aggressive toward Nezer. Jaymie knew the handyman would never commit murder, but the police had video evidence that Bill had threatened Nezer. They couldn't ignore it.

As always, questions teemed in her mind. She circled the Emporium and mounted the outside steps, getting to the top and facing the scarred wood door, painted brown some years past but faded and battered by sun and wind. She knocked. Jacklyn Marley answered. She looked relaxed and happy, not at all as if she worried she was a suspect.

"Hey, Jacklyn, can I come in?"

"Sure. *Entrez-vous, mon ami.*"

Jaymie followed her into a small living room lined with bookcases that were filled with books, interrupted only by a smallish flat-screen TV. Three doors to other rooms were all closed at the moment. There was a shabby sofa in the middle and a coffee table piled high with books. A laptop was open, and several notebooks filled with a nearly illegible scrawl were haphazardly spread across what was left of the tabletop, floor and a hassock. As her eyes became accustomed to the mess, Jaymie noticed a pair of white cats sitting on a ruby velvet pillow in a deep window. Both had turned to gaze at her, unblinking, one blue-eyed, one green-eyed.

"That's Alexandra and Rasputin," Jacklyn said, after noticing the direction of Jaymie's gaze. "Sister and brother. Raspy is the green-eyed love, and Lex is the blue-eyed doll. She's deaf, but Raspy hears for both of them. It's weird . . . I'll call and they will both instantly come to me, even though the vet swears Lex is stone deaf."

"They're beautiful. My daughter has a tiger-striped sweetie and I have a Yorkie-Poo, a rescue. I did have a tabby, Denver, but when I got married and moved I rehomed him with Valetta. He now lives like a king." Jaymie found a spot on the edge of the hassock as Jacklyn plunked down in front of the laptop. "What are you working on?"

"A couple of grant proposals. I need to make some dough, and soon."

A grant did not sound like a quick way to make money. The heritage society had applied for several, and it took months, sometimes years, to even get a rejection. But it was an opening. "Which brings me to what you were doing last night on Evan Nezer's computer. Did you find out anything? Does . . . did Evan owe you money?"

Jacklyn gazed at her steadily. "Are you going to tell the police about what I was doing?"

"I don't know."

The woman shrugged and went back to work.

She wasn't inclined to answer, and Jaymie couldn't promise she'd keep quiet about Jacklyn's illicit activities. "Did you find anything in all the stuff you copied from his computer?"

"I . . . haven't had a chance to look at it all yet."

The pause was telling. "What was Evan like to work with?" Jaymie asked, keeping in mind his theft of work from a woman he was married to. It had, for her, put his accusations against Finn Fancombe in a new light. If he would steal writing from his wife, why would he not steal from a student?

"He was smart," Jacklyn said. "He had his own worldview, and while he was arguing it, it was difficult to counter him. He believed that unfettered production and consumerism were the solution to every first world problem . . . unemployment, poverty, hunger . . . even inequities in education."

"How so?"

"It's complicated. Simply put, I guess it comes down to producing and selling more goods to create income that helps everyone eventually." She shrugged. "I've tried to explain it before but it sounds dumb the way I put it."

"I don't know a lot about the economy," Jaymie admitted. "But I do know that in my grandmother's time you used something until it fell apart, then you fixed it and went on using it, or someone else fixed it and went on using it. But industry has been producing more goods cheaply, and building in obsolescence."

"What can I say? He made a compelling argument. He believed a lot of things that on second thought had me shaking my head. But he sure made them sound good at the time."

"Like . . . ?"

"Like . . . well, he thought shame was a good thing. That women *should* be ashamed of being pregnant out of wedlock, for example."

"That's awful!" Jaymie said, taken aback.

"I'm not defending the guy's philosophy, I'm telling you what he thought."

"Interesting. How about him? Was he ashamed of carrying on behind his wife's back and then splitting up with her to marry the woman he was carrying on with?"

Jacklyn smiled. "He justified it by saying that Sarah was crazy, and he had a right to find some joy when he was married to a lunatic. I think he felt that shame was for other, lesser beings."

That explained a lot. Nezer was someone who was content with twisting the rules when it suited him. "So Nezer talked about his affair and marriage to Bella while you worked on the book?"

"Sure. He seemed completely at ease with his behavior and could justify everything. But then, he always was at ease with his behavior. Even when he was cheating people," she said, her mouth twisted in bitterness.

"Did you get along with him?" Jaymie asked, eyeing her with interest.

"Sure," she said, her gaze sliding over to her cats. She got up and crossed the room, dropping a kiss on both of their heads. "We got along fine."

Avoidance; that was interesting. Of *course* she didn't get along with him. No one did, from her limited knowledge. So why was she lying? Of course, folks were usually careful not to speak ill of the dearly dispatched. "Except he didn't pay you what he owed. Why didn't you get paid up front? Isn't that how ghostwriting usually works?"

Jacklyn straightened and turned to look at Jaymie. "He did give me a small fee up front, but then convinced me I'd make more if I agreed to work for a cut of the royalties. It's an unusual deal for a ghostwriter, but he made it sound good. I should have known better." She squinted at Jaymie and pursed her lips. "What is this all about? Do you think I killed him?"

"I didn't say that."

"But you're asking a lot of questions. Are you done quizzing me now? I'd like to get back to this," she said, waving her hand at the computer.

That had devolved rather quickly before she got to the part when she asked Jacklyn where she was after the party the night before. Jaymie looked around the apartment. "I'll let you go, then," she said, but didn't move. That, she had found in the past, worked ninety percent of the time; talk about leaving, then change the subject. "Will you decorate for Christmas?"

"No. I only need to look out my window to see décor, right?" Jacklyn drifted over to her front windows that looked out over the village green. "It's such a pretty town," she said wistfully.

"Did you take the job serving at the Nezer party *just* to hack into Evan's computer?"

"Pretty much," she said, sitting down on the sofa.

"What time did you come home?"

"Okay, enough of the third degree," she said, slamming her laptop shut and crossing her arms. She sat back and glared at Jaymie. "Just say it! Say you suspect me. *Say it!*"

"Jacklyn, I was wondering if you *saw* anything," Jaymie said, waving at her window. "You have this perfect view of the village green. His body was found in a display I set up. I'm taking it a little personally."

She calmed immediately and uncrossed her arms, relaxing. "It was probably somewhere convenient to dump the body."

Well, no . . . whoever had dumped him there had set up the scene for maximum effect, but she couldn't say that. "Did you see anything at all?"

"Not a thing. I was beat. I came home, fed the cats and went to bed."

"What time?"

"I didn't look at the clock."

"Who do you think killed him?"

Jacklyn smiled. "His wife. Who else?"

"Which one, ex or current?"

"That *is* the question, isn't it? Fury or gain; which is the motive this time? I have to get back to work, Jaymie." She opened her computer back up.

"I have to say, Jacklyn . . . I *did* hear that Evan got you fired from your teaching job at the college. That, combined with him refusing to pay you . . . people *have* been killed for less." Jaymie was astounded at herself, having the nerve to say that.

Jacklyn stared, her expression stony. "You can let yourself out."

⚡ Eleven ⚡

A POINTED COMMENT LIKE THAT could not be ignored. Jaymie wrapped her coat more tightly around herself as she descended, a cold wind blowing up the stairs. She needed a friend's company right that moment, someone to talk to, to confide in. Valetta was busy in her pharmacy, three people lined up at the counter when Jaymie snuck a peek. She got out her phone as she exited the Emporium, but slipped it back in her purse, unused. She didn't want to pull Jakob away from work at this busy time of year.

But there was one person who would not only be overjoyed to see her but would be thirsty for information on the murder. Someone she could trust implicitly. Someone who might know the players better than anyone else in town.

Mrs. Stubbs was, as usual at that time in the morning, sitting in her room near the window in her mobility wheelchair, book on her lap. It was a Sue Grafton, *Q is for Quarry*. But she wasn't reading, she was looking out the sliding doors to her private patio and beyond, to the tumbling brown leaves along the lawn, and one small oak, still stubbornly clinging to its leaves.

"Hey, Mrs. S.!" Jaymie said and gave her a hug.

The woman's eyes were watering, and she swiped at them with a tissue she held in her hands. When Jaymie commented on the book and the tears, asking if they were related, she nodded. "So sad that that woman died, and yet an old lady like me lingers on."

Such melancholy—something Mrs. Stubbs was occasionally prey to—could not be allowed to continue. The book-loving world of devoted readers had lost a giant in Sue Grafton; there was no getting around it. But . . . " I for one don't think Ms. Grafton would want you or any one of her readers to be downhearted. I think she'd love and appreciate that you are still reading her books."

The woman sighed and nodded, setting the book aside, careful to ensure her bookmark stayed in place. "Maybe you're right."

"I know I am," Jaymie said gently, dropping a kiss on her friend's forehead.

She made tea then, wondering how she could cheer Mrs. Stubbs up, and brought it on a tray with mugs to the small table. Mrs.

Stubbs used the joystick of her mobility chair to wheel up to it. "How about I tell you what we're doing for Christmas? Grandma Leighton is coming to Queensville this year, and she'll be staying right here at the inn. We booked the same ground-floor room for her as last year. That means you'll be able to visit! Invite Miss Perry this time, and her niece Morgan. The whole family is going to be doing Christmas dinner in the restaurant, and we'd love for you to join us. Grandma would like that."

Mrs. Stubbs smiled and put her hand over Jaymie's, veins crisscrossing it, showing as raised blue paths veiled by thin spotted skin, soft and smooth as silk. "My dear, I can see right through you, you know, trying to cheer me up. But I'm all right, just a few aches and pains and feeling old, nothing new." She took in a deep breath and sat up straight. "If I am to continue, I may as well go on with a smile on my face. Now, I heard a garbled account from Edith about some excitement in the village green this morning. Why don't you tell me all about it?"

And so as they shared tea, Jaymie did, all the way through, every scrap, even details she had not told anyone else. Her old friend could keep a secret. She talked about the murder, and about the two Mrs. Nezers' collapses, and following Sarah Nezer home and talking to her. "You often volunteered at the high school back then. Sarah Nezer was a teacher there in the eighties."

"I remember her well; Miss Laughton, as she was still called. English literature was her specialty, though she also taught American literature. She preferred it, if I recall. I liked her, though not many did, I'm afraid. She was very modern, untidy, disheveled. She wore loud flowered pantsuits with big shoulders, and she had big hair and big ideas. *Very* opinionated." She smiled. "I have always liked opinionated women, but most on the school board did not. She saw herself as a Miss Jean Brodie, I think."

"Miss Jean Brodie? Who is that?"

"My dear girl, do you mean you've never read the book or seen the movie *The Prime of Miss Jean Brodie*?" Mrs. Stubbs's hooded, watery eyes held surprised mirth. "It's about a teacher who takes certain students under her wing, hoping to turn them into prodigies of a sort. She thought herself a cut above all the other teachers." She shook her head. "Sarah was like that, one reason many of the teachers didn't like her either."

"Valetta liked her a *lot*."

"That doesn't surprise me. Valetta has always had a tolerance for unusual folk, and a taste for trailblazers."

Jaymie picked up her tea mug and drained it, beginning to feel more human. Talking to Mrs. Stubbs had that effect on her; she was a most reliable and trustworthy sounding board. "Sarah Nezer says she had a breakdown after she lost her second child."

"I knew about her troubles and felt sorry for her. Maybe not having any friends among the staff explains why she tried to make friends out of some of the girls. As strong as she seemed and as bold, it appeared to me that her attempts to make herself out to be better than the other teachers was because she felt so very inadequate on so many fronts. I blame her husband for that." She paused and took a long sip of tea, sighing with satisfaction. "She took hit after hit. She had her son, and then, just as she had regained her balance and came back to teaching, she got pregnant again. That ended badly, as you say."

"You referred to her husband. Did you ever meet Evan Nezer, back then or since?"

"I *did* meet him, at school events. He was a bully and a tyrant. I can't imagine how Sarah coped, married to someone like that."

"I think it broke her, for a time," Jaymie mused, then looked up at her friend. "She told me something and I don't know what to think. Evan Nezer was a tenured professor at Wolverhampton College."

"Yes, I knew that. He was there even then, thirty years ago. I always wondered why, if he was as highly regarded as he said he was in his field of economic theory, he was content to teach at a little backwater nothing of an academic establishment."

"Hmm, yes . . . I'll have to tell you about my conversation, such as it was, with his ghostwriter, Jacklyn Marley. But anyway, that wasn't what I was talking about. He apparently had a couple of highly regarded novels published in the late eighties. Sarah claims she was the true writer. He stole them from her and had them published while she was in a fog after her miscarriage and breakdown."

Mrs. Stubbs frowned and picked at a chip on her saucer with one brittle, ridged nail. "And she's never said anything in all that time?

Interesting that she chooses *now* to say something, after he's gone and can't contradict her."

"But Mrs. Stubbs, we don't *know* that she never told anyone else. I'm going to look the books up and see what was said about them at the time. But, in support of her claim, doesn't it seem odd that a man who was apparently such a good author needed a ghostwriter for a book in his field?" She paused and frowned. "There are so many things I still don't understand. Like . . . why did Sarah take such a poor settlement in the divorce? And why, if her books were published to such acclaim, is she, in her words, 'just writing for herself' now?" She didn't feel comfortable talking about the note for Ben; not until she knew what was in it, anyway. Yes, she was going to read it. She realized she had already decided.

"Did you ask her?"

"I did but . . . she deflected, and I didn't feel comfortable pushing her harder, given what had just happened."

"You're a softie. It's not easy to ask uncomfortable questions."

"It's something I'm working on," Jaymie admitted. "You'd be proud of how I handled Nan. I stood up to her, even though she still scares me a little."

"That woman is hard to take. I find her too pushy, even though I like pushy women."

"She's good for me, Mrs. S. I'm learning to push back. I used to be afraid to stand my ground, but I'm getting there." Jaymie pondered her conversation with Sarah Nezer, and voiced her thoughts, adding, "She still holds a lot of pain from that time in her life. It makes me wonder . . . was the drama when she found out Evan was dead just acting? Did she kill him?" Jaymie knew nothing about the night after the party. Nezer was in a nightshirt, so he was dressed for bed. And yet his body had been found outside. She had no clue, at this point, where he had been killed, but as cold as it was outside, he likely wouldn't have been out in the night in his nightshirt, unless it was very briefly, say, to meet someone. She expressed some of her wonderings.

"All good questions, my dear, to which I don't have answers."

"I suppose I need to find out more, talk to more of the folks involved." And to read the note Sarah wanted her son to have that night.

"That would be a good place to start."

Jaymie told Mrs. Stubbs about the rest of the Nezer party, the varying conflicts, all centering around Evan Nezer. She mentioned the pastor and his physical altercation with his host.

"Pastor Inkerman? Aha!" Mrs. Stubbs exclaimed, raising one arthritic finger in the air. "Very emotional fellow, am I right? Lois and I went to see him talk two weeks ago at a fall church social, and I understood he had written a book. Lois bought one, I believe, and he signed it. He seemed a nice young man, very genuine."

"He *did* seem nice when I met him. But . . . Nezer said something odd, when he was talking about him. He said that the pastor only wrote his book about living a best life through the scriptures to hide his affairs. What did that mean?"

"Was he mudslinging to see what would stick? Some people are like that, and from what little I remember about the professor, he was careless about other people."

"True." *Was* Nezer reliable? Jaymie wondered. Ideas and suspects were mounting. "Do you know where Pastor Inkerman came from, or anything about him?"

"Don't tell me the pastor is a suspect too?"

"He *did* attack the professor. I can't see him as a killer, but he does hate Nezer. If you find anything out about the pastor, let me know." Jaymie sighed wearily and flexed her shoulders. Sitting with her friend was like visiting an oasis of peace away from the brutal crime that had occurred. Even though they had been talking about it and pondering a solution, it had given her a moment to reflect and regain her equilibrium. But . . . she couldn't stay all afternoon. "I'd better get going. I'll be back, and we can chat more!" Jaymie winked at her and departed.

On her way out, she bought a couple of salads from the Queensville Inn restaurant, then walked back into the downtown area of the village, climbing the steps to her sister's store. Becca, glasses on the end of her nose, was peering over them at a sales ledger. She looked up. "How are you, Jaymie? You okay?"

"I guess. I'm tired. I'm crampy. I'm puzzled." She smiled. "And I brought us lunch."

Perched on two high stools behind the sales desk, the sisters slowly ate their salads and drank tea Becca had brewed in the tiny office off the showroom. There was an apartment in back where Georgina lived, but Becca tried never to enter her sister-in-law's home unless invited. So she had a tiny fridge, coffee maker and electric kettle jammed in the corner of the office.

"What was Mrs. Nezer like as a teacher? I'm curious."

"She was . . . cool," Becca said, stabbing a chunk of iceberg lettuce. "I didn't get her at first. I think I was taken aback by her enthusiasm. Kids don't expect adults to get excited about anything, so it was surprising to me."

"How did the field trip to Harriette Arnow's farm come about?"

"It was *kind* of a field trip, but not really. It wasn't official. It was like four girlfriends heading off on a spur-of-the-moment adventure. It was . . . the middle of February, I want to say? A Saturday. We were seniors and felt very grown-up, that she chose to take us. But it was ultimately a bust."

"Was it overnight?"

"Good lord, no. *You* know where Washtenaw County is; the farm was an hour and a half or so away from here. It took a little longer going because we got lost."

"And it was just you, Val and Dee?"

Becca chewed and swallowed the last bite of her salad and nodded. "Mrs. Nezer was pregnant, I remember. She had to stop several times to go to the bathroom."

"Did she already have Ben?"

"I think so."

"That was her second pregnancy, then, the one that ended badly. So sad for her." Jaymie explained what she knew.

Becca teared up. She pushed her glasses up on her forehead and blotted her eyes with a tissue. "That's *awful*. Poor woman. All we were told was that she had a breakdown and couldn't work anymore. It sounds selfish, but I don't believe I thought of her again."

"Kids have their own stuff. And it was your senior year, right? You were thinking of college."

"I guess. Dee was heading to nursing school and Val was already enrolled in pharmacy classes at U of M, but I had no clue what I was going to do. I felt like I was behind, the only one struggling."

"Maybe it's a Leighton thing," Jaymie said. "I felt the same way after high school, that all of my friends knew their future, and I was wandering. I went to college for English lit because I couldn't think what else to do."

"It was Mom and Dad's drama," Becca said, referring to their parents' marital troubles at different points through the years. "I know I never discussed my future or plans with them, not when theirs seemed in constant jeopardy. Though I'd never say that to them, especially not since they seem to finally have it all sorted out, in their seventies." She drank the rest of her tea in one long gulp and set her cup aside. "Why all the questions? You don't think Sarah Nezer killed her ex, do you?"

"I don't know. It's possible. He was not a nice fellow judging by every single person who knew him, including Mrs. Stubbs. And . . . she was close by that night . . . hiding in the bushes beside the front step." She hadn't shared that part of the story with Becca yet, but again she didn't mention the note. It was looming large in her mind, the question marks around it. Sarah's demand to have it back troubled her.

"That doesn't mean she killed him. Maybe she was spying on him and the second Mrs. Nezer. What would be her motive to kill him? It's not going to get her any money."

"Belated revenge as a motive for murder? Jealousy over Ben now making up with his father?"

"Well, don't go snooping around too much and get yourself in trouble." She held up one hand as Jaymie was about to protest. "I know, I know; butt out. Anyway, I want to ask a favor. Since you're here, can you mind the store for an hour? I want to dash back to the house and get a few items I brought from home. My assistant is convinced that some of my online stock will sell better in the store." Heather, her Canadian assistant, was taking more and more responsibility for the online end of Becca's business.

"You go ahead. As long as I can use your computer, I'm good. And can you stop at the Emporium and tell Val where I am? I told Detective Vestry I'd stay in contact. They haven't taken my whole statement yet." Every time she recalled that Evan Nezer was dead she felt a jolt, a kind of "not again" feeling of dread welling up in her. Ever since she had first found a dead body in the summer porch of their Queensville home it had become a part of her world, like the negative energy of that happening attracted more negativity. Not that she ascribed to the theory of attraction, but it *was* bothersome. It felt like her own notoriety was making her a target, in this case leading to the killer planting Nezer in her lovely diorama.

While Becca was gone, Jaymie did some research. Sarah Nezer and her tale of literary theft intrigued her. She looked up the two novels, *Root of the Bitterfruit Tree* and *I Make This Solemn Vow*. *Bitterfruit* was apparently a tale of "a middle-class woman's fall from grace, and her voyage to a new understanding of her true place in American society." It featured a failing teacher, maybe Sarah herself. And it had been hailed in one review as *a triumph of feminist fiction*. "*Root of the Bitterfruit Tree* is a reimagining of the landscape of America through the eyes of a woman emerging from middle-class expectations." It had been shortlisted for a major literary award.

I Make This Solemn Vow was described as a story about a woman's struggle to please everyone, and her journey to understanding after her son was born that in doing so, she was giving pieces of herself away. It did not do as well, with some reviewers voicing their disappointment, saying it felt rushed, and that it needed another couple of drafts before it was ready for publication. It was an example of sophomore slump, another said. Evan Nezer showed great promise, so reviewers should expect great things from him in the future, a "brave new feminist voice from an unexpected source," one opined.

Unexpected source; no kidding.

Sarah had said that the second book was in the rewrite stage when she had her breakdown and was hospitalized for a long period. That would explain the failings of the second book, compared to the laudatory reviews of the first book. Ultimately, Jaymie believed Sarah's claim of having written the two books. Evan never wrote another novel, and given what little she knew about him, it was impossible to believe that he had written a masterwork of feminist fiction.

She was about to start a new search when a result farther down the search engine page drew her eye. She clicked on it, and felt her mouth go dry. The epic feminist novel of the 1980s, *Root of the Bitterfruit Tree*, was in preproduction at a major Hollywood studio. Movie rights to the book had been sold for . . . her mouth dropped open.

Half a million dollars.

Half a million reasons why Sarah Nezer might want to kill her ex-husband.

But . . . did she *know* her stolen novel was being made into a major motion picture? And how could Jaymie learn the truth behind that? She had been ready to write Sarah off as a suspect. Their conflict seemed too far in the past, and she appeared to be at peace in her new life. But this, learning that her stolen novel had netted a half million dollars, that was a powerful motive.

Jaymie checked the *Wolverhampton Weekly Howler* website. A news report had been posted on the front page about Nezer's death. *WC Prof Nezer Offed*, the headline succinctly stated. The story gave the bare bones of the events and the police statement, which acknowledged that the victim had been identified as Professor Evan Nezer, sixty-seven, of Queensville, survived by wife, Bella, son E. Benjamin Nezer, and ex-wife Sarah Nezer. The reporter gave a bio of the professor, including the two fiction books and his most recent work, a comparative study of Victorian economics and social conscience as portrayed in the works of Charles Dickens. The reporter had done his research; there was a link to a review of the recent book that called it *an engaging read with a deeply flawed premise.* From Jaymie's view it seemed that the deeply flawed premise was all Nezer, so the "engaging read" part was likely all Jacklyn Marley.

Becca breezed into the store and hoisted a box onto the counter. "So what's all the commotion over at the Nezer house?" she asked.

"Commotion?" Jaymie asked, closing down her browser and slipping off the stool. "Why, what's up?"

"I drove past and saw Bill Waterman and some young fellow in a confrontation."

"Oh, crap, what now? I'd better go. I'll call you later."

She pulled on her coat as she raced out the door and trotted toward the village green. It didn't look good. Bill Waterman's opponent was Ben Nezer, who faced him, fists clenched. Jaymie pulled her coat closed as she ran, hoisting her purse up on her shoulder.

"I got no problem with you, Ben. I told you that." Bill stood facing the younger man, mallet in one hand, stake in the other. "But if you're gonna start the same crap as your old man, then I'll have to say something."

Jaymie shivered; if Bill had seen Nezer's body with the holly stake driven into his chest he would not be doing what he was doing right now, gesticulating with the mallet and stake.

"All I'm saying, old man, is that I mean to honor my dad's last wishes, and that includes not letting you trespass on Nezer property for any reason!" The young man, his expression twisted in anger, moved aggressively closer to Bill.

"Apple didn't fall far from that nutty tree," Bill grumbled and turned to walk away.

"Coward!" Ben shouted after him.

Bill turned. "What did you say, young man?"

"I said you're a coward who murdered my father. You're a bully and a sneak. You killed him because he dared stand up to you!"

Jaymie was afraid Bill would attack him, but the handyman appeared devastated. "Killed him? Me? I . . . I . . ." His lined face twisted in a grimace and his skin paled.

"Bill, *Bill!*" Jaymie rushed over to him, supporting him as he staggered back. "Someone call 911!"

✂ Twelve ✂

THE CHRISTMAS TREE STOOD as a forlorn icon of a season that could not be started yet, not when there had been a murder, and a well-known and loved Queensvillian was being carted to the hospital, victim of a possible heart attack. Valetta volunteered to call Bill's family—he had kids, one who lived in Wolverhampton and actually worked at the hospital—and others who would want to be informed.

While Val paced back and forth on the pavement below the store talking to Bill's family, Jaymie sat on the steps of the Emporium, huddled in her coat, shivering and teary. The immediate aftermath of Bill's medical emergency had been a blur, but one moment stood out. Ben Nezer, who had so violently lost his father just that morning, stood frozen in place as the paramedics worked on the handyman. He looked stricken, his face twisted in anguish. She felt for him; he had just lost his father. Maybe he even felt remorse for Bill's sudden illness.

She was about to go to him, to reassure him that he could not have known what the confrontation would do to Bill, when a large luxury car rolled up by him. Ben went over to it and had a word through the open window with the passenger, then whirled, heading through the pine trees toward the Nezer house. As the car pivoted on a three-point turn, Jaymie got a look at the driver. It was one of the two college gentlemen from the party the night before. The car headed back the way it had come, no doubt to park by the house.

Her phone beeped; it was a call from Jakob.

"Jaymie, are you okay? I just heard! I've been working all morning and didn't . . . but Mr. Nezer is *dead*? And in your diorama? Oh, *liebchen*, I'm so *sorry*."

His warm, rich voice, so full of love, undid her. He got what she had been afraid to say out loud, that Evan Nezer lying dead in her lovely diorama felt like a slap across her face. To say it aloud had felt . . . insensitive to the real tragedy, a human life lost. But her husband got it without her saying a word. She choked back a sob and took a long shuddering breath. "I'm okay, Jakob, truly, I am. I've been with Val and Becca and visited Mrs. Stubbs."

"Come home, sweetheart, come home."

"I don't want to sit around doing nothing. I'll fret."

"I'll put you to work, then. There's nothing better for the soul than physical labor."

She smiled as tears welled. It was practically the Müller family motto: through work we will heal! "You just want someone to help cut trees!" she said with a watery chuckle.

"That too."

"I'll come. I have a couple of things to do first."

She breathed in deeply. She knew Bella Nezer, despite her collapse, had not been taken to the hospital but had returned to her home in the care of Erla Fancombe. Jaymie walked to the house, circled it and approached the back door. She rapped on it. A moment later Erla, her cheeks bright red, her eyes clouded and her manner brisk, answered.

"Erla, how are you?" Jaymie asked, foot on the doorstep.

"I'm fine. Who are you?"

"I'm Jaymie Leighton. I was here as a guest last night. I wandered into the kitchen with my friends momentarily."

She squinted, then nodded. "Okay. Didn't recognize you out of fancy dress and with your hair down. Look, I don't have a moment to chat. Guests . . . of all days! Folks from the college and I—" A signal buzzed and she looked over her shoulder with a deep put-upon sigh. "That's Mrs. Nezer now."

A year ago or so Jaymie wouldn't have been able to do this, but now she was bolder. "Mrs. Fancombe—Erla—it's not fair that you're stuck with all of this work on a day like today, and after an exhausting evening last night! Let me help. I'm experienced in the kitchen and can take care of things while you help Mrs. Nezer and Ben deal with the college folks." She confidently moved past and glanced around the kitchen. She grabbed an apron from a rack by the door and picked up the kettle. "Tea, for college sorts, I think?" she said, glancing over at the housekeeper. "Mrs. Belcher is among them, I imagine. And there's probably sherry in the parlor. You take care of that. I expect they'll need to consult with Mrs. Nezer about what to do, now that Mr. Nezer is gone. I'll make tea, coffee, and help put together trays. You carry and wait on them."

She looked uncertain, but Jaymie didn't leave any room for

refusal. She found the butler pantry off the kitchen and retrieved a sparkling silver tea set shelved with other silver. She brought it to the center prep table and went to the fridge, taking out a carton of milk and a fresh lemon. She glanced around, then slid a cutting board out of its hiding place, alongside the counter. "Go ahead, Erla," she said, glancing up at the housekeeper. "I'm used to taking care of company and working events. You must be up to your ears, and no one should have to deal with a grieving widow and company all alone."

The woman's thick brows had climbed her forehead when Jaymie said "grieving widow," but she nodded. "I won't say no to the extra hands."

Jaymie texted Jakob that she would be home in a while, that she had stopped to help a friend first. Kind of true; Erla could be a friend at some point. For the next hour Jaymie, at Erla's direction, made tea and coffee, filled urns, filled platters of goodies taken out of the freezer and thawed, and cut cheese and made a ham and pickle spread from one of Erla's own recipes. She got up on a step stool and found serving platters and dishes, some dusty from disuse—maybe they had been there for years in the old house—some clean and stowed away recently. There were gaps, like up in the cupboard where a mess of cookie sheets and cake pans lived, and Jaymie got the notion that even Erla had not had time to arrange the kitchen properly, with the move to the historic house happening so recently and everything being so rushed.

It did look like Erla had been trying to make the place her home and work all in one. There were shelves in one corner holding assorted crockery, like a heavy pickle crock on the bottom, a brown bean crock and a brown earthenware bowl with fancy fluted edges on the shelves above it. There was a needlepoint hung on the wall above it that said *East, West, Home's Best*. Jaymie smiled; she couldn't have said it better herself.

As the housekeeper served and cleared in the parlor, Jaymie started dishes. Erla returned, using her butt to open the swinging door as she carried a tray full of dirty dishes and platters strewn with parsley and crumbs.

"You don't have to do that, Jaymie!" she protested. They had, through the hour, become first-name friends and colleagues. "You've already done too much!"

"Nonsense, Erla. I find the aftermath soothing . . . you know, getting my hands in soapy water and creating order out of chaos."

The housekeeper smiled, the lines bracketing her eyes and mouth deepening. "You said it." She grabbed a tea towel and started to dry, putting dishes away as she did so.

"What were they talking about in there?" Jaymie asked, sliding a glance sideways at the woman.

"I wasn't listening."

"You're a better woman than I!" Jaymie laughed. "I'm so snoopy I can't help but listen in on people's conversations."

"I'm a housekeeper; I try to remember my place and mind my own business."

"Do you live here?"

"I have my own apartment upstairs."

"Did you have that at the last place? I know they moved from a ranch house."

"They had the lower level converted to an apartment. That's where I raised my son, Finn. I don't spend any more time than I have to with them. These people are boring. I tune them out and think of my next quilting project."

"Quilting? I would *love* to see your work. Do you ever sell your pieces?"

"Sometimes. Why?"

"I'm looking for Christmas gifts for my mother-in-law and my best friend. A quilt would be fabulous. You must have to ask a lot, though, right? Val and I have a limit on how much we spend."

"The hand-sewn ones I sell for quite a bit, but I do some custom quilts using fat quarters and the sewing machine."

"Fat what?" Jaymie asked.

"Fat quarters . . . that's a piece of quilting fabric. It's like . . . a measurement. I buy precut fat quarters and piece quilts together quickly. It only takes me a week of spare time to make one of those, so I can sell them pretty cheap."

"Maybe I can see them sometime."

As she finished the last of the dishes and Erla started prepping for the family's dinner, Jaymie put on the kettle again and made a pot of tea just for them. "It can't have been easy working for Evan Nezer, though, truly." She eyed the older woman. "Judging from his behavior at the party he seemed like a . . . difficult person."

"He had his faults, but it's Mrs. Nezer who's the difficult one. Thinks she's queen."

"Did you work in the household when his first wife was with him, Ben's mother?"

Her gaze softened. "I did. Sarah and me . . . we're friends. I've worked for the family for years, and I respect how she fought for her health. It wasn't easy."

Interesting that she considered Sarah Nezer a friend and seemed to dislike Bella. "So you've known Ben for a while, too."

She smiled. "Ben and Finn kind of grew up together; they're a few months apart."

"That's cool. Which is older?"

"My Finn . . . he was such a big baby, eight and a half pounds! Look . . . I got a picture of him." She fished in her purse and brought out a laminated photo. It was of a blonde youngster, skinny and gap-toothed, standing on the edge of the water. She traced his white-blonde hair with one finger.

"He was a beautiful boy," Jaymie said softly.

"Sarah and I took the two boys to Disney World, and even camping once! Mr. Nezer used to go on these seminar tours in England and Canada, and we'd have the *best* time while he was away."

"You must be proud of Finn. It must be more difficult now, though, given how Mr. Nezer treated your son."

Her lips firmed and she squinted at Jaymie. "We were working it out. Finn gets anxious and impatient."

"Understandable! I work for the paper and read the news stories, so I've read all there is that's out there anyway, but there is always more, stuff that doesn't make it into the paper. It can't have been easy for your son to be accused of plagiarism like that, and by his thesis advisor, and the boss of his mom!"

"We were working it out," Erla repeated.

"Finn caused quite the commotion last night, though. It took a *lot* of talking for you to get him to leave. Did he come back? It sounded like he wanted to talk to the professor while the president was still there."

The woman turned toward Jaymie. "I think I can handle it all now," she said stiffly, hand gripping the counter, her knuckles white. "I wouldn't want to keep you from your day."

The dismissal was unmistakable and undeniable. "I'll get going, then." She pulled off her apron and hung it back up in place. "I visited with Mrs. Nezer—Sarah—this morning, you know. I was afraid, after she almost collapsed out front, that she'd be ill, but she seems fine. I'm happy to hear that she has you as a friend. And that Finn and Ben are such good pals. Maybe now, with the professor gone, Finn can get back into the college and finish his master's."

Erla shook her head. "I don't think it works like that. I'm afraid Mr. Nezer dying was the worst thing that could have happened for my son, and his chances. I could have handled Mr. Nezer. I could have *made* him see sense. He had an ego, that's all, and needed to be handled the right way. Who is going to speak for Finn now?" She turned away.

Jaymie pulled her coat on and left, walking back to her SUV. Who is going to speak for Finn now? Erla asked. Who indeed?

• • •

JAKOB WAS RIGHT: there was nothing like physical labor to cleanse the mind.

A Christmas tree farmer's year ramped up in November. Jakob had already cut a lot of trees for precut lots, but that would continue as needed. By now he was starting to get a good idea of demand. But a couple of other tree lots had had suppliers let them down, so Jakob was trying to fill their needs as well as his regulars'. That had forced quite a bit of extra cutting.

Some farmers used separate fields for their cut tree operations and their cut-it-yourself trees, and Jakob was in the process of moving to that model, now that they had acquired another fifty acres of land. But this year, and for a few more years, the operations would be combined until saplings had been planted in the spring and given a few years to grow.

From an employment agency in Wolverhampton he had found a college student, Shannon Parker, looking to make a few bucks. Helmut had pitched in, as had Dieter, the eldest Müller brother. Dieter was a quiet soul, graying and bearded, with a piercing gaze that showed he thought a lot more than he spoke. He lived with his parents since his divorce some years before and had a daughter who was in college in Germany, studying German culture, to the delight of her grandparents.

The day was gloomy, but while the men cut the trees Jakob showed Jaymie and Shannon how to push them through the netting baler, which protected the branches so they could be piled for transport. Shannon was a husky red-haired young woman, strong and capable. Her hair was braided into two long plaits that hung over her plaid flannel work jacket and almost to the waist of her jeans. Jakob told her to tuck the braids up while she worked, so they were now coiled around her head and secured with bobby pins, a woolen tuque pulled over the whole affair.

She and Jaymie worked out a system between them of handling the heavy trees, and then Shannon hoisted them on her shoulder and stacked them neatly at the base of the big oak tree in which the treehouse sat. By the time they were finished the sun was down behind the woods across the road, the long shadows enveloping the brush along the roadside. There was a stack of trees ready for local lots and service organizations, and more had been tagged for cut-it-yourself, which would start the next day. Her muscles ached, shrieking for a hot bath, but at least she smelled nice, kind of like a car freshener, the scent of pine tickling her nose.

"I am going to make a huge pot of coffee for us all and see what I have in the freezer. My kidlet is coming home from her grandparents in an hour, and we need to eat first!"

Shannon hoisted the last tree onto her shoulder and toted it over, neatly stacking it on top of the others. "I'd offer to help, but I know nothing about cooking."

"You don't need to know about cooking to help. You only need to follow orders."

The two women laughed together and Jaymie shouted to Jakob, Dieter, and Helmut to come in to the cabin when they were done. She led the way inside and told Shannon where she could freshen up. Jaymie washed in the kitchen sink, then rustled in the freezer for a couple of the meals she always kept handy for nights like this.

Shannon returned, face freshly scrubbed, braids long and swinging to her waist. "May I help?"

Jaymie set her to cutting a long loaf of French bread into slices, then chopping vegetables, while she popped the two meat loaves into the oven along with a casserole of scalloped potatoes, set the timer, then set the table. She made a compound butter for the bread. They chatted as they worked, and she learned that Shannon was an economics major.

Jaymie glanced over at her. "Do you know Finn Fancombe?"

Shannon looked up, her bright blue eyes sharp and inquisitive. "He was the TA for my Intro to Econometrics course."

"Econometrics?"

"That's the branch of economics that deals with math and statistics to describe economic systems."

Eyes wide, Jaymie smiled. "Okay. I'm impressed. Is that your area of focus?"

"Not at all, though I feel like I should have a solid grounding in it. I'm taking economics because I want to teach it in developing countries. I think if we in the wealthiest countries are going to share that wealth, we need to help modernize the global economy."

"Some people shiver when they hear the words *global economy*," Jaymie said. She didn't understand much, but she did hear discussions when loudmouths like Brock Nibley denounced "globalists."

Shannon smiled, her eyes full of mirth. "Yeah, like we're all Illuminati out for the New World Order, or some crap like that."

"I know people like that!"

"*Some* people don't like to face reality," Shannon said. "We live in the world, and the world is a smaller place than it used to be, with every country on the globe tied to every other one. We can choose to ignore it, or participate and make it work for us, and try to make the world a better, more open, more compassionate place. While keeping in mind cultural differences, of course; I don't want every country in the world to be like every other country. *But* . . . it will require compromise. It's like a giant machine with hundreds of working parts, large and small; to work well it needs to be oiled and properly managed. I want to be a part of it."

"I'm humbled," Jaymie said softly.

"No, don't say that. If you believe as I believe, I feel that every single good person is one cog in the wheel. You both support your local economy, and you're raising a child who will contribute, too."

Jaymie nodded. "I think I get it." She paused, then glanced back over, observing the young woman. "You must know Finn pretty well. It's terrible what happened to him, the expulsion from WC. Do you believe he plagiarized?"

Her blue eyes sparked with anger. "I do *not*. He marked papers, and let me tell you, as one of his students you had better have every footnote properly annotated and backed up."

"Hmm." That supported her own conclusion, that Finn had not plagiarized, that in fact it was Evan who had stolen his work. "What did you think of Finn, as a teacher?"

"He's terrible. So easily sidetracked. He's passionate about American economics and how it's failing the poorest of our citizens, and he tends to get on that topic and head off into the sunset. As an advisor, though, he's great. One on one, you know? He's empathetic and smart."

"Sounds like you like him."

Her cheeks burned and she ducked her head, chopping green onions for the salad. "I guess I do. But he's not interested in me."

"How do you know?"

"A girl just knows."

The guys came in and they ate dinner together, then Dieter offered to go pick up Jocie at her grandparents' instead of waiting for her to be dropped off. Jakob grabbed the business plan he was still working on for the Christmas store and flung himself down on the sofa in the living room.

"Are you in a rush?" Jaymie asked Shannon. "Do you want to go for a walk with me and Hoppy?"

Shannon agreed. Jakob looked up from his work. "When you come back, I'd like to talk to you."

"Okay."

Jaymie and Shannon headed out with Hoppy on a long leash. The little dog had begged for attention throughout the meal. It was getting darker, so they stuck to the road, an abbreviated stroll. In December, once the sun was down it got very chilly.

Shannon glanced at her sideways. "Your husband was worried when he found out what happened this morning. He was so cute . . . asking his brother if he should go pick you up and bring you home, or what."

"He asked Helmut, right? What did Helmut say?" Her brother-in-law was so quiet it was hard sometimes to get a read on him. She thought he liked her but was never sure.

"He told Jakob that you would come home if you needed to. He said if any woman knew her own mind, you were her."

Jaymie smiled into the darkness. Hoppy stopped to bark ferociously, probably at a rabbit in the field along the road. "Let's head back. C'mon, little guy." They turned and headed back toward the cabin. It was one of her favorite views, the cabin in the dark, one golden light shining out the front kitchen window. "I'm so blessed," she said softly. "I waited a while, but it was worth it to find my one guy, the one I know will be mine forever."

As they returned Dieter pulled up and Jocie jumped out of his car, racing to Jaymie as fast as her little legs would take her. Jaymie crouched down and pulled her daughter to her in a strong hug. This was what she needed after the day she'd had. She had been drained, and now she was replenished.

Dieter tooted the horn and drove off, and Jaymie, Shannon, Hoppy and Jocie entered the house. Jocie was sleepy after her own big day, but she insisted on heading upstairs to hide a special parcel she carried very carefully. That would be her craft project, Jaymie's Christmas gift. Jaymie gave her a few minutes, then followed and helped Jocie get ready for bed, tugging her nightgown down over her head and doing her blonde hair in braids. The room smelled suspiciously of jasmine. Jaymie hid her smile and turned out the light. "Good night, sweetie. Family day tomorrow."

When she returned downstairs Jakob and Shannon were sitting on the burgundy plaid sofa talking. Shannon looked up at her with shining bright blue eyes.

"Guess what? Looks like I'll be working the Müller Christmas tree lot this year!"

Jakob smiled as Jaymie approached the back of the sofa; he held out his hand to her and enveloped hers in his, bringing it to his lips. "She did a great job today. And I think she's got the right personality to handle the public. That's the toughest part."

"But will you have time, with exams coming up?" Jaymie asked.

She looked stricken for a moment.

"You must already have your schedule, right?" Jakob asked.

She nodded. "I do."

"As long as you can give that to me tomorrow, we can work around it. How much study time do you need?"

Jaymie smiled as she went to make tea. They'd work it out. As the conversation continued, she offered Shannon time and space in the kitchen for study breaks. It was soon settled and the latest Müller Christmas Tree Farm employee went on her way, ready to be back at ten a.m. on Monday.

Before bed, Jaymie ferreted out her clutch bag, which she had tossed into the closet after the party. She sat down on the side of the bed and got out the piece of paper Sarah had handed her.

"What's that?" Jakob asked, pulling off his shirt and grabbing a T-shirt from a stack of laundry that hadn't yet been put away.

Jaymie explained as he pulled the white T-shirt on over his head and undid his jeans, peeling them off and tossing them to one side.

"I know I should have said something to you at the time, but it would have taken too long to explain. I was going to tell you about it later, but it truly slipped my mind. It was . . . weird. Sarah put one finger to her lips, then handed me this note. It has *Ben* written on it, and it's taped shut."

"Well, open it and read it."

He sat down beside her as she slit the tape with a pair of scissors she kept in the drawer of the nightstand. She held it under the pool of light from their bedside lamp and read it.

Ben, it read. *Don't do anything stupid tonight. There is still time. Just hold tight for a little while longer. Mom.*

Jaymie felt her heart thud. It could be read a few ways, but one thing it could mean was to not kill his father. And she hadn't given it to him. Trembling, she said, "I have to give this to the police."

"You do," Jakob agreed, putting his arm around her and holding her close. "I don't know what it means, but . . . you have to hand it over."

"What if it means that he shouldn't kill his father? What if me not handing it over to Ben meant that Evan died?"

"You can't assume that, *liebchen*. It could mean anything at all. It doesn't mention Evan, after all, does it? And even if it does mean what you fear, and you gave it to Ben, what is the guarantee that he would heed it? This is not on you."

"I wish I knew that for sure."

"The only way to find out is to hand it over to the police."

℘ Thirteen ℘

SUNDAY WAS FAMILY DAY for Jaymie, Jakob and Jocie. Jaymie hadn't slept well. The turmoil and horror of the day before told on her. Jakob looked worried, but she assured him she had survived other periods of mayhem, and she'd be fine this time, too.

She called the police station. Detective Vestry wasn't available, but the sergeant she spoke to agreed that the note was important. They sent an officer out to collect it. Jocie was excited to see the Queensville Township Police Department car, and was wide-eyed as she peeked in the windows of the cruiser as Jaymie handed over the piece of paper in an envelope with her own note, explaining the circumstances of receiving it and telling Detective Vestry she'd be in tomorrow to give her complete statement.

Jaymie then did her best, for the rest of the day, to put it all out of her mind and heart and focus on her family.

Jakob made breakfast, tiny pancakes that Jocie loved, then Kevin and Becca joined them, and they all headed to a farmers' market. It was part family outing and part research for their next venture. Later they all had dinner at the Müllers', Becca and Kevin included. Plans were made for the Christmas season.

But inevitably the cold hard light of Monday brought Jaymie to the grim realization that her diorama was forever stained in her mind and heart with the murder of Evan Nezer, and would have to be dismantled once the police were done. She finished getting ready and sat back down on the bed, staring down at the wood floor.

"What's up?" Jakob said, coming back into the room from the en suite bathroom and grabbing his cell phone from the side table.

"I can't leave the diorama in place," she said, looking up at him. "It's not right. It would be too gruesome a reminder of a horrible crime."

Jakob sat down next to her and pulled her close, holding her. "I hate to say it after all the work you and Bill put into it," he murmured in her ear, "but you're probably right."

"I know I am. I hate when I'm right."

He released her, kissed her on the nose, and pulled her to her feet. "You'll do the right thing. You always do." They descended together for breakfast.

So . . . added to her to-do list for the day was to speak to the police about removing the diorama before the Friday night tree lighting.

After Jakob left to greet Shannon and Helmut, who would be working the Müller Christmas tree sales lot, Jaymie made sure Jocie had her bookbag and homework and was out to the road in time to catch the school bus. The child was excited and full of plans for the winter pageant, in which she was to play a snow globe. How did one play a snow globe? Jaymie had asked her. *Very glassily*, Jocie had replied, with a solemn look that dissolved into a giggle.

Jaymie dressed carefully in festive patterned leggings and a long red sweater. She had bemoaned that she didn't know anyone at WC and so didn't have a line into the college to investigate, but she had forgotten one thing: she *did* know someone at the college. She made a quick phone call to Austin Calhoun, offering him free lunch in exchange for a chat, and drove in to The Junk Stops Here to work for the morning, taking care of the cash desk while Gus trained the two new people, a young couple, ex-military both of them, on organization in the store.

Gus, a big bluff fellow, looked somewhat happier these days. He had gone through a traumatic time in the spring and still had family troubles, but things were looking up. As she finished her three hours and headed out, he waved goodbye to her and turned back to work with the two new hires.

It was a sparkling crisp day, blue sky reaching to forever, and with a crystalline feel. The air was cold enough to make her gasp, but her truck was warm. She checked her phone, wondering if she should drop in on Nan to see where she stood after their last testy conversation, and decided against it.

Jaymie's next stop was Wellington's Retreat, a sweet little hole-in-the-wall café and lunch spot on Wolverhampton's main street. Austin leaped up from his seat near the window, his bright eyes alight with joy. They hugged, put in their lunch orders with the cashier and sat back down.

They caught up: Austin was serious about hospitality. He wanted to become either an event manager or a publicity manager for a hotel or inn.

"You would be so perfect for that, Austin," Jaymie said, examining the glow on his round face. Though he could be gossipy and snarky at times, his general demeanor was cheerful helpfulness. "You've got that effervescence and joyful personality. Have you ever thought about working for a cruise line? You'd be great at that, too."

His eyes lit up. "Not a bad thought! Work and travel at the same time. My mom would love that."

A waitress brought their lunches and set them down.

"What do you have?" Jaymie asked, examining his plate.

"Chicken salad wrap and mug of soup. You were the one who got me started on a mug of soup with lunch. I've lost ten pounds in a year!" he said, smiling.

"Congratulations!"

They dug in and ate in silence for a few minutes.

She glanced up at him as he patted his mouth after taking a long drink of his soup. "So how did things go at the Nezer residence after I left the night of the party?"

"I know what this is about," he said, and his expression sobered. He leaned across the table and put his hand over hers. "I heard about you finding a body; my dear, you *do* have a talent."

"One I'd rather do without," she said.

"I getcha. However, if you're going to find a body it may as well be one of someone so thoroughly unpleasant." He rolled his eyes; they sparkled with mingled malice and gruesome enjoyment. "Now, what you asked. Let's see . . . the college folk were still there when you left, right?" Jaymie nodded. "La Bella was playing queen of the manor and Ben the heir apparent. And then Finn Fancombe, enraged and ready to rumble, reappeared! *Dra*-ma!" He sang the last word on a falling note.

"Oh, dear. Nobody has said anything about that yet. What happened?" She ate her cheddar cream soup and listened as between bites of his chicken salad wrap he told her about it.

"Well, now . . . let's see . . . Mrs. Belcher, the college president, and her two orcs, Carter Crossley and Andy Markham—that's the provost and dean—were toadying to Nezer. It was as thorough a butt-smooching as I have seen in some time."

"Why do you think that is? Why does—or did—the college leadership kiss up to Nezer?"

"The prevailing theory is—and I asked around this morning

before class—that Nezer had brought attention to WC from some high-level conservative commentators. He had been on three different radio broadcasts since the school year started, and with the Dickens connection he was slated to be on a few more."

Say something controversial and that was bound to happen. "I don't think I get it. It was the attention?"

"No, no, my dear . . . it was the *dollars*! And the students. WC has a crummy reputation . . . kind of a third-rate school better known for its florists than its financiers. It's a four-year college that shares its campus with Wolverhampton Technical College, my school, which offers technical courses. That does not give prestige in the academic world. Not that *I* think there's anything wrong with that—I'm what the pretentious students call a Techie—but . . . aca*de*mia!" He turned up his nose and said the word with a fake English accent. "Too *too* snooty, and all that." He rolled his eyes. "Prof Nezer was apparently behind a move to shove WTC off campus. He was going to change WC's rep, make it more serious, you know? Or so the thinking went."

"Interesting. A good reason why Mrs. Belcher and the others would want him alive, I guess, if that was their goal. But what if he was rocking the boat *too* much?" That was vague and unlikely, unconvincing even to herself.

Austin, elbows on the table, leaned across and murmured, "Speaking of . . . there was a faction opposed to Nezer. And guess who was leading that, and all the attendant protests?"

Jaymie was silent.

"Finn Fancombe. Who crashed the party Friday night."

"The actual party, and not just the kitchen?"

"No, my dear, the par-*tay*! After you left. He slammed his way in the front door and went right up to Mrs. Belcher. He said loudly that Nezer was a lying piece of crap, and that if his—Finn's—banishment wasn't revoked, he'd expose some very dirty business in the past."

"In whose past?"

"He didn't say. I guess I assumed Professor Nezer's past, but it could just as easily have been Mrs. Belcher's or even the college's, I suppose."

"Interesting. But going back . . . are you saying that Finn was leading a protest against Professor Nezer when he was reliant on him to help him get back into school? Why would he shoot himself in the foot like that?"

"Finn's a complicated fellow, I've heard. And maybe he thought that he had a leg up with some information that would get him out of trouble. If Nezer was discredited it would help his own case."

"He did tell his mother he needed to speak with Mrs. Belcher," Jaymie said, sipping the last of her tea. "Maybe the college president has banned him from campus. There's a campus police force, right?"

Austin nodded. "Kids in cute uniforms," he said with a smirk. "I stole one and wore it for Halloween, only I wore shorts instead of the pants. That's how pathetic they are, though, that a portly fellow like me could waltz in and steal a police uniform."

"Austin—"

"I put it back! Cross my heart. They're glorified mall cops," he said, flapping his hand. "Not the real thing. So I borrowed a security guard uniform, big deal!"

Jaymie bit back a smile at his protestations of innocence and thought for a long minute. "When did the protests against Nezer begin?"

"Start of the school year, I think. You want me to find out?"

"Could you?"

His eyes wide, he asked, "Are you investigating a murder, Mrs. Müller?"

"Austin, don't you *dare* go around saying that."

He made a pouty face, but then smiled again. "I'll keep it between us. Promise. What all do you want to know?"

"I want to know what students think of Finn; I know he was working on his master's in some branch of economics, and that he was also a teaching assistant. The student I spoke with admired him. But what was thought of him generally? And the timing issue . . . did the plagiarism incident come up before or after he started to protest Nezer's conservative talk-show chats and push to move WC in that direction?"

"Are you seriously thinking Finn Fancombe might have killed him?"

"I'm curious, that's all. Anyway, how did it end with Finn at the party?"

"That's the part I don't understand. Prof Nezer took him aside and they had a chat that started out angry and ended kind of . . ."

Austin shrugged, his eyes clouded with puzzlement. "Finn's anger melted away and he looked . . ." He made a face, struggling to find the right word. "Distressed. Surprised. Like he'd learned something startling and didn't quite know what to do about it."

"And then?"

"And then he left."

"What about Ben Nezer?"

"He was watching everything like a hawk, including the run-in his dad had with Finn. He cornered his father afterward, but the professor shrugged him off and went back to the college administrators."

She felt a sick lurch in her stomach. If only she'd delivered that note to him. Would Nezer still be alive? "I wonder what Nezer said to Finn. Maybe he promised him that he'd take care of the plagiarism thing. That's all Finn was concerned with, it seemed to me. He couldn't afford to let it go." She finished her soup. "Anything else you can find out about Nezer on campus, I'd appreciate."

"I will do it with alacrity!"

She gazed at him wide-eyed.

"*Alacrity: brisk and cheerful readiness.* My mother gave me a word-a-day calendar for my birthday. A current-year calendar. In *November*. She loves me but she's thrifty."

Jaymie laughed and got up, retrieving her coat from the back of the chair. She slipped it on, and the two hugged. "I'll call you," she said.

Her next conversation was going to be more difficult. She headed to the police department, housed in a long, low red-brick building that was backed by the local jail. She asked to speak with Detective Vestry and, after a few minutes waiting, was shown into her office.

It was a sterile little box with a window overlooking the jail yard, enlivened only by some paintings of the St. Clair River and a photo of a boat with the name *TruthSeeker* emblazoned on the side. The detective looked up, held up one finger for a moment, and returned to her computer screen. She nodded, put her computer in sleep mode, and as the screen turned black, turned to Jaymie. "You're here so I can take your statement," she said.

"Yes, that, but other things too. About the note Sarah Nezer handed me." The detective nodded. "And I'm not sure if anyone from the historical society has spoken to you yet, but we decided to hold off on the official opening of Dickens Days until this Friday."

"Wise decision. I had already figured that out when the lighting of the tree didn't happen on Saturday. *And* when I saw the notice in the paper. I am a detective, after all."

Jaymie was taken aback at her acerbity, but relaxed when Vestry offered the briefest of smiles. She was kidding. "But also . . . I would like permission to remove the diorama. It's . . ." She swallowed and tears welled. "It's an unpleasant reminder of what happened. And I don't want it there to give news crews any food for sensationalism."

"I appreciate that, but I can't give you the go-ahead yet. We're still processing the scene."

"But how much more can you get from it?"

"You'd be surprised," she said dryly. "Are you ready to give your official statement?"

"Okay."

"Let's adjourn to an interview room," she said, gathering up her cell phone, clipboard, and pen.

Jaymie knew the reason behind moving; her interview would be taped. The interview room was small, simply furnished with three chairs and a bare table attached to the wall. A video camera was mounted near the ceiling and pointed down at the chair she occupied. Detective Vestry, in a monotone, stated Jaymie's name, the date and time, and that it was an interview of a witness who found the deceased, all for the record. Jaymie went through her interactions with Nezer so far, the party the night before, and then her finding his body in her diorama.

Detective Vestry made notes. They sat in silence, the detective's scratching pen on the paper the only sound. They then went back over her statement. Vestry asked pointed questions, and Jaymie fleshed out some of her answers. Most of the questions were about the Friday evening party. And then: "Explain to me how you came to have the note you gave us."

Jaymie described coming up the walk toward the door, hearing something in the bushes and seeing Sarah Nezer. "She handed me the note and I took it . . . reflex, I guess. And then she hustled away. When I saw the name on it, I knew she wanted me to give it to her son."

"But you didn't do that. Why?"

"I meant to, but with everything that happened, all the things I've told you about, I forgot. In fact, I didn't think about it until the next day, and I didn't have a chance to look at it until Saturday night."

"You opened the note and read it. Why?"

Jaymie rolled her eyes. "Curiosity, I guess."

"What do you make of the contents?"

"I don't know what to think."

Vestry's cool gray gaze flicked over Jaymie. "Come on, Ms. Müller, you can tell me what you thought."

"I didn't know. I *don't* know," she said firmly.

"Okay." Vestry scratched something on her clipboard and checked her phone screen. "Did you see anything suspicious that night, anything to do with the victim's computer in his home office?"

Uh-oh. "Why do you ask?"

Vestry, no expression on her face, said, "Just answer the question, please. It's pretty simple."

She had to say it, but at least she could keep the coat check student out of it. "Now that you mention it . . . I didn't think this was important, but when my husband and I went into the office to get our coats—they were using it as a coat check room—I saw one of the servers at the computer."

"One of the servers?"

"One of the casual servers the Nezers had hired."

"Did you recognize the server?"

Jaymie took a deep breath. "Yes. Yes, I did."

"And . . . ?" Vestry prompted when Jaymie was silent for too long.

Jaymie squirmed in her seat. "It was Jacklyn Marley."

"Did you ask her what she was doing?"

"Have you asked her yourselves?"

"Just answer the question, Ms. Müller."

Jaymie sighed. "I did. She told me there were . . . irregularities in how she was paid as a ghostwriter for Mr. Nezer's book, and she was trying to discover if he was holding back information or revenue from her. I told her I didn't think it was a good idea, but I didn't turn her in. That was between them. My husband left it up to me whether to say anything, and I said we should leave it."

"You're a good friend of Ms. Marley's?" Vestry asked, seeming not surprised by the information.

145

The nervous coat check girl had probably already told all. "No, I wouldn't say that. We met briefly the other day."

"So why were you hiding her activities from us?"

Jaymie sighed. One of Detective Vestry's favorite questioning techniques was to imply collusion or coercion where none existed. "I wasn't hiding anything, I didn't mention it. If you can tell me why I would have thought it relevant, I'll apologize for the omission." She paused, watching the other woman's chilly gray eyes. "What does her being on Nezer's computer have to do with his murder?"

"It was within a few hours of his death, or even less. She appears to have a substantial conflict with the victim and was looking for information by hacking into his computer."

Jaymie was silent; she made good points, but none of this had anything to do with her.

"I'm left wondering what else haven't you told us?"

"Let's see . . . I went to a farmers' market yesterday. I saw my in-laws. I took a walk with my dog." She shrugged helplessly. "I can't relate every moment of the last forty-eight hours. How do I know what you'll think I was hiding when I don't feel like I'm hiding anything?" Jaymie was exasperated, and mortifyingly close to tears.

"I don't mean to badger you, Jaymie, but this *is* a murder investigation. You're not stupid; you're the polar *opposite* of stupid." She rolled her eyes. "Okay, I'll admit something: I value your observations. This will go more smoothly if you tell us everything you know or think you may know. You're a smart young woman and you've been through this before. You know what I mean. Stop worrying about incriminating anyone in particular and tell us what you've witnessed or thought of."

There was so much she had asked and heard and thought about, like Finn Fancombe and his activity protesting Nezer, and his badgering his mother to intercede and let him into the party, and how that related to his showing up later. And about Sarah Nezer accusing her ex-husband of stealing novels thirty years ago, and . . . what else? She shrugged helplessly, weary and discouraged. She could talk all day, but all of this was stuff the police could, and probably would, find out, and that Vestry would no doubt find irrelevant. Jaymie had been accused of telling them stuff that didn't matter in the past, and now of withholding stuff. They couldn't have it both ways. She was getting irritated. "If I think of anything, I'll let you know."

"I feel like you're hiding something, Jaymie. I thought we were past that."

She stayed silent and shook her head.

Vestry's mouth tightened into a grim, thin line. She waited, but when Jaymie didn't say anything else she stood and looked down at Jaymie. "I'll let the historical society know when you can dismantle that . . . what is it, diorama? Until then, stay away from it." She stared down at Jaymie. "But I *am* surprised that you didn't bother to tell us that the holly piercing Nezer's heart was from your very own Queensville home backyard."

❧ Fourteen ❧

JAYMIE GASPED, her breath squeezed from her lungs. "What do you m-mean? How is that . . . ?" She blinked and stared.

"You reportedly openly invited people at the heritage meeting to come get some holly from your backyard."

"For decoration purposes."

"Someone wanted a festive corpse, I guess. They stole a stake from Bill Waterman's workshop and a hunk of holly from your backyard. Either one—or both—of you took part in the murder, or someone is trying to implicate you, together or separately."

Jaymie jumped to her feet and grabbed her purse from the floor under her chair, shaking with anger. "Sure, why not . . . Bill and I conspired to kill him in the most festive way possible! We thought we'd leave his corpse in the diorama we spent hours and hours creating." Tears stung her eyes. "And I did *not* invite people to come get holly. I told them to ask me and *I'd* cut them some!"

Her anger died a little as she turned her thoughts to the heritage meeting. She took in a deep, shuddering breath. "So, Detective, do you think whoever killed him was at that heritage meeting?" She clutched her purse to her chest and leaned back against the wall. "Bella and Ben Nezer were there, as well as Jacklyn Marley."

"We're not wedded to the theory that whoever did it was there, but they knew that your property had holly, and where it was, and where to find a wooden stake. Someone involved in either the killing or in the moving of the corpse had heard about your generous offer and knew—or could find out—where your house was."

"But *why*? Why would they do that? To the body, I mean, and . . . and to me, to take the holly from my backyard. I don't understand."

"It's possible that they wanted the holly to make a point and didn't know where else to get it. Your backyard is private and so it seemed ideal. But think about it, who would go to that length? Anyone come to mind?"

Jaymie plunked back down on the hard chair and considered it. "It seems to me that whoever did that, the killer or an accomplice, wanted to point the finger at someone. But that doesn't make sense.

That's *my* diorama, and I didn't have a problem with Evan." She frowned and looked down at her nails, pulling at a loose piece of skin. "But Bill Waterman built my diorama and helped me set it up. And you haven't found out who set fire to the cider booth yet. Could it be the same person? The arsonist and the killer? And were they trying to single Bill out, maybe?"

"We don't have evidence of that at this point. I'd appreciate it, Jaymie, if you would seriously and deeply think about this, and give us any information or thoughts you may have. I don't mean to make you feel that I don't trust you, however . . . I don't believe you're telling me everything. This is an ugly one; it almost looks like the person wanted not only to kill Evan Nezer but to kill Dickens Days too. Or—I hate to say this, but I want to warn you—it could be a pointed warning to you. Or a challenge. You've become notorious in these parts for your inventiveness in helping the police solve crime. A local hero, of sorts."

"I . . . I never fancied myself a local hero," Jaymie said faintly.

"Regardless, there it is. I spoke to Chief Ledbetter and he's a little worried."

Her heart thudded. Chief Ledbetter, her old friend. She hadn't seen him for a while. "You spoke to him?"

"I'd be crazy to ignore his experience and wisdom. I consult with him sometimes." She was silent for a minute. "Look, Jaymie, I'm not going to pressure you. Yet. But if you think of anything you *forgot* to tell us, we'd be happy to hear it. In the meantime, we have a team at your Queensville house investigating the yard. We ought to be done in a few hours."

"Are you sure the holly came from my backyard?"

"Why do you ask?"

"I saw bunches of it at the farmers' market on the weekend. There are other places to get it, including florists, this time of year."

"We're considering every source. Why don't you go over there now and let us know if your holly looks like it's been damaged. It would help. We have someone there investigating right now."

"Okay, but wait . . . I'll tell you everything I've thought of, but it doesn't amount to much at this point." The detective sat back down across from her and Jaymie told her about Finn Fancombe at the back door of the Nezer residence, and how she'd heard he charged in later, and how Nezer had spoken to him. She told the detective everything else she had considered and wondered about.

Except for one thing: she said nothing about Sarah Nezer's books being stolen by her ex-late-husband and the lucrative movie options on them. She wasn't sure why she held that back, but she was deeply conflicted about it. It felt like it would be a betrayal of a vulnerable woman who had suffered so much. And yet there was the note to Ben . . . she didn't know what to think.

By the time she left the police station, her mood was somber, her thoughts in a turmoil. She drove over to the Queensville house to find Becca and Kevin in the parking lane talking to Bernie, who was taking notes while a police photographer took pictures. Trip Findley, their back-lane neighbor, wandered through his back gate and joined them as Jaymie parked along his fence. There were two police cars taking up other spaces, and an area by their wrought iron fence cordoned off.

She joined her sister and brother-in-law and got caught up. She stood on tiptoe and peered at her holly hedge, planted two years before. She gasped. "They've cut a *huge* chunk out of the middle! Who *did* that?"

"I thought you did it," Becca said.

"Seriously, Becca, why would I? I can't *believe* you didn't tell me about this. When did it happen?"

Becca was silent for a long moment and exchanged a glance with Kevin. "Well, here's the thing—"

"You don't *know*! How can you not know?"

Becca sighed. "I didn't notice it until today. Not everyone notices every little thing, Jaymie."

Jaymie caught the stifled smile Bernie was trying to hide. "Okay, I get it. You've probably come home most often in the dark. It gets dark so early this time of year."

"And in the morning you know what I'm like until the second coffee has kicked in."

"Well, I was here on Friday bringing stuff for the fridge for you and Kevin. I'm not sure what time that was, but I know it was okay then."

"I know when it happened!" The voice was from slightly above; they all looked up. Pam Driscoll, who was managing the bed-and-breakfast next door, was on her back patio, which was slightly elevated. "Friday afternoon. I looked out at about two and everything was okay. I did see you cutting some holly, but you didn't cut much. Later, about four thirty, I was in the kitchen making dinner for Noah and saw the bush kinda pulled apart. I thought it was your doggie or something."

"Thanks, Pam!" Jaymie said. So, between two-ish and four thirty; that gave the police a window of time to ask for suspects' whereabouts.

Bernie headed over to take her statement as Jaymie pondered the new information. This all meant that someone planned the murder and shocking display of Evan Nezer's body, and that the plan was in place before the party. But did that mean that nothing that happened at the party had anything to do with it? Logically that didn't necessarily follow. She couldn't discount that whoever had planned to kill him didn't also have a conflict with him at the party. This was getting more and more complicated by the minute.

Brock drove his car down the lane that moment, arriving to show the house next door. He got out, careful to keep his dark wool trench coat away from the dust on his car. Of course he had to know everything going on, and Jaymie filled him in.

His long, plain face held a look of dismay. "That's crazy! All that elaborate staging of Nezer's death . . . it's weird. Why would anyone go to that much trouble? Why not leave him where he was killed, behind his house's shed?"

Jaymie stared at him in surprise. "How do you know where Nezer was killed?"

"Hah! So Jaymie the great detective didn't know? It's yellow-taped-off. I wouldn't have known either, but I was showing a house with a backyard backing it."

He had to toddle off to show the Walters house to a couple. Bernie returned from speaking with Pam Driscoll, and Jaymie asked her about the area behind the Nezer home. "Is it really where Evan Nezer was murdered? How do you know?"

Her dark eyes held a troubled expression. She shook her head, then glanced over to where Becca was still speaking with Trip. "Look, if I tell you, you won't say anything?"

Jaymie nodded.

"Okay, it is *not* where Nezer was killed; honestly, we don't know where that is, yet. It's cordoned off for another reason."

Jaymie asked why, but Bernie shook her head.

"I'm stepping out of bounds even now, but all I can say is, it is not where Nezer was killed."

Something was bothering Jaymie badly, and she knew she had to sort it out or it would continue to bother her until she confessed to the police. But first . . . she drove the SUV down to the street of small houses near the docks and went to Sarah Nezer's door. The woman was home. She greeted Jaymie with a look of distrust. "Do you want tea again?" she asked. "Or will you be telling the police about that, too?"

Jaymie sighed. "Sarah, I *had* to give the police that note. I couldn't . . ." She shook her head.

"It's okay," the woman said wearily. "It's not important now." She retreated, leaving the door open.

Jaymie followed, taking the open door as an invitation. "I . . . I have a question. I won't take up much of your time," Jaymie said, glancing at the laptop and work spread out at a tiny desk in a corner of the living room.

"You want to know what the note meant. So did the police."

"No, I won't . . . I mean, I'd like to know. But I don't expect you'll tell me."

"I did tell them, but I won't be telling you. But it wasn't advice to hold off on murdering his father until a later date."

Jaymie didn't know what to say.

"Sit," Sarah said, taking a spot on the soft sofa along one wall. It was topped by an original painting, an abstract that looked like a woman with dark skin, hints of blue and purple swirled in confusion, creating an eloquent figure with rounded features and elongated legs and arms. Jaymie sat in a sixties-style chair with a crocheted cushion. "What's on your mind?" the woman asked.

"I wanted to tell you, Sarah, that yes, I gave them the note and told them about seeing you there that night. But . . . I didn't say anything about Evan stealing your work, and . . . and all the money he was making from the movie offers."

"I don't care about money!"

"It was a lot, though, and made off your work . . . *again*! That had to sting."

"Do you think I killed my ex-husband?"

Jaymie didn't answer right away. She examined Sarah, who had her white frizzy hair pulled back into a bun today, and wore a long patchwork skirt and a matching vest over a turtleneck sweater. She glanced around the homey, cozy room, modest and shabby compared to the Nezer home. There were many shelves, with books lining most of them and a small flat-screen TV taking up one space. Above that were family photos.

"I love family pictures," Jaymie said and got up, crossing the room to look them over. There were ones from the fifties, a handsome couple shoulder to shoulder, both with cigarettes in their hands, staring into the camera with intense gazes. "Your parents?"

Sarah nodded. "Both gone now, but never forgotten."

There were pictures of Erla Fancombe and Sarah goofing around on a campsite. It was odd to see a younger, slimmer Erla—pretty and happy—with such a big smile. Better times. There was another of two skinny, tanned boys, Finn and Ben clearly, on a sunny beach, gap-toothed grins on their faces, arms over each other's shoulders. "Do I think you killed Evan?" Jaymie asked, turning back and examining the woman on the sofa. "Not really. But . . . is the note for Ben the only reason you were in those bushes by Evan's house that night?"

"*Our* house! That was supposed to be *our* house," Sarah said, a burst of annoyance in her tone. "He promised me we'd sell that damn suburban ranch-house box and move to the Nezer family home one day, but we never did. Not until the *trophy* demanded it."

The trophy . . . Bella Nezer. So there was a hidden well of anger there, and resentment. "I suppose she'll inherit the house now?"

Surprise and alarm flared in her eyes. "No, Ben will get the house! I'm sure of it."

"But they had been estranged, right?"

"It doesn't matter. Evan would never let that house slip out of real Nezer hands."

"I don't know about that. He let it sit for years, rented out to companies and vacationers, right? He may not have felt as strongly about the place as you think. Does Ben even know where he stood with his father? I mean, if their quarrel was only made up recently he may not have made a will leaving Ben anything."

Sarah was clearly alarmed at the new ideas Jaymie was introducing to her. She seemed distracted. "They *had* made up, as far as I know. Ben and I haven't spoken for a few weeks. That's . . . that's why I was there that night, to give him that note."

"Yes, but you forget I read the note. I know it was some kind of follow up to some conversation you must have had with your son. It told him to hold off. Hold off on what?"

She shook her head and stayed silent.

"Sarah, can I ask you something?"

"You can ask. It doesn't mean I'll answer."

Jaymie had no right to intrude, she knew that. "Sarah, I . . . I don't know why, but I'm usually pretty good at figuring out who killed someone. I don't think you did."

"Well, thank you very much for that," she said, a brittle edge to her tone.

"But it doesn't mean I believe every word you say, either." She sighed. "People hide things for all kinds of reasons. I started wondering, why was Evan ready to sell the ancestral Nezer home one minute, then decided to keep it and move into it the next. It seemed odd, and no matter what you think, Bella could not have influenced that. Now, I know he is involved in changing things at the college . . . trying to up the prestige. The party Friday night was all about that. He had the new money from the movie rights, but why use that on a house he hadn't seemed to care about before?"

Sarah's gaze was blank.

"The house certainly does have an air of prestige, especially with all the money Bella has thrown at it in the last month or so. Maybe that is becoming more important to him now. I wondered if he was being paid off by the college president to help in the transformation of Wolverhampton College from a third-rate college to a more prestigious institute. They were using Evan's book and new stature as a conservative voice to attract funding via a think tank, which would have attracted major donors."

"Okay. What does that have to do with me?"

"Because you would not like him using money from your feminist books being made into movies to finance that kind of cause, would you? Evan was the living, breathing antithesis of everything you believe, wasn't he?"

She sighed and sat back against a crocheted pillow. "Look, not to be rude, but I don't have time for—"

"It made you deeply angry, I'm guessing."

She swiftly raised her eyebrows. "Angry enough to kill him? Is that what you're hinting? I thought you said you believed I didn't do it."

"I said it and meant it. I don't think *you* killed Evan."

"Look, I don't want to be rude," Sarah said, a troubled expression on her face. "But there is no reason on earth why I should be answering questions from you. I haven't done anything to be ashamed of, and Ben hasn't either. If I were you, I'd be looking for who else Evan had angered lately. He was always launching lawsuits; why hasn't anyone mentioned that?"

She asked Jaymie to go, as she had somewhere she had to be. Jaymie was out the door and on her way to her SUV in two minutes. Sarah was rattled, but why? She wasn't at the meeting where the holly was mentioned, but Ben was. Was she so sure Ben didn't kill his father? What else could the note mean? Was Jaymie wrong? Were mother and son in on it *together*? Was that why the death was staged the way it was?

Sarah had raised one interesting point, something that had slipped Jaymie's mind until she said it. Evan Nezer was known for launching frivolous lawsuits, one after another. His court costs never amounted to much because being a lawyer, he represented himself, from what Jaymie understood, so all he paid were filing costs. As far as his lawsuits against Dickens Days had gone in the past, judges had dismissed the suits as frivolous, but who else had he sued lately? She got out her phone and texted Nan. If anyone could find out, it was the *Wolverhampton Weekly Howler*'s reporter.

Jaymie returned to downtown Queensville and parked near the Emporium. Crime tape was still up at the diorama, fluttering disconsolately in the breeze, which was stiffening. An officer sat in a car nearby. Another police car pulled up and Detective Vestry emerged, then headed up the side stairs to Jacklyn Marley's apartment. Uh-oh. Well, she'd told Jacklyn she couldn't keep her computer hacking a secret, but it seemed that she hadn't been the first to tell them that anyway.

Jaymie sat in her vehicle, trying to figure out what was going on.

As she had reasoned, though it appeared that the planning for Evan's murder had been done before the party, it didn't follow that the events that took place there had no bearing on it. Maybe there was something in the evening that confirmed or refuted her Sarah and Ben theory. She didn't want it to be true; she liked Sarah, and didn't want Valetta's good memories of her to be tainted. But liking her or not had nothing to do with guilt or innocence.

There were other suspects in her mind, and she needed to eliminate them before coming to any conclusions. She couldn't spend all day at it either; she had responsibilities. She checked her watch and got out her phone. It was three. She had time to make one more quick trip.

Wolverhampton College was a collection of long, low three-story red-brick buildings, all connected by glassed-in walkways and joined by a central administrative building on a large patch of land on the other side of town. She had been expecting to wait until the next day but had texted Austin to see if he had discovered anything. He might have, he texted back. She drove into the campus — she knew it well, having attended a few lectures and seminars there in the past — and parked in the visitors' lot.

Wolverhampton College shared social accommodations, like the library, food court and recreational facilities, with the adjoining technical college. Austin met her in the large glass atrium at the back, overlooking a terrace, where a Starbucks and a Tim Horton's competed for the coffee dollars of stressed and weary students. They both got steeped tea and retreated to the huge wall of windows that overlooked the terrace and garden, now expertly put to bed, shrubs and bushes wrapped in burlap and flower beds mounded with mulch. Outdoor tables and chairs that normally dotted the terrace had been removed to storage, leaving only cement benches around the perimeter separated by planters, garbage cans and smokers' receptacles. Two smokers were huddled on one bench, shivering as they puffed.

"I only have half an hour before my last class of the day, event management," he said, tearing open a packet of sweetener and stirring it into his black tea.

"I won't keep you long. What have you learned?"

"I asked around, and talked to one of my good friends here; she runs the school paper and has been doing some digging on the college administration. There is definitely something up with President Belcher, she says, because the woman was an academic star once; she was provost at a very well-known upper-crust college . . . you know, one of those New England tony places where everyone is called Biff or Skippy or Heather."

Jaymie smiled. "Go on."

"She left there abruptly three years ago. Her official statement was she was leaving to spend more time with her family."

"That's what they always say."

"Political code-speak, right? And it almost always means some kind of scandal hushed up. My friend thinks her downfall was sexy in nature, but c'mon . . . you've seen her. Even her nighties are probably tweed."

Jaymie stifled a chuckle. Austin's cattiness was funny, but she tried not to be malicious about other women. "So, what do *you* think?"

"Financial tomfoolery or academic fraud."

"Like embezzlement, you mean, or her background isn't what she said it was?"

He nodded. "Maybe. My friend is checking those things out. It should be pretty easy to uncover, right?"

"I have a connection or two myself. I may set my own bulldog on it," she said, thinking of the *Howler* reporter she had set on a task. "I know of someone who is particularly good at sniffing out corruption and tracking down its origin."

"Speaking of which . . ." He gave her an embarrassed look. "I needed to trade something for info. So I offered *you*."

"*Me?*"

"Yeah, well, your connections. She'd like an introduction to your editor at the *Howler*."

"Oh, okay. That's actually not a problem."

"Thank goodness," he said, hand over his chest. "I thought I had overstepped."

"No big deal. I'll be happy to introduce your friend to Nan. She's always willing to help a budding reporter."

"Goody. I'll keep digging too, sweetie." He jumped up, sloshing his tea. "Air kisses, and I have to run."

Jaymie sat and finished her tea. This seemed like a long shot, running after President Belcher as a possible suspect. It felt like in Sarah, Ben, Bella, Jacklyn, Erla and Finn she had much better suspects. But Chief Ledbetter had always said it didn't pay to become wedded to one theory.

She got home in time to meet Jocie's school bus. Shannon was taking a study break in the kitchen, poring over her econometrics text, which was loaded in e-format on a tablet. She made notes the old-fashioned way, though, with pen and notebook, saying she remembered stuff better when she wrote it down. Jocie was thrilled to sit at the same table and do her own homework.

Jaymie had filled her slow cooker with all the ingredients for loaded baked potato soup that morning, so all she had to do was add a few last-minute ingredients; dairy didn't do well in a slow cooker, so she added sour cream for the last half hour or so. She cut up a crusty loaf of bread, crumbs shattering and falling to the floor as she sliced into the loaf, and grated some cheddar to sprinkle over the soup. Hoppy and Lilibet raced over and cleaned up the bits of food on the floor.

Who needed a broom when you had animals?

She invited Shannon to stay for dinner. Helmut headed home, so it was just Jakob, Jaymie, Jocie and Shannon. Shannon picked Jakob's brain about the Christmas tree business, and his plans to extend the "crop" to nursery trees for sale to landscaping companies. They talked about the holiday store they hoped to have up and running by next Christmas, and how they would be providing space for local crafters in one section to sell their wares.

After dinner, Shannon stayed to help with the first evening of tree sales. Jocie's two best friends and schoolmates had told her they'd be coming by that evening to get their choice of the best of the trees, so after dinner Jaymie made a big pot of hot chocolate and some hermit cookies, experimenting with a vintage recipe and some fun add-ins, like candy-coated chocolate bits and salted toffee chips. She was definitely going to use the hermit cookie recipe for her column, but she thought maybe she'd make it more holiday-festive with a couple of changes. After baking, the whole cabin smelled like Christmas, and it made her smile.

Jocie's friends Gemma and Peyton arrived with their families to purchase their Christmas trees. Peyton's family, though Jewish, decorated for the holidays, choosing to view it as a form of harmless socialization. Jaymie's stepdaughter showed them how she had decorated her treehouse with brightly colored lights. Then they drank hot cocoa and ate cookies at the picnic table near the tree field while the adults chatted and loaded the trees they had picked. A few other locals came by for the first tree sales of the season, but by eight they were closed and everyone, including Shannon, had gone home.

Jocie was exhausted and slightly feverish. Jaymie came down from putting her to bed and confessed her fears to Jakob. "She's a little warm," she said, plopping down on the sofa beside him. "I hope she's not coming down with anything."

"We'll see in the morning. How warm is she?"

"Very slightly."

"It's probably a normal variation, then," he said. "We'll make sure she's well hydrated in the morning, and see."

"How did you get to be such a smart dad," Jaymie asked, curling up next to him and putting her head on his shoulder.

"I had to learn, and quickly, after Inga left," he said. Jocie's mother, a troubled soul, had left him and her daughter to return to Poland, where she had died shortly after. He didn't speak about her often, but made sure Jocie had photos of her mother, and kept in contact with Inga's family. He and Jocie were going to travel to Poland next summer to visit Inga's parents for a week. "My mom has so many kids she can tell me almost anything I need to know. Other than that . . . books. Lots of books."

"I love that you love books," she said, twisting her neck to look up at his face.

"Even if what I mostly read is arborist reports?"

"Even so."

"How are you doing, about your diorama being ruined?"

She sat up straight and turned on the sofa, sitting cross-legged. She told him about talking to the police, and how she hoped to have it dismantled before the Friday start to Dickens Days.

"How is Bill doing? Have you heard?"

"Dee texted me," she said, of her friend Dee Stubbs, who was a nurse. "He's had all the tests and workups. It wasn't a heart attack, they don't think, but angina. It's serious, though. Val says angina is a symptom of heart disease. He's going to have to take it easier. He's out of the hospital and staying with his daughter — who is a nurse — for a few days."

"Are the police any further with the murder investigation?"

She told him all that had happened that day, things she hadn't had a chance to say since they were thrown into the tree lot business right away when she got home.

"Are you relieved you gave them the note?"

She nodded. "*And* that I've talked to Detective Vestry." She shared what the detective had said about thinking she was smart.

"Of course you are," he said, touching her hair, pushing a lock back off her cheek and tucking it behind her ear. "So . . . do you think Sarah was involved in the murder or not?"

Jaymie frowned and grimaced. "I don't know. My heart says no, but . . . she had so many reasons. This murder is personal. Someone hated him."

"Yeah, but that doesn't narrow it down a whole lot. The man made it his life's work to irritate and anger as many people as possible." He yawned and stretched. "I'm beat. Time for bed for this lad. I'm going to be up and gone early to the casual labor office in Wolverhampton," he said. "We need a couple of more people to work the tree lot. I think I'm beginning to burn the darn candle too far down on both ends."

"I agree, Mr. Müller. Let's call it a day."

⌀ Fifteen ⌀

JOCIE WAS FINE THE NEXT MORNING after a good night's sleep. Jaymie got the little girl off to school and saw Jakob away to the temp agency to meet a couple of guys looking for casual labor. An emergency meeting of the Dickens Days committee had been called, so Jaymie dressed warmly and headed in to Queensville. She parked by Queensville Fine Antiques and walked over to meet Haskell and the others in front of the Emporium. It was a frosty morning with a leaden sky, so Jaymie jammed her hands deep into her pockets, her breath coming out in steamy puffs.

"We need to figure out what to do if the police won't allow us to take down the diorama by Friday," Haskell said. "We can't have the site of a murder as part of our festival!"

"But we can't postpone the festival any longer either," Mrs. Bellwood said.

"I agree," Imogene Frump chimed in, burying her hands in a colorful knitted muff. "We're already into December. We have events planned for the heritage house and attendance is always better after we give out flyers at the Dickens Days festival!"

"And it's our second best moneymaker of the year, after Tea with the Queen!" Mabel Bloombury, treasurer of the historical society, said. "Every week we postpone, our donations go down, and that leaves us with less cash to use for events during the year."

"Hold it, hold it," Jaymie said, putting up her hands. "It's just Tuesday. I agree we need a plan in place before Friday, but there is no saying that the police won't wrap this up and let us take down the diorama well before that."

"*You* need to get busy and solve this problem," Imogene Frump said, eyeing Jaymie. "You've done it before; do it now!"

Jaymie shook her head. That was the problem with becoming locally famous: everyone expected her to wave a magic wand and come up with the solution. "The police are doing the best they can. It takes time to follow up on leads and do interviews and check alibis. Let's hope for the best and plan for the worst."

"I can't believe you people are fussing about your stupid festival when my father is *dead!*"

161

Jaymie turned. Ben Nezer was standing just feet away and had clearly heard everything she had said. "We mean no disrespect to you or your father," Jaymie said carefully. "We have to think of practicalities. I'm so sorry for your loss." She examined his face; was it the face of a killer? Was he overreacting to compensate for guilt?

"*Sorry for my loss!*" he snarled, mimicking her tone in a savage way. "What do you know about *that*?"

"I *am* sorry, Ben."

"You're a bunch of ghouls. Spirit of Christmas . . . bah!" He turned and walked toward the Nezer house as the Dickens Days committee members began to whisper among themselves.

Jaymie ran after him and caught up with him on the other side of the row of pine trees, in sight of the house. She grabbed his coat sleeve, making him stop. He turned and glared down at her. "We don't mean to be insensitive. But we — the members of the Dickens Days committee — *need* to make decisions. I'm sure you're being faced with the same dilemma, you and Bella. You are no doubt having to make plans for your father, a memorial or something?"

He pulled his arm away. "Not yet. The police won't release the body. And there are problems. Things we have to work out."

"I do feel so bad for you. I mean, the last time you saw him was at the party, right? He was . . . having a conflict with several people."

Ben turned and stared at the house, a war of emotions on his face. "I had a complicated relationship with my father, as I'm sure you know. *You've* talked to my mom. She's mad at me because I wanted to make up with Dad."

"What do you mean, mad at you?"

"She told me to leave her alone, if I wanted to be with my dad so much. But it was weird, because the idea of making up with him came from her originally. She didn't want me to miss out on that part of my life."

"Her idea? Oh." Questions swarmed into her mind. Why did Sarah want him to make up with Evan? And what did her note mean? What was it she was trying to warn him not to do that night? "So . . . did you stay after the party?"

"Nah. I was in a hurry to leave. I had . . . I had something to take care of."

"So you didn't stick around? Didn't talk to your dad or . . . anything?"

He looked down at her and frowned, not answering. He turned and began walking toward the Nezer house.

Jaymie caught up with him. "So you're not living in the house, then? I thought maybe you would be, since it's so big. But you're a lawyer?"

He stopped again and turned. "What's with all the questions? You and that gaggle of busybodies hated my father. I get that he was difficult sometimes. But you and Bill Waterman . . ." He paused, blinked and shook his head. "And now my father has been taken away from me."

She examined him closely: was it grief he was expressing, or was it all a fraud? There were no tears, but not everyone cried at such things. Softly, Jaymie said, "I'm sure the police will find out who did it, Ben."

"It won't bring him back. I feel like the only person who misses him like I do is Bella. And even then . . ." He shook his head and turned away. "Bella and me; that's it."

"She truly loved your father?"

He turned swiftly to stare down at her again. "What are you saying?"

"Nothing. I didn't know your dad *or* Bella well, but . . . well, there's quite an age difference. Not that that makes it . . ." She shook her head. There was no way to gracefully say Evan Nezer was an unlovable jerk. "I'm sorry you and your dad didn't get along."

He shrugged and turned away.

"My husband and I left the party," Jaymie said hurriedly, before he could walk away again. "But I understand that Finn Fancombe busted in on you all and confronted your dad, but that after a brief conversation Finn backed off. What do you think your dad said to Finn? Was he going to help him get back into school? Rescind his plagiarism complaint?"

"I don't know. He likely said they could talk later, maybe after the party."

"Who do you think would have done this?"

He shook his head. "I don't know. Dad could be hard to take sometimes, but . . . he meant well."

Meant well . . . that was the family line, it seemed, because Ben had perfectly echoed Bella, as if it had been rehearsed. Jaymie did not believe that; if there was anything Evan Nezer meant, *well* was not it.

"Ben! *Ben!* We need to talk," Jacklyn Marley said, bustling up to them. "Oh, Jaymie. It's you."

"What's up?" Jaymie replied, looking between the two.

"Nothing. We can talk later," Ben said to Jacklyn, and strode away quickly toward the Nezer home.

Jacklyn, dressed in a long, heavy cardigan, turned and glowered at Jaymie, bare hands tucked under her arms. "Thanks a *bunch* for turning me in to the police," she said, moving from foot to foot. Her feet were clad only in slippers.

"They already knew about you hacking into his computer, Jacklyn. I confirmed that I saw you. I told you I wouldn't lie, but I wasn't the one who told them in the first place."

"Hmph."

"Did you discover anything? Is that what you want to talk to Ben about? I mean, he's going to be the heir, isn't he, or do you think Bella will inherit everything?"

"Things are *way* more complicated than that," Jacklyn said with a smirk, then whirled and walked away.

"What do you mean by that?" Jaymie called.

"Never mind," she said, flapping one bare hand in the air. "It'll all come out eventually."

What did Jacklyn know that Jaymie didn't? She stood and contemplated; they had been talking about inheriting, and that was when the ghostwriter said things were a lot more complicated than the inheritance simply being between Bella and Ben. What could she mean by that? Was there someone else in the mix?

With a deep sigh, discouraged and out of sorts, she walked back toward the Emporium.

Valetta came out to the store porch to have her morning break. She waved Jaymie over. "Come have tea!"

Jaymie hopped up the few steps and took the thermos top full of steaming tea into her hands. Brooding, she was silent until Val jostled her and asked what was on her mind. Jaymie poured it all out, her confusion over the many possible motives to kill Evan Nezer, and who was implicated.

"You need to get organized, kiddo," Val said. "Don't you usually make a list of suspects at this point?"

Jaymie glanced over at Val in alarm. "It's kinda scary that I have a 'method' to investigate murder. What is going on in my life?"

"What's going on in this *town*?" Val said, casting a cynical gaze over the village. "Maybe until something happened we never knew about all the dark undercurrents in Queensville. Or maybe this is all random crap. However . . . setting aside that, I'm going to get you a notepad and pen, and we're going to work this out."

"And you're going to tell me if the police saw anything on the CCTV footage."

"Yeah. That's a whole 'nother story. I'll tell you in a moment."

Valetta made a fresh pot of tea and got them proper mugs. Thermos tea was okay in a pinch, but there was nothing like a fresh brew to fire the little gray cells of the brain, as Poirot was known to call them. Valetta handed Jaymie a pen and pad of paper, and together they sat in the Adirondack chairs on the store porch.

"So what is it about the CCTV you were going to tell me?" Jaymie asked.

"*Someone* was smart enough to smear the camera lens with peanut butter, even though it's mounted at the top of the roofline. They did it in such a methodical way that they first did the lens of the camera that would have caught them getting up on the roof, and *then* did the one pointing toward the village green."

"That had to be the killer, then, or an accomplice." She paused, then with a sigh said, "So that means the camera caught nothing."

"Not a thing. The peanut butter trick was done earlier, we think the night before."

Jaymie set her tea aside and hopped down the porch steps, out onto the street, neatly avoiding Edith, Lyle Stubbs's girlfriend, who was likely returning from a shopping trip. She turned to look up to where she now knew the front-facing camera was. *And* Jacklyn's windows overlooking the village green. Could the ghostwriter have clambered out her window and done the peanut butter trick? Interesting thought, but if they conjectured that the camera lens was smeared by whoever killed Evan, what was Jacklyn Marley's motive other than pure spite? It could not have been in response to anything she found on the computer because Jaymie now knew that the murder setup had been planned before that night. She returned to the porch and picked up her tea.

Valetta had watched her but didn't comment. "Unfortunately we had no reason to monitor the footage since the arson, so we didn't find out about the smudged lens until Detective Vestry came to have a look."

"We'll figure it out the old-fashioned way." Jaymie tapped the pen against her bottom lip. "One big question I have is if the arson of the cider booth was related to the murder or not." She jotted down her question at the top of the page. "For now I'm going to ignore it, but I have a feeling it's connected. So . . ." Jaymie looked both ways and hunkered down over the pad of paper. "In this case there are so many people who had a motive because Nezer was such a pill. It goes without saying that I know Bill did not kill Evan, but it almost looks like things were being done to make it appear that Bill is guilty."

"What do you mean?"

"Like, planting Nezer in the diorama with holly and a pudding mould."

"That would point more toward you, though, wouldn't it?"

"Maybe. Though Bill is the one who constructed and painted it, and helped me move it into place. So, let's see . . ." Jaymie started jotting down names and motives and anything else she thought of.

Her list started to take shape:

One: Bella Nezer. The wife is always a suspect, and maybe she inherits. Not sure yet about that.

Two: Ben Nezer. Again, family is always suspect. He had been estranged from his father until recently, and he, too, may inherit. His mother is certain he'll get the house because it is the ancestral Nezer residence.

Three: Jacklyn Marley. They were feuding about money that she claims he owed her from book royalties, and may have found something out from his computer. But . . . Nezer dying would complicate things. Or would it? Maybe Jacklyn felt she could work with his inheritor(s) better than him.

Valetta interrupted Jaymie there and pointed to Jacklyn's name. "And . . ." she whispered, "I've heard that once Nezer was done with Jacklyn Marley's services he got her fired from her teaching job at WC. So . . . revenge as a motive?"

"Yes! I forgot about that. But I still don't know *why* she was fired." Jaymie added that information with a question mark after her annotation.

"Something to find out, I guess."

"I know one person I can ask," Jaymie said, and got out her cell phone. She wrote a text to Austin and pressed Send. She continued with the list. "And speaking of being fired . . ." She jotted down the next entry on her list.

Four: Finn Fancombe. He was barred from getting his master's at WC after Nezer successfully accused him of plagiarism . . . after he accused Nezer of plagiarism first! (What gives with that?)

Five: Sarah Nezer. Her ex had somehow compelled her to accept virtually nothing in their divorce. Did he have something on her?

"I'd forgotten about that until I just now jotted it down," Jaymie mused, twiddling the pen between her fingers. She blew on her hands to warm them up. "I still can't figure out why a woman would walk away from such a long marriage with nothing, not even, apparently, her own heirlooms. And she is *still* angry about how he treated her." A thought occurred to her and she jotted it down.

"What does that say?" Valetta asked, squinting over her shoulder.

Jaymie had written a question: *Does Ben inherit, and will that help Sarah?* "Sarah Nezer thinks her son will inherit everything, like I said. That could be a valid motive for her to kill her ex-husband, even beyond any personal animosity. She could have done it for her son's benefit, which might indirectly benefit her." She wrote another note. "Plus, there seems to be an awful long history of animosity between Sarah and Evan. Anger buried can distill into something pretty potent."

"Sounds like one of those true-crime documentaries: *Anger Buried!* Anyhow, is that everyone?"

"Well, no . . . I mean, there *are* others. Oh, yes! One important one, as a matter of fact." She jotted down a name, then added his motive.

Six: Pastor Vaughan Inkerman. He found out at the party that Nezer was the cruel reviewer who had panned his book.

"Has any writer ever killed a reviewer?"

"Don't know. I've read some pretty cruel reviews online. It gets pretty personal at times. My writer friend, Melody Heath, told me it takes her a day to get over a rotten review. She tries not to read them, but sometimes a writer has to, to get promotional quotes." Jaymie chewed on the end of the pen. "However, if we believe that the murder was planned before the party, then Inkerman is out of it, yes? Because he didn't know about Nezer being the nasty reviewer until the party. I will say, from what Nezer said at the party it sounds like he knew something about the pastor, something unsavory in his past."

Valetta cocked her head to one side. "If Inkerman was a *clever* killer he would make it appear that he only discovered at the party that Nezer was the nasty reviewer, when really he knew ahead of time."

"That would take some acting. The pastor seems open and emotional."

"*Seems,*" Valetta emphasized. "But his anger would have festered, you know? Planning the crime gave him satisfaction, foreseeing his foe's downfall."

"Ooh, that's good. But his emotionality *seems* so genuine."

Valetta shrugged.

"And we'd have to believe that a man who wrote a book about creating your best life using scripture as a guide to help folks is capable of murder."

"You never know what's going on inside someone's mind or life," Val said.

Jaymie eyed her. "You do have a darkness to your soul, don't you?"

Valetta waggled her salt-and-pepper eyebrows and straightened her glasses. "Who knows what evil lurks in the heart of man? The pharmacist knows!"

"Where *do* you get your sayings?"

"That was from an old uncle of mine. Something about a radio show back in the thirties."

"So who does know what evil lurks in the heart of man?"

"The Shadow knows."

"Ah. Okay. Anyway, we have to figure out who, among all these folks I've listed, were capable of the murder."

"With or without an accomplice. There is no saying that the killing wasn't done by a combination of people, like Sarah and Ben."

Sarah and Ben . . . like what the note warned, not to do it that night. The note he never got because Jaymie forgot about it. Jaymie's phone buzzed and she looked at it. "It's Mrs. Stubbs. I'd better take this."

"And I have to reopen the pharmacy. I have dosettes to fill that have to be delivered this afternoon." Valetta gathered their mugs and reentered the store.

Mrs. Stubbs, as usual, got cranky trying to understand Jaymie on the phone. The conversation was slow and a little repetitive, but after some awkwardness Jaymie got the message: Mrs. Stubbs had invited Pastor Inkerman to tea in her suite and wanted Jaymie to come as well. Two p.m. "I'll be there!" she said, and they hung up.

She checked her text messages. There were a slew from Nan, and it seemed the reporter had come through, big time. Jaymie read them all, then digested them. Evan Nezer had died by blunt force trauma to the head, a kind of crescent-shaped wound repeated, like the edge of the head of a hammer, or some other rounded tool. And he did not die in the diorama. Nan made a punning reference to Jaymie's *die-o-rama* that she did not appreciate.

There was evidence that he was transported there in a wheelbarrow or some other one-wheeled cart, then dragged into place. The earth was somewhat frozen, and they weren't sure if the cart had one wheel, two, or even four. And it didn't help anyway, of course, because every single homeowner in Queensville had a wheelbarrow or handcart.

Somehow the reporter had wormed his or her way into seeing the official police reports. Bella claimed she was sleeping and didn't hear anything. Evan was in his nightshirt, though; hadn't she felt or heard him get up in the night? Whenever Jakob got up, Jaymie awoke. That was odd. And didn't she miss him in the morning and wonder where he was?

Erla's official statement said much the same. Exhausted after the party, she had gone to bed and stayed there. There was no further information. The official police statement didn't help Jaymie at all. Incidentally, in case she was wondering, Nan texted, Evan Nezer had no outstanding lawsuits going at the present time, so there was no one angry at him at that moment for a legal action.

Becca was at the store today. It was Georgina's day off, and she was on a holiday-related shopping trip with her brother. The sisters therefore had lunch together at the store, ordered in from the

Queensville Inn, and then Jaymie stayed for a lesson from Becca about how to evaluate the condition of vintage china. Though she had already had lessons in how to recognize hand-painted versus transfer patterns, and other elements, her sister was an expert in quality, having been in the replacement china business for over twenty years. Jaymie learned a whole new vocabulary, including *glaze pop* and *glaze skip*, flaws caused by bubbles in the glaze popping during firing, or glaze that was missed in the painting process. She learned about crazing—the fine web of cracks in the glaze that could become discolored with time—and decoration wear, where silver or gold trim is worn away with time and use.

"Finally, I always give my china dishes a good listen," Becca said. She dug under the desk for a little saucer. "Have a look at this and tell me what's wrong with it."

Jaymie looked it over. "I can't find anything," she said, handing it back. "I think you're trying to trick me."

Becca smiled and adjusted her glasses. "Nope. Here. Listen." She brought out another identical saucer and pinged it with her fingernail. She then did the same to the first piece, but the sound was different. "Look, here—" She pulled over a lighted magnifying glass and positioned it. Jaymie finally saw what she couldn't see before, a very fine hairline fracture, invisible except under magnification. "I knew it was there by listening."

"Wow. Cracks that you can't see with the naked eye." She sighed and stood, tugging down her tunic top. "I have to go. I have a tea party to attend with a vicar," she said in a fake snooty accent. She rolled her eyes. "Actually with Mrs. Stubbs and Pastor Inkerman, author of *Living Your Best Life Through Scripture*." She snickered. "Toodles, sis. Hey . . . do you want to come to girls' night tomorrow night?"

"Could I?" Her eyes lit up behind her glasses and her lips turned up in a smile. "Tell you what, can we do it at our Queensville house?"

"Let me ask the other girls. Can you pull it together by tomorrow night?"

"Are you kidding? No problem."

Becca was a neat freak, so the house would be super clean, and she was extremely organized, so planning snacks and drinks for five or so would be no big deal.

"I think I'll drop over at the house right now, before heading to the inn." Jaymie walked out to her car. Before heading out she sent a group text to Heidi, Valetta and Bernie asking if they could do girls' night at the Queensville house, since Becca would like to be included. She then drove to their Queensville home, parking in the parking lane behind. The police were long gone, of course. Jaymie pushed through the wrought iron gate and examined the line of holly bushes she had planted a couple of years before, and that had just started producing berries.

She had carefully followed advice to plant a male holly bush for every few females so the females would produce berries. She had deliberately made it an ornamental choice: three female bushes, then a male, then three more, then a male, then three more females, for a total of eleven bushes along the fence line separating the Leighton home from the bed-and-breakfast next door.

She approached the holly bush that had been savaged; it was the very first one, next to the fence. She squatted down in the frosty grass beside it. Pam had said the damage happened mid-afternoon. It would take a lot of guts to do that, when you could easily be seen. Jaymie examined the damage. The person hadn't even had to enter the lawn, they had crouched down, reached into the yard through the wrought iron fence bars, and pulled or cut the holly branches. She squinted; yes, cut. The vandal had come prepared and had used scissors or shears, cutting a thick branch near the center so they would have lots of holly for their jolly holiday murder scene.

She shivered and stood, looking around. All of the other yards along the parking lane had wood fences. If someone crouched they wouldn't likely be seen at all. It wasn't as risky a thing to do as it had first seemed. It had likely taken under two minutes and could, quite literally, have been done by anyone.

But why? There was a cold well of anger in setting the scene of the crime.

⌔ Sixteen ⌔

JAYMIE PROCEEDED INTO THE HOUSE and looked around. The place was immaculate, as it always was when Becca and Kevin were in residence. Her older sister was tidy by nature, whereas Jaymie was a little messier. She checked the parlor. It was already decorated for the holiday season with some of the Leighton family's prized decorations out on tables: the brass candle chime set, a ceramic house with Santa poised to come down the chimney, and brass candlesticks on the mantel. It was festive, but not overdone.

When compared with the Nezer home it was humble, but she preferred her own hearth to even Bella Nezer's impeccable taste in furnishings and Christmas decor.

So they'd have a few Christmas drinks and some Christmas-themed snacks. Of course her mind turned to cooking. Maybe a cheese ball, traditional at Christmas, and festive if it was decorated with olives and pimento to look like holly. And some sweets . . . she'd have to think on that.

She was such a homebody, she thought as she retrieved a book from her shelf upstairs. As she descended, her mind returned to the murder. The crime, even down to the staging of the scene, felt domestic in nature, and yet at the same time slightly theatrical, including the peanut butter on the camera lens. That was such a do-it-yourself way to cloud the camera, and yet ingenious. Who would think of that? *She* might, if she were trying to hide her identity. It did make her think that whoever killed Evan had also been the arsonist, though. How many criminals did they have roaming the village streets at any given time?

She checked her watch; ten to two. She'd better get moving.

At exactly one minute to two she pulled into the Queensville Inn lot and parked in a visitor's slot. There was a luxury sedan in a lovely mink color parked halfway over two spaces; the license plate was PSTR INK. So, the gentleman had already arrived. Jaymie pasted on a smile and made her way to Mrs. Stubbs's room, tapped on the door and entered. Inn staff had created a little dining area near her big double sliding doors that looked out onto the terrace. Centered on a round table was a vase of pretty burgundy chrysanthemums on a gold tablecloth. Gold and red leaves scudded past and piled up against the glass.

Mrs. Stubbs waved her over. "Jaymie, I'm so pleased you happened to drop in! This is Pastor Inkerman. We were having tea and discussing his book." A copy of *Living Your Best Life Through Scripture* lay on the table between them.

The pastor stood, laying his napkin on the table, and bowed slightly. "Good day, Mrs. Müller. We met at the Nezer party." His intended smile looked a little more like a grimace. "That was . . . that was an unfortunate night," he said, sitting back down.

"How so, Pastor?" Mrs. Stubbs asked. "Jaymie, pull up a chair and sit and help yourself. We have some pastries provided by Pierre," she added, speaking of the Inn's French-Canadian pastry chef.

The pastor waved one hand, flapping it disconsolately. "That *man*, Evan Nezer. He was a dreadful person!"

"I heard about some terrible accident involving him," the woman said as she lifted the heavy teapot.

Jaymie worried through the pouring but would not take away Mrs. Stubbs's hostess duties. Older folks lost so much along the aging path that retaining dignity was vital.

"Yes, he was . . ." The pastor leaned across the table and softly said, " . . . *murdered!*" He sat back, a look between delicious horror and self-satisfaction on his blandly handsome face. "I cannot help but think it was the result of a lifetime of putting people down and giving a negative energy to the world. One cannot live that way without reaping what you have sown."

"Yes, I do know he was murdered," Jaymie said. "I'm the one who found him in the display I had set up for Dickens Days."

"Oh, my dear, I'm so sorry," the pastor said. His cheeks colored a delicate peach. "I . . . I didn't mean to make light of it."

"It's all right. It wasn't a pleasant occurrence, but he wasn't a pleasant man. I don't mean to be cruel, but it appears his death suited his life. The only times I saw him he was berating a handyman, and at the party he seemed in conflict with just about everyone," Jaymie said, pouring milk into her tea. She glanced up at him. "I know he upset *you* badly. You found out at the party he was a critic who slammed your book?"

"What's worse is, I discovered that people I know—people I *trust*—already knew that he was the reviewer who trashed LYBLTS."

"Do you mean your college colleagues, the college president, provost and dean?"

He nodded, swept back his blonde hair and took in a long deep breath. "He was a broken human being who appeared to enjoy hurting folks. I can't help but think that someone he hurt decided to strike back at him."

"Interesting thought. So you think maybe someone he injured killed him?"

The pastor blenched at her frank words. "I . . . it was a sudden thought."

"Did you know him well?" Jaymie asked, exchanging a glance with Mrs. Stubbs.

"He was a professor at Wolverhampton College, and I'm the interfaith chaplain there. As such, we often came into contact at faculty events. He was so . . . so *encouraging* at first when I was writing my book. It felt like an utter betrayal when I discovered he was the author of that *scurrilous* attack."

Jaymie remembered that Nezer had implied there was a whole lot in the pastor's background that belied his "best life through scripture" message. He used the word *affairs*, but that could cover everything from a personal relationship to financial misdeeds. It was difficult to know how to approach that subject, though. "What made you write the book?"

"I've . . . I've suffered through so much in life," he said, his expression troubled. "It hasn't been easy. I never had a father, and was a foster child, pushed from home to home."

"I'm so sorry," Jaymie said. "Did you never know your parents?"

"My mother was too young to look after me when I was born. I knew her, but she wasn't able to take care of me."

"Was foster care tough?"

"At times, but I finally landed in one where faith was the bedrock. They helped me through so much, and I'm grateful. The book is my way of, hopefully, paying forward that faith is central to living your best life." He opened it to a front-matter page and pointed to a simple dedication to the Inkerman family.

"So being a pastor helped? Your faith must be a comfort in times of trouble."

"It's the only thing that got me through sometimes."

"Through what? I don't mean to be blunt, but do you mean the foster care system or . . . something else?"

"Much of it is personal." He tipped his head up and took a deep breath. "But I wasn't always . . . I mean, at one time I was lost. Profoundly, utterly lost. I've made mistakes. I was given another chance." He smiled. "I'm proof that faith and humility are life-changing."

Nice words, but he seemed to be dancing around the issue. She should press for more; she should ask him what "mistakes" he made. She slumped and acknowledged the truth: it just wasn't in her. She'd never be a reporter, that was for sure. Still, she must soldier on. He was a suspect. Where was her backbone? "I'm so sorry you had that trouble at the party," she said, coming at it from a different angle. Motive was one thing, but opportunity was more important. "Where did you go after your argument with Professor Nezer?"

"I went to church," he said softly.

"Church?"

He colored pink on his high cheekbones and swept his blonde hair off his high forehead. He seemed prone to fluctuations in color, and Jaymie sympathized. She had always been an easy blusher. It was getting better as she got older, but still it happened from time to time.

"Reverend Gillis of the Methodist church is my spiritual advisor. I banged on his door very upset. *That* is a gentleman who lives the scriptures. Even though it was late, he took me in and gave me comfort."

"It's nice to have someone to turn to," Mrs. Stubbs said, her tone bracing. "Come on, you two, I ordered the most lovely pastries from Pierre and I don't want them to go to waste."

They chatted about other things while they drank tea and ate pastries, but Jaymie kept coming back to his statement that he had sought help from his spiritual advisor. Nice deflection, but that didn't mean he was there all night.

Jaymie heard a faint snore and glanced over at her friend; Mrs. Stubbs had dropped off to sleep, her head sagging sideways. She smiled, then met Pastor Inkerman's gaze. "Interfaith chaplain: what exactly does that mean?"

"It means I hold group meetings for those of many faiths. Or no faith at all. It sounds contradictory, I know. I have spoken with Sikh visitors, Muslim students, a Buddhist or two, and Jewish students when their rabbi is away. But I've also comforted troubled students and staff of no faith. Some of my most faithful—pardon the pun—attendees are agnostics and atheists, folks who need to talk to someone."

"It sounds lovely," Jaymie said gently. It was what the world needed more of, conversation, not arguments. Honest differences of opinion openly stated, debates where both sides respected the thoughts and beliefs of the other. "Is that what led you to write your book?"

He frowned down into his teacup. His blonde forelock drooped and he swept it back. "No, I think it's the other way around. Writing the book led me to a better understanding of my interfaith duties. As I read the scriptures I began to listen to the heart of them, not just the literal words." He looked up and met her gaze with an open expression. "We can't follow scripture literally. It was written for a different time, a different world, and written by humans, after all, even if we believe it was inspired by revelation from God. We are all different people now, and I hope we're learning from our past mistakes." He sighed. "The book came from my yearning to do better, to *be* better."

She felt the tug of his gentleness; she wanted to believe every word he said. But she didn't know him. Was it genuine, or was he espousing what he thought he ought, as a chaplain? She hated to be cynical, but it would be too easy to be taken in by her wish to believe in the goodness of people. Some folks told the truth, some lied, and some thought they were telling the truth about themselves while hiding a lie. "You spent the night at the pastor's home?"

He looked startled and blinked rapidly. "Well, no, of course not. I . . . I went home."

Interesting pause. "Where do you live, Pastor? In Queensville?" Jaymie took a sip of her tea, watching him over the rim of the cup.

"Wolverhampton. The college has kindly given me a house as part of my pay."

"A house! Are you married?"

"No. I've never been blessed with a wife." He colored faintly. "I've been too shy with ladies, and too involved with my work. Unless a lady is aggressive I don't . . ." He shrugged. "I don't understand romance, I suppose. And . . . and it's difficult sometimes for a man of religion to make the leap between the professional and the personal."

"So how do you look after a house on your own?"

"Oh, I'm *quite* domestic. I learned early to look after myself, and like cooking, part of the reason I enjoy your column so much. I find cleaning and tidying meditative, almost. I'm a neat old bachelor by now, I'm afraid."

"Do you ever wish you'd married?"

"I wish it often, but unmarried young ladies are so . . . choosy. And a pastor is not first in their choices when they are swiping left or right on their cell phone dating apps." He leaned forward with some eagerness. "I noticed you had a friend there, that night, at the party, a young lady named Heidi? Is she . . . I mean—"

"Is she married? No."

"Where does she work?"

"She, uh . . ." Jaymie never discussed Heidi's family wealth, and didn't know how to explain her lack of a job. "Are you interested in her?"

"She appeared so ethereal, so lovely, like a beautiful butterfly among moths. But I couldn't work up my courage to speak with her."

"And there was quite a bit going on that night. You were . . . upset."

"Yes, there was that."

Jaymie was virtually certain that the pastor was not the type of guy Heidi would go for a relationship with, and couldn't encourage him.

But he pulled his wallet out of his jacket pocket and fished around for a card. He handed it over to Jaymie. "Please, give her my card. I'd be most grateful if you would speak with her on my behalf."

"I can't promise anything, Pastor. She's a very outgoing woman. Maybe someone more retiring would suit you better?"

"I think the opposite," Mrs. Stubbs said, rousing herself from her catnap. "It has been my experience that retiring gentlemen are perfectly suited to outgoing ladies." She smiled. "My husband was a quiet sort and left all of the social engagement to me. It worked out splendidly. Perhaps, Pastor, you should be attending local go-go dancing bars to find suitably vivacious potential mates."

"Tell me more about your work at the college, Pastor," Jaymie said, giving her mischievous friend a censorious look.

He was enthusiastic about his work, and he was far more worldly than he at first seemed. He had taken his Master of Divinity degree from the University of Edinburgh, where he had lived for several years. Jaymie gained respect for him as they chatted, and she began to sincerely hope he was not the killer. But . . . he was as domestic as she had surmised the killer was, and the Dickens angle . . . that might appeal to someone who so loathed Nezer's Scroogey ways. Also, she had seen him at the back door later, so even after he stormed out he was still around. Maybe he came back after speaking to Reverend Gillis.

"This has been delightful, ladies," he said, standing. "But I must go. I have a class this evening and early office hours tomorrow."

"I'll walk out with you," she said, winking at Mrs. Stubbs, who winked back.

They departed, stepping out through the sliding doors and walking to the parking lot together, stopping by his car.

"You are an inquisitive and intelligent young lady." He smiled. "I know all about your exploits, you know, from the *Wolverhampton Weekly Howler*. I'll confess, as shocking as it is, I am a bit of a true-crime aficionado." He blushed. "Oh, not that I'm a fan of crime, you know, but . . . I'm interested in the solutions, and you do seem to find the solutions."

His tone . . . was there insinuation there? It was hard to tell, and his face still held the same cheerful expression. "This one is a doozy, though, Pastor," she said, seizing the opportunity to speak of it with him. "The murder of Professor Nezer. It seems that there are more people who wanted him dead than wanted him alive."

"I hope you don't include me in your suspicions," he said, looking alarmed. He leaned slightly toward her. "So *many* people are keeping secrets! Like Ben Nezer and Jacklyn Marley."

"What are they keeping quiet?"

"I thought you might know already," he said with a significant look, brow arched, eyes sparkling. "I married them a month ago, in the college chapel."

❧ Seventeen ❧

"BEN NEZER AND JACKLYN MARLEY ARE *MARRIED*?"

"Oh, dear, I shouldn't have said anything." he said, two fingers to his lips. "I'm a pastor; I know how to keep a secret, truly, but . . . I don't see why those two young people have not celebrated their marriage. It was all I could do at the Nezer party to keep from shouting it aloud."

"You did have other things on your mind," Jaymie said in disbelief. Did he not remember that she was there and knew what concerned him most that night? His violent confrontation with Ben's father at the party kept him from celebrating anything.

"But it is such a *wonderful* event, a blessing, truly," he said with a sunny smile. "I suppose they became acquainted when she worked for his father, you know . . . in and out of the house all the time. Very intelligent young woman."

"You know her well?" Jaymie asked, trying to regain her bearings in the middle of a puzzling conversation.

"I knew her when she worked at WC."

"I have only met her a couple of times, I must say." And one of those times was when she was hacking into the murder victim's computer.

She didn't want to alarm the pastor at how grave and disturbing she considered the news of their marriage, and the new complexion it put on anything to do with their interactions with Nezer. She would never have put those two together. But maybe that was Inkerman's intent. If he had killed Evan, the shocking news of the marriage would deflect nicely, given Jacklyn Marley's past fractious relationship with Evan Nezer. And the pastor had already commented on Jaymie's investigative habits. Perhaps he was trying to steer her away from his own involvement.

He couldn't know that the opposite had instead happened; from being one of the last suspects on her list, this conversation had pushed him up near the top. "What do you think of her?"

"I don't know her well but she's a very attractive young lady. And a good teacher, from what students have told me. Very knowledgeable. Being considered for a full-time position, too."

"Until Evan Nezer got her fired," Jaymie blurted out.

He looked dumbstruck and placed one hand on his chest, in a theatrical expression of alarm. "Is that truly what happened? I knew she was let go, but . . . are you *sure* it was Evan's doing?"

"That's what I've heard."

"How unfortunate. And how complicated. I can't imagine how Ben dealt with his father after the man got his new wife fired."

"You said they married a month ago?"

"Yes, about that. I must go," he said suddenly, clicking the lock release of his car and grabbing the handle, jerking the door open. "I can't have my class and my appointments left waiting."

"But, Pastor, if I could just—"

"No, no, I *must* go." He hurriedly got into the car, started it, and backed out, Jaymie having to jump out of the way to keep her toes from being run over.

Her mind working furiously, Jaymie got into her car, turning up the heat full blast to warm her hands, which had gotten icy as she stood talking to the pastor. She tried to separate her new strong suspicions of the pastor—brought about by her own cynical read of his motives in telling her about the marriage, and his suggestions that Ben must have been angry when his father got Jacklyn fired from the college—from reality. None of this changed the fact that the pastor's motive seemed weak to her, anger over a lousy book review.

Unless there was something more she wasn't seeing.

She absently checked her phone. Heidi, Bernie and Val had all said yes to having girls' night at the Queensville house. She also got a text from Austin saying he had more info if she'd like it. Since she now wanted to ask him more about Jacklyn's time at WC, she checked her watch—she still had an hour and a quarter before she had to meet Jocie's school bus—and texted him to meet her back in the food court and she'd buy him a tea.

"Sometimes I feel like I spend most of my time in you," she said, patting the dash of her lovely newish SUV.

She returned to WC, met Austin at the Tim Hortons, and splurged on a ten-pack of Timbits as well as steeped tea. The food court was crowded, with giddy groups of young people, their loud conversations melding into a babble of youthful noise, interspersed by serious students trying to study for upcoming exams. They found a table away from the others by the big atrium windows again. Clouds were bunching up on the horizon, piling like dark gray mounds of mashed potatoes gone bad. Food metaphors, even ugly ones, were never far from Jaymie's mind.

"Okay, whatta you got?" Jaymie asked, popping a Timbit in her mouth and washing it down with tea. She was going to float home . . . or waddle, given how many treats she had eaten and how much tea she had drunk.

"Well, my dear," he said, leaning across the table, "my college reporter friend has discovered that as it turns out, President Belcher was *fired* from her last job—or 'resigned,' air quotes—because she was accused of taking bribes."

"Bribes? In a college? In exchange for what?"

"My source has not discovered that yet. Still working on it."

"Okay, wait—" Jaymie got out her phone and texted Nan with a very brief description of the info, asking if her bulldog reporter would follow up. "Now, what do you know about the two others, the college provost and dean, Carter Crossley and Andy Markham?"

"Those three are always together," Austin said, plucking a chocolate Timbit from the little carrying box. "I'm just a student, but even I know it's not normal for the president, the provost and a dean to be in 'meetings' all the time."

"What would that have to do with anything?" Jaymie thought for a long moment. Evan Nezer had obviously gone out of his way to hurt people. He seemed both power-hungry and malicious, a bad combination if ever there was one. That might be why Ben and Jacklyn hadn't told him that they were married, the fear that Evan, out of spite, would find a way to destroy Jacklyn even beyond refusing to pay her and getting her fired from the college. Was he holding other information, some secret beyond Belcher's bribery? And maybe that was what Jacklyn was actually looking for on his computer at the party, information Nezer might be holding on to, either to ruin her or the college president.

Austin drank more of his tea. "I say, if Belcher did it before she'll do it again, you know? The bribery thing."

"You don't think she'd be frightened off from doing anything illegal? I mean, if I'd been caught doing something, the last thing I'd do was repeat it."

"Honey, you should know that's not how humans work," he said with a lopsided grin. "Folks always think, *Well, I did it wrong last time but I've learned. This time I won't get caught.*" He popped a white sugarcoated Timbit into his mouth, powdered sugar puffing out in a cloud.

Jaymie nodded. "You are very wise, Austin," she said, smiling across the table at him.

"Call me Obi Wan Austin," he snickered, then popped *another* Timbit in his mouth. He pushed the box away, chewed, swallowed, then said, "Girl, those are lethal! Like crack for a chunky boy like me."

She laughed out loud and impulsively asked, "Would you come to girls' night tomorrow night with my friends?" She felt heat rise to her face and knew her cheeks were going rosy. Eyes wide, she said, "I didn't mean . . . I'm not calling you one of the girls, you know. Of course, if you come it's not a 'girls' night' anymore. I'd love you to meet Heidi and Bernie and my sister, Becca." She paused in consternation. "I hope I didn't offend you."

Austin took a long gulp of tea and smiled across the table at her. "You'd have to do something a lot worse than calling me one of the girls to offend me, Jaymie. I know what you mean, and I would *love* to come to girls' night, even though I'm not one of the girls." He shrugged. "But I don't have a car. I'm living with my mom. She lets me borrow her car to get to school, but she uses it to get to work in the evening."

"I could pick you up! C'mon . . . say yes!"

"In that case, if it's really no trouble, I'd love it!" He took her phone and added his address to his contact information.

He had one more class he had to get to, and then he was going to talk to the reporter for the school newspaper to ask if she'd found anything out. He departed, and Jaymie cleared the table and headed out too. She decided to swing past the office to see if there were any courses she'd be interested in, so she headed down a long hall, only having to ask the way once before coming to a glass and brick central foyer, with big glass doors that led to the parking lot. She had always come in another way, and so had not been here before.

She entered the office that served both the academic and technical branches of the college and asked about extramural classes, and was given the fall course calendar. She flipped through it, noting cooking classes, wreath making, sewing, and other craft classes. Voices raised out in the hall drew her attention. Slinking to the doorway, she peeked out. Finn Fancombe was there, speaking to President Belcher. Her two sidekicks were coming toward them, but not before Finn spoke loudly.

"I want to know what you knew, and when you knew it!" he said loudly. "Nezer told me something at the party. He said he didn't *want* to accuse me of plagiarism, but that you wanted me gone 'cause I was causing too much trouble about the damn campaign you and your goons started to get that conservative asshat talk radio turd to come here to teach."

Nezer was trying to placate Finn? Why? The president, a look of alarm on her lined face, backed away from the young man. She said something, but Jaymie couldn't hear her. Some of what Finn said jibed with things Austin had heard, that the college wanted to be rid of him because he was a troublemaker, a protester against the college leadership.

"You are *lying!*" he bellowed in response to whatever she had said to him. "I thought Nezer was the bad guy, but now I know the truth."

This was intriguing. Crossley and Markham approached from either side and grabbed his arms. Finn shook them off. "I've seen the letters, you know," he said, facing the college president. "The emails, telling Professor Nezer why you wanted him to say I plagiarized. He didn't want to do it, but you *made* him."

"That's absurd," President Belcher said, her tone just the right amount of condescending and placating. "I know you're upset that Evan is dead. We all are, but—"

"No, you wanted rid of me because I'm not going to be silenced. I won't let you turn this wonderful accepting place into some repressive think-tank thought-police state for right wing thugs!"

Jaymie's eyes widened. She strained to hear as the college president muttered to her two colleagues. She could only hear part of what she said.

". . . and get *rid* of him," Belcher muttered.

"No, I will *not* be silenced!" Finn howled.

Finn backed away, hands spread, as the college president urged them to tackle the grad student.

"Get him out of here!" Belcher yelled. "I don't care how."

They were unwilling, Jaymie was pleased to note, and eyed the college president with uncertainty verging on rebellion.

Belcher, her goons mutinous, turned back to Finn. "Okay, look . . . I can help you. Now that Professor Nezer is gone, we can forget the whole unsavory business. You can resume your master's study."

That was a bribe, and it made Jaymie wonder, had Belcher ordered the murder of Evan Nezer? As far-fetched as it seemed, maybe it was the solution. A bell tolled the hour. She had to get going, and soon, Jaymie thought, glancing down at her watch. However . . . this was too interesting.

"I know what your problem is," Finn said, calmer now. Some students wandered past and paused, watching the strange tableau. One raised her cell phone, videoing the confrontation, Jaymie guessed. "You're afraid that all the dirty laundry is gonna be aired, now that Nezer is dead. You shoulda thought of that long ago. You should have talked to me and made this offer before Professor Nezer was dead. Now every word you wrote to him is going to be out there, and everyone is going to know how corrupt this college presidency is. All the graft, all the bribes, all the underhanded dealings. And me? I'm not going to need you, once it's all out in the open. Because I was right all along."

He started to walk toward the doors as Belcher stood watching, unable to react, her fists clenching and unclenching. But he paused and turned back, his face shadowed at that distance. "I know you're worried about what Ben knows and will do or say, now that his father is dead. But you know what? You should be *more* afraid of *me!*" He whirled and left, with Markham, the dean, trailing him out of the building.

What the heck did he mean by that? Jaymie exited the office into the hall, noting that President Belcher and the provost, Carter Crossley, had their heads together and were talking intently. Pastor Inkerman came in the front doors accompanied, surprisingly, by Jacklyn Marley. He hailed President Belcher and took Jacklyn's arm, rushing her over to the college president.

He said something that Jaymie couldn't hear, but whatever it was, the college president reacted badly, stiffening and whirling. She pushed past Jaymie into the office, yelling that she was not to be disturbed for the rest of the day. Jaymie went out to speak with the pastor.

"Jacklyn, Pastor Inkerman . . . what's going on?"

The woman shook her head. "It's nothing. The pastor thinks I should be able to get my job back, that's all. I told him no, but . . ."

Inkerman, his expression grave, said, "There are things going on here and I'm not pleased. Not pleased at *all*. This college should be a place of freedom . . . freedom to protest *and* to tell the truth." His cheeks went a dark pink. "I have a few things to say to the president and she is going to listen."

"Vaughan, please, don't do this," Jacklyn said, her eyes filling with tears. She grabbed his jacket sleeve and tugged it. "She's not going to listen. And you could end up getting fired."

"Did you see Finn Fancombe on his way out of here?"

Jacklyn nodded. "Yes. Things are getting . . . tense."

Jaymie leaned in and murmured to Jacklyn, "Did you tell Finn things? Did you find stuff on Evan Nezer's computer?"

She nodded, tears dribbling down her cheeks.

"What *is* going on, Jacklyn?" Jaymie said, puzzled by the tumult that seemed to be surrounding the pastor, Jacklyn, Finn and the college leadership. Her phone was buzzing, but she ignored it. The real-life drama going on was far more enticing. Should she say something to Jacklyn about her marriage to Ben? Or would that be betraying the pastor's trust? She opened her mouth to speak, but Jacklyn followed the pastor into the office, and moments later they all disappeared behind a door that slammed shut.

Jaymie was left alone in the echoing hallway. It was time to get home; she just had time before Jocie's bus delivered her.

• • •

THE CHRISTMAS TREE FARM SALES LOT, the broad area between the big oak tree with the treehouse and the field of trees, was a busy place. As she pulled up and parked she could see that the crew had loaded thirty or forty wrapped trees on a truck that was pulling away. That was likely for the tree lots in Wolverhampton, Algonac and beyond.

As she got out of the SUV she recognized one of the casual workers Jakob had hired. "Johnny!" she cried, waving at him.

Johnny Stanko galumphed over to her in his size-fifteen boots and grabbed both her hands in his, shaking them vigorously. He reminded her of an oversized puppy sometimes, the way his enthusiasm and clumsiness combined. "Jaymie! How are you? After I helped on the cider booth, your husband said he might have a job for me. He's hired me to work for the season and he's gonna let me choose a tree for myself! I know exactly which one I want . . . that big one out there that you can see the top of!" He pointed out to the tree field.

Jakob had known the way to the fellow's heart, it seemed. He was a big kid in many ways, his past problems due more to poor impulse control and alcohol abuse than any real evil in his heart. "I'm so happy he hired you. I meant to ask you the other day . . . are you still working at the bar?" Though a sober alcoholic, he had worked as a barback for a place on the highway.

"Naw, they got bought out," he said, waving one big hand. "They turned the place into a ritzy joint. I didn't fit in. I stayed to bus tables for a while, but . . . naw. I'm doing odd jobs until I find something new."

"Well, Jakob must have liked you. He only works with people he likes."

Johnny grinned and ducked his head.

"How goes it with you and Cynthia? You're still friends, right?" she asked, thinking of seeing him on the CCTV footage on the night of the arson.

"Sure, we're good buddies. She lets me do odd jobs, too, for her and Ms. Jewel. I've been picking stuff up for them and moving stuff around. And for Mr. Bill, too. You know that, I guess." His expression darkened. "Is he going to be okay?"

"Bill Waterman? Yes, he's going to be fine, Johnny," she said, patting his shoulder. "He's out of the hospital and staying with his daughter right now."

He nodded. "Good. I'm glad. I thought he had a heart attack because of the fire and stuff. Amos was *so* mad at the one who set fire to Mr. Bill's work, the cider booth, you know."

"Amos . . . oh, the fellow who collects bottles behind the

Emporium!" Jaymie was struck by what he said. "Did he see anything?"

"Sure. He saw who did it."

Jaymie gasped. "Did he tell the police? Did they question him?"

Johnny drew back at Jaymie's reaction, blinking and nervously clenching his hands. "Uh, I don't think so. He's scared of police, you know. Like me. They . . . they're kind of hard on him sometimes. They accused him of breaking into sheds, and he didn't do it. So he's not too sure."

"But they must have spoken with him," she said, remembering his appearance on the security camera footage.

"Sure, but he told them he didn't remember."

And the police couldn't disprove that. "But he did see who did it?"

Johnny nodded, looking worried.

"Did he tell you who?"

He nodded again. "I don't wanna get Amos in trouble. He trusts me. If I told you an' you told the police an' they questioned him an' accused him of not telling the truth, he'd . . ." He shrugged and wouldn't finish, his eyes clouded with worry.

"But we need the person caught. Johnny, you do want to see the person caught, right? The fire could have hurt someone."

He nodded slowly. "Let me talk to Amos, an' I'll see if he'll let me tell you."

"Okay. You do that."

Shannon waved and beckoned Johnny to come help her. They were loading trees on another truck. The local little league team did a fund-raiser every year, and Jakob always sold them trees at cost to help them out. The school bus arrived, Jocie disembarked, and life, as always, kicked back into high gear.

☙ Eighteen ☙

TIME WAS RUNNING OUT. If Jaymie wanted her group to have a successful Dickens Days launch, she needed to help the police find out who had killed Evan Nezer. She felt bad even prioritizing the historical committee's needs when there was a real murder of a human involved. But solving the murder would help *everyone*, especially his family, not just the Dickens Days committee.

Wednesday morning Jaymie started with reading texts and emails from everyone she had reached out to. Nan's were interesting. Her bulldog reporter, who never posed a question that wasn't ultimately answered, had gone deeper, investigating the college connection to Evan Nezer, and had a lot of interesting information, but no conclusion.

She scanned the texts from her editor containing the information, some of which she already knew, or had heard hints of.

It seemed that college president Belcher had officially been forced to leave her last post for "undisclosed reasons," but many people were willing to talk to the reporter about it off the record. Bribery was indeed at the heart of it. She was, apparently, a woman obsessed with her own legacy. She had ties to some ultra-conservative groups and was funneling money from them into programs intended to move the eclectic curriculum of the university in a more conservative direction. She was also using the donations to pressure university leadership into naming a new think tank for her; she wanted it called the Belcher Institute. Someone turned her in, and she was let go.

Nan texted a rude joke after that, based on the name Belcher Institute, with a laughing emoji.

But there was more. Speculation was rife that bribery was only a part of her downfall. She had skirted criminal charges when she had funneled many of those generous donations to her own home renovations, calling her house a "university support building." She had been forced to repay every cent. If she hadn't, she would have been charged. She was fortunate enough to know someone on the Wolverhampton College board of governors, which was how she had gotten this job. She might be on her way out once more, though, given her recent behavior. Echoes of her past, it seemed to many. But did it give her a motive to kill Evan Nezer, even if he was blackmailing her somehow? Jaymie didn't see it.

In rapid fire there were more texts from Nan with the reporter's findings:

Jacklyn Marley had been fired from the university for "inappropriate conduct with a male student," but the informant could offer the reporter nothing more, since the identity of the complainant was withheld. Jaymie frowned. Given what she now knew about Jacklyn marrying Ben, it seemed unlikely she would have any kind of relationship with a student, and the fact that there was no gossip about it, no whisper campaign, made her suspicious. Everyone said Nezer was behind it, but how? And why? It didn't make sense.

Nan's reporter also claimed that as part of Finn Fancombe's appeal of his removal from the master's program at WC, he charged that Nezer's claims were absurd, since he had no proof that Finn had plagiarized his thesis advisor's critiques, and that the college was backing Nezer only because they were afraid he'd sue them if they didn't.

That had to be easier, then, now that Nezer was dead. Jaymie sat back and reflected on what she had seen and heard the afternoon before. Fancombe had issued veiled threats, based on some information he seemed to feel he had, and he had shifted from blaming Nezer for everything to blaming the college president for some part of it. Did that mean Nezer had been spurred on to charge Finn with plagiarism by the college president? With everything she knew now it appeared to be, as Finn suspected, a deliberate campaign to shut him up and shut him out of the college.

At the same time the reporter had snooped into Pastor Inkerman's past, and what he found was interesting, though not definitive. The pastor had, at his last posting, become entangled with the wife of a parishioner. Perhaps that was the "affair" to which Nezer had alluded. If so, it was hardly damning, since the woman had apparently been a willing partner in the affair, and other than a divorce on her part, there were few repercussions. Maybe that's what the pastor had been referring to when he said he was bad at romance, unless the lady was aggressive; perhaps the parishioner had pursued him. Was it cynical of her to think it wasn't such a big deal? Maybe for a pastor it would be, though. It was probably enough to get him removed from his position.

Jaymie needed to speak with Bella Nezer. Surely the victim's wife would have some insight into his death. She wished it was clearer who inherited Nezer's money and property. The reporter had been able to discover very little about Bella Nezer and her past, except for the tidbit that she had signed a restrictive prenup upon marrying Evan. That in itself might be a valid motive for murder if she inherited more from a dead husband than she would have gotten from a divorced husband. Pure speculation on her part, though.

And she had work to do, work other than investigating a murder. It was going to be a long day. Gracey Klausner was delayed, so Jaymie worked at the Emporium for an hour longer than she had intended before heading over to Cynthia Turbridge's store. She and Johnny were going to pick up some purchases from an estate sale, things the woman would convert, or "upcycle," for her store. Dickens Days was expected to be a sales boon for local artisans.

Before leaving, Johnny took Jaymie aside, out the back door of the cottage that had been converted into Cynthia's store, the Cottage Shoppe. He shuffled and looked down at the ground, frozen into tufts of browning grass and mud.

"I talked to Amos. He's scared. He did see who set fire to Mr. Bill's cider booth."

"Yes?"

"But he made me promise . . ." He shifted and sighed, his shoulders slumping.

Jaymie watched his eyes. They flicked back and forth, and he wouldn't meet hers. "Tell me, Johnny."

"He's afraid if I tell you what he saw, you'll tell the police and they'll talk to him and he'll get in trouble for not telling them himself."

This was a dilemma. Her curiosity burned and she longed to say that if he told her she'd keep it to herself, but what if it was vital information? How could she justify *not* telling the police? However . . . it didn't do anyone any good locked in Amos's mind. At least if she knew, it might help her figure out if it had to do with Evan Nezer's murder.

"So what are you saying, Johnny?"

"He made me promise. I can only tell you if you promise not to tell the police the information came from him."

"So I can tell the police, I just can't tell them it was Amos who saw it?"

He nodded.

Okay, *that* was a twist; however, if she did tell the police, it was quite possible they'd figure out who told her anyway. She didn't want to get Johnny's friend into trouble, but maybe that was a risk she'd have to take. It was also possible that if she knew who did it, she could use the information to identify him or her from the closed-circuit footage.

"I can live with that," she said.

He sighed and nodded. "Okay. So . . . this is who did it." He leaned in to her and whispered a name.

• • •

THREE HOURS LATER Cynthia and Johnny came back and Jaymie headed out, walking over to the village green. There was no longer any police presence around the tarp-covered diorama. There was no reason on earth why she shouldn't be able to take it down. Right now it was a silent scream, with the yellow crime scene tape flapping in the breeze that scudded a candy bar wrapper along the pavement. It announced, *A murder happened here!* The scene was indescribably lonely.

She walked over and pulled back the tarp covering the open front wall of the diorama. Eventually the police would figure out the truth, but she was on a deadline. She cared deeply about her town and the history of it, and it bothered her immensely that whoever had killed Nezer used her diorama to plant the body. It was a slap in the face of what the historic committee was trying to do, to make something positive happen for their little town.

Knowing who set fire to the cider booth didn't help as much as she thought it would. She didn't believe the arsonist and the killer were one and the same, though the crimes might be connected. She needed to think about it a lot more.

The joyous traditional scene painted on the diorama backdrop mocked her. Happy Mrs. Cratchit, with her hands in the air waving them in excitement, now seemed to be horrified by the dead body under her dining table. Jaymie had felt like there was a message in the scene for whomever cared to read it. Evan Nezer had been planted there, with the pudding mould over his head and a stake of holly planted through his heart to make a point.

But what if that was wrong? What if it had been done to make it *seem* like the killer was someone with a personal grudge against Nezer? She sighed. And maybe she was overthinking the whole thing. Now, if Nezer had been the kill*er* instead of the kill*ee*, the scene would have at least made sense, given his hatred of Dickens Days, but he hadn't killed himself.

She had to stop thinking of the scene as a message and consider the mechanics of it. The murderer — or his or her accomplice — would have had to plan ahead and know what the diorama was. That wasn't necessarily a difficult thing, given that though she had tried to keep it a secret, coyly refusing to discuss it in the historical society meeting, anyone seeing Bill build it in his workshop would have known. Also, she had set up the diorama in public. It didn't give the killer much time to plan, however . . . maybe the planning hadn't been so much in advance, but a hasty use of what she had so providently provided them. Perhaps it was a handy place for the body of a man who hated Christmas, and more particularly hated Charles Dickens and everything he wrote about and stood for. The rest — holly, wooden stake, pudding mould — was last-minute window dressing, like a bizarre and macabre mockery of a festive Christmas display window.

She dropped the tarp back down over the scene. It was Wednesday; she needed this solved before Friday if they were going to be able to hold the first night of Dickens Days and the lighting of the tree without a dark cloud hanging over the festival.

And Christmas was coming. She loved Christmas; this would be the first for her new family. She would not let the gloomy ghost of Evan Nezer, Queensville's resident Scrooge, cast a pall over the whole season. The only thing she could do for him now was to find his killer and turn him or her in to the police.

Humming a Christmas tune to brighten her spirits, she decided to follow up on something she had thought of a few days ago. She was still in desperate need of a couple of Christmas gifts, one for her mother-in-law and one for Val. She *always* got Val something handmade. The previous year she had commissioned Mabel Bloombury, a prolific knitter, to knit a cardigan for Val with a stylized image of her cottage on it. But this year had been hectic and she had not thought far enough ahead to do something like that.

So she would combine asking a crafter about gifts with a little snooping. She circled the line of pines and headed for the back door of the Nezer house. Approaching the home, she heard the sound of two women bickering.

"You *knew*! You must have known." There followed a string of expletives too foul to follow, delivered in a cultured English accent. Bella Nezer was on a rampage. Something dropped and something else crashed.

"I swear I didn't know a thing, Bella. Honest!"

"But you *must* have hidden it. Am I supposed to believe that suddenly Finn, of all the people in the world, comes up with a hand-written will? Dated *five days ago*?" Bella's tone was a shriek at this point. "I can't believe you'd conspire against me like that, you —"

"I did *not* conspire!"

A hidden will? And Finn Fancombe involved? Intriguing. It sounded like an old-time murder mystery, *The Clue in the Hidden Will*. However . . . it wasn't like her to eavesdrop. Jaymie tapped on the door, but the fight went on, the combatants unable to hear her, it seemed.

"You most certainly did! You're a conniving witch and planned this all along. You got your son recognized, and made Evan write that damned codicil. Then you *killed* him!" Bella shrieked.

"I did *not* kill him! I'd never . . . I couldn't kill a lamb. Evan always planned to recognize Finn! We talked about it long before *you* came along and pushed your way in," Erla said, her equable tone taking on a hint of steel. "I didn't want to tell my son until I knew Evan was serious. I *never* pressured him. Evan decided the night of the party, after he found out what *you* were doing behind his back."

Jaymie's interest was piqued: What *was* Bella doing behind Evan's back? Was there a hidden crack in the Nezer marriage, like the hairline fracture in the fine china saucer?

"Me? I was doing nothing! Don't you *dare* point your finger at me!" Bella said, her voice louder, her cultured accent slipping into a growl.

"It was Evan's decision, not mine!" Erla insisted.

Jaymie was confused. Why would Finn be in Evan Nezer's will, especially given their fractious relationship and the professor's hand in getting the younger man banished from the master's program he had invested so much time and money in? And what did "recognizing" him mean?

Bella and Erla were doing some back and forth "did so," "did not," when the answer hit Jaymie. References in the historical romances she read about "recognizing" someone almost always meant that someone was an illegitimate son. Her stomach twisted; Finn Fancombe was Evan Nezer's biological son? It had to be what they meant. *That* was why no mention had been made of Finn's father, no photo, no tale of abandonment or death.

But there *were* pictures and tales of Erla, Sarah and the two boys vacationing together, camping and heading to Disney World. Did *Sarah* know of Finn's parentage? How would she feel if she did, knowing that Ben was not Evan's only child? So if she understood correctly, Nezer had apparently recognized Finn as his son in a handwritten codicil to his will written days before he died.

"You had better be ready to provide DNA," Bella shrieked, all of her playacting "lady of the manor" air gone. "And for a court challenge! I don't believe a word you've said. Evan would *never* have kept this from me! He promised; everything would be *mine*!"

That was a startling statement from a newly bereaved widow, and it piqued Jaymie's interest, given the restrictive prenup she had apparently signed. Was the Nezer marriage in such deep trouble that Bella was afraid she'd be divorced and left with virtually nothing?

Bella must have stormed off, a door slamming and echoing even through the closed window by the back door. Jaymie tried the door and it opened. She walked into the kitchen to find Erla Fancombe sitting at the worktable, her head in her hands, sobbing.

"Are you okay?" Jaymie asked softly.

The woman bolted up, her chair tumbling back, turned over by her precipitous movement. "What are you doing here?"

Jaymie, watching her closely as she swiped at her wet eyes with the back of her hand, said, "I actually was coming to see your quilts." She bent over and picked up the chair, noticing a shattered mug on the floor nearby, likely the result of Bella's temper tantrum. "Remember we spoke of your quilting?"

"I . . . yes, I remember." Erla, on automatic, it appeared, got a dust pan and broom and cleaned up the mug bits, tossing them into the trash under the sink, the remains clanking and tinkling into the bag.

"You said I could come back and see them." Jaymie wasn't sure that had been said, but mendacity was merited in this case. "I knocked repeatedly but . . . you were busy and didn't hear."

The woman wasn't listening, and the quilt excuse didn't appear to be necessary other than to explain Jaymie's arrival. A few things occurred to Jaymie in that moment, and one was to wonder which son was actually older, Ben or Finn. Did that matter? They weren't in nineteenth-century England, after all; laws of primogeniture didn't hold in America. And even in merry olde England an illegitimate son could not take advantage of the old English law of primogeniture. But the birth order might be revealing in another way, like . . . when did Erla's affair with Evan get started?

Erla sank back down in her chair. Jaymie sat down across from her. "I have to confess," she said. "I overheard your argument with Bella."

The woman gazed at her, eyes wide. "We've never gotten along, but now . . ." She shook her head.

"What was the Nezer marriage like, Erla?"

Her gaze shifted away. "I don't talk about my employers behind their backs."

"I guess I'll think the worst then. It's human nature." Jaymie watched her for a moment and said, "What are you going to do, now that Mr. Nezer is dead?"

She sighed and closed her eyes. "I have to leave. But where? I've worked for the Nezer family for . . . thirty-three years. My whole youth given to that . . . that *awful* man." She broke down into weeping again, tears streaming down her cheeks under the hands she had over her eyes.

"I so sorry, Erla," Jaymie said softly. A torrent of emotion had broken down the reserved woman's walls. Maybe it wasn't fair to use the woman's vulnerability, but murder wasn't fair either. It left deep wounds that would never heal, poisoning everything and everyone with fear and doubt. A solution at least gave peace of mind. She was the housekeeper, and who knew more about her employers than the one who made the bed, did the laundry, cooked and cleaned and cared for them all?

Jaymie made a pot of tea. More confidences had been spilled over tea and sympathy than even wine and commiseration. Setting a steaming mug in front of Erla, she said, "I overheard, as I said. So . . . is it true? Is Finn really Evan's biological son?"

She nodded.

"You had an affair with Evan?"

"More a moment of weakness than anything."

"He was married to Sarah at the time."

"I had just started working for them. I was young, stupid. When did I get so old?" She tugged at a lock of gray hair, stared at it, then pushed it back off her cheek. "It feels like forever ago. Those two—Sarah and Evan—had just got married and were not getting along. They were fighting all the time and he came to my room one night to apologize for quarreling in front of me." She smiled weakly. "He could be charming when he wanted to be. I would have regretted it, but then there was Finn. I can't regret it when I got a son out of it, the best thing to ever happen to me, my only child."

"So Finn never knew?"

She shook her head.

"What did you tell him about his father?"

"More or less the truth, that it was a one-night thing, that I'm glad it happened because I got him."

"Didn't he ever want to get in touch with his dad?"

She flushed up to her graying roots. She looked down at her tea and took in a long breath. "I said . . . I lied. I said he didn't give me his real name, that I didn't know how to find him. I regret that. He's angry with me now that he knows the truth. I don't blame him."

But was he angry with his father, too? Jaymie wondered. "The codicil to the will means that Evan was preparing to openly recognize Finn as his son?" The woman nodded again. "But why did he do what he did to him—accusing him of plagiarism—when he knew it was his son he was destroying?"

"It's a long story," she said with a deep sigh. "A long *ridiculous* story of two men and a difference of opinion."

"Do you mean to say this goes back to the work they both did in economics?"

"It does." Erla explained that though Finn did not know Evan was his father at that point, he did consider him a father figure. "How could he not, growing up in his house, with Ben like a brother to him?" She took in a long shaky breath. "His *actual* brother," she amended. "I'm so used to lying about it, it's become a habit. But Finn's work at the college, his master's thesis, completely departed from Evan's economic theory. I don't understand much of it, though he's tried to explain it to me, but it seems like the two used the same data and statistics to come to different conclusions." The resulting argument had led to the break, apparently, and Evan was not the type to let it go. He was vindictive and decided to destroy Finn's career before it even got started.

"Even though he knew Finn was his son?" It was hard to imagine someone so spiteful. Maybe, if what she had learned was true, though, there was more behind it.

She nodded. "He was in a *foul* mood. Said to me that he had two sons, neither one worth a damn."

Jaymie watched the woman's expression, how the flush left her skin and her expression turned hard. "So when *did* Finn learn that Evan was his father?"

"Evan told him at the party that night."

"Why? I mean, why did he tell him, and why then and there?"

"I don't know. Evan was . . . he . . ." She shook her head, tears welling again in her eyes, and shrugged helplessly.

"He liked to control people," Jaymie guessed.

"That's true, but that's not why he told him then and there, not to control Finn. It was all about Ben. He was going to announce that he was Finn's father just to upset Benjamin."

He had two sons, and he was using acknowledging one to hurt the other. What a prince. "Did you know what Evan was going to do?"

"Of course not! I would *never* have let my son be used like that. Finn was intent on speaking with President Belcher at the party. He was barred from the campus, so he thought he could talk to the president here, one on one. But I knew it would irritate Evan for him to interfere with the party. I thought I could get Evan to use his influence to make the college reverse their action but I knew the party was *not* the time and place. I couldn't tell Finn the real reason I wanted him to wait."

Jaymie cast her mind back to the party, and what she had been told about the aftermath, after she and Jakob left. "I heard that Finn came back and confronted Evan. *That* was when Evan told Finn he was his father, right?"

The woman's tears had dried, and she looked uneasy. "You're not trying to pin this on my son, are you? The last thing he would do would be to . . . to hurt his father. I *know* my son. He would have had so many questions. He would have wanted to get to know Evan in a different way, as a father."

Would he? Jaymie wondered. Or would it infuriate him that Nezer had so callously gotten him canned from the master's program even knowing Finn was his son?

Bella slammed open the kitchen door and glared at Erla, then looked at Jaymie. "What are you doing here?"

"I came to—"

"Never mind." She turned back to the housekeeper. "Erla, you're fired. I want you out of here by tomorrow."

"By tomorrow! Where am I going to go?"

"Do I look like I care?" All pretense of a classy English accent was gone. "I won't have a damned liar in my house. Go live with your son, or . . . oh, that's right," she said with a malicious snarl. "He doesn't have a place to live either, does he, now that the shed is off-limits." She retreated, but then came back and slammed open the door. "And you, you busybody," she said, glaring at Jaymie. "You need to get out. *Now.* Erla doesn't have time to talk. She has to pack."

Under the woman's venomous glare, Jaymie nodded and left.

⌘ Nineteen ⌘

HOME. Home was as welcome a thought as a warm blanket on a cold day. Jocie had dance practice, so Jaymie picked her up at school. As they pulled up the drive by the cabin, twilight was gathering, making every scene mysterious, tossing the upper branches of the trees across the road with a rustling that seemed secretive, whispery. They waved to Shannon, Johnny and Jakob, and entered to the madness of Hoppy and Lilibet, who dashed around barking and yowling their pleasure. Jaymie laughed as Jocie tossed her bookbag aside and raced around with the animals, her high-pitched squeals of laughter echoing into the upper reaches of the cozy cabin.

And then peace, animals and child weary at last. Jocie had homework, a project she was working on. Jaymie turned on the light over the table so Jocie could work, and the lights over the kitchen sink so she could chop vegetables for crudités.

As much as she loved autumn and winter, she liked that on December twenty-first she could always say, *And now every day gets longer!* Living where there were four distinct seasons was a blessing. Just when you got tired of winter, spring arrived with blossoms and warm winds that promised summer. When summer got too hot and humid for her taste, she looked forward to fall, cooler temperatures and pumpkin spice everything!

Jocie's project was about that very thing, the change in seasons, so Jaymie brought out her laptop and helped her research why their hemisphere had winter when it was winter, while in the southern hemisphere December ushered in beach weather! They talked about the tilt of the planets, and the earth's orbit around the sun. It was surprising how much one forgot after years of being out of school.

Once dinner was ready Jaymie pulled on a heavy cardigan that hung by the door and went out, watching as Shannon helped a family load a tree on the top of their car and tie it down, while Johnny and Jakob rearranged the cut trees for optimal viewing, all by the light of the floods that topped the electrical pole near the road. They had that day constructed a new feature, a kind of pergola structure from which they dangled various trees so customers could see them. That weekend would be the first of "cut your own," which

Jakob only allowed in daylight hours, but many folks preferred to just come and pick out a ready-cut tree.

When the car pulled away, Jaymie cupped her hands around her mouth and yelled, "Dinner, everyone! *Dinner!*" She needed one of those bells to clang, like you saw in old western movies to bring in the ranch hands. She smiled at the direction her life had taken, from townie to Christmas tree farmer's wife.

She had made a giant pot of chili and had defrosted and baked rolls to go with it, along with a tray of cut vegetables. Johnny was absurdly grateful for dinner; he thanked everyone multiple times. Before eating he ducked his head and said the serenity prayer. Jaymie teared up. *'Tis the season,* she thought, when anything from a Hallmark card commercial to a friend's festive wishes could reduce her to tears. But this was different than holiday sentimentality; Johnny's struggle to maintain sobriety touched her deeply. She said a silent prayer, reminding herself to be careful about judging others, for she had once judged him unfairly, and it had taught her a lesson. She sent him a warm smile.

At the end of the meal Shannon departed—she had an early exam the next morning—and Jakob took Jocie up for bath and bed. Johnny asked if he could help Jaymie with the dishes. She would normally have said no, but she was in a hurry to get going to girls' night and she had a feeling he wanted to help. That somehow, he *needed* to help. He washed and she dried, since she knew where everything went and could put it all away.

"You use nice dish detergent," he said, mounding bubbles in his big rough hand. He blew on the mound, sending a cascade of foam fluttering into the air. He glanced over at her, maybe anticipating censure, then smiled. "It smells nice. The stuff they use at the church dinners smells like a hospital."

"Do you go to church every week?"

"No, just for the dinners. That's where our meetings are," he said, referring to his and Cynthia's weekly sobriety meetings. "I like going to the dinners because I see friends there. Last week that fellow Pastor Inkerman came and talked about stuff before dinner. It was interesting."

"I've met him. What did he talk about?"

"He talked about how some folks go to church but don't follow the scriptures the rest of the week, and how some other folks don't even know they're following the scriptures, 'cause they're just being kind and helpful."

"Interesting. Did he stay for the dinner?"

Johnny nodded as he handed her a bowl. "But not after. He met a woman in the parking lot. She was waiting for him outside the church."

"Maybe he's got a girlfriend?"

"It wasn't a girlfriend. She's a lot older than him. I mean, not that she couldn't . . ." He trailed off, shaking his head.

"I know he has his own car," Jaymie said with a frown. "Did the woman drive him away?"

"Nope. They sat in the car. Me and Amos stood outside for a while having a smoke and a coffee. We were gonna go back in and help clean up. The pastor appreciates it because a lot of the older folks can't move the heavy tables and such."

"So they just sat in her car?"

He nodded. Jaymie wiped the bowl and put it away, then took the next. They were establishing a rhythm. She got the chili pot from the stove and put it in the sink as Johnny lifted his soapy hands.

"I couldn't figure out why Erla would be sitting talking to the pastor. It was weird."

Jaymie jolted and splashed some of the dishwater, dropping the pot. Johnny sometimes left things out when he told a story, and that part hadn't been clear before. "You mean it was *Erla* sitting in the car with Pastor Inkerman? When was this?"

"Uh . . . a week ago. Tuesday evening, I think. Yeah, Tuesday night is the church spaghetti dinner." He scrubbed the pot then looked up at the clock. "I gotta get going. I'm picking up Cynthia for tonight's meeting."

Though Erla's name kept coming up in relation to things, nothing tied together . . . nothing made sense. "Johnny, you're *sure* it was Erla Fancombe?"

"Yeah. I fixed her car for her once; it's an old Subaru with too many miles on it. But she sure keeps it clean. And Amos knows what she looks like, right?"

"Of course. What happened after? Did they drive away?"

"Nope. He gave her something, like . . . an envelope."

"You could see that inside her car?"

"She put the dome light on, you know, to look at the envelope, I guess. Then he got out and went to his own car, a real nice one with a vanity plate." He finished scrubbing and lifted the pot out of the water, which was now grimy and oily. He emptied the sink, carefully rinsed the chili pot in hot water, then handed it to her.

She wiped it dry and put it away on the pot rack over the table. "And that was it?"

"Yup. She drove away too."

Odd. A meeting before the party, and even before the cider booth fire.

And Erla, according to Amos, was the one who set the fire. He had seen her gray hair and the coat she always wore. Jaymie hadn't been able to figure out why. She had assumed the woman was doing it perhaps at Evan's command. But now she wondered . . . had she eliminated Erla from suspicion of killing Evan too fast? And maybe the pastor had a hand in it, even before he supposedly found out that Evan Nezer was his harsh and hurtful critic.

• • •

SHE KISSED JAKOB GOODBYE and headed out, her mind working on the problems and questions she still had. Erla the arsonist; it seemed odd. Why would she do that? But Amos had recognized her by her clothes and gray hair. The why of it nagged more than anything. She wished she had been able to ask Amos questions about it, because something seemed off.

She took back roads and approached Wolverhampton from another direction, easily finding Austin's mom's tidy split ranch on a well-treed suburban street. He hustled out, clutching his trench coat around him and slipping on the icy lane. He hopped in, his round face holding an eager expression. He wore glasses, and she gazed at him in surprise. "What's with the specs?"

"I guess you didn't know I wear contacts most of the time. But one of my eyes is watering lately—allergies or something like that," he said, squinting and pointing to one pink and watery eye. "So I'm wearing my glasses tonight. Don't look!" he said, rearing back and holding his hands up over his face. "Now I feel self-conscious in them."

"Stop it!" Jaymie laughed and pulled away from the curb as her passenger buckled up. "My sister and best friend both wear glasses, so you won't be the only one. When I was a kid I longed to wear glasses. I thought it made you special, maybe because my big sister wore them."

She turned on the satellite radio, tuned to the all-Christmas music channel, and they sang along to "Jingle Bell Rock," Austin showing vocal talent she never would have suspected. "You're good!" she said, glancing over at him in surprise.

"Karaoke Calhoun, they call me," he replied.

"You have to come next time we have a karaoke party at Bernie's house."

She drove to the lane behind the Queensville house. Heidi had picked up Bernie, and Val had walked over with Georgina, who was invited for the first time, so there was just Becca and Heidi's cars to maneuver around in the cramped parking lane. As she pulled into the only available spot she told him of her childhood, growing up in the home with her mom, dad, sister, and her Grandma Leighton. She turned off the engine, and they stared at the back of the house, the long summer porch with its dressing of winter storm windows over the screens.

They could see the lights on in the kitchen, giving the Queen Anne home a warm and glowing appearance, like a Thomas Kinkade painting. "That's where I got my love of cooking, from my grandmother," she said, her voice hushed in the silent SUV. "My mom isn't much of a cook and my sister is barely adequate in the kitchen." The air was crisp and the sky black as they climbed out. Jaymie led the way through the gate and up the flagstone walk, letting herself in through the back door.

They followed the sound of laughter to the front parlor, where it was clear the party had already started. Heidi, Bernie, Becca, Valetta and Georgina were into the holiday spirits; there was a bottle of red and one of white already open, and a couple of martini glasses full of a dark pinkish cocktail. She introduced Austin around, though Valetta needed no introduction and warmly hugged Austin.

"Cocktails!" Becca exclaimed as she fixed one for the two latest to join them. She was already "happy," her round cheeks glowing with bonhomie and Christmas cocktails. Georgina downed hers and asked for another. She sat in a corner of the sofa smiling at them all, swiftly getting, as she called it, potted. She had many more words and phrases for her state: squiffy, legless, sloshed, sozzled, and Jaymie's favorite, drunk as a lord.

Jaymie watched her, worried about her alcohol consumption after what she and Valetta had figured out. Then it hit her; it was exactly zero percent of her business, and if Georgina hadn't earned the right to live her own way at sixty-something, then who had?

Inevitably, they all talked about the murder, the Nezers, the Nezer party and everything else, though Bernie stayed mum through it all. Popular opinion was that Bella had finally gotten fed up with her husband and did him in.

"Come on," Jayme demurred. "If that's so, how did she get him out to the diorama? I mean, she's a sturdy girl, but I'm strong and I couldn't haul a body that far." She didn't share what she had heard, about the handcart or wheelbarrow.

Bernie was listening and smiling and sipping, eyes wide.

"She supposedly claims she didn't hear a thing. Didn't she even notice her husband was gone in the middle of the night?" Valetta said with a snort.

"But they didn't sleep together," Heidi said. "Oops," she added, and eyed Bernie with trepidation. Bernie shrugged.

"How do *you* know?" Jaymie asked.

Heidi giggled woozily and hiccupped. "Where do you think I was the night of the party? I was snooping upstairs! She has a nice room, and the most *heavenly* fur coats, all smelling of Givenchy." Her eyes went wide. "Oh, ugh! I hope they were faux furs."

"With that woman? I'm sure they were genuine furs and she probably skinned the animals herself," Valetta said with a sarcastic edge. She wasn't a fan of Bella Nezer.

"So they don't share a room," Jaymie said. "But maybe they do sleep together."

"Oh, no, they *don't*. She has all her stuff in her side table, you know . . . book she's reading, night cream . . . stuff. And him too . . . he's got a book on his bedside table and his laptop charger plugged in, all that stuff."

"Well, that would explain her not hearing him leave that night," Jaymie said. "But why did he leave his room? Maybe he heard something."

"Maybe he had a lover," Becca said. "Could have snuck out to meet her."

"In his nightshirt? Or . . ." Jaymie thought, maybe he went outside to meet his newly discovered son, for some reason, and they got in a fight and Finn bashed him. It was possible. She chose not to speculate on that. "I don't know why we're thinking that having her own room means Bella didn't do it."

"No one said that," Valetta commented. "We said it would explain why she didn't hear him leaving, if he snuck out without her knowing."

"Yeah, I guess. So many possibilities. Let's talk about something else," she said, afraid she'd say too much if they kept talking. "Something more cheerful."

Work and Christmas and parties were discussed. Austin, who had been silent through that conversation, was a little reserved at first with a group of new people, but he was soon in the thick of it, telling tales of his first semester at WC. The hospitality course, he said, had all the most amusing people, and they relentlessly poked fun at the serious folks in economics and other "uppity" courses at the Perry College branch of WC.

"I've heard that if the president has her way, WC will eliminate all the tech courses," Bernie said, spreading some cheese on a cracker. "I hope not! I've taken a couple of criminology courses there, as well as working on my master's. Chief Ledbetter is going to be teaching an applied police work course next semester." She crunched her snack and chewed.

"Really?" Jaymie exclaimed. "The chief?"

"The technical college actually recruited him. He's also going to be leading an introductory course in policing." She sighed. "I'd love him to do an anti-bias lecture for current police officers, but . . ." She shook her head.

Jaymie knew about her problems with some of the male officers. Many were good, but some were disturbed by the Queensville Township PD's move to being more diverse and balanced gender-wise during Chief Ledbetter's tenure.

"Why did you become a police officer?" Austin asked Bernie. "I mean . . . what do you want out of it?"

As the conversation turned serious, Jaymie headed to the kitchen to get some ice and lingered by the sink. The information Johnny had provided her with, that Erla and Inkerman had been seen together, and that he gave her something in an envelope, had left her uneasy.

Valetta rushed into the kitchen. "I need a cloth," she said, rummaging in the tea towel drawer. "Austin was waving his hands around and spilled Becca's drink. Or maybe Becca has had a drinkie winkie too many and spilled it herself. Georgina is out of it, snoring away in the corner of the sofa." She grabbed a roll of paper towels, then looked at Jaymie. "What's up? You look . . . perplexed."

"I am."

"Hold that thought," Val said. She rushed away to the parlor, where loud laughter was echoing, then returned to Jaymie in the kitchen. "So what's up?"

"I don't want to take you away from the party."

Valetta waved her hand and tugged Jaymie to sit down at the table. "They're all tiddly. Something's on your mind and I want to know what it is."

Jaymie told Val all about what she had learned.

"Finn Fancombe was Evan Nezer's son?"

Jaymie nodded.

"Wow. I'm stunned. And Erla Fancombe set the cider booth fire? Why would she?"

"I don't know. But now, do I tell the police? Do I say something to Bernie? The footage from the store was grainy and dark and you couldn't tell who it was, but . . ." She shrugged.

"I heard through a friend of a friend—don't say I told you this—that the cops had a feeling it was someone in that house because the materials were found there, hidden in the shed out back." Valetta pushed her glasses up on her nose.

The shed, where Bella claimed Finn Fancombe had been living? That was interesting. "Is that why the shed has yellow crime scene tape around it?"

"Yup."

That explained Brock's revelation, but eliminated the shed as the scene of the murder.

"Trouble is, they were common materials from every household," Val said. "You've probably got the same thing here in your shed or basement. They actually wouldn't have thought anything of it, but for the way the stuff was deliberately concealed."

"But in other words they won't be surprised that it's Erla. I can't figure out why she'd do it." She eyed Valetta. "Maybe Evan made her do it?"

"That's a possibility, but why would she go along with it?"

"She may have wanted to keep him in good spirits since she was counting on him helping Finn, his son, get back into his master's program."

"Could he have, though? I mean, once Finn was kicked out for plagiarism, wasn't that it for him?"

"Erla seemed convinced Evan could and would help, and I think places bend the rules all the time, don't they? Anyway, if that's true, Erla had every reason in the world to keep Evan alive." Jaymie thought. "For the time being, anyway."

"So Erla is officially off the suspect list?"

"Not off, just sidelined. Given how angry Bella was about the will codicil . . . I'm thinking she was willing, if not eager, for Evan to pop off and leave her money."

"How about Ben, though; you said Sarah was pretty sure he was going to be left the house and, presumably, money."

"How much money could a college professor have to leave?" Jaymie asked.

"C'mon, Jaymie, you know better than that. Evan Nezer's family has money from way back."

"I never thought of them as being wealthy, I guess."

"That's because for all his pretention, Nezer never shouted it out to the world, but the family owned a ton of land and has investments in real estate here in town and in Wolverhampton." Val knew a lot more than Jaymie about property because of Brock's real estate business. He stayed aware of who owned what and where. "How do you think La Bella afforded to spiff up the Nezer ancestral home so quickly? It costs mucho moolah to get contractors to do a rush job."

"No, Val, I don't think he *did* have money, not until recently. If I'm right, his lack of money was why he was going to sell the Nezer ancestral home. But listen to this . . ." She told Valetta what she knew about the movie options for Sarah's two books. "It wouldn't make him mega rich, but it *would* be enough to keep the big house."

"That kinda gives Sarah a motive to kill him, doesn't it?"

"Yeah, I did think of that, but I don't want it to be her. Anyway, if

I'm right, and President Belcher was using everything she had to attract big-bucks donors and the money a think tank would have meant to Wolverhampton College, he could have a lot of money coming to him in the future."

"Hmm. Okay. Interesting."

"Anyway, if Erla didn't do it, and Finn didn't do it, that leaves me with Bella, Ben, Jacklyn, and Vaughan Inkerman." Or Ben and Jacklyn together, given their previously unknown and still, it seemed, unacknowledged relationship. She wasn't sure she should divulge that info, so she stayed mum. "I can't see Vaughan doing it." She was still troubled by Johnny's information, seeing Erla and the pastor in a secretive meeting and the pastor exiting the car after giving Erla an envelope. "Though I'm not ruling him out." She considered something she hadn't thought of until then. "I remember before we left the party that night, I did see Pastor Inkerman in the kitchen speaking with Erla. What connection do those two have, I wonder?"

"Maybe Erla goes to his church. He's the college chaplain, but he also holds biweekly services at WC in the chapel. One of my elderly aunts decided she didn't like how modern Reverend Gillis was and decided to try out Inkerman, who is the elderly lady's beau ideal, as one of your Regency romances would put it."

"Of course! It's a simple explanation and likely the right one. Maybe he gave her some sheet music, or scripture, and that's what was in the envelope. Anyway, enough brooding over crime. Let's rejoin the party in progress."

They talked and chatted and laughed a lot more, while Georgina snored. Becca put a noisemaker in her sister-in-law's mouth, and as the occasionally snarky Englishwoman blew in and out, the noise-maker amplified her snoring with a raspberry of sound. The whole group collapsed in stifled giggles, but Jaymie eventually plucked if from the poor woman's lips. She already felt bad about laughing at Georgina. At least the woman was staying the night at the Queensville house, so being drunk off her feet was no problem at all.

But finally enough had been drunk and eaten, and yawns took over from laughter. It was a work night for everyone.

"I think I'll have to open the store tomorrow morning," Becca said, eyeing Georgina. "Or maybe I'll send Kevin."

Having stopped at one drink right when she arrived, Jaymie was sober as the proverbial judge. Val, however, after a couple of cocktails and a few glasses of wine, was tipsy.

As Heidi and Bernie exited out the back door together, the police officer called back, "Hey, folks, it's snowing! Be careful when you drive." She took Heidi's keys and ushered her friend down the flagstone path, through the gate and around to the passenger side, Heidi giggling and slipping sideways.

Jaymie followed them and waved as Bernie pulled out. It was indeed snowing, and a wind was whipping up.

Austin, behind her, whistled. "Woo, it is coming *down*! Michigan weather . . . gotta love it!"

"I think we'd better get going too. And if you don't mind, I'm going to make a slight detour and take Val home. She walked here and I won't have her slipping and sliding all the way across town."

"Let's round her up and pour her into the SUV before she slips out the front," Austin said.

Against her protests and with much laughter they herded her to the back door, where Becca hugged them all goodbye, even Austin. Kevin was coming home up the walk. He had spent the evening with Jakob out at the farm, going over the plan for the new holiday store venture, in which he was an investor. "Coming down, out there. Be careful, Jaymie, my dear," he said, shaking the snow off his overcoat as he entered the summer porch. The crystalline pellets melted in the warmth emanating from the house. "Jakob is a little concerned about you driving in this weather."

"We will be careful," Jaymie said, taking Valetta's arm on one side, while Austin did the same on the other. They descended the two steps from the summer porch and picked their way along the swiftly whitening path, flakes clinging to individual blades of grass, visible in the spill of light out the back door. They got a happy and buoyant Valetta to the SUV and into the passenger side, and Austin hopped in the back. "It's not much of a detour," Jaymie said, glancing in the rearview mirror at Austin. "Across the village, a little out of our way."

"Over the river and through the woods," Valetta sang.

He smiled. "Hey, I'm up for anything. It's an adventure. I can't remember when I had so much fun."

As Jaymie carefully navigated the back lane and got them onto one of the crossroads, Val slumped over. She snored lightly and chuckled in her sleep.

"She's a lightweight when it comes to alcohol," Austin said.

"She doesn't drink much. Neither do I."

"I like a nice cocktail, but my mom works in the emergency ward of the hospital. She's seen too many victims of drunk drivers and told me the stories." His tone was grim. "I don't take chances with alcohol or weather."

She checked him in the rearview mirror, a trick she had become adept at since acquiring a daughter. His expression was a little tight with tension. "It's going to be okay," she said. "I've been driving these roads since I was fifteen, with my dad teaching me how to navigate all kinds of weather. It would start blizzarding and he'd say, *Okay, Jay, let's fly!* and he'd take me out for a lesson in braking on ice, or steering into a slide."

"Sounds like you have a great dad," Austin said. He sounded wistful.

"I'm lucky. It sounds like you have a great mom."

"I do. *I'm* lucky."

She made her way through the village, slowing by the diorama.

"Is that the spot where you found the professor?" Austin asked, leaning forward, straining against his seat belt.

"It is," she said grimly. "Dead as a doornail, with a stake of holly through his heart and a pudding mould over his head."

"Can we stop? Pretty please? I want a picture."

"Austin, no!"

"C'mon. What if I promise I won't put it on social?" he said. "Just a *memento mori*."

She braked and shut the motor down, unlocking her seat belt and twisting to stare at him in the gloom of the backseat. "A what the what?"

"*Memento mori* . . . a depiction of something to remind us that we are always close to death."

"Gruesome! Wherever did you hear that phrase?"

"I might be going out with an art professor with interesting tastes in art," he said with a self-conscious laugh. "Our first date was to a graveyard, where we did charcoal rubbings. Not as much fun as it sounds."

"A professor? You're dating a *professor*?"

"He likes his guys cute, pudgy and young," Austin said. "He's not *my* professor, so we're not breaking any rules. I don't think. And we've only been on two dates so far."

"I won't say a word to anyone. Okay," she said, giving in to his pleading expression. "One selfie but no social media!" She checked to make sure Valetta was comfortable, then got out and shut the door behind her.

He got out of the SUV, pulling his phone out of his coat pocket as Jaymie led the way to the diorama. She glanced around; no police presence. She undid the tarp flap, pulling it up and flipping it over the top. Austin was documenting her actions. The interior was shadowed, the light from the Victorian-style streetlight not penetrating the gloom of the three-sided diorama.

Austin stepped in and held up his phone, in selfie mode, and took a pic as Jaymie stood off to the side, uncomfortable about aiding and abetting a selfie at the scene of a murder. It felt disrespectful, but as long as he didn't post it, she guessed there was no harm done. Austin looked at his cell phone. And screamed.

๔ Twenty ๕

"**WHAT'S WRONG?**" Jaymie cried.

Austin whirled around and used his cell phone to light the back of the diorama, where a figure could be seen lying in a fetal position.

"Oh *no!*" Jaymie cried, and knelt down by the figure. It was Amos. Had he found a convenient corner to curl up and sleep? Not likely, given the frigid temperature. "Shine that over here," she said. Austin switched to a flashlight app and shone the light down. "Amos, *Amos!*" Jaymie said gently, one hand on his shoulder. "Are you all right?"

The man moved and groaned, then whimpered and curled up tighter. Jaymie grabbed the cell phone and pointed the light at his head. "There's blood!" she said. She handed Austin back the phone. "Call 911."

"Don't even *think* about it!" Those shrieked words were followed by a whack, the sound a dull thud, and Austin fell to his knees with a groan, his cell phone dropping from his hand and skidding across the damp grass.

Jaymie froze and looked up, her heart thumping like a bass drum. Erla had the brown fluted bowl from her kitchen in her hand, and Austin had a crescent-shaped cut on his forehead. He was not unconscious but he was hurt, whimpering and holding his forehead, his fingers bloody.

"Erla, we were just . . . we're . . ." Her mind finally caught up to speed. "Oh, *you* did this to Amos! And . . . and . . . you killed Evan."

The housekeeper looked distracted and upset and afraid all at once. But she still held that heavy bowl . . . but it *wasn't* a bowl, Jaymie realized. It was an antique pudding mould. She should have recognized it in the kitchen, on the shelf above the pickle crock, but though she had seen photos of the older crockery moulds in person she had only seen metal pudding moulds up to that point.

"*Why* did you have to interfere? Why did *he*?" Erla said, pointing down. Not to Austin, Jaymie realized, but to poor Amos, who was groaning, and now semiconscious.

"How did he interfere?"

"Tried to extort money out of me," she said. "He said he saw stuff he shouldn't have."

As impossible as it seemed, mild-mannered, quilt-making, loving mother and housekeeper Erla Fancombe was . . . a killer? It felt surreal, impossible, *absurd*. Her stomach churning, Jaymie realized that she had made the deadly mistake of identifying with Erla so much that even though she was officially considering her, emotionally she had discounted her as a suspect. So though Erla was on the list, Jaymie kept pushing her off, finding any reason to ignore her. "Did you . . . did you *really* kill Evan Nezer?"

The cell phone light flicked off. The diorama was dark, with just the faint glow of streetlights from outside the three walls dimly illuminating the interior. Erla hummed a weird, tension-filled drone of agitation, swinging the bowl back and forth. Her eyes were huge, like mirror saucers. Glossy tears welled in them. "Why did you have to come along right now? I'm going to have to k-kill you, too! I don't *want* to. You're a nice girl, but what else can I do?"

Jaymie's stomach twisted as she watched the woman, unsure how to defuse this moment. "You can just walk away. I don't know anything at this point. Let me just get Amos and Austin some help, and just . . . walk away."

"I wish I could," she sobbed.

Jaymie took a deep breath, trying to calm her heart rate and breathing. "Erla, think this through. You can't bash all of us dead and leave us." Her voice was trembling despite trying to steady it as she evaluated how best to tackle the woman. Having been in similar predicaments in the past, she knew to keep the woman talking while trying to figure out an escape plan. How to keep them all safe and take out Erla?

She was weeping now, tears running down her seamed face, her nose running. "Why did you have to *ruin* everything?" she sobbed, her voice clogged with tears. "Nosy parker! You, and him, and Amos . . . why can't you all leave it alone? Evan was a jackass. *Everyone* hated him! This was his own fault."

Jaymie readied herself; if Erla kept crying and got more emotional it might be possible to tackle her. She didn't have a gun, she had a pudding mould, for heaven's sake. Austin gazed up at Jaymie, tears welling in his blue eyes behind the glasses, askew on his face. She shook her head slightly. *Stay down*, she mouthed. "Erla, *please*, let us go. You could get away, you could—"

"And go where?" she cried. "*Where?*" The word was ragged, edges torn, her voice guttural, a cry of despair.

Jaymie tried to get to her feet and yet stay in a crouch, so she'd be ready.

"This is the only home I have, the only one I've ever had. And that man . . . that woman . . . those two . . . they were going to . . ." Erla shook her head and straightened, taking in a deep breath, glaring down at Jaymie and gripping the heavy crockery pudding mould in one strong hand. She was calmer, and that was not a good thing. "Even before Evan died, that *witch*, Bella, was forcing me to retire. She wanted a younger woman, she said, to take care of *her* house. No pension, no nothing."

Blast it; the murdering housekeeper loomed over her, a bad position from which to tackle her. The moment had passed. She would have to create another before Erla summoned the fury to attack Jaymie.

"What does Bella wanting you to retire have to do with you killing Evan?" Jaymie asked bluntly, but even as she said it, she realized . . . it was money.

"Shut up. Just . . . shut up! You don't know what I've been through!" She was beginning to cry again.

Erla was worried about money and her time of influence was running out at the Nezer residence. It was all about the codicil and Finn's inheritance! Erla didn't care about her son getting his master's—which would have required Evan to be alive—she cared about his *inheritance*. If she left the house, Evan, without her to influence him, could have changed the will back at any time. And for Finn to gain the money from the will, Evan Nezer had to be dead. There was, Jaymie realized, another possible reason it couldn't wait, or at least . . . this was the moment to discover if her sudden supposition was true.

She shivered, the cold seeping into her bones and her thighs burning from crouching. The ground was frigid, and poor Austin was beginning to shudder. Jaymie needed to find a way to finish this. "Finn isn't Evan's son, is he?" she said softly.

The housekeeper stared at her, worry in her eyes, her mouth

stretched in a grimace. "It doesn't matter. Finn is in the will now. They can't take that away from him."

Jaymie wasn't so sure about that. If Evan's inheritors discovered the truth after his death, and they could prove that the codicil was only in effect because of presumed paternity, there would surely be a legal challenge. "But Evan *would* have changed it if he knew the truth, right? As a lawyer he started to get suspicious. Did he add up dates finally, all this time later, after so many years had passed? Did he finally figure out what I did, that there is no way a two-months premature baby would be eight and a half pounds?"

She watched the woman, who had consternation on her face as tears dried in sticky trails on her cheeks. Erla shook her head but remained silent.

Time had seemed to slow, and Jaymie's thinking clarified. Images flashed through her mind: the pudding mould on the shelf in the kitchen, cleaned up and put back in place, and what Johnny and Amos had seen, the envelope passing from the pastor to Erla. And she remembered something else: the Nezers had their mail rerouted to the college for the time being. Who worked at the college besides Evan? Pastor Vaughn Inkerman. "It wasn't possible years ago, but did he . . ." Jaymie's eyed widened. "Evan got a DNA test done, didn't he? Their mail was still being routed to the college, so the results were sent there and Pastor Inkerman intercepted them for you."

"You shut up," Erla said, her voice shaking, and the heavy pudding mould in her hand shaking too. Her face was shadowed by the diorama walls, so she had become just a raw, fury-filled voice. "You shut *up*. You do not know the crap I had to put up with for years from that man: the put-downs, the criticism. And I took it all because Evan said someday he'd make sure Finn was taken care of. And then he went and got him ejected from the master's program! Finn was crushed, and all 'cause Evan had to be right. Even if he wasn't right, he had to be right. Even if he had to *cheat* to make it seem so."

She was getting herself wound up, anger taking over from fear and anguish. Jaymie eyed Austin, who was progressing from frightened to terrified. Amos was paler, the scourge of hypothermia upon him. What was she going to do? The falling snow was thickening, blowing into the enclosure. How could she end this? If she screamed, would anyone hear her? Not likely. There'd be no windows open this time of year, and the diorama walls muffled sound.

Maybe someone would pass by and she could shout. Where were all the dog walkers and health nuts when you needed them? The housekeeper was prowling back and forth, mould still firmly in hand. Jaymie was younger and possibly stronger, but there had to be a better way to end this than rushing her and risking worse injury to the two men and herself.

Keep her talking. "But, Erla, Evan was going to help get Finn reinstated into the master's program, right?"

"Hah! Not even high-and-mighty Nezer could do that. I heard those folks talking that night, the night of the party. They didn't know, but I heard 'em 'cause they came into the back hall to whisper and plot. Evan had talked to them all right, like he said he would, but Mrs. Belcher didn't want none of that. She said the college would look tainted if it did so, and she had other fish to fry. She'd been in trouble before, but this time was different. She said she was going to find some way of diplomatically telling Evan it was a no-go. He didn't *really* care, she said, not about Finn Fancombe."

She swayed on her feet, swinging the heavy pudding mould. "She was right about that. Evan never cared for anyone but himself. That woman, President Belcher . . . she wanted some high muckety-muck fellow from some organization that wanted a place to put some kind of tank . . . I don't know what that meant, but it had something to do with money and the economy and . . . I don't know. But they weren't about to let Finn back in to *stain their reputation*." She spat the last words, but then took a deep breath, steadying. "So that's when I knew. I had thought Evan might have to die because of the codicil and the DNA test; I couldn't delay indefinitely. But I knew for sure that night. And it was perfect, so many folks peeved at Evan."

Jaymie shivered. She had been in trouble before, but here she was backed into the diorama with walls on three sides, two wounded fellows and a crazy lady in front of her wielding the unlikeliest of weapons. It would be funny if it wasn't so frightening. And she didn't know what to do.

She edged forward, away from Austin. "I can't figure out how you did it, though. I mean, I know how you killed him—the pudding mould over the head—and you staged it here, in the diorama. How did you know about that?" Her gaze darted around. Was there something in the diorama she could use to clunk Erla over the head with or throw at her?

"You think I don't know everything going on? People talk in this town, and I listen. I overheard Amos telling that Johnny fellow about your little scene. I guess he heard it from Bill Waterman, who always gave Amos coffee and food and cigarettes for helping him around the shop. They shifted your diorama in the shed after he painted it, and Bill explained what it was. When it was set up, I knew all about it, and knew exactly how it worked. I always loved that story, you know, *A Christmas Carol*. Loved the old black-and-white movie, with that Sims fellow, so I read it once, too." She loomed into a ray of light that came through a crack in the diorama. She smiled, an awful, angry smile. "You know, Ben was in the play at school. So was Finn. Finn played Bob Cratchit, but Ben played Scrooge. Hah! His dad never showed up to the play, though. Evan Nezer Scrooge, I called him once."

A nervous giggle burst from Jaymie. "I thought of that too!"

"Yeah, so it was perfect." She stilled, and her eyes unfocused. "An hour after the party I was still in the kitchen, working. Of course. Cleaning up other folks' mess like I've done my whole life. They never cared or even noticed how hard I worked. Evan came downstairs after a fight with missy Bella Butter Wouldn't Melt in Her Mouth and wanted some hot milk. He had indigestion after all that rich catering food, and he didn't trust no one but me to get it for him. Not after Miss Bella giving him sleeping stuff a coupla times so she could sneak out!"

"Sneak out?"

"Sure. She had a boyfriend or two on the side. What woman her age wouldn't with that old fool in her bed? He figured it out and found the sleeping stuff in her bedside table. She swore up and down it was for her, but . . . he had his suspicions. I knew all about it. Shoulda heard the fights those two had."

There was malicious glee in her tone. That, then, was what Erla had meant when she said to Bella that she knew what the supposed mistress of the house was doing behind her husband's back.

"Anyway, I knew it was time," Erla mused. "It was perfect, like a gift from God telling me I was in the right." There was a reverent hush in her tone as she pondered the universe's instructions. "I was *gonna* take him up a warm drink, and then have to haul him all the way down the back stairs, but instead he just . . . delivered himself to me. So, good old faithful servant Erla fixed him some milk with a good dose of Bella's sleeping pills crushed into it. I had 'em ready, see. He went to sleep right there in the kitchen, just dropped to the floor. I dragged him out the back door and bashed him over the head with the pudding mould until he was dead. I had a wheelbarrow ready and trundled him through the trees to your dio-whatcha-macallit. Easy from there to plant him with that decorative pudding mould over his head."

And hammer a stake of holly through his heart. So cold, so calculated. "You planned it ahead of time. You got the holly from my backyard."

She chuckled. "Bella was talking about it to Evan . . . making fun of you, you know, copying you offering holly to anyone who wanted it. She was trying to jolly him up lately. Making fun of the lower orders, as he called you all, was one way to entertain him. It wasn't hard to find your house, and even easier to slip down that alley and steal the holly."

Jaymie, despite the danger, was thinking things through. "But, Erla, why the fire? Why set the cider booth ablaze."

She swayed into the sliver of light once more, her face twisted in anger. "I never did that, you know," she said, her voice gritty with anger. "Those cops . . . they questioned me about it, but I never did it."

"But Amos said . . ." Ah . . . aha! Amos said it was Erla because of the coat and gray hair. But anyone could don a gray wig and borrow a coat. She had a sudden thought. "Bella did that, didn't she? Whoever did it used your coat, and she's the only one who could, other than Evan, and I'm pretty sure he would have taken credit for the arson if he did it."

Erla was startled. "*That's* why my coat smells of smoke!" she said, taking the lapel with her free hand and pulling it up to her nose. She smiled, an eerie look still. "Well, she won't be a problem anymore.

Maybe she'll even get the blame for all of this!" She brightened. "*Yes!* That works out!"

"You think she'll stand for that? She'll tell the cops the truth, and you'll be up for it. C'mon, Erla, you know she won't let an accusation . . ." Jaymie trailed off as she saw the triumph on the woman's face. "Oh, *no*; what have you done to Bella?"

She nodded, then shook her head. "No, you don't understand . . . *poor* Bella. She did it all, you see, even this! Oh, my goodness!" She giggled, a squawky sound. "It's all so perfect. Thank you for pointing that out. The note she wrote . . . her suicide . . . I wanted to shut her up and get her out of the way, but this will all work out."

Jaymie started shaking, remembering Bella threatening Erla with DNA testing and a court challenge; now Bella was about to pay for that threat with her life! Erla was hell-bent on her path. There was no way out of this alive, not unless Jaymie did something soon. Was there *any* human kindness left in Erla Fancombe? At first she had seemed not to want to hurt them. Could Jaymie appeal to that side of the housekeeper? "Erla, *please*, let us go!" Jaymie said, clasping her hands together in prayerful pleading. "I don't know what else to say, but I don't think you're really a killer, not ingrained. You were pushed into it by years of abuse from Evan Nezer."

"Don't make me over into a victim," she growled. "I'm no *victim*," she said, raising the pudding mould over her head. "I will survive—"

"Tell that to Miss Gloria Gaynor!"

There was a thump, and Erla dropped to her knees and keeled over as an arc of blood sprayed the diorama walls. Jaymie looked up to see Valetta standing triumphantly—if wavering a little—behind her, holding a shovel in her hand, a tool no Michigander who drove would be without in their car in the winter months.

"Yes!" Jaymie said, bolting to her friend and hugging her, as Austin leaped to his feet and pulled off his coat, draping it over poor Amos.

"We need the police," she said, snatching up Austin's cell phone. "This madwoman has done something to Bella Nezer."

✒ Twenty-one ✒

"I WISH WE'D BEEN ABLE TO DO THIS YESTERDAY," Jaymie grumbled, shivering. She hadn't had enough coffee yet. Two cups was a necessity or she just wasn't awake. It was Friday morning and the lighting of the tree and new official start of Dickens Days was that very evening, so they had no time to spare.

"I'm glad you're here to do it at all," Jakob said, swinging a hammer and knocking one side wall off the diorama. He had been grumpy since finding out everything that had happened—the danger to Jaymie had been real and he was horrified by it—but was starting to mellow a bit now.

"I know, I know," she said, giving him a side hug. "But I *am*, so let's do this!"

Thursday had been taken up with giving a complete police statement, and visiting poor Amos in the hospital, where the police had taken his complete statement, as well as checking in on Austin to be sure he was all right. Shaken and hurt, though not critically, he had taken Thursday off from college but was back at it now, as he had exams to write. He texted her that his art professor boyfriend was suitably impressed and comforting to him, and had made a fuss over Austin, with the bandage on his forehead.

Thursday also happened to be St. Nicholas Day, and though not Catholic the Müllers set aside that day to celebrate some traditional German St. Nicholas Day customs with the children. Jocie and her cousins stayed with their grandparents and received in their shoes a few small gifts, in Jocie's case books, her favorite present, and Katzenzungen, little chocolate-covered biscuits named "cats tongues" for their shape. Jaymie was grateful for the distraction it provided for Jocie, so she didn't have to explain what happened.

Jakob's brothers worked the tree sales lot Thursday while her husband helped her through the follow-up to the attack. Jaymie learned during her talk with the police how Amos had happened to be in his predicament. After his close call—he was in the hospital still for hypothermia and the injury to his head, which matched Evan's perfectly—he had decided to shed his secretive ways and tell everything he knew and everything that had happened. He rejected Erla's accusation that he was blackmailing her.

He had seen what he didn't understand at first, Erla with a long-handled window squeegee, coming from behind the Emporium. That would have been her smearing the CCTV camera lenses with peanut butter, the police figured. He then saw, as he meandered the village streets in the wee hours of Saturday morning, Erla fussing around the diorama the night of the murder. It had taken him a while to believe that she had killed Evan, and he had simply asked her why she did it, he claimed.

She had told him to meet her at the diorama and she'd tell him everything. She brought the bowl to kill him, there could be no doubt about that. She was talking now, and had made a complete statement as part of what would likely be a plea deal of some sort. Her reasoning was that the pudding mould, a weapon hiding in plain sight, worked once, and would work again. Austin's desire for a selfie at the murder scene had saved Amos's life.

Fortunately for Bella, when the police broke down the door to the Nezer residence and bolted upstairs with paramedics following, she was sleeping soundly, but that was all. Erla had given her pills crushed into her meal, but had miscalculated the amount needed to kill her. She had recovered swiftly, fast enough to confirm that the suicide letter was not legitimate.

Unfortunately for Bella the police found the gray wig that had fooled Amos, and she was arrested for arson. The police would never have focused so closely on the Nezer household in the arson case, but Bella had hidden the gasoline she used to start the fire in the shed. The police were suspicious of the lengths someone had taken to conceal so common a liquid, but before the wig was discovered and Amos had provided the information he had, they had been unable to establish which householder had been responsible. Bella had lawyered up and been released on bail, but Jaymie suspected that if Erla hadn't killed Evan, Bella would have. Rumor had it that Evan had talked with his lawyer about divorce, though he had not instituted paperwork yet. He caught Bella cheating, and that voided the prenup, which had a "no cheating" clause in it.

Without a confession they could only guess at many things, including why she had set fire to the cider booth wearing a gray wig and Erla's coat, but Jaymie speculated that Evan was stalling at getting rid of Erla, and Bella was anxious to have the woman out of her home. Erla was in the way of her plan to kill Evan herself, she had thought. If Erla was arrested for arson, Bella must have thought, the housekeeper would be gone for good. The arrest hadn't happened, but Bella couldn't push for it too hard or her own guilt would have become obvious.

No one would ever know the whole truth of that. Even if Bella *had* considered killing her husband, would she have gotten up the nerve? It was interesting to Jaymie that Bella had been the one to invite so many people her husband did not like and would potentially clash with, like Valetta, Jaymie and Vaughn, with Brock as an unforeseen bonus. It almost looked like Bella was setting the scene for there to be numerous suspects in his murder. But they'd never know, and you couldn't convict anyone on what they might have done, given the opportunity.

Jaymie packed the bits and pieces from her diorama into totes and stowed them in the back of the SUV. Bill Waterman hobbled toward them, looking weak but better than he had. Neither Jaymie nor Jakob had allowed Bill to help, recruiting Johnny Stanko instead to disassemble the diorama structure and tote it to Bill's barn for storage until they could figure out what to do with it.

"I got it open, Jakob, Jaymie," Bill said. "Johnny, I got that handcart we can use and you young fellows can haul it up the hill okay, I think."

"I guess I should feel lucky that we can do this at all," Jaymie said. "Since it was the scene of another crime."

"No mystery about this one though," Valetta said, joining them, tea mug in hand. "We know whodunit, so the police didn't need to keep the scene closed off, once it was processed."

"My heroine!" Jaymie said, throwing her arms around her friend.

They stood together, Jaymie with one arm slung over Valetta's shoulders, and watched the diorama walls being carted off by Jakob and Johnny. When the guys returned, Jaymie hugged her friend and freed her from her grasp. "See you tonight for the first night of Dickens Days?"

"You betcha." Valetta headed back to work.

Ben and Jacklyn, heads together, came around the bend from

behind the line of pines that concealed the Nezer home. They stopped to eye the gathered townsfolk, then exchanged a look and headed toward Jaymie.

"Hey," Jacklyn said as they strolled toward her, hand in hand.

"Hey," Jaymie said back, unsure what else to say. How did one say how sorry one was that a late father-in-law had been murdered by his housekeeper? But she *was* curious. "So . . . a little bird told me that congratulations are in order and you two are married. True? Rumor?"

Jacklyn smiled, then laughed—which completely changed her appearance, making her appear younger—and looked over at Ben, who stood silent and unsmiling. "Not *exactly* true. We, uh . . . didn't sign the official documentation, so we're not legally married. It was for larks that time around." She sobered and sighed. "Ben wanted to tweak his dad, so we did that with Pastor Inkerman, then got photos, but we're not legally married."

"Are you going to?"

She shrugged. "Maybe."

"So, is your relationship why Evan got you fired from the college?" Jaymie asked, something that had just occurred to her.

Jacklyn shrugged. "Maybe, but I don't think so. We never let him know how close we were. I believe he suspected I was starting to put two and two together, about that fishy stuff at WC."

"That's what you were really looking for on his computer that night."

"No comment," she said with a ghost of a smile.

The school newspaper had just that morning come out with allegations against the school president, the provost and dean, concerning their use of donor money. It looked like President Belcher was going to again be looking for a new job. Sooner or later she was going to run out of academic establishments that would have her. The *Wolverhampton Weekly Howler* had given the student reporter from WC a byline in their paper for their own reporting on the school scandal. Jaymie had affected that by sending the young aspiring reporter to Nan with her introduction.

"I knew Evan too well, how his mind worked. I never did find out what student accused me of inappropriate behavior; I don't think there was one. It was in Evan's fertile and vindictive imagination, and the president went along with it. I would have fought them on it eventually. I was planning to, but things were . . . complicated." She glanced at Ben, who was still tight-lipped. She appeared to decide not to go further impugning his dead father's character. "Anyway, here's a fun fact: did you know that the estimable Pastor Vaughn Inkerman was born Vaughn Fancombe?"

Jaymie blinked. "What?"

"The good pastor is Erla Fancombe's firstborn son."

Staggered, Jaymie took a moment to absorb that information. "Wow. Did not see that one coming. I figured out that Finn, despite what Ben's dad at one time believed, is *not* Ben's brother." She paused, then asked, "Does Finn know who his father is?"

Jacklyn and Ben exchanged glances. "I don't think he does," she answered. "I don't think Erla would ever have told him, because she was counting on Evan coming through for him as his 'father.'"

"That's too bad," Jaymie said. "Maybe she'll tell him now. Or . . . maybe not."

Ben looked uncomfortable. "I don't know what to think. Finn and I always got along real well. He was taken in for questioning, you know, but both he and his mom say he was not involved in the . . . the murder of my dad."

"Do you believe him?"

He shrugged and squinted off to the sky. "I don't know. My mom says that she can't believe Finn would do anything to hurt me. She's going to bat for him. She can't help Erla, but she wants to help Finn."

"Does anyone know how he is, with his mom in jail?"

Jacklyn said, "He's going through a rough time. I feel for him. He was a great TA at WC. His students loved him, and I believe he'll come through this okay, but his mom's trouble is going to be hard for him." She squeezed Ben's arm to her side and looked up at him. "I'm glad your mom is standing by him. That's what friends do."

He nodded.

"Speaking of your mom," Jaymie said, watching Ben's face. "There are all kinds of wild rumors about her. Maybe I shouldn't ask, but I'm going to, and you can tell me to shove off if I'm intruding. Why did your mom walk away from the marriage with basically nothing?"

"I didn't want anything."

Jaymie whirled. Sarah, dressed warmly in a heavy coat and wool gloves, had glided up silently and now got off her bicycle. Ben hugged her and Jacklyn smiled. "I don't understand. You were entitled to half."

"I know there are rumors that Evan had something on me, that he had blackmailed me to walk away empty-handed. But I didn't want a penny. I wanted a clean break from everything, all of my past. I spent years in and out of hospitals and therapy and on and off all kinds of meds until we finally found the right combination. I found a good place and I want to stay in it. The best therapy was letting go of it all, but it wasn't easy. I don't expect anyone to understand. It was a blow, I'll admit, when Evan and Bella moved into the big house." She glanced over her shoulder, through the pines. "I had always longed to live there. I imagined redecorating, making it beautiful again." She sighed. "But that is Ben's to do now." She smiled at her son. "I have my writing and my books and my little home down near the river."

"Mom, you can live with us, if you want."

Jacklyn looked startled.

"I wouldn't dream of it," Sarah said with a smile that took in Jacklyn.

"But at least we're going to get you the rights to the books back, so you'll have the movie options. And whenever a movie is filmed from a book, the book sells big time. They're going to film one of them right here, in Queensville!" Ben said, his gaze shifting to Jaymie.

"Wow, exciting! So you'll be the acknowledged author finally?"

Sarah nodded. "I told Ben I wasn't worried about it, but he insisted. We're working it out."

"As your financial advisor I demand it! You should get all the recognition *and* money you deserve."

"And the pastor, Erla's other son?" Jacklyn said, her gaze shifting between Sarah and Ben. "I've heard he claims he did not know what was in the envelope Erla had him steal from the mail room at the college. The one labeled *DNA results*."

"It sounds like you don't believe that," Jaymie said, eyeing Jacklyn.

"I don't know what to believe," she admitted.

Jaymie considered it. "I'd bet he didn't know. It's a cynical world, but I think he's honest."

Jacklyn took Ben's arm. "We'd better get going. We have to clear out my apartment. I'm moving in to the Nezer house!" They walked away.

Sarah lingered on a moment. "You know that note I gave you that night, the night of the party?"

"Sure," Jaymie said, her curiosity itching. "What did it mean?"

"I knew they had gotten married," she said, looking back and watching her son and his almost-wife. "He wanted to tell Evan, to stick it to his father. But I learned a long time ago, it was best not to goad Evan."

"Oh! So the note meant not to tell his dad that he and Jacklyn were married."

She nodded. "I know you were suspicious, but what could I say without telling you what it meant? I wasn't going to break my promise not to tell anyone about them." She walked away, following her son to Jacklyn's apartment.

She'd better get home herself, Jaymie thought. She had some goodies to bake for the first night of Dickens Days. The lighting of the tree would likely bring lots of people into town.

· · ·

O come, O come, Emmanuel,
And ransom captive Israel,
That mourns in lonely exile here,
Until the Son of God appear.
Rejoice! Rejoice! Emmanuel
Shall come to thee, O Israel.

THE METHODIST CHURCH CHOIR sang their haunting rendition of the old carol, which drifted in the chill air along with the crisp snowflakes that danced and fluttered. As they sang, Reverend Gillis, dressed in a handsome navy wool trench coat over a black shirt and white clerical collar, a hand-knitted scarf trailing around his neck, circulated through the crowd, inviting all to come to his church. He stopped by Jaymie, who stood with Jakob and Jocie; he bent down and solemnly shook the little girl's hand, then straightened, pushing his comb-over to one side as the breeze teased it loose.

"How are you, Jaymie?"

"I'm good."

"My friend Pastor Inkerman wanted me to give you a message." He put one hand on her shoulder. "He wanted to say he is devastated by the fear Erla Fancombe put you and your friend through, and hopes there are no hard feelings toward him for what he failed to reveal to you, his relationship with the woman."

"No hard feelings." Jaymie paused. "What about his relationship with his brother, Finn? Does he have one?"

"He didn't in past. Vaughn respected his mother's desire for folks not to know he was her son, so he couldn't exactly reach out to Finn, but he is now."

"Reverend, was Vaughn telling the truth, though? Was he with you that night?"

"He was. He was sorely in conflict with himself. You know, regardless of what others may be saying, Inkerman really is his surname, given to him by his adoptive family. And despite his mother's assertions—she is, unfortunately, a bitter woman—he does know his father, and is working to establish a relationship with him. Erla was so young when Vaughn was born; I suppose she did the best she could for him by giving him away. When she was pregnant with Finn—they don't have the same father—I think she decided that she wanted to keep him, but maybe Finn's father was not in the picture, or maybe she decided he was bad news. I don't know the whole truth."

"It's sad. For Finn, I mean, not to know his father. Maybe Erla will tell now; I hear she is talking a lot about everything. I hope the pastor is okay?"

"He is. You know, Vaughn came to me that night in great turmoil. He found hate in his heart toward Professor Nezer for the man's attacks on his book, and he wished to expunge those feelings from him. We stayed up and talked for hours, and so I told the police."

It relieved her mind to hear it. "So how did you help him?"

"I gave him a very human piece of advice, not even religious. First, you can't control what people think of you. And second . . . when someone is so openly nasty, as Professor Nezer unfortunately was, it behooves us to remember that their wretched behavior reflects more about their inner soul than it does our work or life. I am loath to speak ill of the dead, but Evan Nezer was a miserable man in so many ways."

Jaymie nodded. He had stolen books from Sarah, and cheated on her with their new housekeeper, had lied and plagiarized his supposed son—Finn, whom he *thought* was his son—and cheated Jacklyn out of payment for her ghostwriting, then got her fired from her teaching job. And he was cruel to everyone. *Miserable* was a mild word for his brand of hostility toward the world. "Evan Nezer certainly did not reflect the sense of the season, did he?"

Reverend Gillis smiled. "No, but for that he is more to be pitied than anything. How can anyone see the joy on these little ones' faces and not rejoice?"

Jocie had met up with her friends Gemma and Peyton. The three girls, with Jocie by far the smallest, formed a tight group and sang along, now that the choir had moved to "Santa Claus Is Coming to Town." The reverend moved away, circulating and passing out postcard invitations to seasonal services at his church.

Jaymie noticed the new family in town, Mr. and Mrs. Ibrahim and two children, a boy and girl. They stood at the edge of the crowd, waiting for the tree to be lit. Mr. Ibrahim, who had recently moved his family to Queensville from Detroit, was a custodian at the hospital in Wolverhampton. Their daughter, Noor, was in Jocie's class. "Jocie, Gemma, Peyton," she called out softly. When she got the girls' attention, she pointed to Noor, who gazed at them longingly. Jocie whispered to her friends and nodded, then dashed over to the Ibrahims. She spoke to Noor's mother. Mrs. Ibrahim, her tan headscarf framing a lovely face, dark, almond-shaped eyes and full lips, smiled and nodded as Noor looked up at her. The little girl, also wearing a headscarf of red patterned silk, skipped off with the girls to await the tree lighting.

Jakob kissed Jaymie's cheek and hugged her to his side. "I have to go now," he whispered, and moved off on his own to join up with Bill Waterman. The fellows were in charge of lighting the lights at the appropriate moment, as well as making sure the electricity worked for the cider booth, already being manned by Mrs. Bellwood and Imogene Frump. Jakob was replaced at Jaymie's side by Becca, Kevin, Valetta, Heidi, Austin and others of her friends.

It was a perfect evening, crystalline flakes drifting down to sit in starry perfection on dark woolen coats and scarves, and lovely lights illuminating their picturesque town. The village had been transformed by the heritage committee. Lights were strung outside each shop from the Emporium, through the big bare oak tree, to Bill's workshop, to Cynthia's Cottage Shoppe and Jewel's Junk, across to the Knit Knack Shack and Queensville Fine Antiques, and they were already lit, like pathways of stars.

The only thing left to light was the tree.

Haskell Lockland would usually lead the crowd in a chorus of "Joy to the World" and then call for the lighting, but he and Petty had a prior engagement, made when he thought the lighting would take place the week before. So it fell to Mabel Bloombury. But she passed the torch, so to speak, on to Bill Waterman, who pushed Jakob forward.

"Good evening, everyone," Jakob said, looking handsome in his gold corduroy shearling coat, jeans and work boots. "This time of year is for family and friends to gather, and so we have, all of us, both family and friends of many faiths and customs," he said, with a nod to Peyton's parents, who were Jewish, and the most recent Queensvillians, the Ibrahims. "We've seen tragedy and we've found joy. But the light is always there. Whether you believe in God or follow another path, I think the light is for us all. Everyone count down with me . . . c'mon, kids, you especially," he said, pointing to Jocie and her friends, the group now increased to most of her class. "Ten, nine . . ."

The crowd got to one and the tree blazed with multicolored lights, sending a radiance over the snowy village. The church choir led a verse of "O Christmas Tree," which Jakob sang in German in a booming voice. The night was ablaze and sparkling, shimmering snowflakes drifted down, and it was magic.

☙ Epilogue ☙

"I will honour Christmas in my heart, and try to keep it all the year. I will live in the Past, the Present, and the Future. The Spirits of all Three shall strive within me. I will not shut out the lessons that they teach!"
— Charles Dickens, A Christmas Carol

THE SEASON WAS A FLURRY of Christmas tree sales and parties with friends and family. Jocie and her whole class were treated to a hayride at a friend's stable, and Jocie was a snow globe in her school's winter pageant. Becca and Jaymie's parents arrived from Florida to stay in the Queensville house, while Grandma Leighton was ensconced in comfort at the Queensville Inn to enjoy the comraderie of some old friends, including Mrs. Stubbs and her cousin Miss Perry.

But Christmas Eve dinner and the exchange of gifts was at the Müller farm, a German tradition. The warmth of that family had enveloped all of the Leightons. It seemed they always had enough room for one—or several—more. Jaymie dissolved in tears at one point, overwhelmed by her own good fortune and the wonderful life she had stumbled into. She'd never forget that it was one of her "investigations," when she'd been chased by a villain, that had led her into Jakob's arms.

Christmas day arrived and was celebrated by the Leighton family with dinner at the Queensville Inn. Too much food, too much wine, but just enough happiness to go around. Alan and Joy drove to Canada the day after, taking Grandma Leighton, his mother, back to London and her comfortable retirement home. Becca and Kevin followed soon after.

Jaymie and Jakob were hosting New Year's Eve in the Queensville house this year, and Jocie was having her two friends Gemma and Peyton for a sleepover. It was the usual mad dash to get the house ready, but everyone arrived at the appropriate time, the girls had their "midnight countdown" with the adults at nine and then were banished upstairs to giggle and play with Lilibet and Hoppy, watch videos, eat snacks and fall asleep (maybe; doubtful), and the adults, including Austin Calhoun, who had swiftly become a part of their group, ate, conversed, danced, played silly games, and then toasted with champagne or sparkling cider at midnight.

An hour later they were all gone, wending their way home along snowy roads and paths. Austin went home with Heidi, who had adopted him as a friend and brother. Jaymie watched her cell phone as each person sent a reassuring text that they had arrived home safely. Finally it was just her and Jakob.

"Come with me," she whispered and took his hand. She led him out the back door, across the summer porch, and out to the back flagstone path. The grass was coated in snow, but the path was still bare.

"Darn, I thought you were leading me upstairs," he said, taking her in his arms and holding her against his warm bulk.

"Soon enough, Mr. Müller. But right now . . ." She looked up to the sky, her head leaned back against Jakob's shoulder. The Geminid meteor showers were over—they had seen them in the middle of the month—but there were shooting stars every night. "Let's see one," she said to Jakob. "And wish on it."

"I have everything I need and want," he said, holding her close, breathing in her ear. "But this is good."

The air was crisp, winter well established. Jaymie's cheeks were getting cold, but she stared up at the dark night sky as she had when she was a kid. That was a New Year's Eve tradition with her dad, to go out after midnight and wish on the first shooting star of the new year.

Finally she saw one and closed her eyes, whispering. Then she turned and kissed her husband, looking up into his face, only visible by the spilled light from the kitchen through the summer porch. "I love you," she said.

"I love you. So . . . what did you wish for?"

"I can't tell you that. But, I can tell you I've never in my life been happier. All I want now in my life is for this to continue."

"I second that emotion," he said.

"What?"

"It's the title of an old song! Don't you know it? Smokey Robinson. My oldest brother has always loved classic Motown. How can you not, living in Michigan?" He sang a snatch of it, and the lyric was perfect for them and their love.

"Yup. That's how I feel."
"Here's to the new year, Mrs. Müller."
"And to you, Mr. Müller."
Kissing is an excellent way to stay warm, they discovered.

Vintage Eats

Holiday Hermits: The Perfect Cookie for Any Platter
By Jaymie Leighton

As you may know, lately I have been doing some work with spices, given that Queensville, unbeknownst to me, is the spice capital of the USA! Captain Jonas Perry, one of the founding fathers of our village of Queensville, was a spice importer who traveled the world in search of the freshest spices to import. If you are curious about spices and want to see more, visit the Queensville Historic Manor any day of the week and see our spice grater collection in the classic 1920s kitchen I established there last year.

Hermits are a special cookie to spice lovers. Cinnamon, allspice, cloves . . . this fragrant and deliciously evocative blend will have you thinking holidays in no time. If you're feeling festive, you can add a little nutmeg, too! I'm giving it a special holiday twist by adding in dried cranberries, a jolly and colorful addition. With or without that, they are the perfect picnic cookie, after-school snack and all-round best pairing with cocoa or frothy milk. The hermit cookie is the king of cookies and ideal for any occasion. With all of that being said, here is my take after reviewing dozens of hermit cookie recipes, vintage and modern!

I have such a *tough* job!

Holiday Hermit Cookies

½ cup unsalted butter
1 cup light brown sugar
2 large eggs
½ teaspoon vanilla extract
1½ cups all-purpose flour
1 teaspoon baking soda
¼ tablespoon salt (Note: if you use salted butter, as I did, omit the salt!)
1 teaspoon ground cinnamon
½ teaspoon ground allspice
½ teaspoon pumpkin pie spice (omit if you prefer or if you don't have this, or substitute allspice)
¼ teaspoon ground cloves
½ cup chopped pecans (or walnuts if you prefer)
1 cup dates, chopped (the original recipe I had said to pit the dates, but I bought them already pitted and chopped; I just chopped them more finely)
1 cup sweetened dried cranberries
1 cup white chocolate chips

Preheat oven to 350 degrees F and place rack in center of oven.

Line baking sheets with parchment paper, or use Silpat silicone baking sheet liners.

With an electric mixer or hand mixer, beat the butter and sugar until light and fluffy. Add the eggs, one at a time, beating well after each addition. Beat in the vanilla extract, scraping down the sides of the bowl as needed. I used a stand mixer; it makes baking cookies so easy!

In a separate bowl sift or whisk together the flour, baking soda, salt and spices. Add to the butter, sugar and egg mixture a bit at a time, letting the mixer beat it in. Scrape down the sides of the bowl again, if you're using a stand mixer.

Fold in nuts, dates, cranberries and white chocolate chips.

Drop the batter by heaping tablespoonfuls, spacing the cookies about two inches apart. Bake for 10–11 minutes until lightly browned. Put the baking sheet on a raised rack for a few minutes before lifting the cookies from the pan.

If you are in a hurry, it's great to make the cookie dough and bake it later. I baked a few off, then rolled the rest in wax paper, wrapped that in plastic, and will slice chunks off to bake later. There is nothing like freshly baked! (This worked out great, by the way. Fresh cookies another day!) But hermit cookies keep well; it's been said that the reason they are called "hermit" cookies is that even if one gets away and hides out in the bottom of the cookie jar, it will still be good by the time you find it! I love little legends like that.

The cookies can be stored at room temperature for five days. If you make these up ahead of time, they will freeze well.

These are fat, fragrant, delicious and satisfying with a frosty glass of milk or a cup of cocoa. They truly smell and taste like the holidays!

Happy Christmas, everyone, or *Frohe Weihnachten*, as my in-laws say!

✏ About the Author ✏

Victoria Hamilton is the pseudonym of nationally bestselling romance author Donna Lea Simpson.

She now happily writes about vintage kitchen collecting, muffin baking, and dead bodies in the Vintage Kitchen Mysteries and Merry Muffin Mystery series. Besides writing about murder and mayhem, and blogging at Killer Characters, Victoria collects vintage kitchen wares and old cookbooks, as well as teapots and teacups.

Visit Victoria at www.victoriahamiltonmysteries.